Acknowledgments

Thanks to my first readers of the fine Austin writers' group Cryptopolis: Steve Wilson, Matthew Bey, David Chang, Patrick Sullivan, Sharon Casteel, Jane Hixon, and Fred Stanton—where would I be without you guys! I also want to thank the Cryptopolis North writers Martin Owton and Gaie Sebold for their comments and suggestions. And always, my thanks and love go to Ben, Kim, and Aidan. You guys are the best family a writer could have.

One

The evening sun set through the tall trees that ringed Red Gold Bridge. Shafts of sunlight shot through to the ground, turning the stone of the stronghold a deeper shade of gold. Spray from the forest stream that cut beneath the stone arch, rebuilt now after the winter's war, was caught in the sun, and a perpetual rainbow dazzled in the mist.

Joe and Arrim trudged across the arch of the bridge, Joe feeling weariness deep in his bones. The road was already in shadow behind them, and the mountain rose ahead, the wall and the great gate rising thirty feet over their heads. A slice of the setting sun illuminated the red gold of the stone, and the iron and wood of the gate caught some of the glow.

Off to the side was the smaller postern gate, the one everyone used these days. The two guardians headed that way, threading through the steady stream of smallholders heading back to their forest holdings. Once the smallholders would not have dared to travel the Wood when the sun was so near to setting. It was thanks to Arrim and Joe that they could now.

Small men and women in their drab forest clothes gave

them half bows and shy smiles. Arrim bowed back, the movement coming easily to him. Joe had introduced his own custom. He shook hands with one or two people he had come to
recognize on his patrols through the woods that kept the forest settled and quiet.

The forestholders came to the stronghold on the banks of
the Aeritan River to trade every few days, bringing in baskets
of mushrooms, dried fish, and dyes made from the plants that
grew in clearings only they knew. They brought in freshwater
pearls and smoked eels, thick clay, the charcoal and firewood
that would be used by smiths to fire their forges, and the spicy
roots that were used to make vesh, what Joe called the national
drink of Aeritan. Their goods were prized all over Aeritan,
and the forestholders traded them for what they needed: forged
tools, textiles, and food, mostly protein they couldn't get for
themselves. The forestholders lived in dark, secret clearings in
the Wood and knew the forest better than Joe and Arrim. They
stayed away from the portal at its center, though. They left that
for the guardians.

Waiting his turn to duck through the postern gate, Joe
caught movement and looked up. Lady Sarita was watching
them from over the wall, thirty feet up.

Like him, she wore the clothes from her old life, T-shirt
and jeans. She held a cup in her hand. Vesh, probably. He
heard that she had missed it, back in New York. He waved
and smiled.

Of course, she didn't wave back; she wouldn't have, even
when she was Mrs. Hunt, owner of Hunter's Chase, and he
was just the barn handyman.

Then Lord Tharp joined her, and Joe's grin faded. He hurried after Arrim and ducked through the low arch inside the
wall. Instantly he was plunged into darkness, the only light
a narrow swath coming from the courtyard inside the wall.
Even though Lady Sarita had come back to Tharp after years
of living on the other side—and it hadn't been too bad a life
there, that's for sure—she and her husband stalked around
one another like a pair of pissed-off cats. Joe didn't work for

Lord Tharp, but he didn't want to make him hotter than he already was, where his wife was concerned.

Man's got a serious problem, if he thinks he can keep her on a short leash. Joe hadn't known Mrs. Hunt before she was Mrs. Hunt, so to speak, but she had run her stables at a profit by keeping a tight hand on the wheel. She wasn't the kind to put up with someone trying to run her the same way.

His stomach cramped with hunger. He looked forward to a hot meal, his first in a half month, and a bed with blankets and furs instead of a thin bedroll on a mattress of leaves. Arrim threw him a look as they emerged into the courtyard, already half in darkness. Joe shook his head at his look of inquiry.

"Just thinking of a good hot meal."

"Thank the forest god that's all we have to worry about tonight." He grinned. "And maybe a girl who thinks to curry favor with the forest god by being sweet to a guardian. Your Corinna, even."

Corinna worked in the kitchens and had her eye on Joe almost since the day he came to Red Gold Bridge. She was a broad, pleasant-faced woman about his age, and she had made her interest clear. And Lynn could be on the moon, for all they could ever be together. So far, though, Joe had just been friendly and nothing more. He made a noncommittal noise.

"I'm gonna clean up. See you at the kitchens."

Joe dumped his gear in his guardian's cham-ber on the inside wall of the stronghold. He stretched, welcoming the relief of the pack off his shoulders. Guardians didn't carry much, just a bedroll, dried food, and water, but the constant weight put a strain on his shoulders. His old boots were *not* meant for walking, but he was loathe to give them up. They were in much better shape than Arrim's hobnailed boots, and guardians didn't exactly draw a salary with which to buy new shoes. The job was its own reward, which sucked as far as Joe was concerned. He had never made much money back home, but at least he had been able to buy the essentials. Now he got room and board after a fact, but little else.

He stripped his shirt and washed himself at the basin of clean water left for him in the small room. The soap was a lumpy chunk that hardly raised a lather. *Be nice to have a shower,* he reflected, rinsing off and drying himself with a threadbare cloth. A nice hot shower and a good close shave, instead of using a straight razor that he about cut his own throat with. Instead he got standup baths, long nights out in the weather, jerky for breakfast, and biscuits for dinner.

And the beer was bad, too.

Still, it was like the woods *knew* him. When he set foot in the forest, the woods called to him as if he were home. He sure never saw woods like this where he grew up in central Texas, just thorny mesquite and papery cedar. Not even the cotton-woods back home that lined the creek beds with green were forest like this one. Here the trees closed out the sun. Only small shafts of sunlight reached the damp, cool ground that smelled of decaying leaves. The meadows were bright with green and yellow grasses, and in spring they were studded with a small purple flower like the bluebonnets back home. Creeks ran all summer long, even in the drought of August, or what he felt was probably August. He forgot the new season names that he had learned, and he had lost track of time. All he knew was, it was summer now, and the gordath had settled down. All last winter though, things had been bad, and Joe wasn't sure he was going to be able to take it.

Back then, the gordath had racked the woods, each earthquake cracking the frozen ground and breaking up stone. He and Arrim trod softly, letting their minds reach out to touch the uneasy portal, and slowly, slowly, it closed up. Finally, there was nothing left but traces of the gordath's fury.

He and Arrim marked where trees had fallen and let the forest smallholders salvage them for firewood and for their new houses. One smallholding had been completely destroyed, its houses fallen and the trees toppled as if a missile had flattened the little hamlet. When they came upon it, Joe had been struck by the quietness of the small settlement. It had still been winter, and the snow covered up the fallen houses, but someone had raised a pile of stones to the dead, leaves scattered across the top and around its foot. Joe stood shivering in the cold, but a strange sad peace held the tiny village, as if it were still being soothed.

"The forest will grow up around it," Arrim said, startling him out of his sad revery. "Vines will cover all this, and saplings will rise from the forest floor."

"That's it?" Joe said. He thought of funerals back home and of memorials on the side of dangerous roads, their crosses faithfully marked with plastic flowers.

Arrim pointed to the cairn. "This is all the forest god requires. Then he takes back his own."

Joe still felt the situation called for something, so he fashioned a small cross, lashing it together with a bit of string from his supplies, and laid it against the snowy pile of rock. Maybe it would confuse the forest god and maybe it wouldn't, but he liked to think of the little cross there, slowly decaying and returning to the forest, the emblem of a foreign god. He hadn't been religious back home. He wasn't sure what had happened to him here in Red Gold Bridge, except they had gods for everyone and everything, it seemed.

It was just another way he was learning to think in Aeritan.

The little village was not the only victim of the gordath. Joe began to recognize other places, older places, that had once been cleared and were now vine-covered, their sentinel trees standing around a rough clearing, old stones in a rough pattern humping under a growth of moss. Last winter had not been the first time the gordath flung itself open in a burst of energy, nor the first time the forest god took back its own. Gordath Wood was full of these mementos to the dangerous portal that hid at its heart.

Joe finished washing up and put his old T-shirt back on, the material worn and faded. It was only a matter of time before it fell apart completely, and he would have to turn to Aeritan clothes. One of the smallholders had patched it for him once when he and Arrim had stopped in on their holding in the western part of the Wood. She had taken one look at his outlandish T-shirt and his jeans, and laughed outright, shaking her head.

"Give me that for mending," she scolded, and he looked startled, but he slipped the shirt off over his head. She sat down and mended a tear under the arm while he sipped vesh and the kids giggled at his pale skin. She bit off the thread and handed it back to him. "Come back with enough cloth, and I will make a proper set of clothes for you."

He looked at the heavy trousers everyone else wore and hoped that his jeans held out for a while. He knew that a shirt like Arrim's would suit him better. He knew why he resisted, though, and it was for the same reason that Mrs. Hunt wore her rich lady's version of his outfit.

Forget the portal; once the clothes were gone and they went native, they could never go back.

The door opened, and Arrim ducked in.

"I have a bad feeling," the guardian said.

Shit. Arrim's bad feelings tended to come true.

"What? What is it?"

Arrim grinned. "That they'll run out of bread in the kitchens before we get there, Guardian."

Joe rolled his eyes and pushed past him. "Arrim, where I come from, you know what we call people who make jokes like that?"

"Funny?"

"Stupid."

Red Gold Bridge was no longer at war, but the stronghold still felt like a barracks. The courtyard was full of men and horses and oxen. You had to be careful where you walked, and the stench of unwashed people and manure overwhelmed Joe. He was used to the forest, not this. The stronghold was a major port on the river, and it attracted everybody who wanted to do business throughout Aeritan. There were merchants from other holdings, many of them women with their hair neatly tucked under kerchiefs, and farmers, wagoners, coopers, wheelwrights, armsmen. Everyone fell back to let the guardians walk through, but this time it was different. The forestholders respected and liked the guardians. The strongholders mixed their deference with suspicion. Guardians were neither lords nor smallholders, and their relationship to the woods made everyone uneasy. The stronghold had been built as a way to hold off the gordath, after all, and its denizens never got over their wariness.

The kitchens were full of bustle, too, the business of feeding the stronghold never ending. Joe and Arrim threaded their way to a table, grabbing fresh flat bread, puffed and golden from the skillet, and bowls of the rich, spicy poultry stew that the Red Gold Bridge kitchens were famous for. The stew was like vesh, in that the combination of herbs and spices were exotic yet familiar, comforting in their fullness. He piled soft smoked cheese on top of the stew along with some sweet onions that reminded Joe of the 1015 onions the Aggies grew back home, and odds and ends to round out the meal. Corinna looked up from the dough she kneaded and smiled in greeting.

"Good day to you, Master Guardian," she said. Arrim, not subtle, elbowed Joe. Joe ignored him.

"Hi, Corinna," he said. He nodded at the bread. "Looks good." She beamed. She reminded him of home, too; her hair and eyes had a Hispanic look to them. She could be one of his cousins. And just like he felt nothing for his cousins, he felt nothing for her. Not her fault; she just wasn't Lynn.

Joe and Arrim stood at the hearth, scooping up stew with their flat bread as spoons. They weren't the only scavengers in the kitchens. There were a few kids and a handful of Captain Tal's guard, sitting by themselves at the old scarred wooden table over by the wall. They gave Joe and Arrim hard looks and turned back to their beer and soup. That was another thing. He reckoned he could do with friends about as much as anybody. It was hard to be either looked up to or distrusted.

He ate, thinking it would be good to get out of the stronghold and back to the woods, even though they had just arrived. That's where, after all those years of being on the move, he felt he belonged the most. He could feel the restlessness of the gordath even now, like an extra heart beating alongside his. As soon as he concentrated, the thrumming ceased. Sometimes he wasn't sure what the gordath wanted from him.

He glanced around and saw Corinna looking at him. She smiled and ducked her head a bit shyly.

"Should we prepare a handfasting?" Arrim said, half teasing, half in earnest. "She's a pretty one, a good cook, give you good babies."

Once he had thought about that with Lynn. She was the first woman he ever imagined he could settle down with. The gordath had other ideas though.

"I guess I should get my footing first, before I think about marrying," Joe said evasively. Arrim snorted.

"Marrying, now? You're a guardian, not one of the lords." At Joe's blank look, he said, "Marriage is for the Council, not us. *We* handfast—promise, before the grass god."

"Yeah, I don't know that I get the difference, Arrim, but no, I'm not planning that far ahead."

One of Tal's guards got up, and with an ostentatious look at the two guardians, he went over to Corinna, giving her a winning smile. She smiled back, blushed, and they had a conversation over the bread, with him swiping a loaf from the oven, tossing it to take the heat out of it, and her giving him a mock scolding.

"She's trying to make you jealous, that one," Arrim said, and Joe rolled his eyes. He'd had enough.

"Jesus, Arrim, give it a rest. You like her, you talk to her."

Joe pushed past the guards more roughly than he had to and left the kitchen behind. Almost immediately the temperature plunged. Joe made his way through the stone fortress, automatically heading back to the outer walls. He was restless, the thought of the mountain overhead oppressing him. He paused on the top of the stairs that led up to the walkway on the wall. The air had turned thick with twilight, the barest of sunsets filtering through the shadows. He could hear the rush of the river like a distant wind. He turned south to go down the other set of stairs, his boots tapping softly on the ancient stone. He was the only person on the walls.

The walkway led around the rose tower, which jutted out from the mountain, its own winding stairs carved out of stone and patched with mortar. Climbing rosebushes trailed up along the wall. In the spring they were thick with small white wild roses. Lynn had been imprisoned in that tower.

Joe stopped along the gallery, leaning on the wall. It was his favorite place in the stronghold. Here a series of columns faced out toward the river, light and air entering in through the arched openings. The setting sun made the river sparkle until his eyes hurt. Across the river the Aeritan headlands rose above the banks and faded into the distance. He could see the barest line of a road, white against the dark hills, dipping and curving along the line of the terrain.

It was hard, missing Lynn. They had only had a few short months to get to know each other. Sometimes he dreamed about her apartment over the barn at Hunter's Chase, its white curtains wafting in the breeze from the open windows while they made love in the evening after the day's work was through. He told himself not to think about it, but it was no good. She was an ache that was ever-present. Only the gordath had more of a hold on him, and he knew that the gordath would use his yearning for Lynn as a wedge to pry itself open.

Can't see her, can't hold her, he thought. But he could still go visit an old friend.

Red Gold Bridge's stables were in twilight except for a couple of glowing lanterns secured firmly by the main barn doors and the last remnants of the sun coming in through the high windows. A few grooms played a complicated game of cards and dice near the entrance, where the sun still lit up their table. They looked up.

"Guardian," one said in greeting. They were used to him.

"Evening," Joe said. He jerked his head at the big box stall on the side with the best light and the best air flow. "Just going to have a talk with Pride."

"One of these days you'll have to sit in with us," another groom said, as he always did.

To be fleeced within an inch of his life, for sure. Joe knew he would be lucky to come out of a game with his boots, his belt, and his shirt.

"On payday," Joe promised, as he always replied. They laughed and let him be.

Pride. They didn't call him Dungiven here. The town the big Irish hunter had been named for didn't exist in this world, so the stallion had been rechristened Pride. Dungiven had heard his voice, and the big horse turned around in his stall to greet him, his liquid eyes catching a bit of light. He snorted out, whuffing gently against Joe, his oaty breath warm and thick. The horse's muzzle was dark, the black turning to gray and then almost white. His nostrils flared, and his ears pricked. Joe rubbed his big cheek, and the horse snorted again.

Mindful of the grooms' presence, he didn't say aloud what he was thinking. *I miss her, too.* He didn't know horses the way Lynn did, but he sometimes thought that Dungiven looked over his shoulder first before looking at him, as if expecting Lynn to be right there beside him.

Dungiven snorted again, and his ears cocked forward, just as the grooms exploded out of their seats. Joe turned as Mrs. Hunt came in.

She acknowledged the grooms and their startled cries of "My lady!" with a graceful nod, but she came straight over to Joe and Dungiven.

Joe tried to keep his expression neutral. If she were here, Lord Tharp wouldn't be far behind, and he didn't want to have to deal with the man and his jealousy. Hearing them fight or watching as they punished each other with icy silences was bad enough. *She never should of come back.* He wondered why she did. She could have just pointed him and Arrim in the right direction, after all. Likely it had been out of guilt for opening up the gordath all those years ago and causing a war over her disappearance. He and Arrim had talked about it and decided that they better keep her away from the woods in case she had a change of heart and started things up all over again.

She stopped a few feet away from him. He didn't know if she had come here to talk or just to take in the horse, like him, so he waited for her to make the first move.

"Joe," she said in her even voice.

"Ma'am," he said courteously.

She didn't say anything for a while. He studied her, her face lost in the dim light. She came up on Dungiven's off side and laid her hand against the stallion's neck. The horse's skin quivered, but he stayed still, one ear tilted back—not flattened, as when a horse is angry, but attentive.

"You come here often," she said. It was a statement, but it was so close to a come-on he almost laughed. She couldn't have known that. Or maybe, since she had lived seven years in New York, she knew exactly what it meant.

"Yes, ma'am," he said. "I just like to keep an eye on him." Dungiven was one of them, after all. He didn't say that to Mrs. Hunt though. He didn't think she would like being lumped together with the barn handyman and a horse.

She gave a small laugh, and he could sense the grooms' shock. "He reminds me of home as well."

Busted, he thought. She knew exactly why he came to the stables, and it wasn't just to check on the big horse. But her words bespoke a dangerous homesickness. Aware of the grooms' interest, Joe tried to be tactful. He kept his voice low.

"Ma'am, best you don't think of New York as home."

She looked at him over the horse's mane. "Perhaps," she said, and he knew that would be the most he would get. She gave the horse a final pat and turned to face Joe head-on, her expression lost in the darkness of night.

"I should go. Eyvig will wonder where I am, and I know you are not comfortable with me here."

He was about to protest, even though she had the right of it, when she forestalled him.

"Sometimes, I just need someone to call me Mrs. Hunt. Or ma'am."

He heard the smile in her voice, overlaid with the faintest of tears, so he gave her what she needed.

"Good night, Mrs. Hunt."

"Good night, Joe."

He watched her go, the grooms so shocked at the familiarity of their conversation that their card game was forgotten. Joe sighed. Their meeting would be all over the stronghold in no time; the only thing that ran faster than the river in Red Gold Bridge was gossip. God only knew how Lord Tharp would take it. Well, he and Arrim would be out in the woods soon enough, and Tharp would just have to stew.

Joe woke in his small cell, groggy and disori-ented, with only the faintest memory of a dream to disturb him. He lay shivering with the blankets kicked half off, the rest a tangle, and tried to figure things out. It was pitch-black, the small fire on the hearth having gone out while he slept, and the darkness pressed down on him. His vision played tricks on him, making him think he could see sparks and flickers of light, so he closed his eyes. The cold stronghold air rushed over his bare chest, chilling him.

What woke me? He couldn't remember his dream except for a sense of foreboding. He sat up, untangling himself from the twisted blankets, and groped for his candle and rough matches. He scratched the match on the wall, and the light flared, the acrid smell of sulfur making his eyes water. He lit the candle and set it into the sconce on the side of the bed. The darkness retreated sullenly as his eyes adjusted.

Even before he reached out, he could sense it. The gordath was open.

"Shit," Joe swore under his breath. A sorry-ass excuse for a guardian he was. It should have been the first thing he thought of. He reached out tentatively. It wasn't like the last winter, when he first encountered a full-on gordath that had been out of control for months. Back then, the power was like a roaring turbine, overwhelming, dangerous, malevolent. This felt urgent but distant.

His gear sat at the foot of the bed. Joe put his feet on the floor and cursed again at the cold. He searched for his socks, found them, and put them on, then his jeans and shirt. It was too cold to stay naked, and he wasn't about to cower under the covers until morning. As he drew on his boots, he tried to shake the last remnants of sleep from his head. He grabbed the candle, holding it carefully so as not to drip wax down onto his fingers, and pushed open his door, just as Arrim stood about to open it, dressed and ready to go with his own candle, his pack slung over his shoulder.

"Good," the other man said, with no other preamble. He jerked his head. "Let's go, Guardian."

Joe grabbed his pack, glad he had kept it ready. He followed Arrim, their flickering candlelight throwing crazy shadows on the wall, glistening where the walls were damp. He wasn't sure whether to be pissed off or worried. A little of both, he thought. He didn't know what time it was, but if he wasn't going to get a full night's sleep after two weeks of deadheading through the woods, he was going to have to have a come-to-Jesus talk with whoever was messing around with the gordath.

And if it were Mrs. Hunt, he was going to be seriously pissed.

The tall, narrow house stood in a clearing in Gordath Wood between three tall trees, its rough stone weathered by time. It looked ancient, as if it were older than the forest itself. Narrow, vertical slits scarred the old stone. Its slate roof was broken. Where leaves had fallen and decayed, creating soil, a garden of moss and other plants grew among the slate. The house looked like a tor, a jagged mountain upthrust from the forest floor. The gordath, the portal between the worlds, was centered on this house. Joe knew that it lived in two places, at the end of a run-down lane in hunt country in upstate New York, and here, in Aeritan. Once the guardians lived here, Arrim had told him, but they had abandoned the house to live in Red Gold Bridge between patrols. He didn't say why, but Joe figured that it was because the guardians felt the same thing he felt every time he was near the place. The power of the gordath was most on edge here, most alive, most conducive to opening. It was dangerous to be too close to it, even if your job was to keep it closed.

The clearing was quiet, dark. It was high summer in Aeritan, but the forest stayed cool.

"What do you think?" he asked Arrim, keeping his voice low.

Arrim gestured toward the door. "Make sure no one's here. I want to take a look around the clearing."

Joe pushed open the heavy wooden door, putting his shoulder behind it as the door stuck. The wood scraped across the threshold with a dull squeak. The bottom floor was a bare room, and the cold from the stone floor seeped into his old boots. A fireplace hulked at one corner, debris collecting on the hearth.

There were a few remaining cartons that had once held shells for the guns that Bahard had run from New York to Aeritan, but the boxes were empty, and the cardboard had gotten clammy and fallen apart. The guns themselves—well, no one knew what had happened to them. The Aeritan Council had confiscated what they could at the end of last year's war, but Joe knew how that went. Plenty of guns to go around. At least there was a shortage of ammunition, and he doubted that Aeritan had the technology to make more. The smiths and metalwrights were good, but there was only so much they could do, and making modern ammo was beyond their capabilities. Nothing to stop a little reverse engineering, though, he thought. An enterprising Aeritan engineer could probably figure out how to make a decent facsimile of a modern gun if they took one apart.

The air inside was cold, and the house felt abandoned. Joe headed up the narrow stairs. Cold light spilled in on the landing, more debris in the corners and beneath the windows. At the top, he pushed open a door to one room. Empty.

The gathering emptiness in the house pressed down on him, and the gordath throbbed along with his heartbeat. It lived, he thought. Maybe it wasn't like a human, or even an animal, but it lived.

He thought he could perceive an extra edge this time, a malevolent intention. It wanted to be open, and it knew Joe was its enemy.

Joe opened the next door and looked around. Something compelled him, and he stepped over to the narrow window, leaning on the rough sill to get a better view. The ground was very far below. To his eyes, everything looked ordinary. There was the clearing, and the door in the ground to the root cellar—he could just make out the iron ring half submerged in fallen leaves that pulled the door up and open. The trees shot straight up into the overcast sky.

He frowned into the distance, between the trees. For a second something flickered, and he thought he could see . . .

Then it was gone, and he couldn't tell if he had really seen telephone wires or if it had just been his eyes trying to make familiar sense of tree branches. He knew better than to look again. To distract himself and break the gordath's hold, he turned away from the window. In the corner of the room stood a cask hidden by shadows and covered with debris that had blown in from the weather over the past seasons. It wasn't that big; it stood about knee-high on four ornately carved legs. Joe went over and brushed off the leaves and dirt composting on it. It looked like a lady's jewelry box, even had a pretty little clasp on it. He tried to lift the lid, but it stuck. The lock was mostly decorative, though, and no match for his knife. He gouged at the lock and snapped it free. The lid creaked open.

Joe stared down at the stacks of American currency neatly arrayed inside the chest.

"Joe!"

Arrim's voice rose faintly from the clearing, startling Joe. He came back to himself and hesitated. *The money's worthless here,* he told himself. Only good for starting a fire, or maybe stuffing inside a lumpy straw mattress. So why he wanted to grab it and stow it in his pack was beyond him.

He went over to the window. Arrim looked up at him. "Find anything?" he called out.

"Nothing," Joe shouted back. "Nobody's been here in months."

At least, not since Mark Ballard hid his payment for running guns between New York and Aeritan on the Aeritan side of the gordath. It was better than a bank and easier than laundering money. No one who would know what it was worth would ever find it, and it was safe until Mark needed it. Until now.

And I can't take it. Carry that money around long enough, and he would go crazy. Carry that money, and it would take no effort at all for the gordath to open, unlocked by greed, desire, and homesickness. He should burn it, but he knew he wouldn't. Instead, he lowered the lid to the little chest and left it behind.

He came down the stairs again to find Arrim kneeling in the clearing. The guardian swept his hand over the dirt and twigs as if he were looking for something. Joe watched him, puzzled. The master guardian could be closemouthed with his secrets. Joe could ask him what he was looking for, and all he might get was a vague, "I don't know," or "What do you think?" It was maddening, and it forced Joe to rely on his own intuition, which, he suspected, was the point.

Arrim stood. "All right," he said. "Ready?"

Joe nodded. He closed his eyes, gathering his strength.

"Don't get lost in the woods," the forestholders said. "You never know where you will end up." The gordath reached out and gathered in solitary travelers before they knew they had been taken. That's what had happened to Lynn last year when she rode Dungiven home through the Wood by herself. *Probably didn't even know what had happened to her,* Joe thought. Not till she came to Red Gold Bridge, and probably not even then . . . He mentally shook himself and refocused. As if it knew it was being thwarted, the gordath hummed harder, but that could have just been because Joe was concentrating now. He could feel Arrim gathering his own strength, and their breathing synchronized. He and Arrim and the gordath all breathed together the same, until he lost track of just which one he was.

When he first closed the gordath back in the winter, he knew instinctively what to do. The gordath had been out of control, but in a way, that made it easier—brute force answered with brute force. He and Arrim had joined forces, and the gordath backed down, folded in on itself, and closed up. This time it was like trying to hold water in his cupped hands. He couldn't get a handle on it. The more he tried to grab hold and force it to stay still, the less control he had. Sweat ran down his face and soaked his shirt.

"Dammit," he muttered, losing the connection. He could hear Arrim shift beside him and knew that the guardian was having the same trouble. Joe tried again, and his shallow trance broke even more easily this time. Joe opened his eyes and looked up, disgusted. Arrim snapped a curse of his own. He looked at Joe, his wild hair damp and matted.

"What's going on?" Joe said, frustration leaking out of his voice. "Why can't we close it?" He thought of the money and felt a pang of guilt. *Dammit, is this my fault?*

Next to him, Arrim muttered, "Forest god. I think I know what's happening. Thrice-bedamned meddlers."

"Arrim, you aren't making any sense."

"We're trying to close the wrong gordath."

"The wrong—" Joe stared at the other guardian.

Something zinged over their head and thunked into a nearby tree. A crossbow bolt.

After the first moment of paralysis, Joe and Arrim turned and bolted for the door. The clearing erupted as armed men swarmed out of the woods. Bolts thunked past them, breaking on the stone walls of the house or thudding into the door. Joe recognized they were deliberately shooting high. Men shouted, and Joe and Arrim hit the door at the same time, scrabbling for the bar and pushing.

They weren't fast enough. First Joe was hauled back and then Arrim, and they were dropped to the ground, a sword at Arrim's throat, a loaded crossbow at Joe's. His chest heaved as he struggled to control his breathing, a rock pressing into his back. The treetops almost closed out the sun, the sky white with summer heat. *Where the hell is Tal?* Wasn't that the way it always was—never a cop around when you needed one?

There were about a dozen men, dressed in rough leather and metal armor. They were masked, all were armed, and about six of them had crossbows, cocked and ready. His hunting knife and Arrim's old machete, used when they deadheaded through the woods, were taken, and then they were pulled up roughly and their hands tied behind their backs.

When they were secure, one man approached them. He was masked like all the others, but his armor was finer, his boots sturdy and well-made. *You can always tell a lord in Aeritan,* Joe thought. *Just look at the shoes.*

Of course, not even Lord Tharp carried a handgun the way this man did.

The leader spoke through his mask, his words muffled. "Guardians. Do as you are told, and you won't be harmed."

Joe glanced over at Arrim. The man nodded. He was pale and kept swallowing. Joe knew how he felt. This was bad. They were in big trouble.

It got worse. Another man stepped up next to the leader, dressed in hunting camo and carrying a nice hunting rifle that Joe would have coveted when he was younger.

"Joe Felz," said Mark Ballard with a grin. He was bearded and shaggy, and he looked like he had seen better days, but the unearned cockiness was still there, although Joe had to admit, the rifle backed him up. "Never thought I'd see you here. This must be a step up, right? You got tired of shoveling horse shit?"

Joe nodded at him cordially. "Mark. Still brownnosing?"

Furious, Mark swung on him, but the leader pulled him back by the collar of his heavy hunting jacket, now stained and weathered after a year or more of constant use. The leader stood in front of Mark. He didn't say anything. He didn't have to. Mark pointed at Joe.

"If he mouths off to me again, I'll kick his ass."

The masked lord said, "If you disobey my orders again, I'll have Drav kick yours."

Joe guessed that the man he referred to was the hulking guard who turned around at his name. Drav grinned under his mask, and Mark folded. Joe shook his head. It was cold comfort that Mark Ballard was barely better off than him and Arrim, but he'd take his comfort any way he knew how.

The leader jerked his head at the house. "Go find your coin and hurry and don't take long. We are far from welcome here."

Coin, huh? Uh-oh.

Mark sulked, but he went into the house. Joe waited, his skin prickling. He had no doubt what Mark was looking for, but what the man thought he was going to use American money for in Aeritan, he had no idea.

The clearing stayed quiet while they waited on Mark. Joe looked around, taking in their kidnappers. They were professional soldiers. He and Arrim were well and truly screwed.

They all watched as the pretty little chest sailed out of the top floor window and fell to the forest floor, its legs and lid smashed open. When Mark came out again, he was whistling. He ruffled the last of the stacks before shoving the money into his pack.

"Sweet," he said cheerfully. "A hundred grand, just like I left it. Hear that, Felz? Hare and I are going into business together, and you and your buddy here are going to help."

"Don't use my name." The leader—Hare—spoke tight little words that screamed of rage. Mark looked startled.

"What? It's not even your real name."

Joe barely kept from rolling his eyes. *Shut up, man,* he thought, but he knew Mark wouldn't. Hare's voice was still barely under control when he spoke again.

"Are you through, Lord Bahard? Maybe you would like to visit Red Gold Bridge again, and tell *Lord Tharp* of our plans? Or perhaps we can take our leave, now that we have what we need, and get on with it."

Mark just shrugged. "Yeah, I got what I wanted. You have the guardians. We're set."

Joe and Arrim were pushed into line, separated by several guards, and hustled off. *Crap,* Joe thought. *What have we gotten ourselves into?*

Two

Night had fallen over Hunter's Chase. Lynn
finished her walk-through of the hill barn, peeking in on the
horses drowsily finishing their hay, a few already dozing. The
warmth of the barn, with its aroma of wood shaving bedding
and oats, the heavy scent of horses and manure, enveloped
her. She took a last look around, turned off the light, and
pulled the heavy doors together. Outside, the stars twinkled
faintly in a light-drenched sky. It never really got dark anymore, not even out in the country. She remembered the night
on the plains in Aeritan, the stars a cold, burning swath across
a strange sky.

Was Joe looking at those stars? Was Crae? Sometimes,
lying in bed alone, she thought of the choice she could have
made with Crae, implicit in their stolen kisses. She could
have stayed in Aeritan with him, and then only one man
would have haunted her sleep, not two.

Maybe it was better not to have to make the choice. Sure, it
was the coward's way out, but how could she be happy with
Crae if she knew it meant she could never be with Joe?

Unwillingly she let herself turn to the barn apartment, its

windows dark and lifeless. She had loved Joe. She was pretty sure he had loved her.

If I had to do it over, she told him silently, *I never would have ridden home through the woods last year. Not if it meant never seeing you again.*

And as a consolation prize, she got Hunter's Chase. Now that had been a surprise, when Lady Sarita signed over the stables to her. In a couple of ways, the gift had been more of a curse. The business of running the stables had been a sobering experience. Lynn sometimes felt the harder she worked, the faster she fell behind. On the other hand, the beauty of the place seeped into her, and she felt blessed that she had the guardianship of it. There was no other word, she reflected, even if *guardian* had taken on a load of new meanings since last year.

The air was cool, flowing, the heat from the midsummer day long gone. The cool raised goose bumps on her bare arms. Lynn rubbed her arms absently as she headed down the gravel path to the house, its warm lights inviting. Headlights caught her eye as a car turned up the drive, rumbling slowly over to the main barn.

Whoever it was parked next to Joe's old car, still sitting there from last year, Queen Anne's lace growing up around the wheels. Lynn tsked in annoyance. It didn't look like a client's car. Who would be coming to the barn at this hour?

She walked over as the person got out of the old station wagon.

"Can I help you?" she called out.

The woman turned, her features indistinct. "Are you Katherine Hunt?" she said, her accent tinged with something foreign.

Lynn's blood ran cold.

"She isn't here anymore," she said carefully. "I'm Lynn Romano. I own Hunter's Chase."

The woman sighed. There was just enough light for Lynn to make her out. She was older, in her fifties, her face fleshy and strong. She had once been very beautiful and still had remnants of it.

"Then maybe you can help me," she said, and Lynn began to peg the accent. "I'm really looking for Joe Felz. I'm Isabella Felz. He's my son."

You are an idiot, Lynn, **she told herself as she** brought in two cups of coffee, decaf for Mrs. Felz. She should have told her Joe was gone, and she had no idea where, and sent her on her way. The woman sat in the living room in the low light, looking around at all the silver cups and ribbons, the photos of horses past and present, the old elegant furniture that had Mrs. Hunt's stamp all over it. She smiled at Lynn's approach.

"Oh, thank you," she said. "You are being very kind."

"I wish I could help you," Lynn said, taking the other chair. "But Joe left last year."

"He didn't say where he was going." It wasn't a question.

Lynn shook her head, forced herself to sip so she wouldn't say too much. Mrs. Felz sighed. "That was him. He never told us where he was, even as a boy. He had a tree fort in the cottonwoods along the creek, and he'd sleep up there for days. The day he got his license was the day I knew we wouldn't be seeing him for much longer."

Tears stung Lynn's eyes. She had known nothing about Joe.

"We got mail from an address in Connecticut, so I started there. I drove up all last week. But his landlord said that Joe had been in jail, that he had murdered someone. And he didn't know what happened to him, that he thought he might have jumped bail." Mrs. Felz put down her coffee and groped for a tissue from her pocket. She cried for a few minutes, and her next words were almost indecipherable. "He couldn't have. Not my Joe." She looked at Lynn. "Is that what you meant, when you said he left?"

Lynn didn't know what to say. "No, I—well—" She stopped,

warning bells going off in her head. Whatever lie she told could only get her deeper in trouble, and this mother, who had driven all the way up from Texas, was not about to leave any stone unturned. "I knew Joe, and he wouldn't have killed anyone. He worked with me, and he was a good man." *I loved him, and I wish I could tell you that.* It was hard; every step was dangerous.

She found a tissue from the box on the table between them and handed it to Mrs. Felz. The woman blew her nose and wiped it.

"Why didn't he take his car?" she said thickly.

"His—car?"

"That's his car, isn't it? The one I parked next to? If he was running away, I mean."

Lynn didn't say anything, pressing her lips tightly shut. Blood hammered in her temples. At her silence, Mrs. Felz looked up.

"Yes, it's his car."

A frown furrowed deep between the woman's eyebrows. "So why didn't he take it?"

"I don't know." At Mrs. Felz's confusion, Lynn threw up her hands. "I don't know! He went away, and I don't know what happened to him. I wish I did. Like you, I hope every day that he's okay."

"Oh," Mrs. Felz said. A smile appeared. "You're the girl."

"I beg your pardon?"

"I talked to him last summer—he called. He hardly ever did that. He told us he met someone. His daddy was upset, of course, because he knew it was one more thing to keep Joe from coming back, but I was happy for him."

"He told you about me?"

"Not much, but I could tell he was happy."

Despite herself, Lynn smiled. Mrs. Felz started crying again.

"I'm so sorry. I am just so worried about him, and I miss him, and I want him to come home."

If he did his job right, he would never come home.

Joe's mother got herself together and stood. "Thank you. You've been very helpful. Do you mind telling me how to find a motel?"

There was nothing for miles, and she would surely get lost on the country roads trying to find her way to town. Lynn sighed.

"I have a better idea," she said.

It was strange to see a light in the apartment over the barn. Lynn watched it until it flicked off, and then she went up to her own bedroom. She had made sure the apartment was kept clean, in part because she knew that at some point she was going to need a barn manager. It was perfect for Joe's mom. Mrs. Felz carried up her small case and thanked Lynn as if she had given her a suite at a fancy hotel.

As she crawled into bed she thought, *This is a very bad idea. Very bad.* Mrs. Felz was asking all the right questions. It was only a matter of time before she started to put things together. She'd never get the right answer, of course, only the logical one—that Joe was dead and Lynn had something to do with it. She stared up at the ceiling, lost in the darkness, and listened to the beat of her heart.

Oh, Joe, she thought. I wish you were here.

Driving home from the horse show, Kate rested her head against the window of her mom's car, the cool of the summer afternoon pleasant against her skin. She was still in show clothes—midnight blue jacket, fawn-colored breeches, and white shirt—but her stock was unpinned, and her hair hung in limp strands around her face. She had tossed her boots in the backseat, along with a few ribbons she had won with Allegra, the Hunter's Chase mare she was riding for Lynn. Her stocking feet were propped up on the dashboard.

It had been a good show. The mare was difficult and moody, nothing like her sweet Mojo. But Mojo had died on the battlefield outside Red Gold Bridge, and so Kate had been working with the difficult horse. The riding mostly made her parents happy. She figured that way they could think everything was back to normal. And it had gotten fun again, but she could already tell it was no longer her whole life, the way it used to be. *B.A.—Before Aeritan,* she thought.

She moved restlessly against her seat belt. Her back itched. Her mom glanced at her.

"Are you okay, honey? We can call Dr. Gilbert if the skin grafts are bothering you. She said there are some things she can give you."

"It's not that bad. I probably just got some dust down my shirt."

"Well, take a shower when you get home."

Kate nodded, rubbing her forehead against the window. Her mom went on, keeping an eye on traffic, "So, did you get a chance to look at those college Web sites I bookmarked? And you also want to take a look at your résumé. I was talking with Miranda Bolton, and she said Sophie has been putting together a portfolio of all of her extracurriculars, and I think that's something we should do, too. It's not too early to start, and we don't want to leave it till too late."

"I know," Kate said, trying to face down rising panic. "I just—it's hard to think about all of that." Every time she thought of junior year—the make-or-break year, as everyone kept on saying ominously—she wanted to run shrieking for the woods.

"Well, you know, it's something colleges want nowadays. Your grades are good, your test scores are good, but Harv— colleges are looking for something extra. And I'm afraid that you've spent so much time on riding, that hasn't left much time for putting in community service."

Well, let's see. I extracted bullets from bodies without anesthesia and sewed them up, I helped set broken legs, I made all sorts of medicines and drafts to fight infections that soldiers died from anyway, I rode a horse into battle as a courier, and I stole a car. What would Harvard think of that?

Kate took a breath. "Okay," she said. "I . . ." Her voice trailed off as her mother slowed for a red light. Kate caught sight of someone standing in the long shadows on the side of the road, and she turned to look as her mother stopped the car.

Tall, dark, longish-haired. His clothes . . .

His clothes were Aeritan clothes.

Time stopped. She looked up, her eyes drawn upward without her control. He looked back at her, his eyes as black as his lank hair.

"Go! Go, Mommy, go! Drive!" Kate heard the screaming, realized it was herself.

"Kate!" The car jerked forward but slammed to a stop as Mrs. Mossland realized cross traffic was still streaming.

"Drivedrivedrivedrive! Mom, please go!"

How had he come here? How had he gotten through?

"Kate, my God . . . What is it?"

The light turned finally, and the car sped forward, Mrs. Mossland trying to talk to Kate, and Kate lost in her tears.

"It was the general, Mom. It was him."

She knew her mom was talking to her dad in the kitchen downstairs. Unable to sit still, she paced around her bedroom in her old pajama bottoms and a tank top, her hair wet from her shower. Pictures of Mojo stared at her from shelf space all over the room, intermixed with blue ribbons and silver cups, horse posters and model horses, and a few stuffed animals from her childhood.

When she first got back from Aeritan, she had walked around her room this way for hours, everything unfamiliar, her anxiety making her pace like a racehorse. Only gradually, when her brain reset to Earth mode, could she be soothed and take comfort again from her memories.

Sighting General Marthen made her feel as if she were back in camp once more.

Colar sat at her computer desk, still in his shorts and T-shirt from lacrosse practice. His forearms were thick from practice—well, she thought, she supposed that they were pretty well-muscled from swordsmanship, too.

"You sure?" he said.

She sighed, adjusting her tank top strap. "I don't know. Sometimes—sometimes I think I see him everywhere. But this was different. Only, he was in the long shadows—and he, it just—"

"You can't keep something like the portal closed forever," he said thoughtfully.

"Why would he come here?" She felt another jolt when she remembered the way he looked at her through the windows of her mom's car. When he had her beaten in the center of camp, he kept his eyes on her the whole time. She felt an overflowing of rage and despair, of hatred and helplessness, once again. *I will kill him,* she thought. *I have to kill him.* But she couldn't; he was a general, a warrior. She couldn't hold her own against him. She glanced at Colar. *He'd fight for me,* she thought, and in the next moment she thought, *No.* Because he would lose, too. He was a warrior, but he was also a kid.

And what am I, a princess who needs a champion? If Marthen were here, she needed to deal with him herself.

"He came because of you," Colar said practically. For a second his face went hard, and he looked like his father, Lord Terrick.

"I don't want him."

Colar laughed a little. He swiveled in the computer chair. "The first thing we need to do," he said, "is find out if it was really him."

"How do we do that?"

He grinned. "We scout."

When Kate met Colar last year, he had been a scout in the general's army. From his look of anticipation, it seemed like one of the things he might be homesick for. Lacrosse and basketball were okay, but Colar was so much *older* than the rest of the kids their age. So was she, for that matter. It got hard to sit in class last spring after everything that had happened in camp.

They both looked up at the sound of footsteps on the stairs.

Her dad knocked and poked his head in. "Kate, we need to talk. Cole, can you excuse us, please?"

"Yes, sir," Colar said automatically, getting up, and Kate caught her dad's pained expression. No matter how often he had invited Colar to call him David, he wouldn't. He called his own dad sir. He was hardly going to be so familiar with her dad. Even if the Mosslands had become his parents now, or foster parents at least.

Except, if she *had* seen General Marthen, then somehow he had gotten through. And if he went through, then Colar could go home again. *I could go back, too,* she dared to think, and for a moment she almost forgot to breathe. Did she want that? *Could* she want that?

When Colar left, her dad took his spot at the desk. "Your mom told me what you thought you saw," he said finally.

"I saw him," Kate said. The lump in her throat made the words hard to get out. "You have to believe me."

"Kate . . ." He sighed, raked his hands through his hair. "Kate, we can barely believe what happened to you last winter. Now this? Look, it's time to move on. You can't keep going back to this—this story."

"What, you think I'm making it up out of some sick *need*? My back, Dad! You saw my back! You saw what happened, what he ordered them to do to me!"

"Kate, calm down. Look, it's not that simple. Even if he is here, how do we go to the police about him? No one will believe it, and that means no one will take it seriously."

"You mean no one will take you seriously," she said, bitterness in her voice. A part of her knew that it was to their credit her parents had taken in Colar. They'd had to call in a lot of favors and lie to a lot of people about where he came from to make it happen. After all, he was a boy from nowhere, with no record of his past, of his parents, of even ever being in "the system." It took a lot for her parents to make a new life for him, a legitimate life.

They never once said a word about what that meant for her mother's career trajectory as an influential prosecutor or her

father's plans to be named CEO of a Fortune 500 company.
One whisper about the son fostered under strange circumstances, and it could all be over for them.

She knew all this, and it still hurt that they wouldn't believe her about what happened last year.

"So what you're saying," she began through her tears, "is that because no one else will believe us, you won't believe me."

"Kate, I do—your mom and I, we do believe you. But you have to understand how far-fetched this all is. And you said that thing was closed, that no one else could come through. And now—this *general* is here? How are we supposed to take this?" He drew a breath. "Your mother and I have decided. We should have done this sooner, but better late than never."

They're sending Colar away. She stared with dawning horror at her father.

"We think you need to see a therapist."

Colar of Terrick, heir to the House of Terrick
in Aeritan, but now just Cole Mossland, went downstairs to the kitchen. Something smelled good, and he was reminded of the kitchens back home. The cooks labored all day for the people of Terrick, the householders and the lords, visiting villagers, and wandering peddlers, men-at-arms looking for work, farmers, crafters, others. The kitchen at Terrick was never quiet and never dull. As a kid and even just before he went to war with his father, he liked to sit in the kitchen and hear the wanderers' tales, especially in the winter when the land was shut down by sleet and ice.

Here the kitchen was empty more often than not. The Mossland family usually lived on takeout. Colar liked Indian, himself. Its spices and scents were the most like home.

Tonight Mrs. Mossland was cooking. Kate told him her mom used to cook all the time, that she loved it and could putter in the kitchen all day, stirring, chopping, tasting. It was her rest and her joy, just as his own mother loved to work the wool from their sheep into thread and then cloth, dying, weaving, shaping. She had special songs for each part of the work that she said worked the blessing of the grass god's daughter into every fiber. He didn't think Mrs. Mossland sang to work blessings into her food.

Mrs. Mossland looked up at his approach. She and Kate had the same fine, straight hair and the same nose and mouth, but Kate's eyes were her father's, as was the cast of her face.

Mrs. Mossland's face was flushed from the heat of the pots. Steam rose from a bubbling pot of pasta, and in a gleaming skillet she was sautéing shrimp in butter, garlic, and wine. His mouth watered.

"Oh, hi, Cole," she said. She made an apologetic face. "Is David still upstairs with Kate?"

Colar nodded. "Can I help?" he asked. He hadn't known till he came here that he liked to cook. Back home his only role in the kitchen had been to run in, steal dinner, and run out with his brothers and sister, the cooks shouting at their backs.

"Sure. Do you want to put together a salad?" She nodded at the butcher block table where all the ingredients waited, freshly washed.

The knives were dull again. No one in the family seemed to know how to keep them sharp except for Colar. He got out the sharpener and set to work, the dull scraping the only sound between them. Mrs. Mossland seemed almost lost in thought, but he could tell what was on her mind the way she kept glancing at the kitchen door.

The silence didn't bother him. He honed the knives and thought about what Kate had discovered. The general had come through, looking for her, most likely. His cheeks heated as he remembered what the scouts had talked about, how the general had taken Kate to bed. He himself had seen her coming from the general's tent late at night. And the general had her flogged when he found out she and Colar had kissed. *My fault,* he thought, but he couldn't stop thinking about her, and it was all mixed up with some idea of stealing her from the general.

Instead, it had gotten her so badly beaten that she would bear the scars for life, even with the skin grafts the doctors here had performed.

"Cole?" Mrs. Mossland said, and he startled. He loosened his grip on the knife. The knife was sharp. He set to chopping bell peppers.

So he could go back. The question was, did he want to? There was no place for the son of the lord of Terrick in this country, to be sure, but that didn't mean there wasn't a place for Cole Mossland, age seventeen, foster son of the House of Mossland.

School, for one. Going to school was a foreign experience. He had never been with so many people his own age, all in one place. And what they learned! He could read and write in Aeritan, but the math he was learning now was far beyond anything he ever could have been taught, even in Brythern, the seat of learning. As for science, he couldn't ask half the questions he longed to, because most of the time they were so elementary they were about things everyone else here already knew. But he devoured the books, once his brain reset from going through the portal and he could learn to read again. There were so many marvels here that he had thought of them as magic when he first encountered them. But it wasn't magic. It was technology, and it could be used by anyone, developed by anyone, and the basic principles were taught in his books.

Could he leave this behind? He dressed the salad and put the bowl on the table. The shrimp scampi waited, steaming in a bowl of hot pasta, and Mrs. Mossland pulled bread from the oven. The table was set; there were even small glasses of wine for Colar and Kate.

"Ah, there you are," Mrs. Mossland said with false brightness as Kate and her father came in. Both were subdued. Kate looked as if she had been crying. "I thought we were going to have to send out a scouting party."

Kate and Colar exchanged glances as they slid into their seats. The chatter continued, light and inconsequential, throughout dinner, but Colar's thoughts were far away, to a life he had thought closed to him.

Three

The high windows of the house at Trieve, some paned with wavering glass, glinted in the rising sun. The fields at the foot of the terraced steps were wreathed in early morning mist, a soft gray just tinged with the palest yellow. Crae's breath smoked, even though it was high summer. Trieve was a mountain holding, and the air kept its chill. He wrapped his half cloak around himself, slung his crossbow and bolts over his back, a sword hanging in the scabbard at his belt, and headed for the barn. The old building hulked in the dawn light. It was older than the house itself and had once served as the house for Trieve's lords, when they had been holders themselves. Now it loomed in the mist, an ancient structure of stone and timber.

He pushed open the great door and was enveloped in the smell of the byre: horses, cows, manure, hay. Crae sneezed.

"Good morning, my lord," said one of his men.

"'Morning to you," Crae said. The cows lowed, their bags heavy with milk, and the men chivvied them outside to the milking barn on the lower terrace. The cows went willingly;

they needed the relief. Crae watched them go and then pushed open the half door to his horse's box.

"So there boy," he said. The gelding nickered at him. He was one of Stavin's horses, actually. Hero. Stavin's daughter Tevani had named him. The big chestnut horse, his coat and mane a red brown, was tall and sturdy, tall enough for Crae, who stood a head taller than his friend had.

Not a day went by that Crae didn't think of Stavin and his death on a snowy road on the outskirts of Red Gold Bridge, or his friendship, or the fact that everything he now called his own once belonged to Stavin.

Hero was well-groomed already. The grooms had brushed him and picked out his feet. Crae lifted them anyway out of old habit. When he was captain at Red Gold Bridge, a year and another life ago, he was only Captain Crae, and if he didn't take care of his own mount, no one else would.

He tacked the horse up himself. Hero fought the bit sulkily, tossing his head, then settled down, and Crae led him out. He knew that the horse enjoyed his early morning rides as much as Crae did, who liked to scout the lands surrounding the house as he used to patrol around Red Gold Bridge. He cleared the barn and mounted up, just as a little voice called out to him.

"Lord Crae!" Tevani came running up, slowing as she had been taught before she got too close to the horse's hooves. She waited, hands on her hips, at four years old looking like her mother and father both. She wore thick leggings under her thick skirt, a half-buttoned shirt over all, which still had butter and crumbs from her breakfast on it. Her face, too, it looked like. And her hair . . . Crae winced. Jessamy, her mother, was likely looking for her at this minute, ready with a wet cloth, a hairbrush, and a scolding. "I want to go, too!"

He leaned down to talk to her. "You're covered with butter, Tevani. Lady Jessamy will want you to go back to the house and get cleaned."

Tevani smeared herself more in trying to wipe up her breakfast. "Lord Crae, please take me with you. Please? Mama is only busy with Jori, and Calyne tells me I must be a good girl, and it's easier to be good when I'm riding. And Snowflake is too small," she added, referring to her pony and preempting his suggestion.

If he took her up he would only incur Jessamy's wrath all the more—not that it was hard to do. But she looked so forlorn, and he had always been too easy with her. *I must be sterner,* he thought, but it never seemed to be the right time. Stavin had always spoiled her rotten, too.

"All right," Crae said. "But only for a little, and then you must go into the house. Agreed?"

She hopped up and down. "Yes! You are the best lord of Trieve after my father!"

She couldn't have seen him wince. He dismounted, picked her up, and swung her into the saddle. He mounted again behind her. She immediately took the reins, her hands at the proper angles. Hero snorted and threw up his head but obeyed when Crae added pressure behind the girth.

"Can we gallop?" she said as they went down the terraced slope, Hero half sitting before jumping down each level. Tevani rode it well for someone whose legs were so short she couldn't really straddle the saddle. She was a good little rider though. Born to it, fearless, with an instinctive sureness in her that horses responded to. *Not sure where that came from,* Crae thought. Stavin didn't have the attentiveness, and Jessamy was an indifferent horsewoman.

"Not downhill, Tev. Maybe at the bottom."

"Here?" she asked at the next level.

"The bottom, Tev. When we reach the road."

She giggled at each of Hero's little jumps, and Crae decided that the company wasn't so bad after all. She chattered happily, and he listened with half an ear, as the fog burned off and the sun rose behind them, making their shadows impossibly long.

When they reached the road, Crae took the reins and pulled up Hero to let the horse rest. It was hard riding the terrace. Downhill required concentration and balance. Uphill was even worse, not just because of the incline but because each level was at just the right height and length to keep most horses from taking a comfortable stride, especially one carrying an armed rider.

It was an effective defense.

After a bit he let Tevani have the reins again, and they began walking along the road, Hero's hooves clopping pleasantly along the hard-packed dirt. A tumbledown stone wall, holding back uncultivated scrub and second growth, followed roughly along the road as it wound around the foot of the hill, meeting a rougher road that undulated through the scrub, lost in the sunrise and the fog. He knew that road. More than half a year ago he had ridden it with Lynna. It led to the plains, and beyond that Red Gold Bridge, and beyond that, Gordath Wood. And beyond that, he thought, to somewhere else, where she now lived and he could not go.

Hero snorted and shied. Crae thought he heard a crack or a rustle, and old habits leaped to the fore. Even as Tevani giggled at the sudden movement, he reached behind himself for the crossbow, cursing his ill luck for bringing her. She hampered him—she could be in danger—he could not load a crossbow with her in front of him.

All of this he thought in a flash as he caught Hero behind the girth with his heel and faced the sound.

Just a stray sheep, he thought, even as a head peeked over the tumbledown stone wall, and then another. *Not crows. Not crows.*

They were crows. Holdless, ragged men, they had been plaguing the countryside for months after the war set off by Red Gold Bridge.

Crae could not ride fast enough up the terraces without being swarmed by crows. He would have to hold them off so that Tevani could escape.

Crae swung over Hero's haunches, crossbow up, knowing that he was doomed. He drew his sword with his other hand and spared a glance for the girl, her small face white and frightened now. She had the reins. Her little legs were in perfect position.

"Ride, Tevani!" he roared. He smacked Hero on the hind-quarters, and the horse squealed and bolted, Tevani's scream as high-pitched. She stayed on, though, as Hero carried them both away from danger.

As the crows boiled over the wall at him, he could think of only one thing: if they didn't kill him, Jessamy surely would.

There were six crows. Crae dropped his use-less crossbow but took two of the bolts from the quiver, holding them point out, the sword in the other hand. The crows carried staffs and mauls. He took in all the information he could, backing up to the terrace to keep any from getting behind him.

They came on, grinning, the odds in their favor. They were all ragged and skinny, their teeth brown and broken. Lordless men, he thought. Lawless men. A murder of crows.

Two broke ahead and attacked, swinging their makeshift weapons, no less deadly for all that, and nearly taking one another out before they reached Crae. He grinned, too. That was the problem with mobs: they could be as dangerous to one another as they could to their prey.

He ducked a swinging maul, the momentum taking the man around with it, and brought up the crossbow bolt. It caught the man in the back, and he screamed. Crae took the other man with his sword through his belly, coming in under the staff. It smacked down on his arm, but by then he had already skewered the crow, and the blow lacked force. Crae kicked the man off his sword and back at his fellows.

The rest came on, but by then he had killed or maimed the two.

They gave wordless cries of rage and fear. Crae roared back. A staff caught him a ringing blow, and light crashed in his head. He stumbled backward, knocked off his feet. He lost his sword and cursed himself for giving them another weapon, a good weapon.

He struggled up, only to be knocked down again. His right arm was useless, and a maul crashed down on his shin. *Forest god, help me . . .*

No. There was no forest god here.

Our Father, who art in heaven . . .

Where had those words come from?

Lynn had said them in the forest when they had come upon the smallholding that had been crushed by the earthshaking. She had summoned her god from across the portal to help the forest god lay the dead to rest.

He had to summon . . . he had to summon his own god. But he had no god. Not the forest god of Red Gold Bridge, or the sky god of Wessen. Nor the gods of any lowly captains . . . Crae scrabbled for his remaining crossbow bolt and drove it upward, catching one of his attackers in the thigh. The man screamed and dropped back.

Three. I can take three. He pushed himself backward and grabbed the maul by the middle of the shaft. He could hardly lift it, one-handed, but the crows fell back.

"I am Lord Crae," he said. He pushed to his feet, balancing on his good leg, shaking with effort. "This is my land. Mine!" He lifted the maul over his head, barely able to control it, the weight almost taking him over backward. He roared again, as wordless as the crows. "I am lord of Trieve! I summon the lord's god! I am Crae of Trieve!"

Something happened. Something changed. The light was different. The crows were different. A blazing went through him. The pain faded, though he knew that was just the blood pumping hard in his veins. When he had been raised by the Council and given lordship over Trieve, they had told him, "It is the will of the high god." He had felt nothing then.

Now he felt it, the high god's will, like a light going on inside his head. Trieve was his, but more, *he* was Trieve's.

Had Stavin ever felt this? Had Jessamy?

He roared again. "This is my land! Begone!"

They backed away and fled, leaving behind their two dead and one maimed. The man he had hamstrung tried to crawl off, and Crae watched his laboring progress. He lowered the maul and let it drop, and looked with dazed disinterest at the blood dripping between his fingers.

As he stood there, a thundering of hoofbeats rose up behind him, and Trieve's men—his men—galloped down the terraces to his rescue. They saw the crows, and some gave chase, shouting. Another went to kill the man still crawling, his sword raised.

Crae held up a hand. "Wait."

They all turned to look at him, at the bloody, ruined figure of their lord. "Bring him to the house. I want to talk to him."

Then everything went black.

When he woke again, he was in his own bed in his own chamber. It had been the one he had been used to when he guested at Trieve as Captain Crae, Lord Stavin's common friend. It had not seemed right to move into Stavin's chamber, even though it was his now. And he and Jessamy, though married, did not share a bed. She had been near to giving birth to Stavin's son at the time of their wedding for one, and Jori was still a babe. Crae looked around, awareness of the present coming back to him. The horse doctor Truarch was there and Calyne, Trieve's housekeeper. His arm was bandaged and splinted. He used his other hand to feel his head. Bandaged as well. The horse doctor bent over him when he saw Crae move.

"Stay still," he ordered. "You almost got killed."

"I know," Crae whispered. It was all his voice could do. He turned his head. "Tevani?"

Calyne came up to him, putting a cool, careworn hand against his cheek.

"Fine, fine, Lord Crae," she said, her eyes wet. "She was frightened, but she rode straight home and told us you needed help. She's been begging us to let her see you."

His mouth moved tiredly in a smile. "Tell her in a few days." He didn't want her to see him like this. He remembered something else. "Does the crow live?"

Calyne and Truarch exchanged glances. The horse doctor replied. "He lives, Lord Crae, but we don't understand . . ."

Crae hardly did himself. "Where is he?"

"In the storeroom by the kitchen. It has the only lock, and Vanar, the blacksmith from the village, gave us a stout chain as well."

Crae nodded. "Keep him as well as you can." He fought the weariness, managing to ask one more thing. "Jessamy?"

"She wants to let you rest," Calyne said, a little tremulously.

"I need to talk to her."

"She . . . the baby . . . Lord Crae, you are still not well, and she is still tired, and her brother is coming . . ."

"Send her in."

It would enrage her to be summoned, but he needed to talk with her. *Enough of this pussyfooting around. Trieve will suffer if I do not take up my lordship.* He remembered little of the battle, but he knew what had happened. He had called on the high god, and the high god had answered.

He slept a bit then and was roused by voices and the crying of the baby boy. Crae opened his eyes, and there was Jessamy sitting by his bed, hushing the baby and studiously not looking at him.

He waited until she looked up. Her color rose, and he saw that her kerchief was askew. She never could keep it right as a good lady should. Her shining brown hair peeked out over her forehead. Her brown eyes met his, her mouth straight with displeasure.

"Well, are you satisfied?" she snapped. "Taking her out there with you, then leaving her to ride home by herself for help? She's four years old, Crae! You endangered her life. You have no idea of all the things that could have happened to her."

"Do you want to go home to Favor?" he said. He still could only whisper, and she had to lean forward to catch his words. When they struck home, her lips parted. She paled.

"Are you sending me away?"

The baby squalled, and she looked down at him, soothing him with a broken whisper. Crae made an impatient movement with his good hand, though he couldn't do much.

"Not . . . what I meant," he managed. "I meant . . . is Trieve your home? Or is Favor?"

Her brother was lord of Favor. He had been on the other side of the Aeritan war, siding with the Council. Jessamy's husband had sided with Lord Tharp and Red Gold Bridge. The rift had driven the family apart.

"Trieve is my home, Crae. You can't—you can't mean to send me away. The Council—when we married, that voided the Council resolution against me."

"I'm not sending you away. Listen." He was losing his strength. "Something happened when the crows attacked. I called on the high god—and he came."

Her voice was impatient. "Of course. When the Council elevated you, you took the high god as your god. That is what the summoning is."

"No." He struggled to speak. "This was different. I felt nothing when the Council named me lord." He couldn't explain to her what he felt, and not just because he had no strength. "Tell me of the summoning."

She sighed and rolled her eyes. "When we are called, or summoned, we become lord in the place of our father—or sometimes our mother, though that is rare. Lady Wessen, I believe, is the only one of her generation. Regardless. My brother became Favor. I did not. If I had been, I would have been Lady Favor. But, Crae, you know this, because when the Council called you, that was the same as being summoned."

No, it was nothing like. The Council ritual had been nothing like being summoned, if his battle with the crows were any indication. And Stavin, who would talk about anything, had never once mentioned his summoning. Crae's head hurt, and he struggled to keep awake. He was not naive. He knew all men nudged their gods along sometimes and made sure they moved in the right directions. But he had to get to the bottom of this.

"Did Stavin . . . ever speak to you of his summoning?"

"Oh, Crae, for goodness' sake. Why would he?"

His eyes closed, and he sank closer to sleep. He tried one

last time. "Jessamy, which of the children will be Lord of Trieve after me?"

She was silent for a long time, and he opened his eyes and peered at her. She had the grace to turn away from him when she saw he was looking at her.

"Of . . . of course, if you have . . . a child, perhaps that child . . ." Her voice faded away. He knew what she meant without her having to say the words out loud. To protect her own children's right, Jessamy would see to it that he never had children. He had been elevated to lordship, but it was a sham, or supposed to be. The lords expected that he would die without issue and leave no legacy.

His weakness was a mercy, and he gave in to it. He heard her get up and the door close behind her, and then sleep overtook him, drowning his bitterness.

At length he healed, but slowly. It took days for the headaches to fade and the bruises to turn from violent purple to green and yellow, and weeks more before his leg began to heal. Truarch had set his leg in a complicated cradle of bandages and splints, keeping the bone straight so it wouldn't reknit awry. Crae knew it would never be the same, despite all of Truarch's good care. He would be the crippled lord ever on. Well, he could still shoot a crossbow. That was his strength. So long as he could still shoot, he could still lead.

Tevani came in to see him, brought by Calyne. The little girl ran to him and buried her face in his side.

"I'm sorry, Lord Crae," she said tremulously.

"Tevani! Don't take such liberties—" Calyne scolded, but Crae raised his hand and shushed her.

"You did well, chick," he said. "You were very brave. Did you ride hard?"

She lifted her head and nodded, her cheeks wet. She looked so like Stavin. *She is the closest I will ever have to a child,* Crae thought. *So I will raise her as I see fit.* "Hero is your horse now. See you take care of him well, and he will take care of you."

The little girl stared at him, her tears forgotten.

"Yes, Lord Crae," she said.

She cannot call me father, he thought. *So it will have to do.*

It didn't take long for Jessamy to hear what he had done. She came in as he was helped to his feet by the horse doctor, her kerchief and her skirts flying.

"How dare you," she said, and her voice shook with her anger. "How dare you make such a decision! She is my daughter! You cannot do this!"

Crae looked at the doctor and the housekeeper, and with a gesture he motioned them to leave. They hesitated, looking from him to her and then backed away, hastily gathering up the doctor's draughts and nostrums.

"That is well," Jessamy said. She rolled up her sleeves. "It is time we had this out." She squared her shoulders. "I've overlooked you spoiling her, because high god knows—" She caught herself at the invocation but then went on. "High god knows with the death of her father, she could use some extra kindness. But this. This? First you let her ride out with you, with no men, no weapons to speak of, nothing to protect her with, and now you give her her father's warhorse?"

"He's not a warhorse," Crae pointed out mildly.

"What are you thinking?! She barely comes up to its knees. And you give it to her!"

"She proved she could ride the horse. He's worthy of her. A lord's daughter . . ."

"But not your daughter."

The words rang in the chamber. He let them settle between them like the dust motes slanting in the window. The sunlight fell over his bed, across the floor, and over the large chest that held his gear. Jessamy looked around, and he saw that she could see the mean chamber for what it was.

"So. You've made it clear, you are lord here now. But the children are mine to raise."

Crae began to feel dizzy again, so he sat on the bed. He doubted the weakness was lost on her.

"I am lord," he agreed. "And it is time I take up my duties.

I left it too long, out of respect for Stavin and you. But the land—Trieve—doesn't care about the lords who've gone before, Jessamy. It only cares about the now. I wonder . . ." He stopped for a moment, lost in thought. What if Stavin had not died? Would he ever have been summoned, perhaps to another land? Favor, or Kenery, or even Red Gold Bridge?

He looked at her, his unwilling wife. It had been long since he had been with any woman, and the last time he had so much as kissed one had been Lynna. And they had both known, even then, that they could never be with one another, and their love would be for nothing.

Now he wanted to bed his best friend's wife—no, his own wife—with as great an urgency. And he had no doubt she had a revulsion of him that was as equally great as his desire. But they had to come together. Trieve demanded it. They could not rule together if they could not pull together.

"If I were not Crae, could you treat me as lord?" he said.

"I treat you as I would any lord," she replied stiffly.

"No. You treat me as if I am still the upstart captain, your husband's disreputable friend. For that alone you cannot forgive me, let alone live with me."

"I told you, I cannot love again. Not like that. Not the way I did with Stavin." She said it quickly, as if she had practiced it for this moment. He expected that she had prepared for a lifetime of rejections, at least until he stopped asking. And then she could scorn him for seeking love elsewhere.

"I'm not asking it of you."

She stared at him. "Then what are you asking, if not—?"

He lifted his shoulders. "True. I am asking you to bed me, but not as Stavin's replacement. Not even as Captain Crae."

"You know that it—that's impossible."

"As your husband. Lord of Trieve."

She bit her lip. He waited, watching her war with herself. She could not be happy with her lonely bedchamber. She was young still, and Stavin had often been indiscreet about the secrets of his marriage bed.

"What of your wounds?" she said finally.

"They will heal."

"Now?" she managed, swallowing.

"Jessamy."

"I just—I need more time."

"We don't have a lot more time," he said, emphasizing the *we*. "We have a holding to rule. As husband and wife. Why do you think the crows came here, Jessamy? They are lawless men, lordless men. They seek lordless lands. If we are at odds, Jessamy, what of Trieve?"

She hesitated and then finally said, "I—can't. Not right now. Or even soon. But I will think about it."

He watched her rush off, and he sighed. He couldn't force her, nor did he want to. *I didn't choose you either,* he thought resentfully, as she fumbled the door closed behind her. Alone, he lay back on his bed, resting. The pain had come back, and he wanted to let it ebb before he walked down to visit the captured crow.

The captured man's accommodations were a bed of straw in a storeroom off the kitchens. He was shackled to the wall and given food and water and a chamber pot. From the smell of his small prison, the chamber pot had not been emptied in a while.

One of the kitchen boys opened the door when he saw Crae coming. Crae still walked heavily with the aid of a stick. He nodded to the young boy, but inwardly he cringed.

I need a proper guard, such as I had in Red Gold Bridge, he thought. He had been neglecting his duties as lord, and now he needed to make up for lost time. Crae ducked into the small storeroom. The smell of waste and unwashed prisoner came over him. A window high above let in some light, and a few candles burned on the wall. Not a prison such as in Red Gold Bridge, but a bad one nonetheless.

The man was crippled from Crae's crossbow bolt, but no one had been able to come near him to tend his wound, and it festered. He stared sullenly at the lord through fallen tangled hair, his face narrow and pinched under a wild beard. It was hard to tell how old he was.

"Do you have a name?" Crae asked.

Nothing.

"What brought you to Trieve?"

Silence.

"Why did you attack me?"

Again, silence.

"Who is your lord?"

The man raised his head. His eyes burned in the dim light. His face had a sheen of sweat under the beard, the sign of a fever. The wound would take him if he didn't get help. "The lord of all Aeritan is the lord of crows."

Aeritan hadn't had a high king for more than three hundred years. The man raved. Crae tried again.

"But someone leads you. Who is he?"

"The god of crows."

There is no god of crows, Crae almost said but held his tongue. Were these men called, as he had been? To what purpose would a god call forth lawless men?

"Were you summoned?"

The man grinned, his teeth a crooked, mashed mess. It was why it was so hard to understand his words. "He whispers to us, tells us we can do what we want to all the pretty lords and ladies. And we do. We kill and we ravage, and our god laughs."

Crae looked down at his prisoner, sickness in his gut. He had kept him alive almost on a whim, to find out something about the lordless men. Now he wasn't sure if that hadn't been a mistake.

Still, he had to find out the secrets of the crows. He waited, and the man stopped his tormented giggling. *He is a man,* Crae thought. *Not a creature. But he acts like a creature of the dark tales. High god, help me uncover this thing.* Feeling as if he were groping in the dark, he said, "Will you let our surgeon treat your leg?"

The man looked up, surprise in his ravaged face. His lips parted as if he meant to speak, but the words wouldn't come. *Yet there's intelligence there,* Crae thought. He stumped backward to the door, and said to the boy, "Fetch Truarch." The boy ran off.

While they waited, the man was silent, his eyes on Crae. The wait seemed an eternity. At length the horse doctor turned up, carrying his kit. He looked at Crae with surprise and no little respect.

"He says he will let you treat him now," he told Truarch.

"Lord Crae—" Truarch swallowed what he was about to say. Instead he knelt next to the crow. Crae knew the bravery that took. The crow, though, never attacked, not even when Truarch cleaned the wound, as excruciatingly painful as that must have been. When Truarch finished, wrapping a bandage around the leg, the man's face was gray with pallor, but he had neither fought nor screamed nor tried to bite.

Truarch stood, and the crow fell back, exhausted. Crae himself felt as if he had just run all of the terraces to the house, so intent he had been on Truarch's work and the crow's pain.

"Crow," he said, and the man turned toward him. "I give you guesting in the House of Trieve."

He thought later that of all the things he had done, that had been the high god's doing the most. The crow's eyes flew open, as did the doctor's and the boy's, the only other two who had heard him. Guesting was the obligation of the lord, and it was not granted lightly. It would be all over Trieve in an hour, what he had done; a part of him thought of Jessamy's reaction with wryness. He gestured to the others, and they left the crow to his meager cell.

He was still thinking about it when he returned to his chamber after the night meal. Jessamy did not join him, and he ate in the kitchen with some of the men, discussing his plans for a guard. Trieve had been able to call up all of three hundred fighting men when Stavin threw in his lot with Red Gold Bridge last year. Nearly all of them had died, in part because they were mostly farmers and smallholders. Stavin had never seen to the training of his men.

Crae had discovered that Stavin had not done much to keep Trieve well in hand. *No, I knew that before,* he thought. *But it was not my place—the place of a captain—to say anything, even though we were friends.*

They sat at the table long into the night, over tankards of Trieve's good beer and some stronger drink, talking over his plans.

"Swords, crossbows, hand-to-hand fighting," he said, ticking off what they had to learn. The grooms and the housemen leaned forward, eyes shining, and Crae grinned. The boy who sat watch at the door to the crow's prison was with his father, hanging on his elders' every word. It was good to know that they didn't lack for will, even if they had no training. "It makes no sense for only lords to learn to fight." His grin faded, and he nodded at the storeroom door. There was naught but silence coming from the crow. "They are our enemy now."

"We only ever heard tales of them before," a young farmer said, in for the night from one of the far villages. "Tales the children frightened each other with. Now the tales are constant; they rove everywhere and fear nothing."

"When you go back to your village, let everyone know I need men," Crae said. "We'll start training tomorrow." His head went dizzy again, and he grimaced. He needed a captain for this task, but he would have to get them started. He could not delay before he could engage an experienced soldier.

"Are you well, sir?" someone said. They looked at him anxiously. It was a different sight than when he had first arrived as lord. They had been cautious then, not sure of who he was and what he meant for Trieve and for them. Now they put their hope in him and needed him to be well.

"I will be," he said. He had to be.

He was more than a little drunk when he limped back up the stairs to his chamber, his leg aching from his exertions. He pushed open the door and stared in surprise.

The room was bare. The hearth had been swept. His bed had been stripped, and his chest of belongings, with his clothes and his gear, was gone.

"Oh, sir," said Calyne, hurrying up with an armful of linens. "Lady Jessamy had asked us to clear out your old room and be moved to Lord Stav—the lord's chamber."

She had, had she? Jessamy had made some sort of statement with the move, but for the life of him, he could not figure out what it could be. He turned and followed Calyne. Stavin's room was large, with two glazed windows overlooking the terraces. A few candles burned in sconces over the bed, and Crae couldn't help breaking out in a grin at the grandness. This bed was long enough for his lanky frame, and its carved bedposts rose to the high ceiling. His humble chest sat against one wall, and a huge desk dominated the other. The books on Trieve's history that he had been reading before the attack had been placed on a bookshelf above it.

He had to steel himself to cross the threshold. It felt like a desecration; he felt like an imposter, even with the summoning still quivering somewhere below his heartbeat.

Calyne left him, and he undressed in the semidarkness. Hardly knowing what compelled him, although he knew he was drunk and restless and lonely, he opened his chest. Even in the half dark he knew what he was looking for and found it beneath the rest of his clothes and papers. Far below at the bottom he felt for the cold little thing that Lynna had brought with her to Red Gold Bridge. It was wrapped in her white shirt, the one she wore all the way to Trieve when they looked for a guardian last winter. He knew it by heart, its fine material and plain buttons, and the neatly sewn-up tear in the sleeve. He had made that tear himself when her arm had been broken by a crow's heavy staff and he'd had to make sure the bone did not pierce the skin. She couldn't wear the shirt after her arm had been set. And so he had kept it in his chest, neatly wrapped around the cold black device.

He pulled it out. The little device felt strangely light yet substantial. It was made of metal, or glass, or some other smooth material. It was hinged at one end but he dared not lift the narrow lid. The last time it was open the thing shrieked to wake the dead. He had managed to silence it, but he didn't know how, and he wasn't sure he could do it again.

If Lynna knew he had it, she never mentioned it. She had, after all, left it behind as a distraction when she made her escape from Red Gold Bridge.

Both Lynna and the stranger man Bahard had said the devices could be used to call upon someone. Bahard had said they didn't work in Aeritan, though. Too bad; he was almost befuddled enough by drink to try. He could see himself opening up the small device and calling out her name. Lynna. Lynn. If he summoned, would she come?

And if she answered, what then? He was married, a lord. She could have no place here, nor he with her, in her country.

He wrapped up the little object in the shirt and replaced them both at the bottom of the chest. Then he put himself into his solitary bed, hoping he woke without as much of a hangover as he seemed to be in store for.

Four

The underpass where the black road crossed over the highway was filled with litter and stank of men, excrement, and whiskey. Marthen's nose twitched as the smells finally reached him in his stupor. He moved his hand feebly, his first thought for his small jug of harsh whiskey. It was still there, tucked next to his side. His next move was for the handgun. It, too, still rested in his trousers pocket, heavy and substantial against his side. Relieved, he opened his eyes and looked straight up at the concrete bridge above him. Pigeons cooed and strutted, their perch stained with droppings. The saddle created an uncomfortable pillow and strained his neck.

The bridge hummed with the rush of traffic overhead, the rhythmic thudding of tires over the concrete seams echoing along with his aching head.

Carefully, he turned his head first to the left. Nearby, a handful of men squatted over their few belongings: ragged blankets, bags stuffed with cans, a wheeled basket. He turned his head the other way, his tangled hair falling into his eyes so it took a moment for his vision to clear.

"Nice saddle," came a voice in his ear.

A pair of dark blue eyes, bright like a bird's, peered back at him, inches from his face. Marthen waited for his close-range vision to clear. The man continued to stare at him. He had gray hair, a lined and sunken face, and a bulbous drunkard's nose. Once Marthen could gauge men as well as he could run a battle. Now he couldn't tell if this man were a simpleton as well as a drunkard. He waved his hand peevishly.

"Help me up," he ordered, his voice raspy. The man put an arm under Marthen's shoulder and lifted him, then scooted back to give him room. Marthen waited for the world to stop spinning and then said carefully,

"Where am I?"

"Under a 684 overpass. Or as I like to call it, the crossroads of despair."

Marthen stared at him. Those were not the words of a simpleton. A strange feeling came over him, one he couldn't identify. "Is that in North Salem?"

The man snorted. "Close enough. Why? You rich?" He glanced at the saddle.

Rich? Like a noble? He looked at the man more closely.

"No, not rich." Not noble. "I must find someone."

It sounded so weak to himself that he half expected the man to laugh at him. His strange acquaintance remained solemn.

"They won't have you," he said.

It was Marthen's turn to laugh, a dry little croak. "That was made clear to me." Lord Terrick's parting words had assured him he would stand in his way if Marthen attempted to petition the Council for Kate Mossland. He knew he would be blocked in this world as well. No matter. He had been boxed in before and slipped free.

Marthen had traveled months to find her. He had sold his warhorse, then his gear, and finally his sword, all for whispers of this portal, rumors in dark places paid for by coin passed secretively from hand to hand.

He kept the saddle and the gun. The saddle was all that remained of Kate Mossland in Aeritan. The gun was a gift from the Brythern lord Hare. Marthen knew that Hare played his own game, and the gun was meant to set Marthen in motion as if he were the lord's playing piece. Marthen took pleasure in thwarting him. He would use the gun for his own purposes.

Marthen fumbled for the small jug of whiskey. It still had a few swallows. The man's eyes were fixated on the bottle now. Marthen handed it over, and the man took a small sip. Marthen felt a surge of the old triumph. He wished he still had Grayne, his competent aide-de-camp, but his lieutenant had left him many months ago. Then again, it hardly mattered. Grayne would be all at sea in this strange world, no better than Marthen himself.

"I saw her. She was in a—car," he said, using the unfamiliar word that he had learned from her last year. "I came for her, and saw her, but I don't know where she went or how to find her again."

It had been unbelievable. He had stepped out of the gordath in the woods and into this new world. He hadn't walked far before he saw the marvels of the world she came from, the brightness, the smells, the rush of noise, the cars moving so quickly on the roads so black and smooth.

He waited on the side of the road, hungover, weak, and unsure, still disoriented from his passage through the gordath, when a car slowed and stopped near where he stood on the verge, half in the trees. And through the glass of the window he saw her, and she saw him. Their eyes caught. He took in her burgeoning surprise, the realization, and the fear.

The car sped off, but not before he thought he saw her scream.

It was another day before he understood his impossible luck and how he could not be so lucky again. Not even the soldier's god—not any god—would be able to find her in this place. He was on his own.

He wasn't sure how he ended up underneath this bridge, but maybe it was another kind of luck.

"You don't look like the romantic type," his new friend said. He handed back the jug, and again his eyes fixed on it.

"No." Marthen took a much smaller sip but didn't hand it back. "Help me find her."

The man jerked his gaze away from the whiskey back to Marthen's face. "What? Jesus, you at least need a name."

"I have a name. Is that all I need?"

"Shit, man. I don't know. You have an address? Where she lives?"

"She lives here."

The man gave him all of his attention now. "If she lives here, she isn't going to give you the time of day. Who is she? Ex-wife? I'm telling you, you mess with the townies, more than just asking for a buck, you are in trouble."

They had gotten some attention now from the other men under the bridge. Marthen thought it was like the old stories about crows who lived under bridges and accosted travelers on their paths with riddles. These men were not crows, though. They were drunkards and broken, sad and lost, but they didn't have the madness of the crows.

Once he commanded an army of tens of thousands of men, including the wild crows of Aeritan. Now he had these sorry men.

He made himself stand up. The overpass stretched overhead, and the rushing traffic was like the wind in the high pines of Temia, the thudding of the tires like a drumbeat. They all looked at him, and he felt again the fullness that came when he addressed his army before battle. He began softly, and they had to strain to hear him over the cooing of the pigeons and the incessant traffic.

"So you are pent up beneath this bridge," he said. "You hide here, you drink here, you *stink* here."

Someone laughed, and someone else shushed him. He looked at the man who had first helped him. He already thought of him as his lieutenant. The man's attention was fixed wholeheartedly on him now.

"How are you called?"

The man blinked uncertainly.

"Gary." Close enough to Grayne. The soldier god was smiling on him—or laughing. Marthen bent low.

"Do you like your prison, Gary? Your crossroads of despair?"

Gary had a strange expression, as if he knew what Marthen was doing, and he was falling for it anyway. *He is no simpleton,* Marthen thought. *But I have no need of simpletons. At least not in my lieutenants.*

Gary leaned in low, too, and their conversation became private. "I don't know what you think you are doing, but you are crazy if you think you can start a revolution. These guys are hard up, but they'd sell their own mother for a drink or a hit. If you cause enough trouble, you will bring the cops down on all of us, and believe me, this is paradise compared to a real jail."

"So you do like your prison," Marthen said, loud enough for the others to hear. "Do you want to stay?"

"I—no! That's not what I mean . . ." Gary trailed off uncertainly.

"Anyone else? Anyone else want to stay under this bridge until they come to roust you out? Burn you out?"

There was a rumbling of discontent.

"I'm looking for a woman," he told them. "She is not yet full grown and lives with her parents. Her name is Kate Mossland. Help me find her." He paused. He could see their confusion and indecision, and he contained his impatience. Once he had commanded crows, and that took promises and strength and cunning. He could bend these men to his will. Once he had Kate Mossland, he could still use these men for his purposes. This time, his army would not be disbanded.

From the back someone held up his hand. He was still young, his face not as weathered as the rest of the men, but it was fair on its way to becoming that way.

"So, you mean she's still a teenager? 'Cause, yeah, school's out, but all the kids hang out by the lake in the summer." He glanced around and shrugged. "I could show you where."

"Lynn! One of the horses is loose," Mrs. Felz called from the kitchen. Lynn glanced over from the living room, where she was going through the mail. Bills, insurance—who knew there was so much expense to owning a horse farm?

"I'm coming," she called back and hurried out the front door. She looked down the drive, where the kitchen window overlooked the entrance to the farm. Sure enough, there was a chestnut horse meandering along the drive, browsing on the tall weeds along the verge.

It wasn't one of hers. Someone must have lost a horse from a neighboring farm, and it wandered over here.

"Shoot," she said, half under her breath. She didn't like strange horses coming through. Whose ever it turned out to be would be informed, in as friendly a way as possible, that they needed to keep their gates shut. She headed back through the kitchen, grabbing a halter and lead rope from the hook in the mudroom, and let herself out the back. Mrs. Felz followed, wiping her hands on a dish towel. She had been doing the dishes.

That was another thing; it seemed like Mrs. Felz planned on staying. First she tidied up the barn apartment, then she took Lynn's house in hand, and now she just made herself useful. Lynn couldn't bring herself to tell her to leave, and Mrs. Felz seemed perfectly happy to do things. When Lynn brought it up tentatively, Joe's mom had just smiled and said, "If it's all right with you, I'll stay till I wear out my welcome. My husband, Abel—well, let's just say it's more peaceful here right now than home." Lynn lost her courage and left it like that.

She walked up to the horse, keeping her stride slow but purposeful. The horse kept grazing, but it swiveled its ears toward her to keep track of her progress. It was a gelding, and it was starving. Its backbone stuck up, and its ribs showed. Automatically she registered its conformation—probably part quarter horse with maybe some Thoroughbred. It was a little more than fifteen hands, too small for her but a good solid size. Smallish feet, the head the shape that quarter horse breeders called the bulldog type, with its short jowls and wide forehead. Nice-looking horse. Too bad she wanted to kill its owner for letting it starve half to death.

"Hi," she said, when she got close enough. "Hey there, boy. I've got something better for you in the barn." She held the halter and lead rope behind her back in case he was halter-shy. He raised his head and looked at her and snorted. He was clearly uneasy but hadn't tried to trot off. She stopped and waited, turning her head to the side. She wasn't a horse whisperer, but sometimes if you just didn't look a horse in the eye, horses found it easier to approach you. She breathed easily as if she had nothing better to do than stand in the sun, just as if she were a horse herself. Then she ambled forward a few steps, not quite toward the horse. He made to turn on his haunches but she placed herself in front of him. He turned the other way, but she was there, too, all the time still far enough away that she was no threat.

The moment he gave in, she knew. He lowered his head, swiveled his ears at half alert, and waited. She came up to him, put the halter on, and patted him soothingly. He had cuts all over his face and flanks, some quite deep, as if he had been flayed. They were recent, too, scabbed over but still fresh. Lynn gasped a little. What had happened to him? Who could have done this?

"Okay, boy, easy, easy," she said. "Let's head over to the barn, and I'll get you water, hay. You want a carrot? I can get you a carrot."

He waited patiently, flicking an ear at her nonsense, and she clucked to him and started leading him back up to the barn. She would put the word out about who might have starved, beaten, and misplaced a perfectly good horse, but she wasn't sure what she would come up with. She was confident that none of her neighbors were the type to treat a horse this way.

So what about her other neighbors, the ones who were a bit less—local? She frowned and stopped, taking another long look at the strange chestnut. In Aeritan, horses were no pampered luxury. She had never seen one treated as badly as this one, however. For instance, Crae had been good with horses. He hadn't coddled Briar, and granted, the poor creature had been shot out from underneath him, but he had been a good man with that horse.

She knew one way to find out. She slid a hand down the horse's foreleg, leaning slightly against his shoulder. Obediently he lifted his leg when she came to his hoof. She took one look at the crudely made horseshoe, so clearly not a modern model, and set his foot down again.

"Shoot," she said again.

Either someone was making hand-forged, piece-of-crap horseshoes in some sort of weird bid for authenticity—

Or the gordath was open again.

The sound of a car coming up the drive made her turn around. She didn't recognize the car, a dark green Jaguar; had one of her clients gotten a new one?

The Jag parked in a cloud of dust, and a man got out. He was middle-aged, balding, wearing a polo and khaki slacks. It took her a moment, and then she placed him. What was Mike Garson doing *here*? He was the owner of the Continental, the restaurant and bar that the riders, owners, and grooms all hung out at. He had been Mark Ballard's boss. Lynn grimaced. The less she had to think of Mark Ballard, the better. She looked at the skinny starved chestnut and pinched the bridge of her nose. Garson came over to her. He glanced at the horse, who was clearly not a show horse, and a look of distaste crossed his face before he pasted on a smile and held out his hand.

"Well, Lynn Romano," he said. "Just the person I wanted to see. Mike Garson. I don't know that we've met before, though I know you from your patronage of my little restaurant."

She reached out and took his hand with his artificially strong handshake, and said, "Mr. Garson."

"Oh, call me Mike. I don't have much use for formality. You know, Mark Ballard used to talk about you all the time. He was quite taken with you, you know."

Enough that he tried to have me killed so as not to ruin your little gunrunning scheme. Perhaps some of that crossed her face, because Garson stepped back. The horse, too, caught the tension and threw up his head and snorted.

"I need to get him to the barn," Lynn said shortly.

"Fine, fine, I'll just wait at the house."

Actually, why don't you just leave. She clucked to the horse and left Garson behind, hoping he got the message.

She didn't have enough grooms to run the farm the way Mrs. Hunt had run it, when Lynn was barn manager, so she brought the chestnut gelding into the stall for new horses, an isolated loose box in the far corner of the lower barn. She would have Dr. Cotter come and vet him out and also do a Coggins test . . . *Damn strays,* she thought. She pulled apart a fresh bale of hay and gave him a flake and put fresh water in the bucket. The horse took a long drink, Lynn watching to make sure she wouldn't have to pull away the bucket before he made himself sick. But he only took a few swallows and then, his muzzle dripping, nudged Lynn as if to say thanks. She shook her head and scrubbed him under his long, tangled forelock that hid his eyes.

"Red, you are lucky I have a soft spot for strays." Counting Joe's mom, this was her second one in a week. She hadn't ever had the opportunity to indulge that side of her character before, but given the chance, she clearly took to it. And she thought *Joe's mom* could be dangerous. If the horse was a sign that the portal was open, they could all be in trouble again. *What's going on, Joe?*

The horse dropped his head and went to work on the hay. Lynn watched him for a minute, then closed the bottom door and went up to find out what Garson wanted. Heading back to the house, she felt a spark of anger. Garson was nowhere in sight, the front door just swinging shut. He had let himself into the *house.* Anger deepened into fury. Well, she would set him straight about that. Then he came back out, almost stumbling. Mrs. Felz came right behind him.

"Why don't you have a seat on the veranda? Lynn will be right there, and I'll bring y'all some iced tea." Her voice was gracious and warm, but it was made of steel. Lynn bit back a grin.

"I see you've met Mrs. Felz," she said. She glanced at Joe's mom and raised her eyebrow in surprise. Mrs. Felz winked and then gave a public smile to Garson.

Garson looked between the two women, trying to figure things out. He could hardly demand to know more about Mrs. Felz, but he had to know something was up. Lynn hadn't said what she was, only who she was. Mrs. Felz wasn't dressed for housework. She wore jeans, sneakers, and a big floppy straw hat, as if she had been gardening. Which she had been, in fact. For the last few days, she had been taking care of the flowers in the tubs and beds all over the farm.

Garson looked back at Lynn, forcing a smile. "Well," he said. "Iced tea. How—southern."

"Yes," she said and sat. He sat opposite her.

"I'm glad you found some help, though of course, you know, it can be difficult to run a big place like this. Katherine was very capable, and I know she left the farm in capable hands."

Katherine. Garson knew all of the owners, of course, but that seemed oddly familiar. Did Mrs. Hunt know they were on a first-name basis? Lynn waited.

"But of course it's so much for a young, single woman to take care of. I'm not sure what she meant by it. Surely she couldn't have wanted to saddle you with all of this."

He smiled meaningfully at his own pun. Lynn was struck by a sense of disaster.

Mrs. Felz popped out with tall glasses of amber tea, topped with lemons and rattling with ice. She set the tray down with a bright smile.

"Homemade," she said.

Instant, Lynn knew. It was all she had in the house.

"Thank you," she said, slightly strangled. Whatever Mrs. Felz was doing, it had her almost as baffled as Garson. She sipped her tea. Instant tea or no, it was still good, sweet, slightly acrid. A taste lingered almost veshlike on her tongue. For a second she forgot Garson's presence, even Joe's mom, and Aeritan came to her as powerfully as a kiss.

"So, I thought I would ask how you were doing and see if you needed any help."

She came back to this world with a thud.

"Help?"

"Lynn, let me be frank. I'm a businessman. In fact, the restaurant business is probably tougher than the horse farm business. I know that you've lost clients and boarders due to last year's troubles. I think everyone would understand if you needed to let the place go. Now, I'm not here asking to buy it right away. I just want you to consider the possibility, so you won't feel trapped and maybe make a hasty decision. The fact is, this place is a lot of work, but it's worth a whole lot more than you think. I think you could make a tidy sum—"

She felt the fury rise from somewhere inside her, and for a moment she couldn't speak. When she could finally reply, she said only, "I think you are being presumptuous, Mr. Garson."

"Now, Lynn—"

"I'm wondering what makes you think the farm is in trouble?"

He paused, took a sip of tea. When he spoke again, his smile was avuncular. "I'm sorry. I think I started off on the wrong foot. That's me; my directness always gets me in trouble, or so my wife says. I don't mean to imply that you are unable to run your own business."

"I'm not interested in selling."

"No, of course. But you see, things can turn so quickly. I understand this. And as I said, I want to make sure you don't act in a panic but consider all your options."

"To sell to you," she said.

He nodded judiciously, as if accepting the possibility, now that she mentioned it. "That would be one option, yes."

Lynn kept her voice from shaking with a force of will she didn't know she had.

"I won't do business with anyone who has ever hired Mark Ballard."

She silenced him. He stared at her, openmouthed, gasping a little. His teeth were crooked and nicotine-stained, she thought with a mean sense of satisfaction. When he spoke, his anger rivaled her own. He still tried to control it. "I'm offering you a lifeline and a business opportunity. Just because you had a bad breakup—" He broke off, laughed, all pretense at civility gone. "Seriously, young lady, is this about the one who got away?"

No, it's about the man who wanted to have me killed because he was in a business deal with you.

"I don't need your lifeline," she said evenly. "I don't need your business opportunity. I just want to run my horse farm." A thought struck her. "And if I find out that you are behind any attempt to make it hard for me to stay in business, I'll let everyone know about this conversation. You made your offer. It was turned down. Out."

He slammed down his drink, and the tea slopped over the side of the glass onto the table. "I didn't think you were stupid, Ms. Romano. I suppose you just have a lot to learn about business. Enjoy your education."

Mrs. Felz came out of the kitchen and sat down with Lynn as Garson stamped off to the Jag and drove off in a cloud of dust. Mrs. Felz shook her head.

"Some things never change," she said.

"What?" Lynn said.

"Honey, that conversation is the same one rich men have had with farmers since farming began," she said.

Lynn gave a half laugh. She was a farmer now, eh? Hard to believe. Land was a blessing and a curse. She gazed out over the farm from the shady porch, half of her mind far away. The green fields, the fences, the horses grazing lazily, all the peace of it came over her. She couldn't sell, not to Garson, not to anyone. She was a guardian now, for what that was worth.

Just like Joe in Aeritan, both of them keeping the land safe and sound. It wasn't easy, but it was worthwhile. Only now, if the chestnut gelding was any indication, Joe wasn't doing his part of the job. Lynn twirled the empty glass between her fingers, the condensation cold against her fingertips. She didn't want to fret in front of Mrs. Felz, but the question of the red horse niggled at her. *Maybe I was wrong about the horseshoes,* she thought hopefully, but she knew she wasn't.

"If Joe were here, you two could keep the place together," Mrs. Felz said wistfully. Startled, Lynn looked over at her. The woman made a self-deprecating face. "Don't mind me. I'm just an old woman living in her dreams. I always hoped Joe would get married someday, but I know he wasn't the marrying type." She shook her head.

Truer words were never spoken. Hunter's Chase had probably been the longest Joe had been anywhere in the past few years. She wondered if he missed it. Now that he was a guardian and tied to the woods, would he miss the open road? *Does he miss me the way I miss him?*

"I think—if he ever finds what he's looking for, he might settle down," Lynn said carefully. Not with her, and not where she would see him again, but he might find someone—a smallholder perhaps, or a strongholder. He deserved that. *Let him go,* she told herself. *Let him go.*

Mrs. Felz rested her head against the back of the chair. "I suppose I have to go back," she said abruptly. "If only to tell Abel I didn't find anything." She sighed. "He made it clear he didn't expect me to. Anyway, I know you don't want me here, and you've been kind enough to let me stay, but I've outstayed my welcome, I can tell." She forestalled Lynn's protest. "I only want a few more days, just until I can figure out where to look next. Then I'll go, and I promise I won't bother you anymore."

"All right," Lynn said, trying to hide her worry. Mrs. Felz would be gone soon. She hadn't found out anything so far, and she would give up soon and go. Right now, though, Mrs. Felz was the least of her problems. After all, she was just a mother trying to trace her lost son and find out the truth behind his disappearance. Lynn had a hostile businessman and an open gordath to worry about. *At least it will take my mind off the bills,* she thought dryly. She pulled out her phone to call the vet to look over the new horse, trying to figure out what to do about the portal being open and what that implied. She told herself that Joe and Arrim would get it back under control. In the meantime, though, she thought she should go out to the old house on Daw Road and check on things, no matter how dangerous that could be. The last thing she needed right now was to end up back in Aeritan.

Even if Joe was there. And Crae. No, much better to stay here.

Kate and Colar pulled off the road and in to the gas station at the intersection where she had seen Marthen. The streets here were busy, the major route leading to Connecticut, the cross street almost as busy. Along one side of the road was a small shopping center. The place where Kate had seen the general was a stand of woods fronting a residential area.

They parked at the back of the gas station and looked around. It was hot, the road and parking lot radiating midday heat. Colar was the first to put on his sunglasses, and Kate fumbled for hers. She glanced at him and felt the usual shock; in T-shirt and board shorts and sandals, he looked like everyone else.

Well, and so do I now, she thought. She wore a tank top over a lace cami that covered most of the scars on her back and a denim miniskirt. Her hair was held up in a ponytail, the brown and gold highlights gleaming. Only the scars on her shoulders and back said she was anything different from her outside appearance. She nodded at the stand of trees.

"He was right there," she said. "Kind of in the shadows."

Colar nodded. "They'd be longer at that time of day. Let's ask inside."

He followed her in, and the door beeped at them as they entered. An Asian man looked up from the counter as a few shoppers collected soda, chips, and cigarettes.

Kate hesitated, smiled at the counter guy, and went to the back.

"What are you doing?" Colar whispered.

"We should buy something. Plus I want people to leave."

He looked dubious, but they each picked out a soda and went back to the front. While they waited to pay for their drinks, a few more people breezed in. Kate's heart sank. One was Maddy Street, a girl from school, with another girl she didn't know well.

"Oh, hi," Maddy said, brightening when she saw them. "What are you guys doing?"

They held up their drinks in unison.

"Cool. Sarah and I are going to the lake. A lot of kids are going to be there. You should come." As she said it, she looked mostly at Colar. The other girl looked at Kate and said, "Hi. We used to go to middle school together?"

"I remember you," Kate said. Sarah Decker. "Hi. Where do you go now?"

"Chatham." It was a very posh private school. "Are you still into horses?"

Kate nodded. The line moved up. Maddy continued to chat up Colar, who was smiling at something she said. Maddy was animated and flirtatious, and Kate felt a sharp pang of jealousy. *He's my foster brother, that's all. Just my foster brother.* "You were, too, right?"

"Yeah, some. I outgrew it though." The girl heard what she said and half laughed. "Oh my God, I am so sorry about how that came out."

Kate had to laugh. "No, it's okay. I probably should have outgrown it, too." She shrugged and automatically lifted a loose strap back onto her shoulder. Colar was at the counter and paid for the drinks, handling the money with aplomb. She saw Sarah looking at her scars, but the girl didn't comment. Then Maddy saw and gasped.

"What happened to you!"

"Bad—car accident," Kate managed. She flushed. *Should have worn a T-shirt,* she thought.

There was an awkward silence. Then Maddy hurried to pay for their supplies, and she and Sarah fled, probably too uncomfortable to wonder why Kate and Colar stayed back. "Okay, see you, try to come to the lake," Maddy called out as they headed out the door.

The counter guy was looking at them, this time a quizzical expression on his face. Kate took a breath.

"Hi. We were wondering if you saw someone here the other night, around four or five p.m.? He'd be dressed really weird."

"Like in these clothes," Colar said. He opened his phone and showed the man a picture of his clothes from home—heavy boots, half jacket, leather and mail armor—laid out on his bed. He had taken it that morning. The clothes were still stained with his blood, but you couldn't tell that from the picture.

The man nodded. "Like a Renaissance festival actor," he said, his accent thick but not impenetrable.

"Exactly," Kate said. The man scrutinized the photo, and she added hastily, "Those are just the type of clothes; his were a little different. They were more ragged." She hadn't gotten a close look, but Marthen had seemed much the worse for wear since she had known him as the meticulous, obsessive general. She added, "This guy would be in his forties, and he has long black hair."

The man pursed his lips and shook his head slowly. He handed back the phone. "Sorry."

"Okay, well, thanks." She and Colar turned to go.

"But if I see him, you want me to call you and let you know?"

They looked at each other. Colar spoke first. "Yes. That would be well."

He did that sometimes; the Aeritan in him came out in his words. The Asian man heard and made a face. To him it would sound archaic or a put-on. He probably was already regretting helping a pair of snotty high school kids. Oblivious, Colar gave the man his number, and they hastened out.

"Have fun at the lake!" the man called out behind them.

"So what now?" Kate asked.

"We're not done. We need to look around." They went around back to the Jeep, but instead of getting in, they crossed the road to the stand of trees, scurrying to beat the traffic. The temperature immediately plunged. The trees were pines, dark and green, brown needles a thick carpet underfoot. Colar held her back and scanned without stepping onto the area. Cars whizzed past them. Through the trees she could see a neighborhood of big houses fronting an algae-coated pond. Just some guy, she thought. Just some guy, and now my dad thinks I'm crazy and I need to see a therapist.

She shivered in the shade. She wanted to get out of there. "Forget it. Let's go," she said. "We should probably go to the lake."

"Wait," he said. He knelt and looked at the ground, frowned. He pointed. "What does that look like to you?"

"It better not be gross," she said, gingerly kneeling next to him. A pattern was pressed into the needles and sand, more a suggestion than anything. He got up and stepped around it, then put his foot next to it. His sandal made a distinct tread pattern, one that was identifiably shoelike. The other pattern was broader, less defined. Smudged—or an Aeritan boot, handmade and ill-fitting? Back in the camp, Kate could have been killed for her fine riding boots alone, if someone was crazy enough to go against Marthen's protection of her.

"Okay, I see your point," she said, getting to her feet and dusting off her knees. "But I don't know, Colar. It seems awfully—unconvincing."

"Maybe," he said. "But it's a start." They looked around a bit more, but it was clear that there was very little to see.

The intersection was really far from where the gordath had been anyway. How had Marthen gotten all the way over here—presumably on foot—without raising attention?

Had she really seen him, or was it time for a shrink after all?

She thought back to her glimpse of the man in the shadows

and shuddered at the way his eyes had met hers. Colar nudged her.

"What?" he said.

"Just thinking—you know."

She didn't have to say more. They both had ghosts. Sometimes she saw the way his hands whitened when he held his fork and knife or a pencil when he was doing math homework. *Maybe a therapist wouldn't be a bad idea for either of us,* she thought. *Except how could we tell them anything?*

He nodded and looked around some more, scanning the parking lot, the traffic, and the few people on foot. "Someone had to have seen him. He would have stood out."

She laughed a bit sourly. "Maybe we should put up a wanted poster."

"What?"

"A poster that has a picture of people with their names, the crime they committed, and the reward money. The police put them up. You'll see them around sometimes."

She could see him filing away the information, and his interest sparked an idea. She added, "You know, we could check the police station, see if somebody else did see him and called about him." The police would make it known that he wasn't welcome here. Kate felt a twinge of shame but at the same time was thankful for her safe little town. "Like you said, he'd stand out," she explained. "I think he'd frighten people, even without them knowing, well—"

"That they should be frightened," they finished together. He gave her a quick grin. "I think even Captain Artor was frightened of the general."

Kate laughed. The irascible scout captain spent most of the campaign laid up with a broken leg, but his temper was the worse for all that. The captain had never frightened her though, despite his cursing and bluster. Her laugh trailed off. The general had struck fear to the marrow of her bones. She knew he was obsessed with her, and also knew he hated himself for it. *He hated me and wanted me, and the flogging was only the beginning.* If Marthen had gotten what he wanted, she doubted she would have survived with her mental health and her spirit intact.

She turned to Colar and smiled gamely. "Let's go to the police then, and see if they know anything."

"What is this, a scavenger hunt?" the officer at the front desk said. "Look, kids, I don't have time for this."

The police station was calm and quiet, very little activity. Somewhere a radio blared in ten-code in the back, and someone else answered.

"We just wanted to know if you got a suspicious person report in the last couple of weeks," Kate said.

"The log isn't available right now. Beat it."

"What's going on?"

It was the lieutenant, the detective who had talked to Kate at great length about her abduction last winter. He still wore the same careful suit and had the same quiet, piercing manner as before. His eyes took in Colar, obviously well and healthy, a far cry from the wounded boy who had been in the hospital for weeks.

Kate bit her lip. She had forgotten about this guy. He had investigated her and Lynn's disappearance, and he was not happy with the loose ends their reappearance had left him with.

"Hi, Lieutenant. They want to look at the log."

"Anything in particular?" Spencer asked.

"Yes, sir." That was Colar. He looked straight back at Spencer, giving him look for look. Even in his shorts and sandals, even as a seventeen-year-old kid, he was bigger than the spare lieutenant. Not by much, but with a hint that his growth was yet to come. Still, his manner held nothing but respect and politeness.

"We thought we saw a suspicious guy in the neighborhood, but we weren't sure. So we wanted to check and see if anyone else had called it in," Kate said. She added, "Sir." From her it was much less convincing, and she flushed.

Spencer looked surprised. "Most people call nine-one-one

for that, and we check and see if there have been similar calls," he pointed out. "Did you call?"

"Umm, no. But we didn't want to, well, call a report in on a neighbor."

He nodded. "That's usually what it is. Someone walking a dog. Or raccoons in the garbage. We get lots of raccoon calls. Next time just call it in. People are understanding." He was about to turn away.

A part of her knew it was better to let him go. Making a report could bring up all kinds of questions. She could just imagine her parents' anger and frustration at the renewal of the press, the inquiries. The police had to be satisfied with the official story, that she had run away and gotten mixed up with a dangerous cult, the same cult that had raised Colar. If she tried to say anything else, no one would believe her.

But if she didn't report it, who knew where Marthen would end up next? *Or who he could hurt on his way to me.* She would have to be very careful.

"Well, can we make a report now?" Kate said. She could see Colar looking at her now, out of the corner of her eye. *Trust me,* she thought at him.

The lieutenant turned back. The front desk officer looked between them. Lieutenant Spencer gestured to the officer.

"Go ahead."

Kate took a deep breath. Now she wasn't sure exactly how to describe him. She had to be very careful. There was so much Spencer couldn't know about the events of last fall.

"I saw him last Saturday evening near the convenience store," she began. "He's, well, he's about in his forties. Long black hair, about to his shoulders. His clothes were kind of old-fashioned . . ." She trailed off. The front desk officer hadn't even begun to type anything in at the computer in front of him.

"Was he doing anything?" Spencer asked in his dry voice. "Did you see him commit a crime?"

"No . . . not right then."

"Hmm. Being old and wearing old-fashioned clothes isn't enough."

She knew what she would have to say, and she knew how she had to say it. Kate pushed down her revulsion and took a breath. She twirled her hair, and when she spoke, her voice was a little lighter.

"It was, like, the way he looked. Like he didn't belong here?" She bit her lip and looked away. The desk officer looked a little more alert. He looked up at Spencer, his hands poised. Even Spencer hesitated for a moment.

"He was staring at her," offered Colar. "He kept on looking at her, like he wanted to—well, you know. We were worried that he was going to follow us."

Oh, good one, she thought.

Spencer raised an eyebrow. "Why didn't you call right away?"

"Because, well—he hadn't actually done anything. Like you said. Only, the more we thought about it, the weirder it all got?" Kate put in. This was getting easier.

"Did you tell your parents?"

"No," Kate said, her voice small. The front desk officer made a disparaging noise that meant, *Stupid kids.* "We weren't sure what to do. We didn't want them to worry."

"Have you seen him since?"

She shook her head. Spencer glanced at the other officer.

"All right. You've made a report. We'll keep an eye out for him."

She felt an explosion of relief that it was over. She couldn't trust her voice to betray her.

"Thanks," Colar said, and they hurried out into the cool summer air, both taking a deep breath when the doors closed behind them. They didn't speak until they got into the Jeep and pulled out of the driveway and down the road.

Kate let out her breath, letting her hands on the wheel steady her. "Well, what do you think? Was that worth it?" The wind whipped her hair around and the words out of her mouth.

Colar considered. "If he believed us. Do you think he did?"

She thought about Spencer. "I think we made him curious. I just hope it's about the mysterious stranger and not about us."

"He's a hound," Colar said.

"What?!" Kate was half-shocked, half-laughing.

"He's on the scent. I could see it, the way he looked at us. I think we put him on the track behind us, not just Marthen."

It hadn't been an insult then but rather an observation, an Aeritan one. "Well, what's he going to find if he follows us? That we went through this portal thing last year? We could swear to all that in court, and he wouldn't believe it."

"If there's one thing I've learned from your mother and father, that would be a worse problem than if he did."

She winced, but she couldn't deny the truth of it. She slowed at a stop sign and checked for traffic, tapping the brakes and then accelerating.

"So we can't give him anything to be suspicious of about us," she said. "We have to be as normal as we can so he focuses on finding Marthen."

"Easy enough then."

Even with the wind taking their words away, she could hear his bitterness. Sometimes it was hard to remember that Colar was ever anyone except for Cole Mossland, teenage boy, lacrosse player, honor student. He played his new role so well. But how it must chafe to be Cole Mossland and not Colar, heir to the House of Terrick. She bit her lip.

"Colar—"

"Forget it." He kept his face turned away from her. "Let's be normal. We should go to the lake."

The lake would have kids their age, kids they knew like Maddy and some other friends. The lake would be normal. She kept her voice light.

"Sounds good. Hold on." She slowed, looked in the rearview mirror, and swung the Jeep into a tight U-turn in the middle of the road. A car coming in the opposite direction honked at them, but she stepped on the gas, and the Jeep burst forward. Colar grabbed the roll bar.

"I hate the way you drive!" he yelled into the wind.

"Can't hear you!" she hollered back. The only thing better than riding was driving. Then police lights in the mirror caught her eye, and she felt an instant of panic. *Oh shit.* If she got a ticket, her parents would kill her. Panicky, she slowed and pulled over. She glanced over at Colar and felt a measure of guilt. So much for staying away from the cops.

Instead of pulling in behind her, the cruiser screamed on by, for brief seconds the siren unbearable, and then the sound twisted in the distance. Colar and Kate stared at each other, and she started to laugh with a mix of relief and guilt.

"It wasn't us," she said. Colar just shook his head.

"You got lucky," he said, but he grinned, too. "Don't press it."

"Yeah, I think you're right." Last winter she had pressed her luck, all right. With Colar coming up with a distraction, she had stolen Mark Ballard's old jeep out from under him from his supply camp in a daring daylight raid. Turned out the jeep held a cache of weapons and tech that General Marthen put to good use in the final battle.

Her stock had risen immensely, until the general had found out she kissed Colar and had ordered her beaten in front of the entire camp.

And now he was here looking for her.

Her good humor faded. Kate swallowed against her fear. She put the car in gear and rolled back on the road, accelerating sedately. They arrived at the lake parking lot a few minutes later. The beach was small, and the water was usually filled with little kids and their moms, as well as the usual crowd of teens at their own section of the beach. Not this time, though.

The patrol car had been joined by a couple of cruisers as well as an ambulance. Kate and Colar stared at the scene as she pulled over to the side. A sickening premonition seized her. She caught sight of Maddy at the same time that the girl saw them. Maddy ran over to them awkwardly, a towel wrapped around her as if she needed it for comfort, not just to cover her bikini.

"Oh my God, Kate!" she said. Horror had wiped the girl's face of color beneath her tan. "They said they were looking for you."

halted at the bottom of the crumbling porch and decided to go around the back.

The backyard was overgrown, seedlings encroaching on the cultivated space. The police had cleared the backyard of the skulls and barrels as evidence, and the only thing left was a ragged rope swinging from a tree. There was a boarded up window at the base of the cellar. She held her breath and tried to concentrate. She felt nothing, no nausea. The earth didn't shake. The house was empty and dead, the crowding forest silent and without menace. If she went back into the Wood, she could wake it up. After all, Lady Sarita had not been a guardian, and she had managed to walk through the worlds.

But she had been seeking escape, Lynn argued with herself. She had been seeking relief from a terrible marriage and—Lynn thought—a deep loneliness.

And what are you seeking? The thought came unbidden, and she warned herself: *Be careful.* If she let herself think of Joe or Crae, she could end up walking between worlds, too. She breathed lightly, trying to whisk her thoughts away, and walked a few steps deeper toward the woods. She wouldn't go as far as the pignut trees, she told herself. She would stop before she got too close. She just wanted to see—she just wanted to make sure—there was no opening between the worlds.

Last year, at night, she had been on the trails less than a quarter of a mile away from here, when the gordath reached out and snared her. Now she was at the epicenter.

The grasses reached up to her knees and, mindful of ticks, she was thankful for her jeans. The trees pressed in on her, the thin saplings on the outskirts giving way to the giant trees, the hickories and the tulip trees, that stretched straight and true into the sky. There was no trail here, and she halted inside the coolness of the woods. The air was thick with underbrush, and she let her eyes find a route through the woods. The ground was covered with brown, decaying leaves and the scent of the soil was rich and vital; she breathed it in deeply. Outcroppings of rock jutted up in the woods. She could hear water trickling, even though the small streams should be dry this time of year.

That's the stream where I found Arrim! she thought. *It's right through there.* Lynn took a step forward before she halted herself by main force. She could *not* go into the woods.

Leaves rustled overhead, and she looked up through the greenwood. A squirrel leaped from a branch and then scampered down the trunk of a tree to scold her.

"Yeah, yeah, I'm going," she said.

Other than the squirrel, the forest was in a deep afternoon sleep. Even the cicadas had stopped singing in her presence. There was no gordath here. Nothing. The woods were just that—woods. She had a sense that she could walk through the whole forest, deadheading straight through to Pennington Stables if she wanted to, and she'd arrive safe and sound.

That was the only thing that would prove the gordath wasn't open. The problem was, what if she was wrong? What if it was trying to manipulate her into going in? What about the red horse?

"Of course, statistically speaking, horses are more likely to get dumped off," she said out loud. The squirrel stopped for a moment as if amazed at her ability to talk, and then resumed its chattering. "It's not quite so often that a hole opens up between worlds and one walks through. So I will go as far as those three trees, and then I will walk back. And that will prove—something."

Lynn took one glance back at the house. She barely stood outside the border of its backyard. The three trees hulked about twenty-five feet into the Wood. She could see their trunks. Lynn took a deep breath and walked, counting off her paces.

When she stood beneath the trees, she touched one as if she were a kid playing tag and the tree was home. It was cool and rough to her fingers. Overhead the wind soughed, and she could hear the sound of distant traffic from the highway. She turned around to look back at the house. It was the same as before, small, falling apart, the paint on the siding flaking, which she could see even from this distance.

She had to admit it to herself. The gordath was closed. Lynn trudged back to the house and around the front to her

car. She opened the door and let herself in, wincing in the
baking heat. She sat there for a moment and then started the
engine and pulled away. Only then did she allow herself to
acknowledge her sadness.

Joe was right on the other side. And Crae might not even
still be alive, though she shied away from that thought. She
could never know and would never find out. *Damn that thing,*
she thought. The gordath hadn't opened, but it had awakened
a terrible need. *Maybe that's what it does,* she thought bitterly. Opens the hole inside you first. She knew one thing for
sure: If she ever approached the gordath again, she would be
like Lady Sarita. She would find a way to disappear.

Drav, the big Brythern guard, aimed a kick
at a skinny dog that skulked near camp, and Joe rolled his
eyes. Drav was the camp enforcer, intimidating Joe and Arrim whenever he could, trying to beat the shit out of them
when he thought he could get away with it. Lord Hare re-
buked him when he thought his man had gone too far, but it
was never as soon as Joe could have wished for. Mark tried to
egg Drav on, too, but it soon became clear that it was the
quickest way to make Drav stop. Mark might have thought he
was Hare's right-hand man, but whenever he tried to give any
orders, he was pretty much ignored. He mostly sat around in
camp holding his rifle and pretending to sight it and sulking.

With Joe and Arrim off-limits, Drav took out his frustra-
tions on the dog. It was obviously lost and looking for hand-
outs. It scuttled around with its tail between its legs, flinching
when it got a kick or a rock thrown at it. It had belonged to
someone, because it kept expecting kindness. *No kindness
here,* Joe thought. Nothing sadder than a lost dog.

Well, he and Arrim were pretty sorry and sad right now.
They had been bound and driven by the Brythern soldiers for
two days deep in the forest, with little pity for their pains.
They were kept apart so he and Arrim couldn't talk, and
when he asked, no one, not even Mark, as hard as it was for
him to keep from boasting, told him a thing except they were

captives, they were to keep quiet, and if they made trouble, they would be killed. Hare kept the handgun in a holster at his belt, along with a sword and several wicked knives.

The dog whined and hid in the shadows outside the camp, and Drav cursed and threw a stick at him. A yelp came from the dark, but the dog kept itself hidden. Good, Joe thought. He sat on his haunches; his hands, bound behind his back, were tethered to a tree. As always, Joe tried to work his hands free, but though the rope slipped up and down his wrists, it was clear it wasn't going to untie itself.

"Hey," he yelled out to no one in particular. "I have to piss!"

"Piss your trousers," someone growled. Ballard laughed.

Asshole, Joe thought and settled back. His guards had fallen into a routine anyway. They would be let up in an hour and be able to relieve themselves. It was the one time their hands were untied, but there was no chance for escape, not with three Brythern swords at his throat while he went about his business.

Even without any answers he could figure out some things. They had been kidnapped because they were guardians, and so he was pretty sure that they weren't going to be killed, no matter how much trouble they made. It looked like Mark was up to his old tricks. Joe wondered if he had convinced Hare to cross the Aeritan border just to pick up the cash, and he and Arrim were a bonus catch, or if they were the point of the raid.

The last thing Arrim had said before they were captured was that they were trying to close the wrong gordath. Joe hadn't had time to figure out what it meant. Now it looked as if Hare and his buddies had a portal of their own. And since Mark was involved, chances were that he was making another bid to run guns across this new gordath. Was Garson standing at the ready at his end with another stockpile, or did they have a different game going? *Dammit,* he thought. Lynn could be in danger. She might not know about Garson's connection to the gordath and the guns. He wished he could get a message to her, wished for a moment that he could have sneaked through the gordath back at the old house. Gone visiting, maybe even gone home. But he was a guardian, and guardians keep the gordath closed.

Well, he thought, at some point Hare had to let his two captives work together, and then they could turn the tables.

For instance, they could open the gordath and duck through, and close it from the other side. Maybe. He sure wouldn't want to open it up here and then find out it couldn't be done. He glanced over at Arrim and caught the guardian's eye. At that moment he got slapped on the back of his head, bringing tears to his eyes. When he could focus again, he saw it was Hare who had given him the wallop with his gloves that were made of hard leather and sewn together with metal rings.

"No signaling," the man ordered. Mark and the guards laughed. Joe sat back, his head still stinging, but he kept his silence.

All right, he thought. *There has got to be a way out of this. I'm a guardian, dammit! I have to be able to do this.*

He couldn't think of a damn thing. Even if he could fight, he couldn't fight armed men. If he could get his hands on the gun—Joe knew how to shoot a gun as well as the next good ol' boy, but he sure didn't know how to fight with a sword. It was all moot anyway, since he was trussed the way he was. He glanced over at Mark. Mark just watched like Hare while everybody else made camp. Hare didn't know it—or maybe he did—but Mark was a liability. His brand of cocky put him at a disadvantage, because he always thought he was smarter than everybody else.

I'll have to play him, Joe thought. It was hard when Hare kept a no-talking rule for his captives, but Mark couldn't shut up about his schemes. Joe could be patient and wait for Mark to spill. He'd wait for the gordath, too. He felt out for it. It was stronger here, and it thrummed along with his heartbeat. It didn't feel any different for all that it was a foreign gordath, but he could tell there was something different about himself, something darker, something harder inside of him.

Hare got up and disappeared into the woods. Joe hoped he fell in his own shit.

Drav caught his attention. He had a bit of meat and was holding it out in the direction the stray had disappeared, making kissing noises to call in the dog. Joe jerked up, sickened.

At length there was movement in the woods, and the dog crept out. Joe saw the man's other hand reach up to his knife hilt. The dog cringed but kept coming.

"Drav, leave the dog alone," Joe said. He jerked at his bonds. Anxiety rose in him.

"Shut up, Aeritan pig wife," the guard said. He went back to luring in the dog, which inched slow step by slow step to sure pain.

"Yeah, shut up, Joe," Mark said.

"Drav, hold," said one of the other guards, disgust clear in his voice.

"Piss off."

"Drav, let. The dog. Be." The disgusted guard stood.

"Why don't you let Drav be?" someone else shouted righteously.

"Yeah," Mark said. "It's just a dog. Christ. Let him have some fun."

Joe held his breath, but Drav's sadism warred with his dislike for Mark. He gave him a disgusted look and continued to sweet-talk the dog.

The rest of the guards were standing now, some on Drav's side, some for the dog.

Joe got up and angled closer. He glanced at Arrim across the camp. The man was on one knee, and he looked sick to his stomach. Joe gathered up as much slack as he could in his tether.

"There's a good boy, come to play," Drav said in a falsetto. The dog touched its nose to the meat.

Joe jumped.

The rope pulled him short but not before he rammed into Drav's side, taking him off balance. The knife flashed up into the air, and Drav landed on top of him as Joe was jerked back.

Drav roared and thrashed, and the rest of the men jumped in, kicking and hitting. Joe grunted with pain, but he could do nothing to defend himself. He curled around himself, but they just took it out on his back.

"Hold!" It was Hare. He made himself heard over the me-lee. The beating slowed, but Drav took the opportunity to get up and kick Joe in the ribs one last time. Joe cried out as he felt something crack.

"I said hold!" Hare raised his gun and shot into the air, the report rolling away into the woods.

It got their attention, and the forest went dead silent. Joe rolled over to his good side, trying not to cry, blood streaming from his nose. He couldn't see, couldn't move beyond that, but he could listen.

"What part of hold, Drav, don't you understand?" Hare's voice had gone soft.

"He jumped me!"

"And he was punished. But I can't have him killed. Now, I know you are one of the best men I have. Loyal, brave, a dirty fighter."

"Yes, sir. Thank you, sir."

"But these two men are more valuable to me alive and uninjured than dead—and if I have to shoot you to keep them that way, I will."

Another deep, ringing silence. Hare raised his voice. "And that goes for the rest of you. Mensare, fix him."

Mensare was the small band's medic. He said, "Yes, sir," and Joe felt him drop to his knees next to him.

He heard rustling, and then Hare knelt, too. The Brythern leader reached out and turned Joe's chin, forcing him to look up. Joe made himself open his good eye—the other one had already swollen shut.

"If you try that again, I will have your friend beaten as badly as you just were," the man said. "We won't kill you. We'll just make you wish we did."

Shut up, Joe told himself. *Shut up, don't say anything, just shut up.*

Instead, he rasped out, "You can stick your gordath up your ass."

Hare didn't say anything. He stood and walked back to the fire. Mensare ripped away Joe's thin T-shirt and began working on him, wiping away blood, salving his wounds, and wrapping his torso to bind his ribs. Joe gasped or grunted, depending on whether the medic stung or hurt him, but the pain settled to a steady throb. Mensare caught his eye. In a low voice the man said, "You aren't very bright, are you?"

Joe couldn't laugh so he settled for a snort. "Yeah."

Mensare grinned quickly and rummaged in his bag. "Trying to save a dog like that. You know he'll do his best now to kill that dog in front of you."

"I know." His sense of humor faded.

Mensare said, "Eh, doesn't mean we'll let him do it."

"Have Ballard order him to," Joe managed. This time Mensare full-on laughed and then covered it with a cough. He began smearing Joe with a liniment of some nasty cream. Joe got a whiff of something that almost smelled familiar, as if the ingredients in the cream were the same as something on a drugstore shelf. Mensare caught his expression.

"Bruisewort," the man said. "You'll still hurt like hell tomorrow, but the bruises fade faster."

Joe remembered his mother's mother, his *abuela,* putting arnica on his bruises and singing a charm over them. How did that song go? He closed his eyes and let himself fall into the memory as Mensare finished his efficient ministrations.

He slept fitfully, the pain waking him periodically. It was full dark, the fire banked. He could see the shapes of men standing guard. The stars shone down through the narrow spaces between the trees, and the night had gotten cold. Joe shivered. He couldn't move much, and he ached from head to toe. His vision blurred, and he felt nauseous. *The bastards gave me a concussion,* he thought woozily.

He heard the smallest sound behind him, a tiny footfall

here and there. Joe froze. The guards never reacted as they talked softly to one another. They remained facing outward. The footfalls came closer, and then he felt a wet nose nudging his back.

Oh God. Joe kept still, willing the dog to go back into the woods. Instead the dog settled at his back, and warmth spread into him. Joe still had his hands tied behind him. He used his fingers to stroke the dog's rough fur. The dog licked his fingers once. Joe's fingers found a rough rope around the dog's neck. So maybe it *had* been someone's pet. He managed to grab a scrap of T-shirt behind his back and rip it off at the seam where it had been hanging by a thread anyway. He twisted the scrap under the dog's rope. The dog whined, and Joe stilled. One of the guards turned toward him, but then turned back. Joe let out his breath and pushed at the dog, but the dog just licked his fingers and settled at his back.

A gordath wants to be open. It goes out of its way to lure lost and lonely travelers, calling them through curiosity or homesickness or a combination of the two. Joe pushed the dog away as roughly as he could with his hands restrained. The dog resisted its exile from the one kind man it had found, but Joe elbowed it hard. The dog whined again, and then, as if it understood, Joe heard it creep off. *Good,* he thought. *Go. Let the gordath find you.*

Joe didn't know what Lynn could do if she got his message, but he felt comforted that she would know he was here, alive, and in trouble. *She'll come,* he thought, looking up at the stars between the dark branches of the trees. *She'll come.*

He woke to the hustle of breaking camp be-fore the dawn. Joe knew right away from the cold at his back that the dog stayed gone, and felt relief. Even if it didn't find the gordath, maybe it would stay out of Drav's reach. He could barely move, and Mensare had to help him to his feet. He staggered like an old, sick man, barely able to keep his body straight. Drav sniggered, and Mark looked at him in disgust. Movement helped, though, and he loosened up. His hands were released so he could eat the bread and meat they gave him and drink his cup of vesh, the spiced drink everyone took to here, even Brytherners, apparently.

Joe looked over at Arrim, but the man didn't look at him. He was worried about Arrim. He hadn't been as badly beaten as Joe—yet—but Joe knew that Arrim wouldn't be able to take it, even if his body survived. The guardian lived for the gordath and the woods. Even during his sojourn in a mental hospital last year, he had survived by dreaming of his beloved forest. *Bastards,* Joe thought bitterly. Arrim didn't deserve this.

"Stay still," Mensare ordered. He checked over Joe's bandages and bruises, his hands brisk and thorough. He poked at Joe's ribs, and Joe stifled a groan. "Sorry," Mensare said under his breath. He raised his voice. "He's fit enough, Lord Hare."

Joe didn't know exactly how bad off he would have to be for Mensare to tell Hare he couldn't walk, but he didn't want to have to find out.

"Good. Everyone on the move." At Hare's orders, the guards broke camp, retied the captives, and headed out.

They took it slow for Joe's sake, and he staggered along with limping steps. The trail they had been following took them out of the woods. The forest thinned, and the trees became sparse while the underbrush got thicker, now that the plants could see the sun. Soon they were walking through bright meadows, the morning sun growing stronger than he was used to in Gordath Wood or around Red Gold Bridge. The land rolled away from them, the sky got big again, and the dirt was gold, baked in the hot sun. Yellow grasses blew in the breeze, and for a second Joe thought he could be in Texas, even down to the stubby pines that dotted the landscape. A range of hills caught his eye, and the lowlands looked like they folded in between them. Here and there he could see settlements, the houses square and low-slung, not like the round little stone houses of the forestholders in the woods outside Red Gold Bridge. Livestock grazed, mostly sheep but a few head of cattle. No people, but he had no doubt their passage was being watched very closely. Probably these folk knew better than to mess with the little band.

The land's familiarity made him homesick. *You could plant cotton here,* Joe thought, scuffing at the trail with his boot. *Maybe need some irrigation, but the soil here looks good . . .* He caught himself up at the irony. He couldn't get out of Texas and leave cotton farming behind fast enough, and here he was.

Well, you can't take the country out of the country boy. Even if he becomes a guardian.

The sun was high overhead when the trail began to rise toward a pass through the hills. The ground grew rocky, and the grasses grew sparse until soon they walked on dirt and rock. They ate on the go, sharing the water and letting the prisoners have their ration. Joe was weakening, though. Hare kept a steady pace, and Joe finally had to stop, all of his injuries throbbing, especially his ribs. His head ached, and his nausea grew.

As the rope grew taut between him and his guard, the man yanked at it. "Move!" he growled. Instead, Joe went to his knees.

They all gathered around. Mensare rolled him over on his back, and Joe kept back a groan as a rock dug into his side.

"He'll have to rest," he said. "He went farther today than I thought he would."

Lord Hare made a disgusted noise. He glanced at Mark. "Lord Bahard," he said with scarcely disguised contempt, "you carry him."

"Me!" Mark protested. The guards all exchanged eye rolls and a few snickers.

"You. It's time you pulled your weight around here."

With a sulk Mark slung his rifle over his back and put Joe's arm over his shoulder, heaving him up. It was almost as painful, but the support helped.

"Thanks, buddy," Joe said, mindful of the forced and unwelcome embrace.

"Screw you," Mark said, for once keeping his voice low.

Resentment leaked through. Just as Joe expected, he couldn't keep quiet. "What the hell are you doing here anyway? How did you become a guardian?"

"Just luck. What about you? How is it being lord and master?"

Mark was too stupid to even know he was being laughed at. He swore again, half dragging Joe up the steep, rocky trail. The sun beat down, and Joe felt faint and nauseous. "Fuck Hare, and fuck the rest of them. I swear, once you open that gordath, I'm going straight through and never coming back."

"So what's the deal?" Joe prompted. "They have a gordath over here now?"

Mark couldn't keep his mouth shut. Once he had a chance to vent his frustration, he let loose. He struggled up the trail, supporting Joe and ranting under his breath.

"Guess there are these things all over the place if you know what to look for. Now Hare wants to run the same deal that I had with Garson. Hell, he even wants in on the oil deal. But the Brythern gordath is worse or something. They tried to control it the last time, and the guys told me that it took out like twenty men and horses. So I told them where we could find you. Well, a guardian anyway. You were a surprise."

His voice turned aggrieved. "I *told* Hare I needed the money that I stashed for this deal. It's seed money, dammit!"

So Hare hadn't believed Mark when he said that's what the money was for. Good for Hare. Joe wouldn't believe him either.

"Sounds like it's quite a deal," Joe said noncommittally.

"Hell yeah. If we bring in the oil men, the same ones Garson contacted last year, and we can keep the gordath open, we can run pipelines from over here back to New York. Man, we pull this off, we'll be fucking rich. Well, me, Garson, and Hare. You'll be lucky you're not dead."

If there was oil; well, and there probably was. The geology over here looked about the same as back home.

"There's just one little problem," Joe said. "A gordath can't stay open."

He could hear the smirk in Mark's voice. "That's your problem, not mine. Not Hare's. Believe me, if he wants it open, you'll keep it open."

How far will a gordath open before it destroys two worlds? Joe had the uneasy feeling that if he and Arrim weren't careful, they were going to find out.

The hike continued. The ground kept rising, and small pebbles rolled under their feet, sending down a constant barrage to the people at the back of the line. Finally, Hare stopped. Mark released him, and Joe collapsed.

The trail ended at a marker, gray and eroded, the carvings barely legible. Joe could read a little of Aeritan writing after the months he had been here. Someone had carved a rose and the characters for Red Gold Bridge. So this was the border, where the countries of Aeritan ended. Beyond this was Brythern.

"Bring the other guardian here," Hare said. Someone pushed Arrim to stand next to Joe. "This is why you are here," he said. "You are to open a gordath for us. You will keep it open until we tell you otherwise. You will control it when it becomes greatly powerful, and you will tell us exactly how it is you do all of this and show us how it's done. Fail to do this thing, and you are useless to us, and so you will die—not, by the way, easily or peacefully."

"I'll tell you," Joe said hoarsely. He gestured feebly, and Hare made a face, as if he knew what Joe was up to, but he bent low anyway. Joe lifted his head. "Just click your heels three times and say, 'There's no place like ho—'"

Hare smacked Joe across the mouth, the leather and chain glove bringing blood to his lips, but, eh, Joe thought, it was almost worth it.

Colar half stood in the Jeep, taking in the scene at the small beach. The police lights continued to strobe, and he couldn't look at them, though he could see it didn't bother anyone else as much. It was much the same as watching TV or a movie sometimes, a barrage on his senses so that he had to turn away. *They grew up with it,* he thought, *but I didn't.* Only sunlight in Aeritan could hurt your eyes, if you were foolish enough to stare at the sun.

Maddy was sobbing, and Kate was trying to comfort her.

"Maddy, it's okay, okay. The police are here. What happened?"

Maddy kept crying, and Kate unbuckled her seat belt and got out. She put her arms around Maddy and held her, and the girl's sobs slowed down and stopped. The other girl, Sarah Decker, was talking fast on her phone, her voice almost as hysterical as Maddy's. She wore a red bikini and her blonde hair glowed in the sun. Colar stared, caught himself, and looked away. And speaking of things to get used to. The girls here were . . . different, to put it mildly.

Kate looked at him over Maddy's head. *What happened?* her expression said.

He shrugged and hoisted himself over the door of the Jeep. Just as he landed, the detective they had been talking with not fifteen minutes earlier came over to them. Spencer looked furious.

"All right. What the hell are you two involved with?"

"What?" Kate said blankly.

"What I mean is, what kind of game are you playing? You tell us that there was some guy staring at you, and now this?"

"Officer, I don't understand."

Colar was beginning to. Maddy had said, "He was looking for you."

"Maddy," he said.

She looked up at him.

"What did he look like?"

"Oh God." She gulped. "There were, like, a bunch of them. It was like the guys you see at the exits asking for change. Only the one in charge, he had, like, long black hair, and his eyes never blinked. He kept on asking for Kate. He said—he said he'd kill us all one by one if we didn't tell him where she was. He grabbed Austin, and he, he, had a gun—"

Austin Emerson. Sophomore, honor student, French horn player. During the school year he and Colar played basketball together at lunch sometimes, pig—or horse, if they decided to skip fifth period. Colar went still and quiet. Austin in the hands of the most feared general in all of Aeritan, who was rumored by one and all to be quite mad . . .

"Is he dead?"

Now Spencer was looking at him. Colar couldn't parse the meaning of his expression, but he filed it away. Shuddering, Maddy shook her head. "One of the other guys, he made him stop. Yelled at him, said he couldn't ki—kill a kid."

"That's enough," the cop said. He turned to Kate. "When you filed your report, Miss Mossland, why did you conveniently forget to tell us that the man we were keeping a lookout for *knew who you were*?"

Kate tried to protest her way out of their predicament. While she was talking, Colar said, "Did anyone tell him where she lived?"

As his words sank in, they turned to look at him one by one. First Maddy, then Kate, whose protests came to a halt, then Spencer. For a moment there was nothing but silence. Then Maddy said in a small voice, "Austin told him. He was really scared, Kate. I'm so sorry."

"It's okay," Kate said. She had regained her calm, though she had lost all color in her face. "Tell him I said so, okay, Maddy?"

Spencer turned and spoke into his radio. One of the cruisers backed up and pulled out.

"Miss Mossland," he said, "where are your parents?"

"They're at work," she whispered. She made her voice louder. "Work."

"All right. Call them. Tell them we're sending a team to the house, but they are to go straight to the police station. You two, drive back to the station and wait there." His voice hardened. "Tell your parents that you and I and young Mr. Mossland here need to have a talk. An honest one this time."

Kate and Colar drove to the police station, followed by Spencer. They didn't talk for most of the drive until she turned to Colar. She was very pale, but her expression was set and calm.

"He's gone to the house," she said. "He wants to set a trap."

"He's in the trap," Colar said. "The police will get there before him." He wished he could be as convinced as he tried to sound. Colar tried to think what the general would do. Even being new to this world, the general had to know by now that he was at a disadvantage. The police had cars and radios and guns. Even the lieutenant carried one. Colar could see it strapped under his suit jacket.

But Marthen had a gun, too, now. And he knew about radios. He used one in the final battle in Gordath Wood. Colar grimaced. Not so much of a disadvantage after all. Knowing the general, the man had another tactic up his sleeve.

He would have killed Austin, if the other man hadn't stopped him. That much Colar was sure about. He remembered the general's order: *Kill all the smiths,* and the brutal murder he himself was involved with. He clenched his fist on his thigh, willing the memory to go away. If it didn't, if he couldn't make the thoughts go away, he was in for another three or four sleepless nights.

Kate came to a complete stop at the intersection and then started up again at the same sedate pace.

"All right," she said, and he looked at her. She had regained her color, and her voice was strong again. "We have less than two miles to come up with a story. They think it's a cult, so we'll have to give them that. Just follow my lead. Yes, we recognized him, but I didn't want to worry my parents, so that's why I lied." She gave a sudden, twisted smile. "That will serve for Mom and Dad, too."

He didn't say anything. He felt his stomach tighten. Lies had a way of coming back and tripping you up. He didn't think the police officer would be put off by easy lies. He would keep coming and coming until he got what he wanted. They were prey, both of the general and now Spencer.

"So he wants us to come back to the cult, and that's why he's coming after me."

Colar frowned. "I think—I think we should say he's coming for me."

She threw him a quick look.

"I'm supposed to be from there," Colar said quietly. "Raised in it, remember? So it would make more sense—he wants me back."

She was quiet for a minute, and the only sound was the engine and the roar of the wind. The police station came into sight, and she slowed and pulled in, rolling to the farthest corner of the lot. Kate turned off the engine and looked at him. Her expression was bleaker than before.

"The thing is—Colar, they might make you go."

He stared at her. "They?"

"My—mom and dad. If they thought the general were your father or something, they might say, well, it's time for you to go home."

Spencer was waving them over, but they didn't move. Colar bit his lip. *My foster sister,* he thought. *She is my foster sister.* He had fancied her last winter, when they were the only two young people in the camp. He still did, but the rules of fostering were strict, and so he had tried to keep his feelings tucked away. He made a decision, slightly numb. He knew he would regret it later, and that he would miss this life terribly. School, friends, girls, sports, cars, and later, college. He didn't belong here, and he was nothing but an imposter. Even the reason he was here—the only reason anyone could give—was one he couldn't understand and never would, not if he lived here forever. But he wouldn't live in this world forever, and it was all a terrible mistake that he was here in the first place. Marthen's coming was a sign from the high god. He would give it all up, return to Aeritan, and become lord of Terrick in his turn.

"That's just it, Kate. If Marthen's here, the gordath's open. I can go home."

It took Kate's parents about forty-five min-
utes to arrive from work and then be filled in on the situation,

including the attack on the kids at the lake. When they found out that she and Colar had gone to the police not an hour before the attack, they were livid.

"Kate," her father had said, low-voiced in his anger. Kate stared back at him defiantly. *No matter how much you want this to be about me being crazy, it's not.* She didn't say that, though, not in front of Spencer. Instead, her father turned toward the officer, his face working with an effort to placate and dismiss. "Officer, I blame my wife and myself. You know, we thought if we just gave her time to get her life back, just let us all get our lives back after what happened last year, but it's clear that maybe we should have given her some extra attention."

Kate gasped at her father's betrayal. She turned to her mother. *Mom,* she mouthed in outrage. Her mother just shook her head slightly, her lips compressed into a thin line. She was pissed; that was clear.

"Maybe," Spencer said, jotting things down in his notebook. "But if you don't mind, Mr. Mossland, I don't think this has to do with your daughter's mental state. She identified someone she recognized from this cult that kidnapped her—and by the way, we never found anything to support that contention—and now he's not only come after her, he's putting other people in danger. So while I can appreciate that you just want to cover this up, I can't do that."

"This isn't a cover-up, and you know it, Louis," Mrs. Mossland broke in, her words clipped. "We'll help any way that we can, but since we don't know what's going on, we don't know what we can do."

"The truth would help," Spencer said mildly. They all stared at him; the response had guilt written all over it. Kate had to keep back a laugh that she knew would sound hysterical and inappropriate. Talk about confirming that she was crazy.

"Officer," she said, steadfastly ignoring her parents and their alarm at what she might say. "I was kidnapped last year by a cult of crazy people. They dragged me all over the place, and I never quite knew where I was. Colar was shot by one of them, and we managed to escape, and I drove home, and that's it. Except now, the leader came after us. I didn't think he would, but he did."

"The kids at the lake said that he had a bunch of other people with him. You know anything about that?"

Kate frowned, trying to look as if she were thinking. Instead, she remembered what Maddy had said. *Like the guys you see at the exits asking for change.* What would Marthen be doing with a bunch of homeless people?

"I don't know," she said finally. "I don't know anything about that. He was definitely by himself when I saw him."

Spencer consulted his notes. "This man, as you described him, was wearing 'old-fashioned' clothes. I remember when you and young Cole turned up last year, Miss Mossland. That would be what you were wearing, too, except his clothes were more like combat gear. Can you tell me about that?" His look included the two of them.

As one, Kate and Colar shook their heads. "No, sorry, it was just what they made us wear," Kate said apologetically.

"But the other men he brought with them, they wore modern clothes," Spencer said. "The kids and the adults at the beach were sure of that. Could be he's recruiting."

"If he's recruiting from among the local homeless people, surely you've gone to question them," Mrs. Mossland said, her voice raised in alarm.

"We have, Janet. And it's a funny thing. All the underpasses from here to Brewster, even, are all empty, except for trash left behind. Like they've disappeared, just like Miss Mossland did last year."

Police lights strobed in the early evening out-side the Mossland house in their quiet neighborhood. Kate and her parents and Colar waited outside while the police checked the house one last time for intruders. Their neighbors watched from their porches and driveways or from behind the curtains in their great rooms, and Kate knew that her parents were embarrassed over the unwanted attention. No one spoke. Kate kept on swallowing against the lump in her throat, trying to keep back the tears. Her father would rather believe she was crazy instead of the truth.

At last the cops finished their sweep of the house, and one came up to the little family huddle, his modern armor with the SWAT logo on it making him look big and bulky. He carried a rifle pointed at the ground, his finger well off the trigger.

"All right," he reported to Mr. Mossland. "It's all clear now, but someone has been inside; the alarm has been compromised, but someone knew enough to call the alarm company and call them off. We checked with them, and that's what they logged. But we checked everything, and there's no one inside. House is clear."

That couldn't have been Marthen, Kate thought. He had someone with him who knew about alarm systems.

"So what we can do is keep a detail here—" the officer began.

"That won't be necessary," her dad broke in. Kate looked at him. Was he crazy? Marthen had pulled a gun on a kid and broken into the house looking for her. Beside her Colar moved restlessly, as if he wanted to say something.

"Dad," she said. "I think—"

"That's enough, Kate!" The look he gave her was one of fury, as if he didn't know her or even like her. Despite herself, Kate cringed. "Officer, we'll be fine. It was just a break-in. They won't come back."

Kate thought the man gave a look that Captain Artor might have given: impatient, disgusted, and derisive. But he just nodded and called his men away. Without looking back, Kate, her mom, and Colar followed her dad into the house and closed the door.

The house was fully lit, every light blazing. Kate's mom reflexively went to turn off the lights but then hesitated. Kate understood. *It feels dangerous,* she thought. *It doesn't feel like home.* As one they began to move from room to room. The police had been thorough; there were traces of their passage everywhere. A chair was out of place, and the pantry door had been left open, but they hadn't violated the house. That had come earlier, and an aura of unsettledness remained. Kate found herself jumping at the least sound.

"I'm calling the alarm company," her dad said. "Incompetents. They're supposed to ask for the password."

Her mom sighed. "David. The password is taped to the underside of the alarm box because we kept on forgetting it."

Her father began to bluster, and Kate had enough. They were in danger, grave danger, and her father had just compounded it with his willful pride. "I'm going upstairs," she called out. Colar went to follow.

"Kate," her father snapped, and Colar halted. Kate looked back. "Don't. You. *Ever.* Interrupt like that again."

Kate felt the color drain from her face. Her father had never spoken to her like that before. Her mother looked as if she were about to say something but turned away. She tried once more.

"Dad, you have to—"

"Not another word."

Fear, anger, and hurt kept her silent. She waited until she could get her voice under control, and when she did, she managed through her teeth, "Yes, sir."

She saw by the look on his face that it had been a direct hit. Kate turned and headed up the stairs. She hadn't slammed her door in years, but she was tempted. Instead, she closed the door and threw herself onto the bed, tears leaking from the corners of her eyes into her ears. Her parents thought she was crazy and that she needed a shrink. They'd never believe that Marthen was truly dangerous. How was she supposed to keep them safe if they refused to listen to her?

We'll just have to find him first. What they would do with him was another story, but they would have to find him and stop him before he attacked again.

Crying about it wouldn't help. Kate got up, wiping her face, when something caught her eye.

Draped neatly across the back of her desk chair was Mojo's old saddle, the one she had left behind in Aeritan.

Six

Crae limped out of his chamber before day-
light had broken, only to almost be bowled over by a
householder rushing by with an armful of cleaning supplies.
He flattened himself against the wall as she stammered out,
"Oh, sorry, Lord Crae! Excuse me, and Calyne wants you to
not return to the upstairs until this evening, please my lord
and thank you!"

Bemused, he watched her go, her words floating behind
her, and shook his head, tightening up the strings at the throat
of his shirt as he headed down the stairs. He hardly needed
his walking stick anymore, though his leg was still stiff. He
walked, rode, helped shear sheep and move cattle, and sparred
with his men, and rubbed liniment into it each night, massag-
ing the herb-infused grease deep into the muscle. Truarch
told him it would keep the scar from tightening his muscle
like a drawn crossbow. He couldn't tell if it was working, but
the wound didn't hurt as much, even if he did smell like the
hay meadows.

He made his way down the stairs, threading his way between harried householders, each giving him a breathless

greeting and usually some kind of admonition. He was told to stay out of his chambers, the kitchen, the great hall, and the guest chambers. The whole household was in an uproar over the Lord of Favor's visit. He was expected that day. It was one more thing he had to deal with. Crae didn't know the man, except from what he had heard from Stavin, and that obliquely; he had muttered once that Jessamy had gotten all the sense in that family.

He wondered what his new brother would think of him. Favor had attended his wedding, but they had not spoken except for the formal words of family over the wedding cup: "Welcome, Brother. Let us drink to our bond."

Crae didn't really remember much about his wedding, other than the sense of wariness he got from everyone at Trieve, except for Tevani, of course.

He turned to the kitchen, remembered that it was off-limits, and gave a curse. He hadn't eaten, and whatever they were cooking in there for the welcome feast made his mouth water.

Damned Lord Favor, he thought. *Well, it's my damn house, and so it's my damn kitchen.* He steeled himself and was about to pull open the door when one of the cooks bustled up behind him, two freshly slaughtered ducks hanging by their necks from her capable hands.

"Ooh, get that door for me, Lord Crae, please?" she called out, tendrils of brown hair coming from underneath her kerchief. Her dark eyes lit up when Crae held the door for her and followed her in, admiring her figure in her serviceable skirts and a half-laced bodice, no doubt undone because of the heat in the kitchen. Indeed, the heat rushed at him from the ovens, and he was enveloped in warmth and spices. The cooks and their help had been joined by men and women from the neighboring villages, all busy deboning birds and stuffing sausage, kneading bread or patting down flatbread. The kitchen was piled high with sweetbreads and sausages. A basket of the first strawberries waited to be turned into a sweet and savory chutney along with onions, garlic, and dandelion greens. Crae's stomach rumbled again, but he also wondered what this feast was costing him; it looked as if a fair bit of his livestock had been slaughtered to impress his brother-in-law.

"Now, sir," the cook said, throwing an impish glance at him as if she caught him looking at her, "we are all very busy for Lord Favor's visit . . ."

She reminded him of being a captain and being the recipient of a woman's boldness at Red Gold Bridge.

"Vanye, if I don't get something to eat and some vesh, you are all going to be very sorry."

She rolled her eyes, but he could tell she wasn't mad. "Fine. Go help yourself, but stay out of the way. Not that!" she shrieked as he made for some freshly baked rolls stuffed with spiced beef. He held up his hands in exaggerated alarm, and Vanye laughed. Her laugh faded as her attention turned to a point past his shoulder. Crae turned and saw his wife watching him flirt with the householder.

Jessamy's face was stricken, but she smoothed her expression hastily.

"Good morning, Jessamy."

She nodded. "Crae. Vanye."

"My lady." Vanye took her ducks and fled.

"Have you eaten?" he asked.

"Of course, Crae. Where have you been? We've all been up for hours."

"I didn't realize your brother's visit would turn the house upside down and keep me out of my chambers, the hall, the corridors, the kitchens."

"You usually spend all day outside anyway. Get something to eat, but we're all busy."

He sighed. *Not again.* "Why are you so angry?"

"I'm not angry, but if you must know, we're very busy, and it would have been better if my brother's visit did not have to coincide with a crow in the kitchen."

"The crow is not in the kitchen, and I don't see what the visit and crow have to do with one another."

"Because I don't know how I will explain to Lord Favor

why there is a crow anywhere in this house, especially one that tried to kill my daughter."

"I'll explain it."

She snorted. "You? That's not—"

"Good enough?" he finished for her. She reddened. He was peripherally aware that the kitchen had gotten very quiet. Jessamy seemed to become aware, too, because she lowered her voice.

"I wasn't angry before, but now I am. See what you did?"

He couldn't help it. He said, "It's not that hard, Jessamy."

For a moment she looked as if she were fighting tears, and then she turned and walked away. He felt wretched and closed his eyes, wishing for strength. When he glanced around again, all the cooks looked quickly away. After a bit Vanye came up to him with a roll stuffed with minced meat and cabbage and a mug of vesh. She gave him a sympathetic look, but she also jerked her head at the door.

He took the hint and left. Jessamy had already disappeared, but he didn't have the energy to try to find her and placate her. She had always been moody, but lately she had been so on edge that the entire household tiptoed around her.

They hadn't bothered to place the crow's lockup off-limits to him, so he set his stick outside. The boy he had set as guard had a kitten with him and was letting it bat at a string. Crae bit back a smile as the boy, hardly more than nine, saw him and stood straight up, approximating a soldier at attention. The kitten mewed, and the boy shushed him but continued looking straight ahead.

"Um, hello, sir, Lord Crae. I'm sorry, sir."

Well, the crow was no danger, and the only reason the boy was on duty was to call for help if he or the crow needed it. But Crae thought that he should encourage the youngster's instincts.

"Son," he said, "have you checked on the prisoner?"

The boy's face fell. "No, sir. Do you want me to?" he added hopefully. Crae held up a hand.

"When you stand guard, even over a miserable creature

such as the crow, you need to be vigilant at all times. The crows are full of wiles. How do you know he hasn't escaped?" The boy's eyes went wide. Crae kept from smiling as he pressed home his point. "I knew a prisoner who once hid beneath a manger. She would have escaped, too, if I hadn't tricked her."

"How?" the boy said, his eyes wide.

"I pretended to give up looking for her and close the door to the stables behind myself, but I really stayed inside. She thought I had left and stood up from her hiding place."

He remembered suppressing a grin of triumph at Lynn's shock and disgust. She had been upset with herself, but he had been able to convince her he wasn't her enemy—Tharp and Bahard were. He nodded at the door. "Let's see if he is still inside. Has Truarch come to care for his leg?"

"No one has been to see him, sir," the boy said. He pushed back the bolt and pushed open the door, and Crae limped in.

The crow looked up listlessly when Crae entered. The boy lit the two candles on either side of the door and left them alone. The crow lay in the hay, his leg exuding the sick-sweet smell of infection, the chains half-hidden in the straw. The room had become sickly again. Crae regarded him from the doorway. If no one had been to see him, the crow was likely starving, if he was well enough to eat. He slid down as best he could with his stiff leg. The vesh slopped a little. He held out both the vesh and the stuffed roll.

"Here. Breakfast."

The man watched him, unblinking. He was sprawled in the straw as if he had no energy left. Crae set down the food and pulled himself closer, steeling his nerve. *If I call for help, the boy will come,* he thought absurdly. It was foolish to be so frightened. The crow was dying. Even with Truarch's care and remedies, his leg was festering.

"Here," Crae said again. There was a clean bucket of cold water at least, set far from the corner with the slop bucket. Crae scooped up a cupful with the dipper. Supporting the man's shoulders, he sat him up and held the dipper to his mouth. The man sipped obediently, but he felt hot, so hot.

After a bit he croaked something and feebly waved away the dipper. Crae let him back down carefully, and the man closed his eyes.

"Do you wish to speak to anyone?" he asked, feeling a little foolish. The man moved his head in the straw. *No.*

Crae nodded and he sat next to him. "Do you want me to go?" he asked, this time feeling still more foolish. Again the man moved his head.

No.

"All right," Crae said. "I'll stay."

The crow didn't die then but only slept. Crae left when his breathing settled to a raspy evenness, blowing out the candles and leaving the crow in darkness. When he stepped out into the hall, he breathed the fresh air, feeling the sweat bead on his forehead. The boy watched him from across the hall, holding the kitten as it squirmed and purred, biting his fingers. It was a bad job for a kid. Crae decided to set him loose.

"Here," he said. "Go find Truarch and tell him he needs to see to the crow. If he's not in the barns, he will be out with the sheep or in the cow fields." The boy's face lit up at his reprieve, and he ran off. Crae watched him go with a grin, and then his smile faded. The crow was dying. His scheme to learn what he could of the lawless creatures was going nowhere. *I can't capture a hale one,* he thought with grim humor, *and I can get nothing from a dying one.* Maybe Jessamy was right, and it was a fruitless quest. Crae locked the door behind him and went off to find his men. They needed to drill once the morning's work was done.

The sun had come up finally. The grayness of the early morning was giving way to the pale yellow of the sunrise, and the cool air was a welcome change after the kitchens and the sickroom. Meadow birds piped and called. It looked to be a fair day, the air brisk and cool for now, but it might even get some heat later on. Crae arched his back and stretched. It would be a good day for riding out, and he needed to get aboard a horse again and test his leg. Perhaps he could take

Lord Favor around Trieve when he arrived. That might calm Jessamy, to see her husband and brother get along.

On the way to the barn he tossed the meat roll over to the pigs, reluctant to eat it after it had been in a room of sickness, and dumped the vesh in the rosebushes at the back entrance to the barn. He stuck the cup on a stone ledge next to the lintel, hoping he remembered to bring it back.

He looked longingly back at the house, wondering if he should try again for the kitchens, when a tantalizing smell caught his attention. He turned. One of the cooks was bringing food to the men in the barns. She had a pitcher of vesh, some more stuffed rolls, and pickles, it looked like. Crae grinned, retrieved his cup, and followed his breakfast into the barn.

The breakfast fueled that morning's arms work. He set his men to battling on the lawn at the top of the terraces, using wooden swords to start with. Crae went from pair to pair, keeping an eye out and sometimes stopping combat to give advice on positioning and tactics. It was maddening that Stavin had not taken care of this when he was lord. He would not have lost as many men as he had. He had grieved over them, true, but he would have done better to have prepared them for war rather than throwing them into it willy-nilly. Many of these men, now, were brothers or cousins of the men who had died.

One sure thing in Aeritan. There would always be a war, and so there would always be a need for fighting men. He could not fail his men—his House—by allowing them to be lost again. Though he couldn't do it alone. He needed a captain, someone who could focus only on putting together a fighting company. Once he had been such a man, but even he had come to Red Gold Bridge, his old posting, with a fighting force in hand, and taken over another already trained. He had never had to train his men from scratch.

Well, now he had the need. As the sun got high and his muscles loosened, Crae stripped his shirt and tossed it aside.

So did many of the others. He motioned to one of his men, the young farmer Alarin. The man threw him the crude wooden sword, and Crae faced off against his opponent. His weapon was a crossbow, but in close combat that was useless. He was not as great a swordsman as others, but he could handle himself well. He nodded to the other man, and they set at each other, Crae calling encouragement. The swords clunked dully together.

"There, good! Now watch your step—press hard on me as I back up. Good!" He held up the sword, and the man halted, grinning. "Try again. This time you want to keep me from getting my footing, so you have to move faster and harder, like so." Crae attacked, pushing the man so quickly he stumbled. Crae let up. No good at this stage in quashing all of their confidence. "Now you try it." The man nodded and pressed a credible version of Crae's attack.

"Lord Crae!" At the call Crae turned. The other man was not so quick to stop, and he rapped Crae in the bare ribs with his sword before he could pull up.

"Ow!" High god, that stung!

"Oh, sorry, my lord!" The man went from confidence to wide-eyed worry.

Crae breathed hard to get the pain under control. "No harm done. You've got quite a blow there. Good thing we're just playing." The man grinned in relief. Crae canted his head and looked down at his ribs. An angry red mark was slashed across his side. He winced. It was going to raise a good weal. He hoped Truarch had a nostrum for this.

"Oh, sorry, sir," said the man who had distracted them. "Lord Favor's here."

They all turned to watch as Favor and his train mounted the terraces. Their horses were blown, but the riders did not dismount. He heard some of the grooms mutter at that. Crae held up his hand and gave them a stern look. This was one of the Council lords, and they had best be respectful. Grudgingly they subsided, and he let it go, but he made a note to himself that he would need to be harder on them. It was too easy to let them be on equal footing with him—not so long ago he was a commoner, too—and forget they must remember their place. He must not be like Stavin and let things go the easy way. He winced at the memory of Vanye's familiarity and resolved not to allow himself to be drawn into that again.

Crae grabbed for his shirt. It would not do for the Lord of Trieve to greet the Lord of Favor—his wife's brother and thus his brother—naked from the waist up, especially with a livid mark across his side. He pulled his shirt over his head, tying the strings at his neck, and raked his fingers through his hair, then limped forward to give greeting to his new kinsman.

The lord was not much older than Jessamy and looked a great deal like her. He was taller than she, but they shared the same cast of face and the same dark eyes. Favor stayed in the saddle as his horse snorted and shook the froth off its neck, its sides bellowing. He looked down on Crae.

"Lord Favor, I give you greeting and guesting," Crae said. *Get off your damn horse, man.* "Come, take your ease in my house."

"Is my sister within?"

"Yes, of course."

Favor gestured to his men, and they all dismounted, some with a great deal more alacrity than others. So at least he had some men who knew what was due their mounts. Take care of your horse, and he will take care of you, the saying went, but it didn't always happen. Crae nodded to his grooms, and they came over, and there was a great bustle as housemen helped bring in Favor's belongings and the grooms took care of the horses.

Favor led the way to the house, and Crae shook his head and let him go. So his brother would not be courteous. So be it. He had a holding to lead. He turned back to his men, his limp more pronounced from the exercise. The exhilaration from their training had faded away, and now Crae felt the soreness he had been denying. The youngsters looked none the worse for wear, though there were a few of the older strongholders who looked the way he felt. That was a hard thought, and he pushed it away.

"Enough for today," he said. "We'll go again tomorrow." It would be well if they could spar against Lord Favor's men, now they were here, but he knew that could go badly. His men were novices; he had but a quick look at Favor's men, and they all looked battle-hardened. His men didn't need to have their confidence flattened.

All the more reason to get them into fighting shape. With crows on the move and Aeritan's lords always irritable, it was not good to have a weak holding.

Alarin, the young farmer, fell in beside him as he gathered up his gear and his walking stick and stumped toward the house.

"Lord Crae, may I ask you something?" The young man's voice was low. Crae stopped and waited.

"Should we not have fighting men stationed in all of Trieve's villages? I know I have much still to learn, but with all the men here, it leaves our holdings vulnerable."

Crae nodded. Alarin was an earnest fellow, his eyes clear gray and a farmer's tan evident on his face and hands. He was strong and stout, a good man, and a smart one.

"We're racing time," Crae said, keeping his voice equally as low. "I say this not so that you can talk it over in the ale-house, but that you know I am aware of our lack. We need fighting men, and we need them fast, with the crows on the move and any other attackers out there. So, we are going to train as we have been. And I will find additional fighting men, and with the high god's blessing, we will be ready when the need comes."

Alarin nodded, his face determined. He bowed, and Crae went on to the house.

Jessamy had greeted her brother, and they stood together at the fireplace, a cup of welcome already in Favor's hands. Tevani was wild with excitement, jumping up and down. She caught sight of Crae and ran over to him.

"Lord Crae, Lord Crae! My uncle has come! He has the

same name as Jori! Uncle Jori, come see Lord Crae! He gave me Hero!"

Jessamy gave her brother a glance, and Crae figured that she had already told him about his gift of the horse. Favor skimmed over Crae, his eyes lingering on the walking stick.

"Yes, I heard about that. Jessamy, I see what you mean, about the spoiling. Maybe it's a good thing I've come."

Jessamy had the grace to look abashed at that. Crae let the slow burn rise and fall within him. This was not the time to give his wife's brother the trouncing he deserved.

"Come, the welcome meal awaits," Jessamy said a bit hastily. "We give thanks for your safe journey, Brother. We can all talk later. Tevani, ask one of the housewomen to help you into your pretty clothes. Goodness, child, how did you get into so much mud?"

"I never know how it happens, Mama. I think mud likes me."

Several days later, Crae was drilling his men under a bright, midsummer sky. There were no clouds, and the sky was deep blue. It was hot. Sweat poured off him and his men. Their wooden swords clunked dully.

He was furious. Favor's men watched, and he could see them turn to each other, hiding comments but unable to hide their smirks.

He should have been able to ask Favor for help. But when he broached the topic, Favor had taken great pleasure in disdaining his request. "I do not wish to blunt my own men's prowess by setting them at beginners." Even Jessamy had looked at her brother, startled by his response. Crae had seen the way her eyes narrowed, but she had kept her counsel, though she seemed uneasy. A part of his anger was directed at her. She needed to help, and yet she would rather support her brother against her husband. *No, against her home.*

His men had grown unsure under the gaze of the audience, and Crae bit back a curse. Finally he shouted, "Swords up!"

Everyone halted raggedly, still another sign of their inexperience. Crae picked up his shirt where he had left it on the grass and wiped his face with it. He scanned his audience. Let Favor complain if he wanted to, but Crae was going to put his brother's men to good use. He pointed at Breyan, Favor's captain. "You!"

"My lord?" the man said, stepping forward. He finessed the respect due to a lord with his body language that said he answered to one lord only.

"You are Breyan, are you not?"

The man bowed.

"Come, show Trieve what Favor can do," Crae said. He let a mocking tone enter his voice. Breyan bit back a laugh, and his men all gave a chuckle.

"With all due respect, my lord, but your men are not yet seasoned. It would not be good for them to fight us."

"Oh, that's not what I meant, Breyan." Crae tossed aside the toy sword and picked up his scabbard where it leaned against the stone wall of the old barn. He drew it and it rasped out of the scabbard, a satisfying noise after the timid thunking of wood on wood. He waited. "Well? Or don't you think that I can wipe that smirk off your face?" He hoped he could. He was worried about his leg, but he didn't think the captain had anything on him. He was several years older and a bit thicker than Crae, even if he was an experienced fighter. *And right now my anger will carry me when my leg fails me.* He'd blood Breyan to make his point.

Breyan looked astonished. "My lord, I can't—well, *my* lord wouldn't allow—"

"Yes, I would," came Favor's voice. He had come out of the house with Jessamy. "You have my permission, Breyan. Captain to captain."

Crae's men rumbled, and a few stepped forward. He held up a hand and walked over to Favor. "Rather than lord to lord?" he said, loud enough for all to hear.

This time the silence was broken only by the sounds of the wind and the distant baaing of the sheep. Jessamy spoke up first.

"Don't be ridiculous. You aren't going to fight. I won't allow it."

"Of course not," Favor said quickly, though Crae hadn't missed how he had to swallow before he could speak. Crae was taller than he, and the man had a softness about him that spoke of too much wine and rich food.

"Are you sure?" Crae said. He shifted his sword. "Are you sure you don't want to fight me?"

Favor turned pale, and his breath came fast. He gripped his sword hilt, though, and stepped forward gamely. "You forget yourself," he said.

"Crae, stop this at once," Jessamy said. "Jori, *don't.*"

Favor sneered and made a great show of releasing his sword hilt. "For you, Jessi. After all, you are much to be pitied, for what fate has married you to." He took her arm and made to lead her back to the house. She shook off his hand and turned to Crae. She was livid. Crae had seen her angry before, of course, but this was the first time he had seen her in full wrath. She had paled except for two points of color high on her cheeks. He stared back at her, matching her anger with his. *Do not walk away with him,* he thought. *Do not, Jessamy.*

Jessamy kept her eyes on him, eyes that were dark with anger. She gave him a full curtsy, her back rigid, bowing almost to his feet, the elaborate ritual speaking of her fury. And then she turned on her heel and walked away from both of them. After a moment of surprise, Favor followed at her heels, remonstrating, and she shook him off.

Crae watched her go, seething. He walked over to where he had left his gear, pulled out a cloth, and wiped his sword down, even though it had not been used. "Captain," he called, sheathing his sword. Breyan turned to him with a watchful expression.

"Sir."

"In Favor you follow your lord's orders. In Trieve you follow mine. Laugh at my men again, and I will see to it that you are cleaning the stables and shearing the sheep in their place. Is that understood?"

Breyan was rigid with shock and growing anger. When he could finally speak, his voice was tight. "Understood."

"Good. Then pick up a wooden sword, all of you, and fall in. We have a House guard to train."

He watched his men join forces with Favor's, and already the energy of the training center climbed tenfold. Crae watched and called out orders, and wished he could spar, the anger burning a hole in his gut. Better not to, he decided. In his mood he could easily kill someone, wooden sword or no.

Calyne approached him timidly later that eve-ning when Crae sat alone in the great hall, cold air coming in from the imperfect glazing in the windows high overhead. He sat at the desk on the raised dais, going over the histories of Trieve and the accounts, a bottle of strong spirits at his elbow. He had not gone to dinner with the others. Instead, he called for his meal and sat with a few oil lights and a fire on the hearth to cut the chill. He knew he was sulking, knew that he lost what high ground he held in acting so, and still he got drunk and wished them all to hell.

He looked up at the housewoman's approach. She bobbed quickly and then said, "Lord Crae, Lady Jessamy asked that you join her in her chamber."

His first impulse was to say no. He could tell that Calyne thought he would, that or demand that Jessamy join him instead. Crae sighed and stoppered the bottle.

"Tell her I will be up."

Calyne bobbed another small curtsy and rushed off as if she had been reprieved. Crae closed the books and set them neatly away. This was Jessamy's domain anyway, this desk with all of its accounts. She had kept them in Stavin's absence. Trieve had prospered under her control. It would have been a sad thing for her to have left her home and her children's home if the Council had their way last year.

Only by marrying Crae had she been spared that. He supposed it too much to ask that she offer him thanks. No, that was bitterness speaking. It had been hard for her to seek this salvation and harder still to accept it from him, and he understood that. She had never liked him or Stavin's friendship with him and tolerated it only for her husband's sake.

He kicked back his chair and grabbed his stick. He doubted that she was planning to apologize, so he might as well go and see what she wanted.

She sat nursing the baby boy in the low light by the fire and a few candles. Tevani already slept in a small bed next to the larger one that was Jessamy's, and there was a cradle for the baby. The room was crowded and peaceful. Clothes spilled out of a large chest, hers and the children's. The baby suckled sleepily, and Jessamy was herself ready for bed, her hair down around her shoulders and falling to her waist. She wore a nightgown with tiny buttons down the front bodice. It was half-undone now so she could nurse. A blanket lay discreetly over the boy and her breasts. Crae waited, leaning against the bedpost. She had summoned him; she could begin.

She watched him over her son's head. Even in the dim light he could tell she had been crying.

"Thank you for not fighting him," she said, her voice thick. Of all the things he had been expecting, that had been far from it. She caught his expression of surprise, and she gave a watery smile. "Crae, I'm no fool. He deserves a good thrashing, my brother or no. But if you fought him, win or lose, it would be very bad for Trieve. We are in a tenuous position here. No trained men and an upstart lord? It would not take much for the Council to decide they made a bad choice in you and seek to remedy it."

She was right. She put into words what he had been sensing but hadn't been able to articulate. What the Council had raised, they could cast back down. Just like that, they were thinking together. All of his temper vanished.

He nodded. "So what do you suggest? We need allies, men—" If they could not even get Favor as an ally, would any of the Houses come to their aid in the Council or otherwise?

"I will talk to Jori," she said firmly. "He won't go against me, no matter how much he dislikes you." Crae acknowledged her openness with a wry smile, and she gave him one of her own. "And I think we can count on Terrick. I know that House. They are good and honorable. Their son may still live beyond the gordath."

"And Wessen," Crae said. It was his home country, and he knew the formidable Lady Wessen, Sarita's mother. She had been the one who sent him off to lead her daughter's guard, after all. *At which I failed,* he thought, but nonetheless, he felt the grim lady would have forgiven him, now that Lady Sarita was returned.

"Red Gold Bridge is perhaps not our ally," Jessamy said thoughtfully. She dislodged Jori from her breast, hastily covering up her nightdress. She stood and laid the sleeping baby in his cradle. He cried out once and then sank into sleep, and Jessamy gave a sigh of relief. She kept her back to Crae as she buttoned her nightgown, and he allowed himself to admire her form under the nightdress, almost but not completely hidden under its folds. "Unless Sarita can influence Tharp."

"What of Kenery?" he asked her. "Do you think . . ."

She snorted and turned around to him. "I would not trust Lord Kenery to hold my horse for me. Do you know what it took for me to argue him around? A bit of flattery and an appeal to his most false nature."

Crae laughed out loud, then muffled it instantly, hoping he hadn't woken the children. "I had wondered. I thought you just kept talking to him until he finally gave in."

It was her turn to laugh, although more quietly. "There was something of that, I admit." She began braiding her hair loosely. "So our allies are few, our enemies many. But that is the way of the Aeritan lords—how we do squabble." She gave him a smile that was almost impish. "Welcome, Lord Crae, to your new family. So how much longer do you think it will take before we have a fighting force?"

"Months," he acknowledged. "I need a captain, perhaps two. I can't do it all myself. And we need men in all the villages."

"Breyan is a good man," she said. "He was in my father's

guard as a young man, and he took over when Jori became lord. Perhaps he knows someone among his men who could be a good captain. I'll ask him."

"Good," Crae said. He felt a wave of relief and hopefulness. He never thought it would happen, but they worked together, at least for now. Perhaps it took her brother to make Jessamy see Crae in a better light. He wanted to take her in his arms—hell, he wanted to take her to his bed—but he knew better.

Crae stepped forward and kissed her lightly on the cheek. "We will get through this," he said. "Trieve will survive."

She made as if to say something but changed tack.

"It will," she said firmly and formally. "We will. Good night, Lord Crae."

Well enough. They were back to that. He still felt lighthearted, though, enough to tease her a little. He gave her a formal bow, lord to lady.

"Good night, Lady Jessamy."

And then he left her to seek his bed.

Jessamy must have talked to her brother, be-cause Favor sulked the rest of the day. Crae hadn't had a chance to ask her if she had forced Favor into agreeing to ally with Trieve, but he suspected from the man's attitude that she had been successful. Favor never looked at Crae the whole day. He drank hard at dinner, the good beer that was Trieve's specialty wasted on him. Crae was beginning to wish that he could take his meal into the kitchen and at least enjoy the company there, when Favor finally spoke up.

"So, Captain," Favor said sullenly. He glared up at Crae. "You have turned my sister's House into quite an old barn. You give guesting to a crow. That is something new. What next? Marry him to my niece, perhaps?"

Crae looked at him through narrowed eyes. High god, how he hated the man. No alliance was worth this. "Someone needs to find out where they come from, who they are, and why they fight."

Favor spat out a laugh. "They are lordless men, godless men. They are mad, filthy animals. They deserve to be killed where they stand. Instead, you bring one into your house—my sister's house—and stable it in your kitchen."

"Jori, shut up," Jessamy said with deliberation.

"No, Sister! I have had enough of this. I've seen how he treats you. I've seen how he runs your house. He is an incompetent, common captain at arms, and he can't even do that very well." He sneered in Crae's direction and at the stick propped against the table next to him. "Have you seen his men-at-arms? Farmers and shepherds all. Not a soldier among them."

"That is because, Jori, all of our men-at-arms were killed fighting against the army *you* joined." Jessamy glared down her brother. "So it could be said that you put us in this precarious situation."

Favor blustered. "Well, if Stavin had not joined with Red Gold Bridge . . ."

He trailed off at the look on her face. Jessamy was pale, her face like stone.

"Don't you ever disparage Stavin."

"Jessi—"

"Don't you 'Jessi' me! You never call me that except when you want something!"

"He gave guesting to a crow in your kitchen!" Favor's voice was rising.

"It's my house, Jori!"

"It's. My. House."

A part of Crae knew he spoke, but the words welled up from another source. He knew only that he stood, and the same strength he had gained from the high god overwhelmed him again. He put his fists down on the table and leaned over Favor. "Trieve is mine. I will keep this holding as befits its lord, and I will not be gainsaid. You are my kin, but never do you think, ever, that you have the right to question my rule."

Favor shrank back. His throat worked convulsively, and Crae let his disgust creep into his expression.

"Are we clear, *Brother*?"

Favor just nodded.

"Good. Then, I have work to do."

He pushed back his chair with one boot, grabbed his stick, and bowed to Jessamy, as lord to his lady. "My lady," he said. She was furious, he could tell, but she graced him with a nod in reply.

For a moment, as he left them to the remains of their family dinner, he thought that it would be fun to set the crow loose and watch Favor run. Then he sighed. There had to be a way to get through to the man, and he didn't just mean his wife's brother.

The mountain light lingered long into the night in Trieve, the sunset remaining for hours over the jagged horizon, even as the first stars opened in the vault of the sky. Crae walked the perimeter of the house and barn, keeping quiet conversation with his smallholders as they readied for the night. The sheep were in the fold, the dogs keeping a careful watch, the cows in the byre. Crae turned to go back to the house and was surprised to see Jessamy come out to him, a wrap around her shoulders, her hair blowing about under her kerchief. Favor was nowhere to be seen.

"At last," she sighed. "Both children sleep, and I have a few moments to myself. I talked to Breyan, and he said he had a few likely candidates for you, men who have been chafing under his command. You should interview them tomorrow."

That could mean he was eager to rid himself of troublemakers, but Crae understood. He had been a young man of that type himself—ready for his own command. It was how he came to Red Gold Bridge those years ago. It was a small step after that to taking his position under Lord Tharp's rule. He would be there still, breaking heads and keeping peace in the stronghold, if Lady Sarita had not disappeared through the gordath. Once, it was all that he had wanted: his own command in a good House. His ambitions were few: adventure, love, and an honorable commission.

Life had grown complicated, to be sure.

"Good," he said. "And the other? Did he agree to an alliance?"

She gathered her shawl, her hair flying in the rising wind. "Well. He is stubborn. And he cast in his lot against Trieve in last year's war and sees no reason why he can't do so again. But he wants to marry, and I told him if he sets against Trieve again, I would make sure every eligible maid of marrying age knew exactly how windy he gets after dinner, not to mention certain other . . . secrets I have on him."

Crae laughed despite himself. "You are an elder sister, indeed."

She laughed, too. "Oh, we fought so hard when we were young. I love him dear, but he sets my back up all the time."

Mine, too, but Crae didn't say that out loud. They stood companionably for a time, enjoying the rising breeze and the lights from a distant village, a few houses in a fold in the hills far below. He was startled when she spoke.

"There is nothing wrong in the way you treat me," she said abruptly. It took Crae a minute, and then he remembered Favor's temper at dinner.

"I know," he said with equanimity, though Favor's accusation had stung, as it had been meant to.

She laughed a little reluctantly. Again she shook her head.

"Crae, you are the most unlordlike, upstart captain—" She broke off. When she spoke next, her words came jerkily. "I must apologize to you. Your elevation by the Council was not a summoning as I said. It means the same thing, but there is a difference, as you discovered. We are not often summoned nowadays, but the high god appears to be silent on the matter, so the Council does as it wills."

He couldn't find words for a moment. Finally he said, "Is anyone ever truly summoned anymore?"

"It's not something to talk about," she said. "But—I think not, or at least, it is not given the final word. Lady Wessen had to fight for her right to be lord of Wessen. I was young, but I remember my mother being quite shocked that she would go against the Council and insist on taking up her House." She put a hand on his arm. "You must not talk of this to anyone or accuse anyone," she said, and he could hear the fierceness in her voice. "Sometimes the high god chooses—differently, that's all. So the Council makes its decision."

Elevated by the Council and summoned by the high god. It should have cemented his position as Lord of Trieve. Instead, it had only undermined it. If the high god summoned whomever he wanted, then it meant that anyone could be a lord.

The Council wouldn't like that.

Crae and Jessamy turned to each other, perhaps each waiting for the other with the answer, when the door to the great house came open, and the kitchen boy came bounding out, his skinny boyish frame like a sketch in the darkness.

"Lord Crae, Lady Jessamy," he cried, and there were tears and terror in his voice. "Lord Favor has killed the crow."

On the outside of Crae's attention he could hear Favor blustering. He knelt by the dead man's body. Blood pooled out from under him where he lay. It puddled outside the storeroom door, and the straw bedding was thick and rank with it. A crossbow bolt jutted through his torn shirt into his heart. First Favor must have shot the crow from the safety of the doorway as he lay helpless and chained, and then, when it was safe, cut his throat. Favor stood back now, his long knife bloody. Breyan stood next to him as he babbled. Crae caught words here and there—"duty" and "creature" and "filthy" among them—but he mostly concentrated on the crow.

He was just a dead man now, no longer a fearsome enemy, and his secrets and those of his brotherhood died with him. He was younger in death, but so dreadfully ravaged. His leg had never healed, and Crae could smell that rot had set in. He wondered if he should tell Favor that he had done the man a favor indeed, by giving him a quick death, and wasn't that a fine joke.

Crae put one hand over the man's eyes and closed them. He stood, and Favor's babbling died off. Within him, the summoning quivered, and he could feel it in the beating of his heart. He felt something else, too, as if another god spoke to him. *The crow god,* he thought. The crows had no lords, but they followed their god.

And now the man was dead under the sacred guesting, and he could see a dreadful unfolding in his mind's eye. The crow god would tell them his man was dead, the guesting broken, and the crows would come to avenge him.

One part of him—the part that was still Captain Crae—thought, *And so it begins.* The part that was Lord Crae spoke out loud.

"Captain Breyan," he said. The man looked at his lord, then stepped forward.

"Yes, my lord?"

"We must ready all the men. Though Trieve's are yet untrained, I ask you to prepare them for battle. The outer villages must also be warned. Alarin." The farmer stepped forward, on fire with eagerness. "Who is our best rider?"

"Myself, Lord Crae."

"Then take the best horse and warn the villages." The man turned and ran for the stables.

"Now, wait," Favor began, even as his captain bowed. Crae turned to his brother.

"You see," he said, with a soft voice over steel. "You broke guesting—"

"He was a crow, and you are a fool! What possessed you to give him guesting? That was more of a blasphemy than any of my doing!"

"And they will come."

"It meant nothing to him! He was an animal!" He was almost screaming.

Crae shook his head. How could the man not know? Surely the high god was quivering inside him, too, along with the rising fury of the crow god? He could almost see the gathering of crows in the darkness, coming together as one ragged army.

He turned and found Jessamy. She had one hand to her mouth, and her kerchief, forgotten, lay around her shoulders. Her light brown hair gleamed in the torchlight, and tears shone on her cheeks.

"You won't be able to talk us out of this one," he said softly, and she gave a dry laugh.

"How much time do we have?" she said.

"A few hours. I think they will attack before sunrise. We'll need to lure them up the terraces to bring them within crossbow range."

She didn't ask how he knew, so he didn't have to tell her he could sense them gathering at the foot of the terraces. They were a few miles away at most.

The trick would be to bring them within range but keep them from storming the house. He would have to rely on Breyan for that. At least Favor had brought him a good captain. He would thank his brother later.

"All," he ordered, raising his voice. "Prepare. Men of Trieve, follow Captain Breyan."

They jumped to obey, although he could tell there were some who were as confused as Lord Favor.

As everyone left, Favor turned to Crae. This time the bluster had fled, leaving behind only bewilderment.

"He's a crow," he said again.

This time Jessamy answered. She sighed. "He was under guesting, Jori. It binds all of us equally."

Crae thought he could kiss his wife. He just nodded at her, and she gave him a quick nod back. Then she surprised him. She knelt next to the crow and placed her hand over his eyes, whispering the words of farewell.

"The body must be washed and laid out in a plain robe," she said. "My householders and I will do him that courtesy."

"Thank you," Crae said, and this time, he knew she heard what he meant. *Trieve thanks you for your service.* A shadow passed over her face, and he hated himself for having to salt those wounds. But she called for her people to help her, and the moment moved on.

He shouldered past Favor, when the man made a noise that could have been a strangled question.

"Ask your captain," Crae said, too disgusted to be courteous to the man. "Do what he tells you to do."

Seven

The last light of the evening was fading as Marthen surveyed his camp. Gary had set it up just off the woods along one of the reservoirs that dotted the area. Marthen had put the word out—no campfires—and they had obeyed him. The makeshift war camp had a few tents, a neat row of bedrolls, and what little gear the men had was all carefully stowed. He had Gary order a latrine detail, and the man had been surprised, but Marthen thought he saw wary respect in his expression.

A wind blew, rattling the leaves in the high branches above him. Some of the stickiness blew away, and he smelled rain.

Gary came up to him now, his plain features hidden in the twilight. "More guys are showing up," he told Marthen. "I don't know where we're going to put them all." He hesitated. "These tents and shit—it's all going to show up if they send out helicopters or planes. We need to cut brush and drape it over the tents."

Marthen wasn't used to thinking in terms of spies from above. He still wasn't used to the airplanes that cut across the blue sky, leaving long, thin clouds in their wake. If he wasn't careful, the sight of the flying machines would captivate him until he lost track of where he was. He could see now what Kate Mossland had been telling him about warplanes. *If I had those in Aeritan,* he thought, *no one would have been able to stop me.*

Now he looked at Gary. The skinny drunk had grown to be a competent aide-de-camp. He would soon be as quiet and resourceful as Grayne, who had the knack for disappearing until Marthen needed him. He allowed approval to leak into his voice.

"Good. See to it," he ordered. Gary nodded in pleasure.

"Yeah, I learned that when I was growing pot in Tennessee . . ." His voice faded as Marthen turned away. Gary had presented him with a bigger problem, though. Where were they going to put all these men?

The men had showed up just that night, after Marthen and his first little cadre had ambushed the pleasure seekers at the lake. When they heard the sirens approaching the lake, and Gary told him what that meant, Marthen ordered them to scatter. Gary had set the rendezvous place in these woods, and only Gary went with him to the house. They cut through the woods on foot till they came to a quiet street filled with towering houses, all alike with grand windows and ornate doors. Gary led him to the garage and showed him how to break in; Gary showed him the little box that had a silent red light blinking on it. Right now, Gary said, it's calling the police. Marthen waited, feeling the same rising tension, the same sense of overwhelming grandeur he did when he led the charge into battle. He let it fill him, holding back on his impatience the way he had held in his warhorse, knowing that when he gave it release, it would be all the stronger. *Let them come,* he thought. Instead, Gary looked underneath the little box, found the word to say, and spoke into the device that was called a phone.

Gary was invaluable. He said nothing when they moved through the house, and he nodded when Marthen said, "No touching, no thievery." Room after room spread out before him, all filled with furniture, paintings, *things*. Marthen didn't know what he was looking for till he opened a door upstairs and found it.

Her chamber. She had paintings of the small brown horse that she had been captured with last year. There were ribbons, toys, books, a window on her desk that was dark, another window like it on the other side of the room. It was a child's room. Here she was still a child. In Aeritan she was a woman grown. His desire mixed with disgust at himself.

Gary was getting restless, constantly checking the window at the end of the hall. "Come on, man," Gary had urged. "Take something or not; we got to get out of here."

Her bed was messy, the blankets and bedclothes trailing onto the floor, as if she had spent a restless night. Clothes spilled out of a sturdy chest of drawers. The room had her aroma to it, and as Marthen breathed it in, his head began to pound. It had not done that for months. He tried to keep himself steady.

"Jesus Christ, man!"

Marthen grimaced. With the last of his control he set the saddle on the back of the chair and followed Gary downstairs. They escaped out the back door, just as the rising call of sirens sounded in the distance.

And now, this. He had started with about ten men. He had about fifty now. It was a sorry collection of men compared to the thousands he had commanded in Aeritan when he served the Council. They were all from among the bridge dwellers, some old, some only looking that way because of the hard life they led. Gary said that they were mostly alcoholics—"like me," he said, with only the merest chagrin—"and a few druggies, but you won't get many of those," he told Marthen, as if to reassure him, "because they need a steady income and tend to work alone. Which is just as well, because the meth heads—well, you don't want them around.

"So we're mostly just harmless crazy. A lot of these guys, they were tossed out of mental hospitals. Jails don't want 'em."

Crazy or not, they found his camp and settled in without a word. When he made Gary ask about this one or that, they mumbled something about how they heard there was a shantytown, and they were tired of the highway.

"Excuse me!"

Marthen turned to look at a newcomer, pushing his way through the underbrush toward the camp. This man was neither crow nor bridge dweller; that was immediately clear. His clothes were good, and his face was clean-shaven, his hands clean. He struggled through the underbrush into the clearing, one hand half up as if to proclaim himself unarmed, the other gingerly pushing aside thorny bushes. Marthen flicked a hand, and Gary immediately stepped forward, a long staff held across his body. The newcomer flinched and stopped. He scanned the group. Even in the twilight Marthen could tell this man was middle-aged, his hair thinning, his body paunchy and unfit. His eyes lit on Marthen. The man gave a big smile and reached out his hand. Marthen's distrust deepened, and he made no move to take it.

"I'd like to talk to the man in charge," he said. "Name's Garson." Marthen waited, arms folded across his chest. He was in no hurry. The man dropped his hand.

"Mike Garson," the man added. "You're from *there*. Aeritan, right? You might have heard of me. I worked with Mark Ballard and a fellow named Lord Tharp to set him up with a few goodies." He nodded at Marthen's belt where he stowed the gun. "Looks like you got one of them right there."

Marthen kept his expression calm, though his heart started pounding. *This* was how Tharp had gotten his weapons. This man, this bluff, hearty man, who smiled too easily and offered his hand without a care, this man had set into motion one of the most devastating wars in Aeritan.

Marthen needed this man.

"What do you want?" Gary said. He glanced back at Marthen as if to check in, and Marthen shoved down the irritation. Reassurance indeed. The man was like a dog.

Garson looked from Gary to Marthen. "I have a proposition," he said. "For your boss. See, I think we can help each other."

"So let's get this straight," Garson said. He and Marthen sat together, Marthen on his tree stump and Garson on a lumpy boulder covered with moss and leaves. "You came from Aeritan after that girl, the one who disappeared along with Lynn Romano." His pleasant face got hard when he said her name, then smoothed out. The other woman, Marthen thought. Yes, he had seen her at the battle in Gordath Wood last year. She had taken Kate Mossland and young Terrick away. She was full-grown. Hardly old, but in this world it was hard to tell.

"Not just for her," Marthen said. He had learned from Gary's attitude and now from this man's that Kate Mossland was off-limits in ways that would—could—hurt him. She was young, and she was wealthy. Both of those things he knew. Had she been an Aeritan woman of good blood, and he had gone after her as a robber bridegroom, his life would be forfeit. Who knew that in this world it was much the same thing, except that it was not her wealth that protected her but her *youth*?

"Right," Garson said. He looked and sounded as if he were fighting distaste. He looked Marthen over. "You planning on taking her back to Aeritan?"

"That depends," Marthen said, his voice dry. "Do you intend to provide me with means?"

Garson laughed. "I could. I could. And you want to go back to Aeritan and set yourself up as a warlord. Could be— that's what Mark said was going on, the few times he came back. It'd be easier there than here. I don't know if you've guessed, but we've got pretty strict laws against mercenary generals over here." He slapped at a few mosquitoes that landed on his broad forehead.

"But I'm not just going to give you guns. I need a few things done first, and a few promises. I arm you, and you are working for me, for one thing. And for God's sake, don't touch the kid till she's legal, okay?"

Marthen didn't bother telling the man he had no interest in serving him. He said only, "What do you need done first?"

"Yeah. Well, you know that woman who the kid came back with?" Once again, Garson's face twisted in disgust. "She owns Hunter's Chase Stables now. She inherited it from the other lady, the one who came from your side and who went back. That lady stole what was mine. Stole it right out from under my nose. She must have been watching and waiting, waiting for Mark to come back through with my first payment, because he left it there for me, and I never saw a dime, because she got to it first. Well, she's out of my hands. But Lynn Romano is still there, and she's got the money. I know she has." He looked straight at Marthen. "You and your boys take care of Lynn Romano for me, and I'll get you your guns."

Marthen was silent for a moment, considering. Under his steady regard the man shifted uneasily, rubbing his hands along his plain trousers. When he was ready, he said, "I will receive the guns first, before I act on your commission."

Garson laughed. "Smart man. I'd do the same myself. But only a few, just to whet your appetite. You'll get the rest when Miss Romano is no longer a problem."

Marthen watched him go off and went back to regarding his growing camp. He didn't need an army to take Kate Mossland. He needed an army because he was a general, and he was meant for conquest. With the girl at his side, nothing could stop him. This time he was starting with crows, but that was because he knew what crows could do. They fought with mauls, but their best weapon was fear.

He thought back to his last terrible months in Aeritan as a sloppy drunk searching for a gordath. Now he knew it had all been necessary. It had led him to his crows, to his army.

The buzzing in his head started again, and with great difficulty he kept it under control. *Not yet,* he thought. *Soon, but not yet.* Soon it would be time for the reins to be loosed and the spurs to be applied. Soon it would be the time for madness to lead to war.

* * *

Lynn woke to the sound of rain pattering on
the roof. She lay in the darkness, the wind blowing in through
the open windows, bringing a smattering of cold rain with it.
The air smelled wet and wild. She lay there for a moment,
coming awake. She needed to close the window to her bedroom so water wouldn't get all over the floor. She groaned and
pushed herself out of bed. The floor was damp already, and
she winced.

"Yuck," she muttered. She fumbled with the sash. It was
stiff but finally came down with a clunk.

The rain and the cool were abruptly cut off, and the bedroom became unpleasantly humid. She pushed back the curtain
and looked out. The farm was dark, the only light coming from
the lightning flashing on the distant horizon. She counted seconds until thunder rumbled. The storm was pretty far away.

She told herself to go back to sleep, but she was wide awake
now. Plus, in the silent house she could hear an irregular *tink
tink tink*.

The roof was leaking. "Great," Lynn said. She turned on
the light, wincing against the brightness, pulled on her robe
over her pajama pants and tank top, and went to investigate.

The house was old. Someone—probably before Mrs. Hunt—
had updated the interior and modernized the plumbing and
electric, but the bones of the old house remained Victorian
farmhouse. It was surprising that it hadn't leaked sooner.
Lynn padded over the wide floorboards, turning on lights as
she went. The drops sounded louder in the hall, and she
flipped on the light switch even as she realized she was standing in water.

"Shit!" She jumped back, heart hammering, staring first at
the floor and then at the ceiling in dismay. A damp patch had
formed around the trapdoor entrance to the attic.

She had never been up in the attic. It hadn't seemed necessary. She didn't have a lot of stuff, so she hadn't needed stor-
age, and she had been hesitant to roam all over the house; it
didn't even feel like it was hers, after all these months. Ex-
ploring it felt intrusive.

She heard a knock on the door and Mrs. Felz calling, "Lynn? Are you all right?"

Lynn went out to the living room and opened the door. Mrs. Felz stood there in her robe, wet from her dash across the driveway. Lynn let her in.

"I saw the lights," she said, pushing back her wet hair. She looked wild and frizzy, for a moment like an exotic beast with a woman's broad, handsome face. "I wanted to make sure you were all right."

Lynn felt both irritated and guilty for it. "No, no. Sorry to have woken you. The rain woke me, and then I heard that I had a leak."

"Oh, honey, I was awake. I've always loved listening to the rain."

"Well, it's in the attic. I'm just going to get some towels and a bucket." She led the way back to the mudroom, where some old ratty towels and a filthy mop bucket were kept. Mrs. Felz clucked at the water in the hall. Lynn wiped up the water and placed the bucket under the leak.

"Oh, you'll have to check and make sure it hasn't ruined anything in the attic."

Lynn had been hoping to leave that till tomorrow, but it wasn't like she was going to get much sleep. And if they could find where the water was coming in, she could put down another bucket and then call out the roofers. Just another expense. She sighed and tugged the cord that opened up the trapdoor. How had Mrs. Hunt run this place, and drive a Mercedes, which Lynn had already sold, and pay her household and barn staff?

The stairs folded down with a squeak. No one had been up there in a while. A rush of air, musty and humid, poured down at them. Lynn looked up into the gaping hole. She looked at Mrs. Felz, who was peering up into the attic with interest. Lynn suddenly felt how nice it would have been to have Joe here and not his mother.

After going back to the kitchen and rummaging for a flashlight, she took her first step onto the rickety ladder. Holding her robe like a lady in a long gown, and with the flashlight in one hand, she ascended into the attic, stopping with the upper half of her body in the attic. She swung the flashlight slowly.

The beam of light showed a high-roofed room, beams and floorboards rough and unfinished, thick with cobwebs. There was the detritus of many years all around. A stack of broken chairs filled one corner. Lynn remembered the gala from a few years ago when a horse had broken loose and run through the spectators, turning over chairs as everyone ran for their lives. There were also odds and ends of life. A cardboard box with a jumble of paperbacks spilling over the top; those couldn't have belonged to Mrs. Hunt. Old lamps. A pile of rectangular picture frames.

There was a wooden chest. Lynn shone the flashlight on it. It was flat, old, handmade. Antique, she thought, but she knew it was much more than just an antique. She hoisted herself up and into the attic. From below she heard Mrs. Felz.

"Did you find the leak?"

"Not yet," Lynn called back. She stood, ducking under a hundred-year-old beam, and went over to the chest. It had a motif of roses carved in it.

Lynn had seen those roses before, and she would never forget them. They were carved over the doorframe of her tower prison in Red Gold Bridge.

She tugged at the lid of the chest. It came up heavily and fell back against the wall. She shone the flashlight on the contents. At first she thought it was filled with linens, but the light caught on something and winked and reflected back at her. Lynn reached in and pulled aside the cloth. A rope of pearls shone back at her, a red jewel in the clasp blinking like a star in the light of her flashlight. One by one she uncovered the rest of the treasure. There were gold necklaces, or what she assumed was gold. An honest-to-god whatsis, silver tiara, only slightly tarnished. More pearls. *What?* she thought, repressing a hysterical giggle. *No diamonds?* Oh, here they were, in a small flat cloth that was tied with a ribbon. There were coins as well, in leather pouches like the one that Lady Jessamy had carried at her belt as lady of Trieve. And underneath that . . . copper, silver, and gold bars shone under the flashlight, along with other metals she couldn't recognize. She could be looking at titanium or platinum, for all she knew. All precious, not for jewelry, but for manufacturing. Forget the pearls; there was a fortune here in industrial metals.

There was an irregular lump beneath the rest. Lynn lifted it out and unwrapped the cloth, and a handgun gleamed under the flashlight's beam. Her heart started pounding. *Oh shit,* she thought. Things were complicated before. Now they were much more complicated.

Lynn was still holding the gun when Mrs. Felz poked her head up. "What did you find?" she called. Taking her time, Lynn set the gun back in the chest and closed it as if there were nothing in there.

"Nothing," she said. "I think I'm going to have to come up here when there's more light."

"That's probably a good idea," Mrs. Felz said. She backed down to let Lynn climb down. Lynn took one last glance at the chest before she made her way down the ladder and closed the ceiling trapdoor.

Well, I guess that explains how she was able to afford this place. It was one question answered, but it raised a couple of others in its wake. Sure, it was obvious where the treasure had come from. Crae had said that Lord Tharp had funded his war with Lady Sarita's dowry that she had left behind when she initiated her gordath divorce.

The treasure was hers to begin with.

But what the hell was it doing here? And how did she get a gun to go with it?

Eight

It was before dawn when Alarin returned, his horse trembling at the end of the charge up the terraces. Alarin flung himself off as soon as they cleared the last ledge, almost as done in as his horse.

"I've warned the nearest smallholdings." He reported in where Crae waited with the rest of the men in the main hall, gearing up. Everyone was surrounded by crossbows, bolts, and swords, and what armor they could scrounge. The more experienced of Lord Favor's men were eating. Alarin gulped thankfully at the ladleful of water someone brought him and drank deeply. He splashed the rest on his head and chest and then continued. "And sent out a few youngsters to raise the alarm among the more far-flung villages. They are also looking to their own defenses, sir, though if the crows come through any one village, there might be nothing they can do."

"They're as ready as they can be, as are we," Crae said. He clapped the young man on the shoulder. "You did well. Now grab a weapon and report to Captain Breyan."

The man nodded and took off in Breyan's direction. They had worked it out between the two of them, Lord Crae and

Favor's captain. Of the eighty or so men they had, Crae would take two-thirds and station them at the bottom of the terraces. They would be spread thin, and he hoped that the crows would as well. Luckily, the crows were mob fighters, with handheld weapons that were crude and inexact. They would be at a disadvantage against trained fighters.

Crae had only about thirty of those, and they were mostly Favor's. He shook off his despair. No matter how many times he counted his men, the numbers never changed. They went into battle with only a few soldiers, and that was the truth of it.

He glanced up at Jessamy's entrance. She barely gave the fighting men a glance as she threaded her way over to him. All the men looked up to watch her and then him. He knew they all wanted to see how their lord and lady fared together. If the two of them failed to convince, it might spread uncertainty throughout Trieve. And Trieve could not withstand such a thing.

"We've readied the torches and oil," she told him, her voice low. If the crows broke into the hall, she and the householders, mostly women, had to be able to fight.

"Good. Where are the children?" He kept his words private. Besides Tevani and Jori, there were four more small ones that needed to be protected.

"The old barn." She smiled at his look of surprise. "You'd be surprised at the nooks and crannies of this place. I don't think Stavin knew them all. The old barn has a trapdoor that leads to a root cellar. It's big enough for two of the housewomen and all six of the children."

He nodded, then said, "Jessamy, you must join them."

"This may be your House, Crae, but it is my home. I will defend it."

"Jessamy, I order you—"

She laughed at him, and after his first shock he had to fight a laugh at his own expense. *The summoning only takes you so far,* he thought—*point taken.* "All right," he told her, close to her ear so no one else could hear. "But stay back until necessary, and if I or Captain Breyan gives you an order, you obey it."

She bobbed a curtsy. "Yes, Lord Crae," she said in a meek voice, making sure he heard the sarcastic tone. He watched her go, and then came back to himself.

Bells caught all of their attention, the deep tolling coming from the villages to the south. Everyone looked up. The crows were on their way. Crae took a deep breath.

"Heed me," he called out, making his voice reach the ends of the hall. "As we planned. All the men with me, to the bottom of the terraces. Those with Breyan, take the top third." He paused, then let his full anger reach into his voice. "Do you know what the crow told me? He said they ravage and kill, *and their god laughs.*" He let that sink in, and he could see their faces darken. Muttering rose in the hall, and men gripped their sword hilts. "We'll see who is laughing, and it won't be their god. No mercy, boys. No prisoners. Kill them all. *Kill them all.*"

He thrust his sword into the air on the last words, and they echoed his cry with their own, with a scrape and a clash of their own swords. The sound rang in the hall along with their cheers.

They were ready, even the young ones. The veterans had taken them in hand, though he knew what that was like; it was hard to think of the shepherds and farmers of Trieve as anything but shields to stand between themselves and a crow's maul.

Not a good way to go into battle, he thought, as he led his small band out of the doors, the armor fitting with a comforting yet constricting weight on his back and shoulders, the nosepiece of his helm limiting his vision. But if anyone ever came up with a good way, he hoped they would let him know.

It was still pitch-dark outside, and he paused them on the second level to let their eyes adjust. "No one look back at the house," he called out. It would take that much longer for their eyes to adjust if they looked back at the lights. They went down terrace by terrace, their armor clanking. Slowly they could make out a detail here and there, as a few stars shone through. The night was mostly overcast though, and there was no moon.

The night was split by ululating screams that, even though Crae was expecting it, sent a shock of fear down his spine. The crows came in a loud rush, deadly, skinny shadows in the dark.

The soldiers answered with a cry of their own, but their advance was disciplined. Crossbowmen crouched and loaded and shot, loaded and shot, their deadly bolts zinging into the crowd of crows on the lower terraces, their goal to thin the mob. They could not shoot at the advance, for fear of hitting their own men in the dark. Crae heard the screams that said some of their shots were true.

Still the crows came on, and Crae estimated there were several hundreds scampering up the terraces. He braced himself on his good leg as a crow leaped on him, swinging a maul. He ducked, letting the man's momentum carry him around, and then slashed down with his edge. The crow fell, and Crae pulled out his sword, and followed with a backward slash as another crow came at him, and another. He drew in breath and let it out in a shout, his war cry lost in the cries of the men and the crows around. Everyone was screaming; everyone was in a frenzy.

It was dark, chaotic. He used both his sword and shield as weapons on the next man, and the crow's scream was cut off into a dying gurgle. Overhead he heard the crossbow men from the top terrace fire, and the bolts pinged and thunked into the attacking wave. Crows dropped. One crow threw himself at the soldier next to Crae, and the man went down. Crae thrust his sword in the crow's back, then kicked him off his sword. The soldier stayed still, and Crae fought over him, taking a bruising hit to his head. His helmet rang, and he staggered. A crow screamed and came up in his face. Crae, his bad leg giving way, fell backward. With the last of his strength he thrust upward, catching the man under his ribs. The crow screamed again, gurgling, then fell on top of Crae.

He roared with frustration and pushed at the dead weight that lay athwart him. Someone pulled the body off of him and hauled him to his feet. It was Alarin. The farmer was covered with blood and dirt, and his helm was dented. Without speaking they set their backs to each other, swords and shields up, moving as one like a deadly beast. Crae could feel the other man's back against his, armor to armor, and they gave each other support as they thrust and hacked.

Still the crows came on. They flowed over the terraces, a never-ending wave, and pushed the men back to the upper terraces. Crae stumbled over an armored body as he was forced backward by the sheer volume of crows. There was but one more terrace before the lawn at the doors to Trieve. If the crows reached the lawn, there would be nothing to stop them from breaching the house save householders with nets and flaming vats of oil. *We kill and we ravage, and our god laughs* . . . Crae drew breath into his lungs, and he could feel Alarin behind him shift to give him more support.

"Trieve, attack!" He roared. "Trieve, redouble!"

He heard roaring in his ears, and for a moment thought he was about to lose consciousness. But no, it was the roar of his men, answering his cry, his men and Favor's, fewer than one hundred brave souls. Yet they answered his call, and the line of crows wavered, and they slowly pushed forward, backing the crows off the terrace.

And still the crows came on. Even as he used sword and shield to repel each crow in front of him, more came and more came. *Soldier's god,* he thought. *Will we kill every crow in the country before the night is through?*

Time became measured by breaths and the pulsing of his heart, until he felt as if the world had always been night, and he had always been fighting crows. He could not let himself think of anything else but this moment, the same moment for all eternity. Breath, slash, step, breath, slash. His muscles burned, and he had to lock himself away from the pain to master it. Crae shifted his sword to his left hand; there was no finesse anymore anyway. He fought like a crow himself, bludgeoning and hacking. Alarin slipped behind him and caught himself against Crae's back.

A crow came up in front of him so suddenly Crae thought he appeared out of the air. For a second the man's face was imprinted upon his vision, what he could see: wide eyes, the glint of teeth, a sharpened spear blackened and slick with blood. The crow screamed as Crae lifted his shield to ward off the attack, catching the crow under the chin with the rounded edge. He could feel the click of the man's teeth as he forced his jaw upward. Crae set his shoulder and pushed the man backward, off the edge of the terrace step. The man windmilled wildly and landed hard on his back and lay still.

A space appeared in front of him where the crow had been. Crae waited on the terrace's edge, sword and shield up, Alarin breathing hard behind him, and let the world come back to him, first sight, then comprehension.

Dawn rose over the terraces; gray mist trailed over the battlefield. The top terraces were littered with hundreds of crows. His land was black with them. Far below some crows still lived, but they were fleeing. He would give the order to track them down later. Crae dropped his hand, his shoulder and back screaming with agony. Sweat stung his eyes, and he squeezed them tight to try to ease the sting. With a shaking hand that was stiff and swollen, he unstrapped the leather strap at his chin and took off his helmet, the better to look around him. The battlefield came in focus now. He could see the last crow groaning on the terrace below him, his hands jerking but his legs curiously still. Crae had seen those injuries before; a man whose spine had snapped lost the use of his legs as if they had been cut off. Crae stared down at him, unmoved. The crow was no longer a danger and would likely die before the day was out. *Whose god is laughing now?* he thought, but he felt neither triumph nor vindication.

* * *

They had won, but the aftermath had just be-
gun. About half of Trieve's men were among the fallen. Crae
knelt beside one of them, a young shepherd. The man gave
little gasping cries. Blood ran down from a gash that had
nearly taken his eye. Crae helped him sit up.

"All right?" he said.

"Yes, my lord," the man said and promptly fainted. Crae
lowered him back down. He limped over to another man. This
one was dead. Crae laid a hand on his shoulder and whispered
a few words the man could take with him to the soldier's god.
He is a good man. A good fighter. He will serve you well.

Crae felt too weary for grief. *If this is all we've lost due to
my whim and Favor's idiocy, I will thank my high god every
day and every night,* he thought. Alarin came up to him. The
young man was covered with blood, but it was the look in his
eyes that struck Crae. His eyes were old, exhausted, and
deeply sorrowful. Behind him trailed many of Trieve's men,
and Crae knew at once what he needed to do. He reached up a
hand. Alarin pulled him to his feet.

"Lord Crae," Alarin said.

Crae clapped him on his shoulder. "Come, Captain. We
still have much to do." Alarin was so tired that his comprehension was slow. But when he understood, the young man
managed a smile and a half bow.

"Thank you, sir. I will honor you with my service."

"I know," Crae said. "Let's go."

Trieve lost about forty men, Favor two. Breyan
reported his deaths, and they set all to fetching and laying out
their dead. The crows they left where they lay; their namesake battle followers could take care of them while Trieve and
Favor mourned their dead.

The householders had not had to show their mettle. Jessamy had her women stow the torches and oil, and the heavy
ropes and weighted nets they had set up to blockade the great
hall. If the crows had broken through, it would not have kept
them out, but it would have stopped them, perhaps long enough

for the householders to escape. The children who had been hidden away in the cellar were reunited with their mothers and fathers. Jessamy hugged her children fiercely. Jori wailed, and Tevani clung to her mother with one hand on her skirt, sucking her thumb. Crae went over and patted both children clumsily, but Jori cried harder at the sight of him in his armor, and Tevani wouldn't speak. Jessamy surprised him though; she touched his arm briefly, and their eyes met. He squeezed her fingers clumsily through his heavy glove and then went to see to his men and she to the ordering of the household to tend the wounded.

The battle was over, but the day was long. Crae sent squads out to ride to the outlying villages to rout the crows that had escaped to ravage the smallholders. He and Breyan set the men to building a rough palisade of sharpened stakes midway up the terraces. If the crows came back that night, they could keep them at bay. *Attacking under the cover of dark works both ways,* Crae thought grimly. He stayed in armor, though it stank of blood, sweat, and oil. His leg shrieked with pain, and he staunchly ignored it, though he knew his limp worsened as the day progressed. He moved between terrace levels, supervising the defenses. Alarin set a work detail to move the corpses of the crows to the bottom terraces. *We cannot bury them,* Crae thought. *There are too many. We will have to burn the bodies.* The idea sickened him, but he had no choice.

The word came back; the squads had run down a few handfuls of surviving crows and made short work of them, and the surrounding villages were clear. Everyone let up a drained and ragged cheer. Breyan came over to Crae under cover of the noise. He was still in armor, too, his helmet under his arm, and he sported a stained bandage around his dark and gray-streaked hair. He grinned.

"Not bad for a lot of farmers and cowherds," he said cheerfully.

"Not bad with your help," Crae said. "My thanks, Captain." He frowned. "How much longer will we have you?"

"I wish I could stay, Lord Crae. I could give you some of my men, with Lord Favor's agreement."

Crae grunted. He didn't want to be beholden to Favor, but he had little choice. And it was the least the man could do, after getting them into all this. Not that Favor would acknowledge that.

"I will ask Lord Favor," he said. "We could use your men. I would stake my life that the crows will come back."

"I would set a watch all around the perimeter night and day, and have the villagers do so, too," Breyan said. "If they are set on their heels often enough, even crows will back off, find easier prey."

"Probably," Crae said. The problem was, if the crows knew that right now Trieve was at their mercy, they would be unrelenting. He went a little sick at the thought.

"Lord Crae, Lord Crae!"

He turned. One of his men on the work detail came running up.

"Sir—he says, he says he's the lord of the crows, sir. He's at the bottom of the terraces. He wants to talk to you."

The hall went quiet. Everyone looked at him.

"Tell him I will meet with him."

He had Hero saddled and was boosted on board, his leg screaming in agony. Alarin handed him up his sword and crossbow and bolts. Alarin and Breyan mounted up and followed him on horseback as well, as did a handful of Breyan's men.

By rights, Crae supposed he should have had the crow come to him, but he did not want him up near the house. Best to keep him below, at the foot of the hill.

The bodies already stank as they negotiated the last terrace and approached the remaining crows. There were five in all. The lord of the crows, so-called, stood in front of his handful of men, still armed with mauls and staves. Next to him Crae heard Breyan and Alarin arm their crossbows, and their men drew their swords. Crae turned his attention on the crow lord.

He was no less ragged than his men and just as skinny and ill-fed, but he had found a horsehair cap somewhere, with the horse tail still attached. He wore that and a blue cloak that looked as if it had once been Terrick colors. He had no other clothing; he stood before them naked and exposed.

One of Breyan's men sniggered, faltering when Breyan growled at him. Crae felt pity and disgust, along with revulsion.

The man held himself stick straight.

"Lord of the high House," the crow lord said, his accent refined. He did not sound like the captured crow. This man could have been on the Council. "You have something the crows want."

Crae halted Hero. The horse snorted and shook his mane. Crae leaned on the pommel of the saddle, looking down at the crow. "You have left many dead men on my land," he said. "You may go to the first terrace to collect them."

"Not them," the crow lord said, and his smile was sly. "You have another. You took him from us. You promised him something, and we want it."

"It's not yours," Crae said. "I promised him and him alone." Not even a mad crow could believe that guesting was given to an entire people when it was granted to one.

The sly smile widened. "But you broke your promise. You took it away."

He doubted the crow would understand or care if he said, *That wasn't me; that was my wife's foolish brother.* He kept his voice level as he said, "He died under our care, and we washed his body and laid him out with all courtesy."

"You give one of us such a courtesy?" The crow sneered. "This I must see with my own eyes."

Crae didn't want to. He wanted nothing more to do with crows. Let them fester in their madness and fear, he thought. But if showing this man the courtesy they had given one of his own would make him leave Trieve, then he would do so. He found himself bowing his head in acknowledgment. "Come. I will bring you to him."

This time it was the lord of the crows' turn to hesitate. Then he leaped onto the first terrace, a scramble of thin arms and legs. "I come."

Crae gestured Breyan and the others to stay, and they faced off against the remaining crows. Crae reined Hero around and walked the horse beside the strange lord up the terraces.

Everyone at the house turned as the strange couple came up the hill, people watching them climb the terrace. Hero breasted each level next to the crow, whose scrawny legs let him climb each level with alacrity. Still, the crow was breathing hard when they achieved the top, and so was Crae.

He dismounted, wincing as he put weight on his bad leg. He gave the reins to one of his men, catching the man's wide-eyed look, and led the crow lord into the house.

Now the women turned to look, catching a full glimpse of the odd man's nakedness, their faces a mixture of surprise, disgust, and amusement. The crow was unmoved.

Jessamy stood up, wiping her hands, and came toward them. She had the same look of steel that he had seen before. She glanced over the crow, her expression mild but stately.

"I am Lady of this House," she said. She gave Crae the smallest of glances but went on to say, "You are welcome here."

Bless you, Jessamy, Crae thought, his heart slowing.

"He wishes to see the cr—his man," Crae said. Jessamy dipped with full courtesy, spreading her skirts wide.

"This way." She led them to the storeroom.

The smell of herbs and death hit them as they neared the room. The man had been washed and his hair and beard scented, and he lay peacefully in a white robe. Scented candles burned around his makeshift bier; the room had been swept of every scrap of straw and every bit of night soil.

The crow stepped in and looked over the man. His face held no expression as he examined every inch of the body, lifting the robe to see his infected leg and the wound to his heart.

"You promised him guesting; you give him death and burial," he said at last, his voice gravelly.

He grieves, Crae thought in wonder. He nodded. "We will help you take the body away, for your own customs."

The crow made a noise like a laugh. "Bury him here," he said. He turned away, his ragged robe sweeping near the candles. It knocked one down and extinguished it, even as Crae and Jessamy jumped forward in alarm. "Then he will be a part of this land." He cackled again. "You gave him guesting. You made a promise. Now you keep the promise."

The crow lord did not come with them to bury his man. Instead, Crae and Jessamy led a small group of householders to one of the high sheep pastures. The sun poured out its blessed warmth and the meadow birds piped and called as the householders raised a cairn of white stones to the lost crow. He did not know what to say to the high god. Would he even listen if Crae asked him to watch over the man? And what of the mad crow god? Would he even know what to do with a prayer other than one by his benighted followers? In the end, they all stood in silence, Crae still in his bloody clothes, until he felt they had done what they could, and they filed down the grassy hill. Crae looked back once at the lonely cairn at the top of the meadow, silhouetted against the sun and casting a shadow that pointed a finger straight at Trieve. He felt a chill then. It was as the crow lord said. The crow was a part of Trieve now.

It was near midnight before Crae limped off to his bedroom. He ached all over, soothed somewhat by a bath and change of clothes and the beer and whiskey that had flowed—overflowed—for all. It would not make his head better tomorrow, but tomorrow was another day. Now he just looked forward to his bed.

One of the householders had laid a fire for him to cut the chill of the mountain air, and it crackled cheerfully in the dark room. Crae undressed, leaving his clothes where they lay, and climbed into bed. He had just closed his eyes when the door opened.

He raised himself up on one elbow as Jessamy came in. She carried a single candle that she placed in the sconce over the bed with a practiced ease. She wore her white nightdress, and her hair was unbound. It lay around her shoulders and trailed halfway down her back. She said nothing as she crawled into bed beside him and turned to face him, her breathing even and her gaze intent in the dim candlelight. Crae's breath came faster. He touched her hair, twining his fingers in its softness. She bit her lip but made no move. He pulled her closer and kissed her, not sure how she would respond. For a second she resisted, and then put her arms around him, but stiffly, unwillingly, and gave him a peck on the cheek. He drew back, his heart sinking. *This can't work. High god, I can't see how this will work.*

"Jessamy," he whispered. "I will not force you."

"I'm here of my own will," she countered. "It's just—I've never been with anyone except for Stavin. You are so different—I—" She faltered to a stop.

He didn't know what to say to that. He stayed quiet, stroking her hair, letting his fingers graze her cheek and across her lips. She shivered, rigid with tension, but didn't pull away. Crae pulled her close, telling himself that they had time, there was no hurry. He kissed her again, letting his kisses trail down her neck to the hollow of her throat, to her breasts. She gave a little gasp and closed her eyes, and when he returned to her lips, she kissed him back.

Later, when the fire had sunk to red coals, they lay tangled together. Crae lay with his arms around Jessamy, and she wept into his shoulder.

"Shh," he whispered, wishing he could soothe her better. "Shhh. It will be all right."

Nine

The next day sparkled in the aftermath of the rain. Hunter's Chase looked washed clean, the fields bright green, wet with dew. Mist collected in the low places, and the air was crisp. The sky was already bright blue with only a wisp of clouds. Lynn helped the girls who came to feed and turn out, checking the schedule for which clients were planning to ride that morning. All the horses were lively, the good weather perking them up, and as the grooms led them through the gate and unhooked their lead ropes, they trotted up the hill, snorting and shaking their manes.

Lynn went into the red horse's stall and haltered him. "Hey, Red Bird," she said. The horse whickered as she scratched him under his mane, and he rubbed his head against her side, almost knocking her off balance with his rough affection. Mrs. Felz had started calling him Red Bird, which she said was what Texans called cardinals, and it suited him. He was cocky, like his namesake bird, his mane standing up like a crest, and his eyes were bright, lively, and dark.

Her mystery horse had turned out to be a good horse. His Coggins test had come back negative, and the vet had pronounced him healthy except for worms. She had administered a dose, and Red Bird responded almost overnight, though he was still a bit underweight. Lynn herself had pulled his shoes and rasped down his hooves. She was no farrier, but she could do that much, and she didn't want her regular farrier to ask questions about the horse's badly made horse shoes. She wouldn't know what to tell him, for one thing, and she didn't want the best farrier in the region to wonder what the hell she was doing to her horses.

Lynn attached a lead rope and led him out of the stall, his hooves clomping dully on the cement aisleway. This was the first time she would turn him out into the fields; she thought he was ready, healthy enough to hold his own and find his place in the herd's pecking order. She led Red Bird over to the cross country field and unclipped the lead. He snorted and shook his mane and bucked, then trotted forward, his legs shaking a little. Lynn felt a pang. Poor guy. She had kept him limited to turnouts in the sandy dressage ring for his own safety, but a horse was made for wide-open spaces. Red Bird dragged his nose on the ground and then folded himself up and rolled, scratching his back over and over. She had to laugh. He snorted and rolled, and when he got up, he shook until grass and rain and dirt flew off him in a cloud.

"Go run, you idiot," she told him, and he did. He cantered smoothly up the slope, bucking now and again.

A horse is made for open spaces, she thought again, pulling the gate closed and putting the latch in place. So how was Dungiven doing in Red Gold Bridge? The stronghold had been built inside the forest, backing up to a mountain. Not the best place for horses, and the stables there were dark and damp. She should know. She had hidden in a dark stall when she broke away from the tower room. Though a fat lot of good it had done her. She had been promptly uncovered when Crae tricked her into revealing herself.

It could have been a lot worse. At least it had been Crae. If it had been Mark Ballard, would he really have killed her?

She could hardly believe it, even of Mark, but then, it turned out there had been a lot at stake. At least Mark thought so. Not only had he been running guns between here and Aeritan, he and Garson had been planning on keeping the gordath open and selling oil leases.

Mrs. Felz was out gardening when she came back to the house. Lynn waved to her, and Joe's mom waved back with her trowel. The place really looked nice. Mrs. Felz was talking about putting in roses over an old trellis they had unearthed in the toolroom. Which begged the questions: how long was she planning on staying, and should Lynn broach the subject again? *If she stays, I should pay her,* Lynn thought. She guessed she had the money for it now. Except that a trunkful of cash—or the equivalent in gems and precious metals—generally was illegal.

What the hell had Lady Sarita been doing? Lynn had sent Mrs. Felz off to bed and had stayed up for a few hours after her discovery in the attic. She looked through the accounts in the office desk, trying to see if Sarita had been selling off her regained dowry piecemeal for operating expenses. There was nothing that she could see that would account for that. The lawyers might know something, but Lynn didn't want to go to them right away. It was Sarita's own dowry, but how had she come in possession of it again?

Lynn put up the lead rope in the mudroom, stripped her work boots, and went into her bedroom to mull her choices in front of the closet. A sundress would be too obvious, and she didn't want to give the wrong idea. Breeches and shirt, then. Tall boots? No. Hard to drive in. She'd wear her paddock boots. She had just polished them to a shine; like most horsewomen, Lynn took care of her boots along with her tack and was proud of both.

Dressed, she looked at herself in the full-length mirror on the closet door. She wore her fawn-colored breeches, a white oxford shirt, and her paddock boots. As a concession to what she was doing, she let her dark hair down around her shoulders. As always, it startled her a little to see it down. It softened her

face, making her less—intense. Proper, Joe had called her. He
had teased her a little, and she smiled, remembering. *You always wear your hair up, he had said,* catching her in the barn
where it was just the two of them and they had a quiet moment.
*You know it don't matter; everyone still knows what you look
like.* .

Maybe, she thought, her smile fading. But that wasn't the
point. The point was that she had to be taken seriously to run
the farm the way it needed to be run. She was Mrs. Hunt's
right-hand woman.

When she went to see Howard Fleming that morning, she
had to portray something else. She had to be disarming.

When she pulled up to the vast Pennington
Stables, Lynn was struck by the difference between the two
barns. Hunter's Chase under Mrs. Hunt had been no less meticulous, but it was smaller and more intimate than the huge
Pennington. The drive up was white gravel that shone under
the summer sky. Green fields with white fences ran alongside
the long drive, and the red stables sat back behind them.
There were plenty of riders and horses, a lot of expensive cars
in the parking lot. There were grooms everywhere, leading
sleek Thoroughbreds or warmbloods, the cream of the show
world. The jumps in the training rings were brightly painted,
the poles striped red and white, the barrels, the coops, and the
hedges all perfectly trimmed. *Man,* Lynn thought, turning off
her car. *Who could stand it?*

The Fleming house sat on the hilltop, a pile of roofs and
windows. It reminded her of Trieve, which made her think of
Crae. *I should have stayed. He fought for me; I should have
stayed and fought by his side.* Except he had sent her off with
a kiss, and she had ridden away without looking back.

With great deliberation she shrugged off the memory. It
could do her no good right now. Lynn headed up to the barn.
She would ask there for Howard.

Geoff, the head groom Howard had imported from a
British racing stable, turned at her approach. A young groom

watched, holding an expensive Thoroughbred by the halter and lead rope. Geoff tilted back his farmer's cap. With a flick of his eyes, he took in her appearance, and a faint smirk appeared on his face.

"Looking for Howard?" he said, his accent thick.

"Hi, Geoff," Lynn said stiffly. "Yes, actually. Is he around?"

He half hid a snort. "Up at the house." He turned back to the horse and the young groom, continuing his lecture on the proper way to rub down a horse.

Figured. She should have gone straight up. She didn't like Geoff, he didn't like her, and the way everyone talked about her, her visit with Howard was going to be all over the horse community in no time. Well, as if she could keep it secret. She only hoped she could keep the topic under wraps.

Howard had guests. There were several people at the garden at the front of the house, all wearing civilian versions of Lynn's riding outfit: breeches, yes, but not actual riding breeches, and white shirts that were much more expensive but not quite for riding, and boots with heels that were too high and had metal detailing that looked like spurs but weren't quite. *Well*, Lynn thought, *I tried.* But she would never be mistaken for an owner or a client. Underneath it all, she was just a barn rat. That's why Geoff had smirked. She smiled, trying to hide her discomfort.

"Hi. I'm looking for Howard. Is he around?"

The men and women eyed her. "He's coming out in a moment," a woman said finally. Her hair and makeup were impeccable. Lynn thought she might have seen her in a movie or on television. She felt dowdier and dowdier.

"Lynn!"

She turned. Howard came out, wearing his signature breeches and light blue polo, and she actually felt a wave of relief. He came over and took her hand. "What a surprise!"

"I should have called, I'm sorry. I didn't realize you had guests." All of whom were watching intently. "But do you have a minute? Or, is there a time we could talk?"

She hated feeling like a supplicant, that's what it was. Howard cocked his head, looking at her. He nodded.

"Yes, of course, of course. Come on in. Have you met everyone?"

She was introduced as the owner of Hunter's Chase to everyone, promptly forgot all the names, and with Howard's hand at her back, was ushered into the house and his study.

Opulent was the only word. Impeccable, gleaming terazzo floors, light streaming perfectly into the room, books and art carefully placed. He gestured her to a leather chair, and he took the other one.

"What can I help you with?" he said. "Is everything going all right? I should have stopped by sooner, made you feel welcome. All the owners are hoping things go well."

"Everything is fine; the farm is great," she said with as sprightly an air as possible. She set herself up for the first fence. "This is a little strange, I know, but I need to know about Mrs. Hunt. You were friends. What did you know about her?"

He looked taken aback at her forthrightness. Lynn sat back, tossed her hair over her shoulder, and crossed her leg.

"She was a good woman. I was very sad to see her go."

"Was she in any kind of trouble?"

His mouth dropped. "I don't know what you mean." His eyes flickered away.

Be careful, she told herself. She kept her eyes on him, said nothing.

"I don't know," he said again. "She, well, she had lots of friends, or rather a lot of people I didn't know anything about, although I tried to guide her as best I could. There was an innocence about her, I thought. I felt I could help."

"Were you concerned about her?"

"Well, she was a very competent person," he blustered. "I don't know that concern is the right—"

"Did you know her before she owned Hunter's Chase?"

"Lynn, what are you after?"

With an effort, she kept her mind off the chest in the attic.

She said softly, "I think she might have been involved with something and gotten in over her head."

He grew very still.

"Well?"

He stared at her, mouth agape. A part of Lynn wondered where she had gotten her resolve. The rest of her just focused on Howard.

"I heard—rumors," he said finally. "We just thought she had been—set up by someone."

Lynn had heard the rumors, too, from the rest of the stable workers. Sometimes people said it was a horse-mad sheikh, other times this or that politician. Could she have bankrolled herself?

Crae said Tharp used most of her dowry to finance his war. Tharp paid Ballard, and Ballard paid Garson.

"Was it Mike Garson?"

She knew by his expression that it was a direct hit and something more. As if he knew he had given it away, he said, "Interesting fellow, Garson. Did you know he shot most of those trophy animals at the restaurant?"

"Did you try to warn her away from Garson?"

Howard sat back, staring at her, his light blue eyes rimmed with red. He wasn't a handsome man, and he was arrogant and dismissive. The house was ridiculous, too, screaming *too much!* the way it did. When he spoke next, he lost his arrogance, and he was just a middle-aged man. He almost sounded as if he was as much aware of that as she was.

"I did. It was after a dinner one night at his restaurant. Garson cornered her on the way to the ladies' room. I watched as they argued, and it looked as if he threatened her. I went over to put a stop to it, but she said it was nothing. She didn't tell me anything. I nosed around and toyed with the idea of engaging a private investigator."

Oh man. Can you imagine what one could have found out?

"But in the end, I didn't think I should interfere." His gaze sharpened. "Should I have?"

Lynn hesitated. She didn't like him, but he could be an ally in other ways. She didn't think he liked Garson, for one thing. "Mike Garson came to Hunter's Chase the other day, and he offered to buy the place. He said it was too expensive to maintain, and I should just give it up. Some of the things that he said, well, he sounded threatening, like he would make it hard for me to run the place. I thought, if he had approached Mrs. Hunt the same way, maybe it led to her disappearance."

She lied the same way Dungiven took a fence: big and bold.

The effect was instantaneous. Howard was furious. "Charming individual," he said, his voice dry. "What did you tell him?"

"No. Or words to that effect."

He laughed, and for that moment they were equals, owners not just of expensive land but of a piece of a disappearing life. "Lynn, why did you come to me?"

"Because I think she was in trouble, and you were her only friend." Mrs. Hunt or Lady Sarita, whoever she was, she didn't have friends. Not really. But that didn't matter. Whether Lady Sarita knew it or not, this man had been the best friend he knew how to be.

Almost at once the old Howard was back. "You're a sweet girl," he said, leaning forward and taking her hand. With an effort, she kept a grimace off her face as she pulled her hand away. "Is that all you needed? Just reassurance that Katherine had my good feelings? Because my guests are waiting. But yes, I warned her about Garson. I was jealous—a pretty girl like you might think that's funny about a man like me, but I was. And I thought there was something about his attention for her that was—menacing, as if he had some secret or knew something about her. But if it was just pressure to sell, well, you'll have to get used to that. We all get it; even I do."

But Lynn wasn't finished.

"Howard, when you warned her, what did she say?"

"That it was all right, that Garson held no danger for her, and if necessary she could always disappear." Then he frowned. "Well, she actually said, she could always disappear *again*."

Garson, **Lynn thought on the drive home. She** had the windows down, letting the cool air in to clear her head and put her thoughts in order. That's why he came by the farm and wanted to buy it; he knew there was a fortune somewhere on the property. He knew it was there because Mark had brought it over from Aeritan as payment for the guns he was getting from Garson. So how had Lady Sarita retrieved it?

If she went to Garson and demanded answers, he would know she found the dowry and the gun. And if he knew it was somewhere at Hunter's Chase, he would never rest till he got it back. He wouldn't give up so easily, even though she had kicked him out on his last visit. He'd keep trying.

And Mrs. Felz was there alone. Lynn sped up, taking the narrow country lanes as fast as she could. *Damn Garson,* she thought. If Mark was right and there *was* oil in Aeritan, he wasn't about to just let all that go away. He was probably trying to open the gordath again. But Joe and Arrim were there to stop it.

Except there was the case of Red Bird. Why hadn't Joe and Arrim stopped the horse from coming through the woods? What if they couldn't? Maybe something prevented them from keeping the gordath closed. Was Lord Tharp up to his old tricks again? But Lady Sarita wouldn't let him. She wanted the gordath to stay closed. That's why she went back. Unless— what if she were regretting her decision to go home?

The tires squealed as Lynn took the turn to Hunter's Chase too fast, and her little car fishtailed. As she fought for control of the car, out of the corner of her eye she caught the odd sight of several men walking along the side of the road. They were bearded and scruffy, clothes and faces showing they had seen better days. They were definitely not from around here. She toyed for a moment with the idea of calling the police, but the thought was distasteful. Poor or not, scruffy or not, these guys had the right to walk along a public road.

She had bigger problems, anyway. There might not be any earthquakes this time, but it looked like the gordath was open, and Mike Garson was nosing around after Lady Sarita's dowry. She wasn't sure what she could do about either situation.

To her vast relief, Hunter's Chase looked unchanged when she pulled up. She parked in front of the house and got out, her sweaty shirt sticking to her back. She looked around. A few clients rode in the ring, and the rest of the horses grazed in the fields. Mrs. Felz was nowhere to be found, and her car was gone. Lynn went into the house, expecting a note.

Sure enough, there it was, on the kitchen table, held down with a glass full of wildflowers.

> *Lynn. Mr. Garson from the Continental called. Would like you to call ASAP. Isabella. PS. Went into town for groceries.*

He called, eh? And found out she was out? Lynn dropped the note and looked up at the ceiling. She ran for the hall. With shaking hands she pulled down the trapdoor and unfolded the attic ladder, scrambling up as soon as it touched the floor. A wan light came in from the vents at the corner of the eaves, and the air was hot and humid, the heat collecting up here almost visible, it was so thick.

The chest was still there, and she felt a wave of relief. Then suspicion touched her again, and she went to take a look, bent over awkwardly in the cramped space. Sure enough the bounty was untouched, the gun still wrapped where she had placed it, tucked in a corner of the chest. She breathed out hard in the dusty, humid space. She should move the chest. Garson suspected that it was somewhere on the farm, and he would do his best to find it. The problem was, where could she move it to?

She heard the kitchen door creak open and Mrs. Felz call out, "Lynn? I'm home."

Lynn shut the chest and went back down. When she descended, Mrs. Felz was standing there with an expression of surprise.

"Oh. Another leak?"

"No. I mean, yes, well, not sure, actually." Feeling she said enough, Lynn concentrated on folding up the trapdoor. With her back to Mrs. Felz she said, "So, what did Mr. Garson have to say?"

"Nothing much. Still as full of himself as he was when he came to visit." Her voice made it plain she was not impressed.

"You should go home," Lynn said abruptly. She hadn't known she intended to say it.

Mrs. Felz looked at her, confusion and surprise warring with each other. Tears started to well, and she turned away. "Of course, I—I never meant to . . . Of course. I will."

Lynn felt hugely, monumentally, wretchedly guilty. *She's in danger, and she's endangering me,* she tried to tell herself.

She didn't believe it for a minute.

Mrs. Felz didn't say anything else, just went back into the kitchen and continued to unload the groceries. Lynn followed her back in, wishing she could take the words and stuff them back into her mouth.

"Isabella," she started. Mrs. Felz didn't reply, but she banged the cupboards a bit more than necessary.

"Look—"

"No!" Mrs. Felz said. "You are absolutely right. I've overstayed my welcome, and it's time to go home. I don't know what I was thinking." She stopped and turned around. Her face was tired and careworn, the brightness faded.

She's not that old, Lynn thought. *She's younger than my mom. She must have been very young when she had Joe.*

"Listen," Lynn said as gently as she could. "I'm in a whole lot of trouble, and you could be in trouble, too. I think you should go, because I'm worried things are going to get dangerous around here."

Mrs. Felz didn't answer right away.

"It's that Mr. Garson, isn't it?" she said finally.

Lynn nodded.

"Can you call the police, tell them he's harassing you?"

The police suspected that she faked her disappearance last year so she could somehow end up owning Hunter's Chase. She doubted they would be sympathetic to any unfounded—and unfoundable—accusations against a pillar of society like Mike Garson. All that was too hard to explain though, so she just shook her head.

"And if you are here alone, what good is that? Don't you see how foolish you are to keep to yourself?" Mrs. Felz's eyes sharpened. "Does this have to do with Joe?"

Lynn stayed silent for a second too long, and Mrs. Felz sat down at the kitchen table. She began playing with the note that she had left. She spoke very quietly. "Are you ever planning on telling me what happened to my son?"

Sure. He went through a gateway between worlds to find me, and you know what? He stayed behind there because it turned out he knew how to control it and there aren't too many people with that talent. Now the gateway is open again, and I am worried that it means something happened to him.

She didn't say any of that. Instead, she said, "I don't know what happened to your son. But I plan to find out."

The morrim nestled against the side of a rocky draw, supported on several small boulders and tangled with deadwood and papery vines. Green thornbushes and brush curtained over it, and the rock was covered with moss. It looked like an ancient rockslide. Only the energy emanating from the rock indicated what it was. Joe could feel it from where they stood, about thirty paces away and looking up. He glanced over at Arrim, and the man met his eyes briefly and looked away.

Back in Gordath Wood, the ancient morrim was matched with Balanced Rock, its mate in North Salem. Where was this morrim's twin, and where did the gordath between them lead? Joe remembered what Mark had spilled, that Brythern had tried to control the gordath out here with disastrous results. Hare's men all stood back nervously now, behind him and

Arrim. He almost laughed. At last, the Brytherners were starting to get scared, as if finally catching on that they were out of their league. Well, maybe he and Arrim could use that to get out of this fix.

"Guardians," Hare said. "Get over there and tell me what you know."

Their guards pushed them forward, and they stumbled a few steps to the morrim, looking up at it. Climbing up would be a bitch, Joe thought. The rock pile looked half-supported by the ropy vines and roots, and he thought he could see some three-leaved poison ivy to boot. Crap. He hoped Hare didn't want them to go up there.

"So what do you think?" Joe said to Arrim in a low voice.

"Hey!" Mark shouted. He turned toward them, slightly raising the rifle. "No talking!"

Joe almost threw his hands into the air with frustration. He looked at Hare. "What do you want, Hare? You want us to control your gordath, then you have to let us work together."

Hare looked mad enough to shoot Mark then and there. Nonetheless, he had to save face. "You talk when I say you can talk, Aeritan." He looked at Mark. "Take the rear guard; shoot anything that comes along."

Mark looked like he wanted to protest, and then he made a face and went back down the trail to stand a useless sentry watch. Joe watched as the Brythern lord rolled his eyes but then looked back at his two captives. "All right. What can you tell me?"

It was the first time since their kidnapping that they had relative privacy. Joe ignored Hare's question.

"Hey," he said, keeping his voice low. "You okay? You hanging in there?"

"Forest god," Arrim muttered. "How can you take it?"

"It sucks, but it keeps them happy," Joe muttered back. "Look, whatever happens, we can't open their gordath."

"I know."

"No games, Guardians," Hare warned from a few steps away. He was getting nervous, Joe realized. He was probably already regretting his decision to let them talk. Joe tilted his head back and focused on the morrim. Under the sounds of the rustling forest, the whir of insects, and the movements of their guard behind them, he could hear the whispering of the morrim, like a radio out of tune. It was maddening the way it stayed on the edge of his hearing, static and words he strained to make out, even though he knew that it was not a language that he knew. Another indication the gordath was alive—the damn thing talked.

Now he could feel the air that came down from the rocky slope. It was cool and smelled ancient, as if it came from a place that existed long ago. Millions of years ago, this granite boulder had been flung up from the earth. At least, back home it was. Here, who knew?

The humming intensified, and he drew nearer so that he stood almost directly beneath the morrim. Behind him he could hear Hare shout a warning, but it was so far away he ignored it. The supporting boulders were dug into the side of the slope, and now he could see how the morrim was cradled on them, almost gently. He climbed a few feet, pulling himself up the vines. If he reached up, he could almost touch . . .

Joe yanked his hand back, scrabbling backward and losing his footing so that he fell on the trail. He looked at his hand, half expecting to see it was glowing or burned from his direct contact with the energy. It was the same as always: dirty, rough, and worn. It tingled, though, as if it had fallen asleep.

"What!?" That was Hare and Arrim both. Joe panted and got to his feet, trying to get his heart to slow down, to beat to a regular rhythm. He ignored Hare and looked at Arrim.

"I think I felt the gordath directly."

If the morrim were the anchors, the gordath was the sail that stretched between them like a spiderweb. Joe knew what he felt was one of the lines that held the gordath in place. If he closed his eyes, he could almost see the line of energy that stretched from morrim to gordath, a dark pulse running beneath the surface. He turned and followed the direction his senses told him. It led deeper into these strange woods that were scruffier, harder, less lush than Gordath Wood proper. The gordath was that way. They had felt it open all the way in Aeritan. No wonder they hadn't been able to close it; they weren't anywhere near it.

Hare came up next to him and looked up at the pile of rock above them, and for once he looked keenly interested in something other than his men, his mission, or making it clear who was in charge.

"Can anyone touch it?" the Brythern lord asked.

Joe and Arrim looked at each other. Maybe the morrim would recognize a nonguardian and zap his ass to kingdom come. Or more likely, it would know it had nothing to fear from the man and reserve its malevolence for the ones it knew could contain it.

"Much as I don't care where you stick your hand, better not," Joe said finally. "You might screw something up."

The man's eyes narrowed.

"Well," Joe said, "you best show us where this brand-new gordath of yours is."

They didn't really need Hare's help. As if touching the lines had awakened something, Joe could practically follow the energy beneath their feet. But he figured the Brytherners didn't need to know that.

The power hummed beneath his boots and into his body, making his ribs ache deeply. It was hard to draw a breath. Dammit, he *needed* to talk things over with Arrim. He looked at the other guardian. Arrim walked carefully, one foot in front of the other, and Joe knew he was pacing the line.

It was so close to the surface, he thought. The lines in the old gordath were so deep and ancient they could be barely sensed. This was new, and it made him uneasy.

He had been yanking the Brytherner's chain when he told him he and Arrim had to be able to work together to control this new gordath, but he had a feeling that he might have been right—and it might still be more than they could handle.

And if we turn out to be useless, we—and the whole world—could be in some serious shit.

* * *

After several hours of walking, it was as if they had reentered Gordath Wood. The air cooled a bit as the tall trees closed out the sun. Joe could hear water falling somewhere and licked his lips, cracked and broken from not enough water, food, or care. The forest got wet again, the loamy soil rich with nutrients. The trail wound down deeper into the woods, and a little pool emerged at the bottom of a hollow, ferns dripping down the cliff sides into the water. He could see dark shadows of fish swimming languidly.

They didn't stop, just kept on walking, the guards pushing them past the water till he and Arrim stumbled.

A half hour later, the trail turned again, and the smell hit him first, and then he registered the buzzing of flies. Joe stumbled backward, choking. Where trees had toppled, their roots had pulled up completely out of the soil, drying dirt clinging to the tendrils. Some trees had broken, the jagged yellow wood weathering in the air. Horses lay where the energy of the gordath had blasted at them, their bodies bloated so that saddle girths had popped open. Scavengers had already started on them.

At least they must have removed the soldiers, Joe thought, covering his nose with his sleeve. He thought of the little smallholding that he and Arrim had come across months ago in Gordath Wood. Only in this clearing there was no peace, just death. Joe looked at Hare.

"What the hell happened?"

Hare's jaw worked. "We opened the gordath, as Lord Bahard said it might be done. Only . . ."

Only they couldn't control it, and it killed more than twenty men, just as Mark had said. Mark began to bluster. "Hey, don't look at me. It worked last year, and I got through just fine."

Asshole, Joe thought. Mark got through, sure, but he couldn't close down the gordath. It took a guardian to do that. Joe shook his head, still sickened by the stench. He looked at Hare.

"You are one crazy bastard, you know that?"

He expected a reaction, even another smack across the face, but Hare just shook his head. His lips pressed together as if to keep back what he wanted to say. Instead, the Brythern lord looked around at the clearing, a muscle jumping in his jaw.

"All right," he said finally. "Open it. Keep it open."

"Jesus Christ, Hare. You've got to be kidding," Joe said, panic rising. The way the portal was humming, all it needed was the slightest touch to open it. Hell, he and Arrim would have to be very careful to keep from disturbing it. It was so on edge all he had to do was reach out with his mind, and it would fly open.

The gordath's vibration increased in intensity as if it could feel his panic. He could sense it whispering on the edge of his mind; if he strained to try to understand, it would lure him in. If he wasn't careful, it would worm its way inside of him and take control.

"Hare," Joe said, his voice shaking. "We all have to get out of here. Now!" Joe tried to keep his mind carefully focused, but it felt like ants were crawling around inside of him. He glanced at Arrim. The man was sweating. Joe knew he could tell how delicate the situation was.

"Open it!" Hare roared. "Open it, and keep it open!"

The ground trembled under their feet, the ferns swaying and the leaves rattling overhead. The forest darkened almost imperceptibly. Joe's head spun with the effort to keep control, and he swallowed the rise of bile in his throat. His knees went weak, and he fell.

God, he thought. *Forest god, Jesus Christ, whoever you are. Stop it.*

Arrim went to his knees next to him. Joe could feel the gordath opening. The last thing he remembered was sharp regret. So the Brytherner would have his way after all, and all of the beatings had been for nothing. He could do nothing about it except to succumb, and the gordath opened wide, swallowing his world.

Ten

"Kate!" her mom called through her bedroom
door. Kate opened a bleary eye. It was morning, and the day
was fresh, the sunlight streaming through her bedroom window. Yesterday's chaos came back in a rush, and when she
looked at Mojo's saddle, still perched on the back of her desk
chair, she felt a sickening quiver in the pit of her stomach. Her
mom knocked again and poked her head in, and Kate made
sure she was covered up to her chin with her blankets. She had
slept in her clothes, and she didn't want her mom to see. Her
mom was dressed in a suit and had her briefcase and keys.
"I'm going to work, sweetie, and your dad's already gone. I
don't want you sleeping in all day. Cole's already up; you
should be, too."

He always got up early. First light.

"Okay," Kate said. "I'm going to the stables today."

Her mom smiled. "Good. Your dad and I talked, and we
think it would be a good idea if we bought Allegra for you.
You seem to like her, and you did get a few ribbons with her
the other day. We'll talk with Lynn tonight—if you want, of
course."

Was that a bribe, or did they think it was a solution?

"Um, okay," she managed.

Her mom was about to close the door when she saw Mojo's old saddle. Her gaze sharpened, and Kate could see her struggle to control her anger. "Oh, Kate. Remember what I said about no tack in the bedroom?"

"Sorry," Kate managed. "I'll take it back today."

Her mom pressed her lips together, as if she wanted to keep going, but instead she nodded. "All right. I will see you tonight. I might be late—we'll order takeout. Cole likes Thai, doesn't he?"

Kate felt a rush of irritation. *Just go!* "I don't know, Mom," she said, her voice level. "I'm sure he'll manage."

Her mother hesitated, then, still determined to let no bad mood foul the day, she said again, "Good-bye, Katie. Call me if you need anything."

Call me if you intend to go crazy again. Kate waited for her mother to close the door and threw off the covers, fully dressed from patrolling the house last night. She and Colar had alternated watches, and he had taken the early morning shift. She had left him at the top of the stairs, his sword in one hand, a cell phone in the other. The night stayed quiet, but she knew that it was only a matter of time before Marthen came back.

What were they going to do? The general had sent a message when he left the saddle: *You aren't safe from me. I can come here anytime.* She didn't know how she was going to be able to protect her parents if they wouldn't believe her or Colar about the danger.

The house was dead silent, and she held her breath, listening, a trickling of fear niggling at her. Her home was no longer a refuge; now she felt as if she were being watched. Kate got up and shed her slept-in clothes, getting dressed in the first clean pair of jeans and T-shirt she pulled out of her bureau. She was clumsy in her haste and knocked over a picture from her shelves. The glass broke with a crack.

"Oh no!" Kate knelt to pick it up, careful of broken glass. She turned it over. It was one of her and Mojo taken at a show just before she had gone to Aeritan. She held him by the reins under the chin with one hand, the other holding up a yellow ribbon. She remembered. They had come in third among some really stiff competition. Most of the other riders had upgraded to better horses, bigger horses, on their way to garnering enough points for Nationals. She was proud of how her little horse had proved himself against some of the toughest competition in the area.

"Kate?" It was Colar.

"Just a sec," she called out, but he opened the door anyway and came in. He carried his sword, lowering it immediately when he saw her.

"I just dropped something," she said. She checked for broken glass, but the picture had just cracked, not shattered. She got up and set it down on the desk.

"I heard it. I thought he might have gotten in the window."

Her window was on the second floor, and there was no convenient tree to climb, like in the movies. But she knew better than to underestimate her enemy.

Colar sheathed the sword. He wore his sword belt over jeans, and the scabbard hung down low by his side. He was wearing sneakers, the laces tucked inside. He touched the saddle. It still had a few black hairs from Mojo's mane stuck in the D rings, and there were splotches of blood and dirt. *Aeritan blood,* she thought. *Aeritan dirt.*

Colar looked as if he were fighting to keep his anger down. His hand whitened on the hilt of his sword. When he spoke, his voice was low. "I don't like him being here."

She sighed and sat back down on her bed. "What are we going to do? He made it clear he's going to come back whenever he wants to. This house isn't safe, and I don't know how to make it safe." A thought struck her. "We're not safe right now. He probably has someone watching us this minute, and he knows my mom and dad are gone."

He walked over to her window, positioned himself next to the wall, and peeked out through the blinds. "He could be," he said. "We patrolled most of last night, and we did have the alarm on, so if he did set someone to watch, they probably had an eye on us all night." He glanced at her. "I set up a deadfall early this morning in front of the garage door. I figured that would be the way they would try to get in first. I put everything back when I heard your parents get up."

"Cole's already up," her mother had said. She just hadn't known that he had been up all night. She probably heard him puttering down in the garage and just thought he was throwing the basketball around.

Kate said, "What did you use?"

He shrugged. "Tools and things from the garage."

Kate almost wished Marthen had tried to get in last night. Maybe then her parents would believe them. As it was, time was running out. They couldn't wait for him to make the next move.

"We have to find him. He's hiding in the woods, and he's got all those homeless men with him. He's got to be camped out by the gordath." She didn't want to leave the house empty, but it wasn't the house that Marthen wanted.

"Then what?" Colar said. He leaned back against the wall. The scabbard looked incongruous against his jeans. *He looks taller,* she thought. *How strange.* "What do we do with him?"

What, indeed? There was only one thing they could do, even if it meant that they could get stuck on the other side. The words came to her as if the soldier's god had spoken them.

"We send him back." *In pieces if we have to.*

Colar's expression was hard to read; he looked as if he was going to say something but stopped himself. Finally, he said, "If we take him through, we might not get back. If you can't go home again . . ."

"I know," Kate said quickly. "Let's not worry about that."

They hurried to prepare. Kate dumped her binders and notebooks out of her school backpack, sweeping out all the detritus of sophomore year. She left the pile on the bedroom floor and hurried into the bathroom. Aspirin, tampons, a roll of toilet paper, toothpaste, and toothbrush, all went into her backpack. Inspiration struck, and she pilfered a few old hotel soaps and shampoos, too. She took the Band-Aids and the antibiotic ointment. *Too bad none of us are taking antibiotics.* Finished, she went back into her bedroom, stuffing underwear, an extra shirt, and extra socks into the backpack. It was full. *The jeans I have on now have to do,* she thought. She bit her lip, thinking, then grabbed a light jacket and a thin sweater. She could roll them up and tie them to the back of the backpack.

There was a good chance they weren't going to stay, anyway. This is just a precaution, she thought. All they had to do was make sure Marthen went back.

That's all? a sardonic part of her mind asked. She ignored that and zipped her backpack shut.

She met Colar out in the hall. He had dumped out his lacrosse duffel bag, and it was full. She knew he packed his old armor, his old clothes. His sword was strapped to the back of the gym bag. "I'll change into my gear when we're in the woods." He nodded at her pack. "Toilet paper?"

Kate giggled, suddenly lighthearted. "Toothpaste, too."

He grinned, and he suddenly looked his age. "Let's get food."

They went down into the silent kitchen and raided the pantry.

Kate checked all of the doors and reset the alarm. Her mom must have left it off when she went out, and Kate clicked her tongue in annoyance. *Well, soon they won't have to worry about it, because Marthen will be gone,* she thought grimly. They went out the garage and loaded up the Jeep. It was eerie, how quiet the house had become. She used to not mind being home alone, but the house would never feel safe again. Suddenly she remembered her saddle.

"Wait!" she said. Colar looked up from where he had dumped the duffel bag. "My saddle. I promised my mom I wouldn't leave it in the room." She felt a sharp sadness. What if she *did* get trapped on the other side?

"All right, but hurry."

She ran up the steps, her hiking boots clunking on the carpeted stairs, and grabbed the saddle from her room, holding it over her arm. She looked around. It was a mess, and it would look like she had been snatched from the house. Her school stuff was all over the floor, and the cracked photo . . . She didn't have time to clean. She would leave a note in the kitchen.

A sound came from the garage, reminding her she had to go. She shouldered open the door and ran back down to the kitchen. They had left the pantry door open, and she closed that, then rummaged for notepaper and pen in the junk drawer. Hastily she scrawled,

> *Mom and Dad. We're okay. ~~We just wanted to check~~*
> *~~We just wanted to make sure the general~~ We'll see you*
> *soon. Love, Kate. And Cole.*

It wasn't enough, but it would have to do. She heard the Jeep start up and went out to the garage. Kate set the saddle in the backseat and climbed in. Colar put the car in gear, and they backed out, the garage door cycling up its chains, the motor a dull roar. As the garage door closed behind them, the house looked like any other house in the neighborhood, silent and empty during the day. Kate listened to the thudding of her heart as they drove out toward the gordath.

In the cold gray light of a Trieve dawn, Crae woke alone in his bed. The side of the bed that Jessamy had shared was empty, the blankets drawn up neatly as if to erase her presence. He had held her until she cried herself out and fell asleep, her head tucked under his chin. She was warm and heavy in his arms, and her hair draped over his chest, tickling him. At some point she moved to lie next to him, and he fell asleep at last.

He was confused. She had come to him, and though at first stiff and shy, she had shared his bed willingly. Then she cried as if her heart was broken.

Did she regret her decision? Or had she cried because of disappointment? *High god,* Crae thought. *Could things get any more complicated?* He sat up, threw off his blankets, and got out of bed. He winced; yesterday's battle made his body one great bruise, and last night's ale did the same for his head. He moved slowly as he dressed, stumbling to get his woolen socks on. The stone floor held a chill, and there would be no fire till that night.

Dressed in his heavy trousers and shirt with his warm overshirt on, he yawned and headed out to the stairs. Time to take stock of the damage and see what Trieve needed. This time he would take a troop out to scout the lower terraces. No need to get ambushed again, though he doubted the crows would try it. They had been routed too thoroughly.

And one of their own was buried in Trieve. That meant something to the crow king. Trieve kept its promise and gave the crow guesting for all eternity. In the tally of potential allies, Crae thought, perhaps the crows would side with Trieve, although he was not sure whether he would lose more by treating with them than he would gain.

He was headed out to the stairs when he stopped, looking down the still-dark hall. Jessamy's chamber was that way. Crae hesitated, then made his way down the hall to her room.

He could hear movement within her door and listened to Tevani's chatter and Jori crying. Then the baby stopped crying, and he knew the babe nursed. Crae knocked.

All sounds paused. He had almost lost his nerve when he heard running footsteps and then the door rattled and opened. Tevani had opened it, pushing against the weight of the heavy door with all her strength.

"Lord Crae!" she shouted and barreled into him. Crae caught her up and, still embarrassed, he entered the room with the little girl in his arms.

Jessamy sat in her chair nursing the baby, her face an *oh* of surprise. She looked straight at Crae, turned red, and looked down studiously.

"Good morning," he said, setting down Tevani. She ran back to her little trundle bed, chattering.

"Are we going riding this morning? I'm not afraid of the crows. I can come out riding with you, can't I? Mama, please say yes. And Uncle Jori says I can ride with him, too!"

Crae pushed down a twinge of jealousy. Favor wouldn't be here much longer, but he had no doubt Favor's offer to let Tevani ride with him was a direct shot at Crae.

Under cover of Tevani's chatter he knelt beside Jessamy's chair and took her hand. She started to pull away but let her hand stay.

"Are you well?" he asked softly.

"Yes. Yes, of course. I—it was such a day and a night," she fumbled. She still wouldn't look at him.

"And last night? Are you well?"

She looked full at him, startled. "Yes, Crae, of course. I—I am sorry I—cried."

The room had gone silent, Tevani having caught on that the grown-ups were having a conversation that she was not part of.

The room was warm and cozy, full of life and comfort. He felt as if he were an intruder. Had he done wrong to come here?

"I wanted to wish you good morning," he said, realizing how inadequate it was.

This time her mouth quirked in a smile, fleeting as it was. She gave his hand a squeeze before bringing it back to tuck the blanket around her son.

"It is a good morning," she said firmly, and the old brisk Jessamy was back. "We have survived the crows, and Trieve is safe. Because of you," she added.

He didn't know what to say, so he just touched the baby's head. He was fair, like his father, though he looked more like Jessamy. But Crae knew that boys often looked like their mothers, and girls their fathers.

If he and Jessamy had made a baby, he would have a child. Crae caught his breath.

If Jessamy noticed, she made no sign. "Here," she said. She put her finger in the corner of the baby's mouth and dislodged him from her breast. She covered up hastily and raised the boy to her shoulder, rubbing his back. "He would nurse for hours if I gave him leave. Greedy little thing." The boy gave a hearty burp, and they both laughed. Jori smiled, too, a wide-gummed grin, the tiniest pearl of a tooth showing through. "Hold him, please, while I get myself together."

She had never given him leave to carry the baby before. Crae took the baby and held him while she got up and called over Tevani.

"Come here, darling; let's get you dressed."

The baby was surprisingly heavy and warm. Crae sat down in the chair and held him face out so he could look around. The baby leaned back against him, and he watched Jessamy alternately scold and cajole Tevani into her thick tunic and leggings.

As Tevani sat on the floor and painstakingly fastened the straps of her boots herself, there came another knock on the door. Calyne bustled in with linens.

"A good morning to you, my lady, little Tevani—oh!" She spotted Crae, holding the baby. "Oh!"

Crae felt something warm and wet down the front of his shirt. "Here," he said hastily, holding out the damp baby. "I think he needs you."

Both women clucked. "Oh, that dear little boy!" Calyne said. She took him from Crae and laid him down in his cradle, her careworn expert hands unwrapping the diaper, taking a new one, and wrapping him up again all before the boy could do more than whimper.

"Thank you, Calyne," Jessamy said. She laced up her bodice. "I swear that this boy goes through twice as many cloths as Tevani ever did."

"Oh, of course, Lady Jessamy. Come, shall I take both children to breakfast with me?"

"No. I, well . . . That is—"

Crae had never seen Jessamy at such a loss for words.

"Yes," Crae said firmly to Calyne. He stood, knowing that he towered over both women. She bowed hastily, and with Jori in the crook of her arm, she took Tevani by the hand, the little girl jumping in her boots. The door closed behind them, Tevani's voice regaling Calyne with the events of the morning all the way down the hall.

"What?" Jessamy said, looking up at him, her chin raised. She looked as if she needed something to do with her hands, now that she didn't have the baby. She had held Stavin's son between them so that he could not get too close to her. And it had worked, until she had come to his bed last night. Now the days of shields between them were over.

He took her hand again, this time lifting it to his lips. She made a small wordless sound. He bent and kissed her. Once again her mouth was stiff at first, and once again she yielded, her lips soft and sweet.

"If you don't come to me tonight," he said, his voice low, "I will come to you."

The first thing he noticed when he made it downstairs was that Calyne's news traveled fast. Everywhere people smiled when they saw their lord.

"Good morning, Lord Crae! A good morning to you, sir! How are you this fine morning, my lord!"

It was disconcerting to say the least. As a mere captain, he had had more privacy, little though he had been able to make of it, for there were few opportunities for love at Red Gold Bridge. Still, it was as if everyone had a stake in his and Lady Jessamy's marriage bed—and come to think of it, exactly what had the grooms and farmers been wagering on the last few months?

The only person who had no great smile for the turn of events was Lord Favor. He scowled at Crae as he came into the kitchens for breakfast and vesh. Crae's general good humor faded.

"Brother," Crae said shortly. He got himself a cup and let one of the maids fill it for him.

Favor grunted. Crae wondered if he had been drinking something stronger than vesh already that morning. His expression was hangdog, and he slumped at the table. Breyan was at his side, and the captain glanced from lord to lord, his expression closed.

"So, you were triumphant," Favor sneered. Crae didn't bother replying. He sipped his hot spiced vesh and waited. His brother-in-law flushed. "Now what? I heard how you gave in to that foul stick who called himself the king of the crows. King of the rats, more like. What kind of man are you, Captain?"

Crae regarded him over his cup. *You are a fool,* he thought. *If I could, I would thrash you and throw you from the top stair; only your sister saves your skin.* When he was good and ready, he said, "The kind of man who made a valuable alliance with a feared enemy. No crow will attack Trieve ever again. And if we are ever attacked"—he put some emphasis in the word—"they will come to our defense. So you see, Lord Favor, I might be more *favorably* inclined toward the crow lord than I am to you right now."

Favor's expression made him look as if he were about to explode. He stood, and Breyan stood with him—to defend him against Crae or to hold him back, Crae was not sure which. "You threaten me," he blustered, "but you have no idea who you toy with. I am a member of the Aeritan Council, Captain, and who we elevated we can cast down."

Everyone in the kitchen had given up all pretense at work. The hot bustling room had become still, the stone walls almost leaning in to hear. Crae set down his vesh. With the utmost care he kept his control.

"You didn't elevate me," Crae said. "The high god did, and until he says otherwise, I am lord here. You would know that, Favor, if you had been summoned, as I was. Instead, you just took the lordship with a nudge and a wink."

Even as he spoke he knew he trod on dangerous ground. He warned himself to take care. From what he knew, he might as well have accused the entire Council of falsifying their right to their lordships.

Favor licked his lips. "And you are ungrateful and unworthy," he said. "I spoke against you from the first, because I knew you were nothing but a common free lance. You resigned your commission and took arms against your lord, you consorted with a low female from an uncouth land, and you conspire with crows against the House of Trieve. I should bring you before the Council on charges of treason and strip you of your rights."

A couple of men growled and stepped forward. Breyan drew his sword and stepped in front of Favor, even as Crae lifted his hand to halt his men. They stood down, but they did not back off.

"Do it," he said. He could barely speak for his anger. "Go to the Council. Tell them what you think of me. Bring war to your sister's land, her children's birthright. All for nothing except your hurt pride and that you can't stand the idea that I married your sister in more than name only."

"You dare—" Favor stopped. When he spoke again, his voice rose barely to a whisper. *"You insult Favor."*

"You've insulted Trieve more than I could ever insult your House," Crae said. He was half-worried, half-thankful that he hadn't worn his sword to breakfast. Favor was armed. He had come to the kitchen looking for a fight, and Crae had handed him the pretext. *Fine. Then we will have this out.* "You insulted this House the moment your horse set foot on the bottom terrace. You brought war down upon us, yes, you, *Brother.* You brought this battle to us through pride and stupidity. I do not take the flat of my sword to your back for three reasons, and they sit upstairs safely *in my House."*

Favor advanced, one hand on his sword, Breyan next to him. Would he have stood so next to Tharp? Crae's mouth twisted. He would have done as Breyan did. A captain served the House, not the man. Breyan's feelings for his lord could not enter into it. He didn't look around, but all the men and some of the women gathered at his back. Some were his newly blooded fighting men, but none were armed.

"You are a false lord, and the Council will treat you as you deserve. We will take Trieve down stone by stone, Captain, and make you watch when we put your people to the sword and torch your fields. That will teach you to think you are better than your station."

"Get out of my House." Crae could barely speak. He turned toward Breyan. "Get him out of here."

"Uncle Jori! Lord Crae!" Tevani bolted into the kitchen, followed by Calyne. "Can I ride Hero this morning with Uncle Jori? Please? You promised you would ride with me—"

Favor growled and turned on his niece as the little girl ran up to him. Crae knew what he meant to do: simply swat the child away. He knew Favor could not have meant to hurt her. But the man drew his sword and swung it at her with the flat end. They were in such close quarters that Breyan and Crae fouled each other as they jumped in. The sword caught Breyan across the shoulder and down his chest, and the man dropped. Crae caught the rest of the arc across his shirt, the tip scraping his skin as he threw Tevani out of the way. The little girl screamed as she thudded to the stone floor, her cry cut off on impact.

Then there was nothing else but shouting—Breyan in pain, the women and the men in horror. Crae grabbed the sword from his brother-in-law and raised it over his head. Favor's eyes went from confused to pleading to terror-stricken, but he could make no move as Crae plunged the sword into his chest almost to the hilt.

Blood blossomed on Favor's fine shirt, and he sank to his knees, the sword jutting out from his chest. Crae let him drop, and the blood pooled beneath him on the stones. All around them the men and women of Trieve moved, some to pick up Tevani to keep her limp body out of the flow of blood, some to draw Breyan away and wrestle his sword from him. More men came in, drawn by the commotion, more women. Jessamy came running in, stricken at the sight of her daughter.

"Tevani!" she shrieked. "Tevani! High god, she can't be dead! She can't!"

As if from far away, Crae heard the others reassure her

that the child hadn't been bloodied but had been pushed aside and had fallen. He heard Tevani's gasping cry as she regained consciousness. Crae let the flood of panic swirl around them. He and Favor were in a world all their own. He watched as the life failed in Favor's eyes and the man fell forward, the dead weight of his body pushing the sword through his back.

High god. Help me.

His god was silent though, or at least Crae could not hear him over the buzzing in his head.

Eleven

"Hi, Lynn," Nancy called from behind the counter at Toomey's as Lynn entered the low-slung feed and supply for some odds and ends for the farm. Nancy was about Mrs. Felz's age, and she had worked the feed and supply store for twenty years or more. "Jim wanted me to let you know that he's got in a new batch of dewormer and he hasn't gotten your order for grain, and was wondering what was up."

Crap. She had forgotten. *Dammit, I need a barn manager.* "Hi, Nance," Lynn said. "Sorry, that was my fault. As long as I'm here, let me put that in. And, er . . . how quickly can you get that out to me?" Toomey wholesaled the grain and hay for most of the area farms.

Nancy tsked. "I'll put you on the list. Hey, so what's this I hear about you finding a new horse?"

News traveled fast, that was for sure. She knew she wouldn't be able to keep Red Bird a secret for long.

"Yeah, it was strange." *You have no idea how much,* Lynn added to herself. "I'd put up flyers to see if someone lost him, but I don't think they should have him back. He was pretty badly mistreated."

Nancy raised an eyebrow. "And he just wandered in? He must have known a good thing when he found it."

"Yeah. I've put him up and had him vetted out. Nothing wrong with him that food and time won't cure."

A new voice chimed in. "Your mystery horse? I heard about that."

Lynn looked up to see Sue Devin, one of the local riders who ran the cross-country club, with a basket of supplies in hand, wearing jeans, a long-sleeved shirt, and hiking boots. Lynn smiled. She liked Sue, a no-nonsense woman who was in her seventies and looked and acted as if she would live forever. She used to be a member of the hunt club and was one of its foremost riders, until her husband died and Sue gave that up. She was still a fixture on the horse show circuit, though, with her big rawboned bay gelding, the aptly named Chocolate Moose, who was eighteen if he was a day and still jumped as if he was ten years younger.

"People are terrible," Sue went on. "Are you going to try to find the owners?"

"I was planning on turning them in to the ASPCA if I did," Lynn lied, a feeling of inevitability coming over her. Well, people would forget about the horse soon enough, as soon as the next news tidbit came up.

"Wait, if she keeps him, doesn't that make her a horse thief?" Nancy teased. "Do we get to hang her?"

"I think they only hang horse thieves in Texas," Sue said.

With an effort, Lynn kept any reaction off her face at the mention of Texas.

"So tell me about him," Sue prompted. There was nothing better than a new horse to talk about.

"Blocky, nice square build, looks like he has some quarter horse in him. About fifteen hands," she added. Sue made an *Oh well* face. Like Lynn, Sue was tall. In the horse show world, anything less than sixteen hands for a tall girl didn't look good in the show ring.

"After all this, you've bought him, I think. I wouldn't worry about the owners coming forward," she said.

Nancy rang up Sue's purchases and said, "Are you off to perambulate?"

"Indeed I am," Sue said. She caught Lynn's confused expression. "You youngsters. Don't you know what a perambulator is?"

Lynn shook her head, half laughing. "A baby carriage?"

Nancy pushed over the receipt and said, "It's a fancy title for people who don't do anything except hike," she teased.

"Hush, you. We do more than hike. We walk the town borders between Connecticut and New York and make sure that the borders are secure."

Lynn felt her mouth drop. "Wait . . . you what?"

Sue stowed her packages in a big canvas tote with a jumping horse cross-stitched on it and chattered on, oblivious to Lynn's reaction. "It dates back to the Colonial era. All of the Connecticut towns used to have them. Now we call ourselves the perambulators, but we haven't been official for, goodness, twenty or thirty years. As Nancy says, we just hike."

"So, you're like . . . guardians, right?"

Sue considered that. "I hadn't thought of that, but that would be a good way to put it. Well, I have to run. Oh, and Lynn, let me know what happens with that horse of yours and if you find his owners. I'd love to give them a piece of my mind."

"Wait!"

Sue turned around with a quizzical expression at Lynn's urgency. Nancy waited with Lynn's purchases, also as surprised.

"Sue, this is really important. Where do you hike, exactly, and have you been in the woods recently?"

Sue was smart; Lynn had always known that. The woman's expression changed from quizzical to sharp. Lynn held her breath.

"If you aren't busy today, why don't you come out with us, and I'll show you. I'll swing by the farm and pick you up."

Lynn nodded, watching her go. The door tinkled behind Sue, and Nancy finished bagging her purchases. Remembering, Lynn turned to her and took the bag.

"I just wish I knew what was going on, but no one ever tells me anything," Nancy groused. She gave Lynn a sharp look of her own. "I'll tell Jim to schedule you for a shipment."

"Thanks."

Lynn got into her car, heading home on autopilot. So there were guardians in the area. Who knew—especially since they didn't seem to know themselves. How much did perambulators know about the woods in the area? Did they know anything at all about Gordath Wood? From what Sue said, it was a Connecticut tradition, not a New York State one, but in this part of the region, it could be hard to tell where Connecticut left off and New York began, especially on the trails. She supposed that was the point of having perambulators, in pre-satellite-mapping days. What if those long-ago selectmen had established perambulators in Connecticut not to guard against border encroachment from New York but to keep an eye out for something more dangerous?

On the other side of Gordath Wood, they had guardians who knew what they were doing and how to keep the gordath closed so it wouldn't consume the worlds. Over here they had old folks who liked to hike in the woods. She didn't know how much she could tell Sue. She didn't know how much the older woman would believe her. But maybe it was time for the perambulators to know what they were really up against.

Lynn looked through the binoculars across a forested tract in Connecticut at what Sue Devin had said was the border with New York State. She couldn't tell. The woods were divided by roads and houses, and one great empty field swooped up toward the sky as if it wanted to meet the clouds. Next to her Sue consulted with her fellow perambulators over maps and binoculars. They were a hearty group of a half dozen middle-aged and older enthusiasts, all amiable, with water bottles, bird books, hats, hiking boots, and walking sticks. Lynn was the youngest by about thirty years, and they treated her with good humor and a touch of pity—the latter, she suspected, because she could barely keep up. She wasn't used to walking, she wanted to protest, but instead saved her breath. She needed it. They hiked some steep and rocky hills in their duty to patrol the borders of Connecticut towns.

The summer air was still under the trees, their leaves hanging limply in the midsummer heat. Cicadas buzzed rhythmically. The sound was soothing and peaceful. If she had a hammock, she would have wanted to swing easily and fall asleep.

The last time she fell asleep in the woods, things hadn't been so peaceful, she reminded herself. She lowered the binoculars and handed them back to Sue.

"So is that High Hollow?" she asked Sue, gesturing toward the sweep of open space.

Sue nodded. "And over there is Stone Brook," she said, pointing to the west. "And behind that—"

Hunter's Chase. And Gordath Wood.

As promised, Sue had come by to pick up Lynn, who had brought along a filled water bottle, some granola bars, and her old sneakers from the back of her closet. She had wanted to fill a backpack with provisions, just in case, but she'd held back. They wouldn't be hiking anywhere near the gordath, after all.

They didn't keep to a trail, exactly. "Too easy to get lost," Sue quipped, and the rest laughed. "We have to be careful though; we stick to trails where we know there are endangered species." She pointed out several on their walk: here a salamander in a damp swale, there a kind of fern. There were flowers and other plants as well, and plenty of invasive plants, which caused a fluster of consternation and some ruthless weeding that left the bad species pulled up by their roots and drying in the sun.

"And up here is a special treat," Sue told her. She accepted one of Lynn's granola bars. "If you look over here, there's a glade of old-growth forest tucked away. Whoever logged this area hundreds of years ago left a nice little swath."

Lynn felt a prickle go down her spine. This is what she had come for. "I'd love to see it," she said casually, and Sue led the way. They picked their way off the trail down a rocky slope.

The rocks in the area were legion, brought by glaciers, left behind when the ice retreated. The morrim in Aeritan had been one such boulder, and so was the morrim in North Salem.

She saw immediately what Sue meant when they reached the little swale, and she knew at once that she looked at a piece of Gordath Wood. A glade of six huge trees, ancient and gnarled, squatted in a semicircle, one, the tallest, almost split in two by an old lightning strike—or some other force. It had sheared off a half of the trunk and several branches, but it did not kill it entirely; that cloven branch rested on the ground, but it still carried green leaves and life. Thin grass threaded between the trees and around a fat, squat boulder that hulked in the center of the little clearing. Soil and leaves mounded around its base.

Bet it's supported by smaller rocks, if someone wanted to dig under it to find out. The shiver down her spine increased, and she felt a momentary dizziness. She took a few steps closer, then stopped. Was it whispering to her? She didn't want to hear it if it was. To turn her thoughts, she said to Sue, "What do you know about it?"

"Well, it's hard to say. These trees are old oaks, and their DNA suggests they are related to trees in Gordath Wood itself. That's not so unusual, but those trees are singular; there don't seem to be any oaks in the area that have the same genetic code. It's like they came up through acorns from—from, well, I don't know. We also know there are these pocket ecosystems that you find in odd places where the surrounding conditions don't usually support these species, and yet here they are. It's odd that this little glade is here, so close to Gordath Wood. Maybe a long time ago all these woods were the same forest."

"I like it," Sue finished, still gazing at the little glade. "It's a mystery. It makes me a little homesick." She laughed a little. "Well, nostalgic anyway." She straightened herself up briskly. "And then I remind myself that I have better things to do than think about the past. But I wanted you to see it."

"Thanks," Lynn said. "Is it okay if I—I mean, there aren't any endangered species around it, are there?"

"Oh no, no. Tread as you wish. I'm going back up to the overlook, and we'll come and get you when we're done."

Lynn was about to say, *Wait!* when Sue headed back up the trail, leaving her face-to-face with the old morrim. It didn't mutter or sing. It looked just like a big rock that was half-buried in the composting woods. The feeling of peace and silence in the woods deepened, and she felt the same melancholy again. She looked back once, but she couldn't see Sue and the others, though occasionally she thought she could hear their voices.

Or the morrim's? she wondered. No, the sound was too prosaic. It didn't carry the same menace as the last time she heard the muttering of a live morrim. She walked forward, her sneakers scuffing through the grass, and laid a hand on the cool, rough, lichen-covered rock. She felt a faint tremor, and then the rock went still.

She gasped. For an instant the morrim had responded to her touch. Energy had zinged into her hand as if she had touched a live wire. She turned around and looked back up the trail to the ridge, trying to imagine the sight line to Hunter's Chase and Gordath Wood on the other side of the New York State line. In between, somewhere, there was the gordath . . .

Wait a second. *This* morrim wasn't attached to the one in New York. That morrim was Balanced Rock, and it anchored the gordath between itself and the old morrim high up on a ridge in Gordath Wood in Aeritan.

So what gordath did this morrim connect to?

"Shit," Lynn said out loud to the empty glade. "There's more than one."

As if her recognition sparked something in the gordath, she felt the tremor again, only this time it shocked her from toes to head. The old oak trees rustled, and the grass bent with a shiver from a wind that came from nowhere. The hair lifted at the nape of her neck. In an instant Lynn had an impression of a flare that ran from the morrim straight into the woods, like a line of underground lightning. Then it was gone, and the atmosphere subsided.

"Lynn!" Sue called her from the trail. "Are you ready? Henry thinks a storm might be brewing . . ." She trailed off. "Are you all right?"

Lynn backed away from the morrim and began to run back up the trail, her breath coming hard.

"We have to go," she said. "Get everybody together, Sue. We have to get out of here."

Sue gave Lynn a strange look, but she said nothing to the others as they hastened down the hill from the old morrim. The strange weather had blown over, and no more was said about an impending thunderstorm. Lynn kept looking back as if she could see the morrim behind her, but it was hidden in its little glade.

When they got to the parking area, everyone said their good-byes and got into their cars with promises to meet again. Sue and Lynn faced off in the empty lot. They were both sweaty and grimy and tired.

"Goodness, Lynn," Sue said finally. "What on earth is going on?"

Lynn drank the last of the water in her water bottle and carefully tossed out the last drops onto a dusty Queen Anne's lace poking up at the edge of the lot. "Sue, why is it called Gordath Wood?"

"Lynn—"

"Everyone always said the woods were named that because some Colonial guy in the sixteen hundreds called it God's earth. But what if it wasn't? What if the name of Gordath Wood came from the same place the oaks come from? Somewhere else?"

"Well, I don't know how that could be, although anything is possible, I suppose."

Sue was humoring her. Lynn smiled and screwed the cap back on her water bottle. "Yeah, you're right. Listen, as long as you think I'm crazy, can you do me a favor?" Sue began to protest, and Lynn waved her off. "I mean it. A promise even."

"I'll try." Sue sounded dubious.

"Stay away from that little glade. In fact, maybe you and the rest of the perambulators can find other borders to patrol for a while."

She half expected the older woman to protest. Instead, Sue just said, "You know, that's what Joe told me. Last year, after you disappeared. Stay off the trails. I didn't understand then, and I certainly don't now. But Lynn—I think that's not such a good idea."

Now it was Lynn's turn to look confused. Sue went on. "Whatever happened last year, with the earthquakes and Balanced Rock coming off its supports, and my goodness, that was more frightening than the earthquakes, I think—" She paused and got herself back on track. "What I mean is, that we perambulators guard the town borders and make sure they are safe and sound. If something is going to happen, like last year, we need to be here."

In Aeritan they were called guardians, and here they were called perambulators. Whatever they did, it protected the borders. She couldn't force Sue or the others to leave their post, and she knew Sue was right; it might be a mistake to try.

"Just be careful," Lynn said finally, and Sue gave her a smile.

"We always are, my dear."

When she got home, the day had become hu-mid and gray, the sunshine washed out. Everything drooped under the heat, from the horses in the fields, standing head to toe to brush flies from each other as they grazed, to the flowers and shrubs that Mrs. Felz had coaxed back to health. All of the clients had gone home for the day, now that it was too hot to ride.

Lynn parked her little car and trudged up to the house. Mrs. Felz sat on the front porch, fanning herself and rocking slowly, iced tea condensing in a glass on the table.

"Oh, that looks good," Lynn said.

"Plenty in the icebox. By the way, be careful in the kitchen. You've got another stray."

The scrawny dog lay in a makeshift bed, a cardboard box that was lined with newspapers and an old frayed towel from the ragbag in the mudroom. A bowl of cat food—all the kibble they had was for the barn cats—and of water was set next to it.

The dog looked up at her and thumped its tail shyly. It was filthy and matted, its longish fur patchy in places. It was a gingerish color, and its tail had once been a plume, but this dog needed a bath, plenty of food, and some patient brushing.

"You're kidding," Lynn said out loud. The dog wagged harder, hopefully. "I don't want you," she told it, getting herself ice and pouring tea from the pitcher in the fridge. "I don't want any more strays." First Mrs. Felz, then Red Bird—might as well name the place Bleeding Heart Barn.

The dog got up unsteadily to greet her with the innate politeness some animals had: horses, too, will rise to their feet when someone comes to their box, not out of fear but out of courtesy.

"Oh, come *on*," Lynn said in despair, but her words trailed off. The dog had something wrapped around its neck; she hadn't noticed it earlier because the rope blended in with its fur. Lynn set her glass down on the kitchen counter and knelt. The dog licked her hands and strained for her face, but she moved its head aside and looked at the rope.

Twisted around the rope was a piece of T-shirt. It was frayed, stained, and faded, and it had once been black with the name of a long-ago band on it. She recognized it because of all the time it spent on the floor of the barn apartment where Joe stripped it off after a day's work.

He had sent her a message from Aeritan.

"Joe," someone whispered, shaking him. **"Hey,** Felz. Get up."

When did Arrim learn his last name? Joe thought groggily. He opened his eyes and tried to focus. It was dark, the sky midnight blue, dotted with stars. The air was chill. He had a fever and shook with ague.

Inside him the gordath hummed. It was closed, but his nerves still felt hypersensitive, as if his skin could not stop feeling things. Memory came back. Who had closed the gordath? Had Arrim managed it? *Because I sure couldn't.*

"Felz. Jesus. Wake up."

He turned his head with great effort. Mark Ballard loomed over him. At least he thought it was Mark.

"What do you want?" he managed. Of all the people he didn't want to see, Mark was up there.

"Just get up, okay?"

Joe sat up, stiffly and in great pain. He looked around when the world stopped spinning. The forest was still in the darkness. They were alone, or at least it looked like it. He couldn't see much in the forest. He listened, but he couldn't hear the sounds of men sleeping. There were only the dead horses and the fallen trees. *I must have been out of it, if I could sleep through the smell,* he thought.

"Where's Arrim?" he whispered.

"Who? Oh. He's over there. Don't worry about him. We gotta go."

Not without Arrim, Joe almost said. "Why aren't there any guards?"

"Never mind. Listen, you gotta do this thing. You gotta open the gordath. We have to go through."

Something was wrong. The last thing he remembered, he had opened the gordath—well no, more like the gordath had burst open inside him.

"Who closed it?" he said.

"Forget about that. You opened it once. You have to open it again. Listen, let's just get out of here."

Yeah, he had remembered that. So why was it just him and Mark? Had everyone else died when the gordath burst open? Had Arrim died?

"Listen, you open it, and you go through, too. You can

close it from the other side. Come on man. I know you don't trust me, but you got to do this. Do it for yourself."

The gordath waited, trembling, wanting to be open. *God,* Joe thought. He could, so easily. He didn't need Arrim. He could open the gordath, and he could go home.

Not without Arrim. He stalled for time. "How was it closed?" Joe said.

"What?"

"Who closed the gordath?"

"I don't know. One minute there was a big fucking hole in the air like usual, and the next thing it slammed shut. You passed out, and so did the other guy. But come on. You can open it again. You have to."

Damn thing closed on its own. Unstable. Well, the only stable gordath was a closed one. They had been given a reprieve, through no ability of their own. But that meant that Hare was no closer to controlling the gordath than he had been before, unless Joe gave in to Mark's cajoling.

"Where are the guards?" he said again.

"Again with the guards. Hare left me with you. Now come on, let's go."

"No," Joe said.

"What the fuck? You like it here? You like getting the shit kicked out of you?" Mark's voice had risen to a shout.

Behind them a torch flared sulkily, and Joe closed his eyes against the reddish light, his night vision shot to hell. He could hear the sound of swords drawn all around them and crossbows being armed.

"Lord Bahard," came Hare's voice. He stepped out of the woods, a silhouette against the torchlight. Another torch flared and another, and they were ringed by smoking, flickering light. Joe raised himself up achily and looked around. He and Arrim had been left to rest where they had fallen, near the closed gordath. Everyone else had camped a bit farther out. A smart move, Joe thought, considering the danger—and the smell.

"You aren't trying to leave me, are you?" Hare said. His

voice was silky, and his men ranged themselves behind him. In the fitful light Joe could see Mark touch the safety on his rifle, a small movement.

Crap, Joe thought. He was going to get them both killed.

Instead, every crossbow came up and aimed straight at Mark, the sharp points catching the dull light.

"Set it down, Lord Bahard," Hare said. After a moment Mark obeyed, but as he did, he burst out, "Screw you, Hare! I've done enough! You promised me the same deal as Tharp gave me, and I haven't seen one cent! I'm through! God damn it, *I want to go home!*"

Hare smacked him. The sound was loud in the night. As Mark stumbled backward, Hare grabbed him by the front of his bulky camo jacket and pushed him up against a tree. Hare was smaller than Mark, but Mark could do nothing against the man.

"You fool," Hare said, and all the smoothness was gone from the Brytherner's voice. "You go nowhere without my leave. Is that understood? One more try, and you are useless to me."

He stepped back, and Mark pressed himself against the tree, cursing. Hare ignored him. He picked up the hunting rifle and handed it to one of his men. "Bind him," he ordered, and with eagerness three of their guards went forward, two to hold a struggling Mark and the other to yank his arms around his back.

"God dammit, Hare!" Mark blustered, but Hare ignored him. He looked at Joe and Arrim.

"Are you strong enough to try again?"

Joe shrugged, though every bone hurt. "That depends. Are you crazy enough to want to go through that again?"

"I tire of your recalcitrance, Guardian."

As if to remind them of the gordath's presence, the ground rumbled, and they all caught their balance. Joe could feel the energy zipping beneath him. *Here we go again,* he thought. So much for keeping the gordath closed. Pretty soon the earthquakes would start up on the other side, and the hole between the worlds would spread. They had barely closed the gordath the last time it burned between the two worlds. He remembered the soldier who fell through into emptiness back then, and shivered. This one was worse, much worse. And if Hare made good on his threat and killed him and Arrim, nobody was going to be able to stop it.

He hoped Lynn knew the gordath was open, even if she hadn't gotten his desperate message with the dog. *Run, Lynn*, he thought. *Don't stick around. Because Arrim and I are in a shitload of trouble, and when this gordath opens for good, we aren't going to be able to control it.*

How far did a person have to run before they could outrun a gordath?

"Well? Why won't it stay open?" Hare asked. He faced his two reluctant guardians under the circle of torchlight that smoked in the little clearing. He sat on one upended tree trunk. The stench of death, of upended trees, and maybe even the stink of energy that came with the gordath, surrounded them. The forest trembled continuously. Hare's men gathered close, all of them, even Mark, fidgeting nervously.

Arrim said, "The gordath is a living being. It can't be controlled, only persuaded." His voice was tired. *He's given up,* Joe thought. Arrim was on the verge of panic. Another beating, or even the threat of one, and the man would break, if he hadn't already.

Hare lowered his voice and said almost gently, "Then why can't you persuade it, Guardian?"

"It's not—this isn't—" Arrim faltered at Hare's expression.

"Hare," Joe said. The Brythern leader shot him a sour look. "Lay off."

"You don't give the orders here, Guardian."

Drav growled and stepped forward, but Hare waved him to a halt. Joe pressed his advantage. "Look, this gordath is too much for us. It's closed now, and it's still shaking all the time." All around them the leaves and grasses quivered, though the air was still. "I don't know what you got us into, and you sure as hell don't know what you got us into, but I think you need to come at this from a different angle. We can't open it and keep it open. You keep making us try, and we might not be able to close it. Now we all know what happens when the gordath can't be closed."

He looked about meaningfully at the dead beasts all around them. But did Hare really know? Joe remembered the earthquakes in New York, so violent that they dislodged Balanced Rock from its support stones and flung it onto the highway. He looked straight at Hare, and the man's expression in the weak light lost its single-mindedness. Hare was starting to think.

For a long moment they were all silent as they waited for him. The constant ceaseless rustling hummed in Joe's bones. Finally Hare turned, and when he looked at them, he shook his head. His voice became thoughtful.

"Do I know?" he said. "Yes, I know. Last winter, the first time this troublesome man"—he indicated Mark, who sulked— "came through and brought his weapons of war, we felt the tremors in the city of Cai-sone. And then, the weapons showed up on our borders, and we knew we had to understand what your country was doing. While Aeritan went to war, our learned men and historians searched deep into our histories and discovered what these tremors meant. It wasn't the first time Cai-sone had felt these earth shakings, and here we were, through no fault of our own, facing them again."

"So," Joe said. "After all that, now you want to open the gordath anyway?"

"To control it, Guardian!" Hare snapped. "The country that controls the gordath controls the world. Your weapons, what this man has told me of your country's mechanisms, its thirst for fuel, all the trade between nations would go to Brythern, not Aeritan."

He controlled his voice. "Our histories tell us of a stranger who came to Brythern generations ago. He wasn't a barbarian like you, Guardian." He gestured to Arrim. "Nor was he from across the oceans. He said he came through the forest. He spoke of distant countries we had never heard of, and he bore many marvelous objects. We still have some of his possessions in the university at Cai-sone." He held out his hand, and one of his men placed Mark's hunting rifle in it. Mark whined and strained toward it, but Drav cuffed him on the back of his head. "He had an ancient model of a gun like this. Not much more dangerous than one of our crossbows."

A flintlock? Joe thought.

"But as much as Brythern marveled at this stranger, he marveled at Brythern, our alchemists and our scientists, our cities and our holdings. He wanted to deliver our country to his god, he said. He was insistent upon that fact, so insistent that finally he was beheaded, and his head was placed on top of the great stone cairns that he said was a gatepost to his world." This time he looked at Joe. "I've met two of you now, from your world, your 'god's earth.' I'm not impressed, Guardian. Not impressed at all."

"Tell him the rest," Arrim said suddenly. They turned to look at him. He swayed, caught himself, but his voice had strength and intensity. "They didn't know what they had. And after they killed the stranger man, there was no one who could close the gordath. It opened wider and wider until finally a great cataclysm struck that marred Brythern, the same one that destroyed half of Gordath Wood as well. You arrogant fool. You killed a guardian, and you let the gordath rain destruction down on the world. And now you mean to do it again." Disgust filled his voice. The guards moved uneasily, muttering among themselves. Joe knew how they felt. Arrim's sudden strength sent a shiver down his spine.

"No," Hare said, as if explaining something simple to an idiot. "This time, we have two guardians. I only have to kill one of you."

"God dammit," Joe said. "Hare, for the last time, you can't control it. The only control is to keep it closed. Once you open it, once you wake it up—it's out of your hands."

"Then I have no need of you, do I, Guardian? For the last time," he mimicked, "if you don't control the gordath, either you or your friend dies."

"And then what?" Joe said. "So what are you going to do? Shout at it? Wave your hands, threaten it with your knife? You are going to cause the same disaster that happened three hundred years ago! All this will look like a party!" He gestured at the carnage surrounding them.

"We can't fail," Hare said. "We won't fail. If we had kept at it, the gordath would be under our rule now."

"Or maybe you couldn't make it work *because everyone was dead*!"

"Christ, Felz, give it up," Mark said with disgust.

Joe fought for control. "Hare, listen. Let me and Arrim work on quieting it. We'll shut it down—yes, shut it down," he repeated as Hare made to protest. "Then we can work on opening it up again little by little, instead of just allowing it to blast its way free. It'll take time, but this way, we have a chance that we might all live through this." He could tell by Hare's expression that the man listened to him, albeit grudgingly. "You want it under control, this is the only way to do it. Otherwise, it's just like last night, Hare, just like a few weeks ago *right here*, and just like three hundred years ago."

Hare said nothing, and Joe held his breath. Finally, reluctantly, the man nodded. "All right. Do your best to quiet it. For now. But when I say it's time to open it again, you will obey. Understood?"

They had been given a reprieve. A pain lifted from Joe's chest. But he needed to ask for one more thing.

"We'll get to work. But maybe you guys could start on burying the horses."

As dawn rose over the woods, turning the sky from black to gray and starting the birds to piping, Arrim and Joe faced the center of the clearing. Around them the guards were set to chopping the fallen trees to create sledges to haul the horses away. Even Mark had been unbound and made to work, complaining soundly. But all that faded into the background as the guardians began their work.

A gordath wants to be open, Joe thought, concentrating. It was the first thing he learned as a guardian. He could see the livid afterimage of the portal against his closed lids. But a guardian wants to close it. He and Arrim were only following their nature. He drew strength from that concept and found himself making a kind of peace with himself and with the entity in front of him at the same time.

Twelve

Lynn drove the small, one-horse trailer around to the driveway in front of the farmhouse, parking it so she could pull out to the street. It was early, the sun barely up, the mist collecting on the fields. The lights were on in the barns for the girls who came to feed, their bikes and old cars parked out of the way for when the clients showed up. The horses were already snorting and whinnying, eager for their morning grain and turnouts, some of the more impatient ones kicking their stalls. Lynn could hear the sounds of rock 'n' roll pouring from the tinny radio in the tack room.

Just a regular morning at Hunter's Chase, she thought, leaving the parked trailer and truck and heading back down to the lower barn. She had already given the girls their orders. Until she returned, Mrs. Felz was in charge.

Just how she was going to tell Isabella was another story.

She had grained Red Bird herself earlier, and now she tacked him up. She put him in a western saddle and hackamore and led him up the hill to the house. He loaded easily into the trailer with only the slightest hesitation. *Good boy,* she thought. An old horsewoman had once told her you could add two hundred dollars to a horse's price if he went into a trailer without fuss. Lynn knew she appreciated it. She tied him with a safety knot and left him with a pat on the rump.

Isabella came out from her barn apartment, wrapped in her tatty robe, a look of puzzlement on her face.

"Lynn, what on earth?"

"I have to go away for a few days," Lynn said. With Mrs. Felz following, she went into the house and gathered up her things from the kitchen: a bedroll, a pack with Aeritan necessities: clothes, matches, aspirin, bandages, toothbrush, toothpaste, and toilet paper, and trail food for her and grain for the horse. She figured that she would get heartily sick of granola bars before she found Joe, but she didn't have time for anything else. It was high-calorie food and would keep her going. That's what counted.

With her back to Mrs. Felz so she wouldn't see, she put the gun from the attic chest on top and tugged the straps closed. Lynn hefted the pack. It would all fit on the saddle. "I'm leaving you in charge." She picked up a fat envelope from the table. "If I am not back in ten days, I want you to open this."

Mrs. Felz took it, dumbfounded. "Lynn—"

"Look, believe me, I know how weird this is. But please. You have to do this for me. Just sit tight, run the farm like you've seen me do it, and ask Sue Devin for help if you need it."

Sue. She needed to call her—well, that could wait. She'd call her at the entrance to the trail to the morrim and let her know what she was doing.

Mrs. Felz looked at her like she wanted to say a bunch of different things but didn't quite know how to begin. Finally she settled on, "Does this have something to do with Joe?"

It was time to come clean. She nodded.

Mrs. Felz sat down heavily at the table, her face crumbling. "So he's alive," she whispered through her tears. "I thought—I thought he must be dead."

Lynn waited awkwardly, and then she set down the pack and knelt by the older woman.

"Please believe me," she said, "It's more complicated than you—or even I—can understand. But the dog was a message. I think Joe needs help."

Mrs. Felz got herself under control, wiping her eyes. "Then go. I'll take care of things here. Call me when you find something out."

"I'll try," Lynn lied. "Now I really have to go."

She picked up the pack and whistled to the dog. It got up, wagging, from its little bed. It was still thin, but a warm night and a full stomach had done wonders for it. It followed Lynn to the truck and hopped in as if it knew what was going on. Lynn threw her gear into the bed and got into the driver's seat.

The farm truck handled the single horse trailer with ease, as Lynn put it in gear, and they bumped slowly down the driveway. She pulled out onto the road and accelerated smoothly away from the farm. She glanced at it in the rearview mirror. She might never see it again. She tried to put that out of her head. The envelope she had given Mrs. Felz contained the papers for signing over the farm to her as well as instructions as to what was in the chest in the attic. Lady Sarita wouldn't mind; she had left it there, after all. She meant it for the farm.

The morning's slanted shadows striped the little gravel parking lot at the trailhead to the Connecticut trail. Lynn parked the horse trailer and got out, the dog jumping down behind her. She let down the ramp and led out Red Bird. While the dog and the horse touched noses, the dog wagging eagerly, Lynn called Sue Devin.

"This is Sue Devin speaking."

"'Morning, Sue. This is Lynn. I need a favor. Well, two favors, actually." While she talked, Lynn strapped her gear and her bedroll onto the back of the saddle one-handed, holding the phone at her ear with the other. It was awkward, but she needed to hurry. She didn't want some early morning walker to come upon her.

"Lynn?"

"I'm at the trailhead to the hiking trail in Connecticut.

Can you come by and bring my truck and trailer back to Hunter's Chase?"

There was a long silence. Then, "Those aren't riding trails."

"I know, and I'm sorry." The perambulators had all inveighed against riders on the hiking trails because horses' hooves cut into the soil and caused erosion. Lynn knew she was committing a cardinal sin. "Please, come get my trailer and bring it back to the farm."

"Lynn . . ."

"I'm going to leave the keys in the water bucket. There's still water in it, so be forewarned."

"Lynn, don't you dare . . ."

"So the next thing is, I want you to call out the perambulators. You need to watch the woods in two places. Up here, in these woods, and over by the old house at Daw Road. Keep an eye out for anything strange. And I think—I'm not sure but I think you'll know what to do."

"Lynn . . ."

"Bye." Lynn closed her phone and put it in her pocket, locked up the truck, and plunked the keys into the water bucket as promised. She flipped the reins around Red Bird's neck. She swung aboard and pushed Red Bird up onto the trail. With luck she would be through the gordath before Sue came to get her horse trailer. With the dog following, she pushed the horse into a trot, and they headed up the trail.

It wasn't a riding trail. It was too rocky, and the trees closed in until she was thrashing through branches and brush that she had not noticed on foot. But they made good time, and Lynn dismounted for the steep climb up to the overlook, taking long strides next to Red Bird as they made their way to the summit. When they got to the top, Lynn let the horse blow, walking him in gentle circles, his coat darkened with sweat. The dog sat, tongue lolling. When they had rested, she turned off to the little glade that held the morrim.

It was as silent as before, the still-long shadows concealing most of the rock except for a slice of sunlight passing over it.

The dog whined and pressed against Lynn's legs. She patted it and clucked to the horse. When they got close, she put her hand on the cool, rough rock.

Just like the last time, energy zipped in a straight line, and she jerked her head up to follow it. As if she could see the underground pulse, she saw where it led: away from the trail, away from the old Gordath Wood, and far deeper into these woods. Along that line was a new gordath, she thought. Go that way, and find a new way into Aeritan. Or . . . somewhere.

Out of habit she checked the saddle girth and then turned to the dog. She fished out the piece of Joe's T-shirt from her pocket and knelt and held it to the dog. The dog nosed it and whined, and its tail tucked under its legs. Lynn patted the dog.

"Show me," she told it. "Just show me."

She mounted up and headed along the line. The dog trotted in front now, occasionally looking back at her. Once it gave a low woof, the first she had heard, when they fell behind. There was even a faint trail, though it was probably a game trail. For now, though, it led in the direction she wanted. She thought she could even feel the energy line zip under Red Bird's hooves. The horse tossed his head and snorted but kept up a long, loose stride. As they headed deep into the heart of the forest, the trail taking them downward where the sunrise had not yet reached, Lynn refrained from looking back. She was not sure she wanted to see the morrim disappear from sight, either because she descended or because she rode from one world to the other.

The last time she did this it was dark, and she rode Dungiven straight through a three-rail fence. She hoped this time worked a little better. She pressed her heels against Red Bird's sides, and the horse broke into a flat-footed walk, a smooth, comfortable gait that could carry them for miles. Lynn settled into the saddle, one hand light on the reins, the other down at her side.

It occurred to her that if it didn't work and she ended up out at the highway, she was going to have a lot of explaining

to do. She had better not think on that, though. It had to work.
With the amount of blood on the T-shirt, Joe's life might de-
pend on it.

Lord Favor lay in the guest bedchamber, his
body washed and scented candles and clean straw surrounding him. Offerings to the grass god, the god of death and renewal, were piled at his feet. Crae stood next to Jessamy as
she offered prayers to the high god for her brother. She was
still pale with horror and woe, her tears for her brother mixed
with her worries for her daughter, her anger at Crae, and her
unrelenting shock.

Tevani had regained consciousness but didn't remember a
thing of what happened. She lay in her small bed, querulous
and crying. Jessamy was at her side as much as she could be.
The little girl was confused, thinking she had gotten injured
by the crows during her and Crae's adventure. It took hard
work from everyone to keep her still and quiet so she could
heal.

Jessamy began crying again, quietly. "He was my brother,"
she whispered brokenly. "He was my brother."

He was a fool, a tyrant, and a petty bully who had struck
out without thinking and almost killed her daughter. But he
was her brother, and he had been Crae's brother. Crae felt a
muscle jump in his cheek.

And now the Council would take sides. Crae saw it all in
his mind's eye, the march to war again. Any of the allies they
had counted on just days before were as dust. The Council
would turn on him as easily as they had granted him a lordship.

He thought he had been Trieve's savior. He had promised
Stavin he would protect Jessamy and his children. Instead, he
brought doom upon them. He had become bad luck to all he
touched. To Stavin, to Jessamy, to small Tevani, even to a
hapless crow. It were best he become crow himself and outlaw, destined to wander ragged and alone. He had broken

Council law, first by daring to presume the high god had touched him, and then to commit a brother killing.

Favor had wanted to see him brought down and broken, and in his death he got his wish. Crae would be broken.

He would send them all away. Jessamy and the children would go to her House with the body of her brother. He would remain and await his fate. Crae turned to tell her this when she crumpled up at the side of the bed, one hand clasping her brother's cold one. She whispered to her brother, telling him private things only a sister could say. "I loved you even when we fought," she told him. "You were my brother. I protected and scolded you, and now you're gone. Please, Jori, please forgive me. I couldn't protect you. I'm so sorry."

Stricken, Crae felt the blood rush from his face. The angry buzzing that nagged at him ever since he committed murder heightened its pitch. He stepped backward, away from her and her blame, and felt awkwardly for the door. He stumbled down the stairs.

No one looked at him. No one spoke to him. He could barely see; he had gone blind, his vision dark. All of the householders fled at his approach, and he staggered to the kitchen, his first thought only for strong drink.

He pushed through the door and stopped dead. There was the place where Favor had fallen, the flagstones whiter where they had been scrubbed and scrubbed of blood. It was a tell-tale of his guilt. Bile rose in his throat, and he swung away, outside.

Even the clear, cold air did not relieve him. The pressure mounting in his head, Crae found his way to the stable. He couldn't trust himself to tack up his horse, so he looked around. He saw one of his men, standing hesitantly, waiting for orders. Crae did not recognize him.

"Get my horse," he ordered. His voice rasped, harsh and implacable.

The man bowed and said hurriedly, "Yes, my lord Crae."

He waited until they brought Hero to him, the horse playing

up and snorting. It took Crae four or five tries to get his foot into the stirrup, and he swung aboard clumsily. Hero neighed and backed nervously. Crae spurred him forward, punishing him with his hands and his boots. The horse bolted, men scattering out of his way, pulling the barn door open just in time. Crae managed to duck under the lintel, and they burst through.

He didn't ride down the terraces. Instead, he reined his horse out and around to the fields. The sheep baaed and scattered, the dogs barked, and the shepherds shouted, but soon they were through, galloping up the grassy hill toward the endless sky. Here and there rocks dotted the hillside, as if they had been sheep turned to stone by a playful sky god. Hero bolted straight out, mane and tail flying. Crae kept him moving with his hands and feet, and when the horse flagged, he kicked him hard again. Up they galloped until they reached the top of the hill.

He pulled the horse up, and Hero snorted and reared. Above them the sky arched deep and blue, a few clouds dotting the expanse. Far below them Trieve spread out, the great house and the outbuildings looking small from his vantage point at the top of the mountain. Crae looked down. The baaing of the sheep reached him faintly, but the only other sounds were those nearer to hand: Hero's deep breathing, the piping of a mountain bird, the wind.

His tears.

He gave a great cry. He fell rather than dismounted and tumbled to his knees, his grief like pain, panting and heaving in his tears. He had lost everything. Jessamy, Tevani, even if she healed. He would have no son, no daughters. He had no House.

I am crow. I am crow. I am crow.

When he came back to himself, he lay on the hillside, the grasses warm against his back, looking up at the sky. It had gathered more clouds, and the sun played chase among them. Even as he watched, a shadow raced across the fields, bending the grasses before it. A chill swept over Crae. Nearby, Hero cropped grass, his reins trailing carelessly around his feet. Once he would never have left a horse like that, where he could step into his reins. Habit forced him to his feet to take care of his horse, and the animal nickered at him, nudging him and forgiving him for his temper earlier.

In his great unrest he had not realized where he was; they had buried the young crow up here. The cairn, a pile of rocks stacked neatly together, hulked a few feet away. The crow's grave was silent and at peace. The sun went behind the clouds, and the wind picked up.

The high god kept his silence, but Crae could hear the words of another behind the silence.

We kill and we ravage, and our god laughs.

This was crow land now, and by his murder he was the crow lord. The Aeritan Council's retribution would be swift. Favor's threat would come true, and no matter how he fought this time, Trieve would be broken, stone by stone.

He saw Jessamy off the next night, the better to travel in the cool of the darkness. They gathered at the bottom of the terraces, where the grooms brought down the two carriages, one to carry Lord Favor's body and one to carry his sister and her children and servants. They harnessed the teams there. Lord Favor's guard surrounded him, dark red sashes cutting across their chests, denoting a funeral train. Tevani was bundled into the carriage, wrapped in a warm cloak, and laid on a pallet of padding and pillows, the better to cushion her. Jessamy sat with Jori on her lap, her face still and white. She, too, wore a red sash, and her kerchief was tied precisely, not a hair peeking out from beneath the cloth. She was so still now, it stayed in place. She looked at Crae over the baby's head, her expression somber and remote. Crae knew there would be no handclasp, no kiss, not even the kiss of lord to lady.

So be it. There was no comfort for a crow. He spoke coldly.

"It is best you return to your old House," he said. "I do not expect to see you back here. I would advise you to petition the Council to dissolve our marriage."

"You turn me away?" Her voice was dull. "Then there is no refuge for me or the children."

"The House of your childhood is your only refuge now," Crae said, lowering his voice so that Tevani would not hear. The little girl didn't seem to be aware of anything except for her hands picking and picking at her blanket. Crae looked at Jessamy. They had fought—and then fought together. They had even taken their first steps toward love. He was crow now, and all that was over.

"Crae," she said, and her voice broke. "Don't do this. Don't send us away."

Didn't she understand? "Jessamy, they will come and tear Trieve to pieces. You cannot stay. Besides—" He could not speak further. *Besides, I killed him. I took up a sword and slew your brother.*

She swallowed her tears and looked away. When she regained her composure, her voice was dull. "If you wish, it must be so, Lord Crae," she said. She leaned forward. "I am ready. Take me home."

He stepped back as the driver whistled up the team, and the horses threw their strength into the traces.

"Captain Crae! Captain Crae!" Tevani cried. Even the driver heard, and he pulled up with a whoa.

"Tevani, hush. You must lie still," said Jessamy. But Crae walked a few paces and opened the door again. The little girl struggled against her wraps, and despite his coldness, his heart ached for her.

"Captain Crae, please take care of Hero for me," she said.

"You must go now, Tevani. Be a good girl for your mother."

Her face crumpled. "I'm sorry I made you hit me," she whimpered.

Crae couldn't breathe out enough to protest. Jessamy snapped, "Drive on, please!"

He watched them go, trundling into the night, Favor's outriders led by Breyan.

Then he turned and headed back up the terraces, the torches
guiding his way up the giant steps. This time there was no
small army to prepare for war, no willing men to lead. He was
alone against his enemies.

Colar knew they were on the wrong track as
soon as they reached the old house at the end of Daw Road.
Cicadas buzzed in the hot summer sun, and when they walked
around the vacant house and entered the woods, the air was
still and humid. The cicadas stopped their buzzing in alarm,
and he could tell they were the only people there. Sweat trick-
led down the small of his back under his T-shirt, and he was
thankful he had waited to put on his heavy armor. He hadn't
wanted to call attention to himself, and it looked like there
was no need for it after all.

"I don't understand," Kate said, frustration in her voice as
they stood by the three tall trees. "He has to be here. Where
else can he be?"

They had been so sure they would find Marthen here, but
the woods were abandoned, the house empty, the gateway
between the worlds closed up tight, as if it had never existed
at all. Colar scanned the ground, looking for any sign he
could, and his heart leaped. He knelt.

"What! What is it?" She knelt next to him. He frowned.

"Someone was here not too long ago," he said. He pointed
out the footprint. "But it was only one person, and the print
doesn't look big enough."

"Dammit," Kate said. "We can't just wait for him to come
back to the house again." Her voice held a strange note, and he
looked at her as she gave a strange half laugh, half sob. "My
mom and dad will ground us for life if they find out we went
out looking for him."

Sometimes Colar thought that her parents were more
frightened of the truth coming out than about the danger. He
didn't understand it, but he didn't understand a lot about this

world. *Though it doesn't matter, since I won't be staying for much longer.*

Although, with the gordath shut tight, perhaps that wasn't true after all. He shook his head in frustration. Marthen had to have come through, and there should be some sign of it. So where was it?

Kate sighed and sat down against a tree, arms folded across her chest. She had ruined the footprint, but he supposed it didn't matter since, whoever it was, it wasn't their man. She looked up at him, her blue eyes clear and her expression worried. She had a sprinkling of freckles across her nose, and her hair gleamed, even in the dim forest light. His heart hammered. *She's my foster sister,* he told himself, but he slid down next to her, letting his shoulder press against hers. She was muscular from riding, but she was soft, too. She moved uneasily, reddening. *I shouldn't have done that,* he thought, but he didn't move away.

"All right," she said, her voice unsteady. "We have to think. Why isn't he here?" She bit her lip, thinking. "When I saw him, it was closer to Connecticut and the highway. That's like ten miles from here. If he came through the gordath, he'd have had to walk all that way."

"Or get a ride."

She shook her head. "Not with what he was wearing. No way would anyone pick him up. And he would have attracted a lot of attention."

Colar nodded. From what little he knew of his new world, he could agree with that.

"And then there are his men," he said, thoughtfully. "The police said they came from the highway, too."

She was thinking furiously, he could tell. "What if there was another way through? Could there be another portal?"

Another way through the woods. Another path home. *There can't be,* he thought first. *How could there be?* But it made sense that Marthen had come through near where Kate had first seen him. But where could the gordath hide itself? All he had seen were roads, houses, and stores. All the towns here bustled day and night, not like the small villages at Terrick's outskirts. "Is there forest near there?" he asked dubiously.

Kate sucked in her breath, her eyes wide. "Yes. Oh my God. It's all protected habitat, and it's just a few miles from the highway. There's old growth forest there, and there aren't any houses or roads, just a hiking trail. There aren't too many places you can hide a bunch of people in the woods around here, but in that forest, you totally could. That's where we'll find his army, and that's where we'll find the gordath. He's there, Colar. He's got to be."

She jumped to her feet, and he followed suit. "Come on. We have to hurry." She headed off, back to the old house and the dirt road where they had left the car, and he got up to follow her. He could see it falling into place. They couldn't manage the army; there were just the two of them, and from what Maddy had said, there were about a dozen men in the ambush at the beach. The police could take care of the crows. He would take care of Marthen. Colar rubbed his sword hand against the side of his jeans. He knew the general had a gun. He didn't care. Ever since the eve of the final battle, when he found out what Marthen had done to Kate, he had wanted to face him down.

And then what? He knew enough that if he killed the general in this world, it would be murder. He could go to jail. No. He would have to go back to Aeritan. He glanced at Kate. She held onto his arm, still trying to tug him toward the Jeep. She had become doubtful now at his hesitation.

"What is it?" she said.

"I'll fight him," he said, and he could hear the anger in his own words. "But I can't fight him here. It will have to be in Aeritan."

Her face changed as she steeled herself. "I know," she said. Her voice started out strong but broke at the end. "But I still don't want you to go."

He didn't know how they ended up kissing, but they did. He pulled her close, and they kissed, making up for months, he thought dazedly, when they weren't allowed to even think of each other except as brother and sister. He wrapped his arms around her, wanting more, wanting to set her down on the forest floor, but when he started to kneel them both back to earth, she made a noise of protest and pushed her hands against his chest. "No," she said, pulling away from him. She was breathing hard. "You know we can't."

He was the son of a lord; he could do what he wished. He almost said that, but instead he stepped back. He held onto her hands, making sure she couldn't go away. "You're right," he said. "Not now. But you can come with me, and I'll petition my father. He'll let us marry, I know he will. He'll be so grateful he'll give me anything."

That was not even close to true, and he didn't know why he said it. His father would be grateful, to be sure, but he was also Lord Terrick. Kate's expression was unreadable, and then she looked away.

"I think right now we should concentrate on finding Marthen," she said, in the general direction of the woods. She pulled her hands from his.

"All right," he said evenly, catching her tone. Was she angry? Just because he wanted her to come with him? Even if they couldn't marry, what of it? In her world people paired up all the time without marrying. Almost immediately as he thought it, he knew that wasn't fair. If they tried that in Aeritan, the whole Council would come down on him and his parents, most likely. And he wanted to kiss her again. "Don't be angry, okay?"

Whenever he talked the way they did here, it always made her smile, and she did now. "I'm not angry, just—Colar, let's not talk about it."

Just then, her phone rang, startling them both. She pulled it out and looked at the display, and her heart sank. "It's Mom." The theme to "Kung Fu Fighting" stopped, took a breath, and rang again.

"Don't answer it," Colar said immediately. Kate grimaced, dithered, and finally flipped open the phone.

"Hi, Mom," she said, looking back at the old house on Daw Road. He could fill in her mother's side of the conversation.

"With Colar. We're off to Lynn's place."

"I'm sorry. Sometimes I don't hear the ring when we're in the car."

"Got it, Mom. We're going to the stables. Bye."

She snapped the phone shut. She looked at Colar and rolled her eyes. "She's going into a meeting to discuss a plea bargain, and then she said she's coming home early. Let's just stop off at the barn anyway. I can leave the saddle, and we can figure out how we're going to do this." He nodded. It was a good plan, and more importantly, Lynn might be able to help them. She would understand they needed to find a new gordath. It would be nice to have someone on their side in this.

The wind lifted the hair on Marthen's neck, and the cooling breeze felt good. The summer air here was damp and hot, and the biting insects were numerous and persistent. The camp had to remain hidden in the woods, and they had to stay in the hollows, but that meant they were in the stillest part of the forest. So the breeze was welcome.

The camp remained hidden, in part due to Gary's management of things. He kept Marthen posted on outside events. So while Marthen felt trapped in his wooded camp, with logs for seating, and shelters half made of musty tents and deadfall, Gary went out and about and brought back the news and sent out men in squads to bring back food and drink from the midden bins.

"The police are keeping a pretty sharp eye out for us," he told Marthen. He had a fresh bottle of whiskey, purchased for him by a sympathetic driver who was just passing through. He nursed it carefully, his old faded khaki shirt and blue trousers covering a body burning with alcoholism. He couldn't have been much more than Marthen's own age of forty years, but he looked twenty years older at least. "Our appearance at the lake, plus all these guys finding the camp has gotten us noticed.

We are going to seriously have to think about moving, but we're running out of woods."

On this side of Gordath Wood, that was true, Marthen thought. If he could get everyone back through the gordath, though, the police would never find them. That was, if the Brythern gordath cooperated. He had been dead drunk when he came across it, led there by tips and rumors paid for with his dwindling coin. He followed the whispers until finally he stumbled through, eventually finding himself in a stand of pines next to a black road, and there, driving by, was Kate Mossland.

First step. Once Garson delivered the guns and the ammunition, he would take care of Garson's commission and ransack the holding called Hunter's Chase. He had already sent out men to scout the farm, and it was a simple holding with no defenses, settled only by women. After his crows killed the women, he would have his men set fire to the house and outbuildings, and that would be that. But he needed an escape route once the attack was complete, because it would bring down the police on them with no mercy. He had to move his men back to the other side of the gordath.

"Gary," he said, "I am giving you a commission. Attend carefully."

The man lowered the whiskey bottle. Marthen went on. "Do you know the place where there is a grove of pine trees, near a pond and where the roads cross at a marketplace?"

The man stared at him, shook his head. "No offense, dude, but you really aren't from around here, are you?" Marthen gave him a level stare, and the man added quickly, "I think so, I think so. I bet I could find it."

"Good. Now let me tell you what to do when you find it."

Gary listened intently, his eyes only slightly wavering from time to time. If Marthen's experience was anything to go by, being drunk could only help. The hard part would be moving fifty men through town without being noticed, so Gary would have to move them well after dark. By then the Hunter's Chase holding would be on fire, drawing attention away from Marthen and his men.

As for himself, it was time to draw in Kate Mossland. While his men were at their work, he would go to her house. Once he had her, his star would ascend once more. He was an outlaw now with only a small army of crows, but he was General Marthen of Aeritan, and he was returning with her and with his own weapons. Let the Council make what it would of that, but this time he would not be thwarted. The girl would be his, and a lordship would be his, and anyone who would stop him would face his crows and his guns.

"Hey!" It was one of his men, standing watch at the edge of the camp. He had Garson with him. "He says he got 'em!"

Marthen felt a rush of excitement surge through him. He picked his way up to them. "Where?" he said. Garson gestured toward the road.

"I've got a crate for you. You'll need a couple of strong backs to bring it up."

Marthen sent two of his sturdiest men to pick up the crates. They lashed it to strong limbs they had cut from deadfall and hoisted it onto their shoulders, and the rest of the men all trailed back to the camp in a ceremonial parade. The men set the crate down, wiping gleaming sweat, and Garson stood back, beaming with pride.

"Just a taste," he said. "Just a taste."

They pried open the crate and pulled out the weapons nestled in straw. Garson was saying something about SKS semiautomatics, but Marthen wasn't listening. He pulled one out, hefting it. It felt better than the small handgun. It felt better than a sword or crossbow. He looked around. His men waited, some eagerly, some uneasy. He caught Gary's eye, and his lieutenant stared at him. He might have been befuddled with drink, but his expression held fear and disgust. Marthen turned away from him pointedly as he loaded the clip. *You cannot back out now,* he thought. *You are my man, and you will serve me.* But if he didn't, if he couldn't, Marthen would replace him. He turned to two of his men. He had marked them as the two most crowlike; they were violent, almost mad. Gary had said that most of his men were peaceful, harmless drunks, but not these men. He would send them to the holding.

Last year in Aeritan he had ordered his outriders to burn down the smithy in every village on the border between Temia and Red Gold Bridge. Burn the smithies, kill all the smiths. This was no different.

Garson was watching him, the same easy smile on his face. "So," he said, dusting his hands as if he had concluded his task. "I'll leave you boys be. I figure you've got a lot of planning to do. You can have your man here"—he indicated Gary—"let me know when you're done, and then we can negotiate on the rest. I'm looking forward to a long and lucrative relationship, General."

After Garson had trudged back to the road, Marthen half expected Gary to protest, to tell him he couldn't use the weapons. Instead the man just looked around him as if he were sickened. He sat by himself, nursing the bottle of whiskey. Marthen felt a prick of irritation. If the man passed out, he would be no good to him. He went over and grabbed the bottle. Gary looked up at him in protest.

"No more. Not until you complete your task."

Self-disgust warred with self-preservation; he could see it in the way the man looked at the bottle. Marthen tasted contempt in his mouth. The man was useless, feeble. "Go," he ordered. "Before I make an example of you."

Gary stumbled to his feet, backing away, falling again. The men laughed, all except for Marthen's two crows. They had already begun to separate themselves from the rest and only watched with dark and distant eyes. Gary finally found his footing and fled. Marthen watched him go. The man would fail him soon. He wondered if he should have had him killed anyway. No, gunshots would bring down attention on his head, and he had no time for that.

He had no doubt Gary intended to go against him. Very well, then. He could use his weakness. Let Gary go to the police to warn them about the pending attack on the farm holding. It would divert their forces, so that when he went for Kate Mossland, there would be no help to be found. Marthen scanned the camp for the next likely man. "You," he ordered. "I have a commission for you."

Thirteen

Dawn broke over the high seat of Trieve, the mists shrouding the terraces so that from Crae's chamber it looked as if the house floated on a gray sea.

He shivered as he dressed, a chill seeping up from the floor. His hearth was cold, the smell of ashes mingling with the smell of leather and sweat-suffused clothes. He got into his warm trousers, his thick overshirt, and drew on his socks and boots.

Stavin's old room was thick with ghosts. Crae sat on the edge of the bed and thought how he had failed his friend. When Stavin begged him to care for his wife and child, he could not have imagined that Crae would kill his brother-in-law and exile his wife.

He went over to the desk and pulled out a sheet of thick, rough paper and a pen. The ink had dried in the inkwell, but he used the last of the water from the pitcher by his bedside, and it loosened sluggishly. He wrote with a careful hand and then waved the letter to let it dry. When it had dried, he took off his chain of lordship and tucked it inside, folding the letter around it. He scratched a match, lit a candle, and, when the wax dripped, carefully sealed the letter. He should have used the seal of Trieve to mark the wax, but it was no longer his by right.

Crae gathered up his pack with his few belongings, his gear, and, stuffed down at the bottom, Lynna's shirt and the little device. He took one last look at the chamber he had so briefly owned, and then shouldered out of the door.

The house was mostly empty, the householders having already fled ahead of the war that would come to their doorstep. He had brought the crows down upon them, and now the Council. Well, as his last act as Lord of Trieve he could protect the house the only way he knew how. Crae went into the kitchens. They were empty, too, the ovens cold. He scavenged for bread and dried meat, stowing them neatly into his pack. He found a jar of vesh herbs and poured them out onto a kitchen cloth, folding them up and putting that in, too. A noise caught his attention, and he looked up.

It was Alarin, his captain. The young man watched him without a word. He wore his leather armor and carried a sword, a far cry from the young farmer he had been. He was all soldier now. He had always been a strong man, well-muscled from hard work, with a strong neck and back. He was still raw, still not yet seasoned, but the battle against the crows had turned him into a fighting man.

Crae nodded to him and went back to his work.

"You are leaving, then," Alarin said, and it was a mark of how young he was that his voice shook the slightest bit.

"If I stay, the Council will come. You know that."

"So! We held off the crows! We have the defensive position. We can hold them off, too."

"Don't be a fool," Crae snapped. The Council would lead an army that would show up the crows for the rabble they were. There was silence. Crae finished tying up his pack and looked at the young man he had made captain on the battlefield. He held out the letter. Alarin made no move to take it, so Crae set it on the kitchen table.

"If you still serve me, you will carry that letter to Lady

Jessamy at Favor, and after she reads it, you will do as she tells you."

Alarin looked stubborn, swallowing, but he looked away, drew a long breath to steady himself, and then turned back. "I serve Trieve."

He served the House, not the man. It was the sign of a captain. Crae nodded. He tapped the letter. "Then know that by delivering this letter to Lady Jessamy, it will serve Trieve."

Alarin relented. He picked up the letter. Crae could tell that he marked the weight of it and the feel of the chain sliding inside the folded package. He looked at Crae, understanding in his expression. Crae went back to tightening the strings of his pack. After a moment, Alarin asked, "Where will you go?"

Finished, Crae swung the pack onto his shoulder. He filled the kitchens with the bulk of his gear.

"Away," he said.

Hero laid his ears back and tried to evade the bit as he always did, then gave in sulkily. Crae saddled him and led him out, the horse weighted down with his pack and bedroll. He pushed aside the big doors of the ancient barn and let in the cold light and early morning air. The fog had lifted, though down in the woods at the foot of the terraces, it still drifted through the forest. He didn't bother to get into the saddle but started walking down the terraces, Hero jumping like a mule for each level. They were both sweating lightly when they reached the bottom, and the crow king was waiting for them. He stood before Crae, all sinewy arms and legs, as skinny as the staff he carried. Now he rested on it and looked up at Crae with rheumy eyes. Crae sighed. He wasn't surprised. He tightened Hero's girth and stepped into the stirrup, swinging aboard. He waited, and the horse tossed his head, attempting to move out. "I knew I would find you lurking around here, old man. What do you want?" He did not need to be pestered. Of course, the crow had other ideas.

"Do you know the law of the crow?" the crow king asked.

Crae shook his head and clucked to Hero to move him out. "I have no time for riddles."

"What Aeritan gives, we crows must take. For we have no House, no land—only Aeritan, and Aeritan alone must sustain us."

It was the first time he had ever thought of the crows in those terms. To be sure they were Houseless, lordless, spurned by all. Were they the true inheritors of Aeritan? Impossible. They were lawless men, most of all, and far from belonging to Aeritan, they were its scourge. He thrust down the thought that he had become one of their company. "I'm going now," he said and pressed his heels against Hero's sides. The crow raised his voice.

"We crows are but harbingers, Lord Crae. Aeritan faces a great danger. It is time you brought it to its end."

That made him stop. Crae turned Hero on his haunches to face the crow. The man had not moved from his spot, still leaning on his staff. "I am a simple man, crow king. Make yourself clear."

"The lord of all crows is coming through Brythern, and he aims nothing more than the destruction of the Council, one by one. He will destroy the fragile truce that has sustained Aeritan for generations. Instead, chaos will take root, and in its wake the crows will reign."

Aeritan under the reign of crows would mean all of the Houses and the holdings under attack. Fear spiked along his spine. Crae said finally, "And if that were so, crow, why do you warn me? Is that not what all crows desire, to kill and ravage and burn? Hear the laughter of your god?"

The crow king looked at him for a long moment. He said, "No one chooses to become crow, Lord Crae. You of all men know that."

That stung. With effort he kept his emotions in check. The crow king gave him a curious little smile. "So now that you are crow, what is it you choose to do? Seek the laughter of the crow god, or seek to save your Aeritan?"

* * *

Lynn never reached the highway, as she had half feared. Instead, she, Red Bird, and the dog wound down off the ridge, entering the deep woods where the sun stabbed through in pale, narrow columns. Mosquitoes and deerflies buzzed incessantly. The air was dank. The twisting trail ran along a marshy area, skunk cabbage and hummocks lifting out of the mud. Red Bird left clear hoofprints along the trail, his footfalls squelching. His tail lashed constantly, whisking at Lynn's legs as he swept away the flies from his flanks, and he tossed his head. Lynn stopped, dismounted, and broke off a leafy branch that she twisted over his bridle. He looked ridiculous, but he tolerated the leaves as if he knew it helped protect his eyes against the flies.

She had to constantly wave the insects away, smacking at deerflies at the back of her neck. That and curses didn't help much. It was hot and muggy, and she and the horse both had dark patches of sweat. The dog panted but trotted along resiliently.

Lynn checked her watch. They had been traveling steadily for about an hour, alternating between a running walk and a trot, and she had let the horse blow when necessary. After all, this wasn't the Pony Express, though she supposed she had the right gear for it. *I don't even know if we're going the right way,* she thought. *I don't even know if we're in Aeritan. All I have to go on is the dog, and who knows what the dog is doing.* She sat back in the saddle and pulled Red Bird up, scanning all around her. The dog flopped down instantly, its tongue dripping.

She dismounted and took a swig from her water bottle, letting the cool water sit in her mouth before swallowing. Then she poured some into Red Bird's mouth, and let the dog lap it from her cupped fingers. Fastidiously she wiped the water bottle onto her shirt before capping it. She had another full water bottle, but they needed to conserve. *Don't know how long I'm going to be out here,* she thought. Last year the gordath had reached out and pulled her between the worlds, and she had walked for hours before she was found by Crae and brought to Red Gold Bridge. Who knew where this portal had deposited her?

She put the water bottle back into her pack and felt a tremor. No, more of a shiver, the ground sliding for a moment out from beneath her. Lynn caught herself. Red Bird threw up his head and shied sideways. The dog put her tail beneath her legs and crouched. Overhead the leaves rattled, then subsided.

"Well," she said out loud, trying for some kind of bravado. "Looks like this must be the place."

She didn't want to be mounted if a bigger earthquake hit, so she shook the reins over the horse's head and whistled for the dog. She patted the dog's head when it responded. "It's okay, pup. You're doing fine."

The tremors reignited her sense of urgency, though. If the gordath was waking up, that meant that Joe and Arrim were losing control. *Hang in there, Joe,* she thought. *I'm coming.*

They were deep in the woods. It smelled wet and rotting. The sky between the tall trees was white, late summer heat bleaching out the blue. The marsh dozed under the buzzing of insects. Out in the distance she could see dead trees, ghostly and stark against the sky. Farther out was a line of blue where the marsh turned to lake, and across from there was another line of hills.

From a distance, it looked beautiful, cool, and inviting. "I could go for a swim," she told the animals. Red Bird twitched an ear back at her, but the dog was having none of it. They trudged on, and now the trail bent toward the lake. For the first time, a cool breeze swept over them. Everyone perked up.

A quarter of an hour later they were on the banks of the lake on a small, shingled beach. A circle of blackened wood and stone showed where someone had already camped there. Lynn breathed a sigh of relief at the sign of life, no matter how stale. The dog went to nose at the water, standing in it up to her belly and lapping eagerly. Red Bird pulled forward, too, but Lynn took him firmly in hand. "Hold on there, sir," she said. She let him drink a little, then pulled his head up and walked him around. A horse that drank too much too fast could give himself colic, and colic could be fatal. She controlled his sips until he was sated, and then loosened his cinch and let him rest. She let herself empty the first water bottle while she looked around. Her gaze sharpened as she caught the sight of some footprints in the rough sand. Her heart sank. She began to walk cautiously around the little beach. *Dammit*, she thought. If she had thought first, she never would have walked Red Bird all over the damn place. She found more footprints where she had never trodden, and there it was, so clear it made her blood run cold: the unmistakable footprint with the narrow heel and spade-shaped sole of a cowboy boot.

Joe had been here.

Red Bird came up behind her to look, and she pushed back against his chest to keep him from fouling the footprint. The boot print and its mate, a more blurred version, pointed toward the woods, away from the lake and the trail. So Joe had gone that way. Sure enough, a trail led back into the woods, wider than the one they had followed. There were no more footprints that she could see, but more importantly, there were no hoofprints. They were on foot, and that meant she had an edge. Lynn cast a look at the sky. It was late afternoon, the sun shining across the lake, casting light and shadow across the water. A heron lifted off as she watched, a fish flapping in its beak. Let the horse and the dog rest, she thought, and she removed Red Bird's saddle so the horse could roll and scratch himself. After that, it would be Pony Express time after all.

Fifteen minutes later, after a granola bar shared with the dog, she was ready. Lynn saddled up, tightened the girth, and swung on board. She gathered the reins, and the horse alerted at once. Lynn glanced at the dog and whistled. The dog would have to follow at its own pace and catch up with her later. She pushed the horse up onto the bank, jumping over a tangle of tree roots and driftwood. It was wide here, and grassy. Red Bird burst into a trot and then a canter.

Good footing for traveling at speed. Lynn put Red Bird

into a hand gallop. His hoofbeats drumming into the soft grass, the horse leaped forward, ears pricked and tail thrashing. Lynn leaned forward in the big saddle, hands moving rhythmically, riding like a cowboy, sliding down along Red Bird's neck to avoid low branches. *Hang on, Joe,* she thought as Red Bird galloped hard along the trail. *Please hang on.*

"She's not here," Mrs. Felz said. The woman sat on the front porch, but instead of rocking leisurely, she sat very still. Her gardening gloves and trowel sat on the table next to her, and her worn hands were clasped very tightly in her lap over a thick envelope. She looked as if she were going to cry or had been crying. "I don't—I'm not sure where she went."

Kate didn't like to talk to Mrs. Felz. She didn't know what Joe's mom knew or didn't know, and she hated the idea that she might spill the beans.

"Did she say when she was coming back?"

Mrs. Felz shook her head, and Kate began to get worried. That didn't sound like Lynn at all.

"And she didn't say where she was going?" Kate looked at Colar. He shrugged. Kate looked around. "Wait. Her car's still here."

"She took the truck and horse trailer and that little old red horse that just showed up—oh, and the dog. A little stray dog. She said—she said the dog might have something to do with Joe."

"With Joe!" Kate exclaimed. "Mrs. Felz, you have to tell us. Where did she go? Did she say anything?"

"Did she say how long she might be?" Colar put in.

A truck and trailer rig rumbling up the drive caught their attention. *Oh my God, she's back,* Kate thought with a breath of relief. But it wasn't Lynn; it was Sue Devin, and she parked the trailer and marched up to the house.

"All right, I need to know what is going on," she snapped, her eyes bright and her short white hair standing on end as if she had been running her fingers through it. "What is Lynn Romano up to?"

* * *

They repaired into the kitchen. Mrs. Felz got everyone iced tea. The curtains lifted sluggishly in the fitful breeze, but the kitchen was cool and dark.

"She told me she might be gone a week or more, and if she was, I was to open this." Joe's mom held up the thick envelope. It was still sealed, as if she was determined to follow Lynn's instructions to the letter. "She said you would help me run the farm, Miz Devin, while she was away, if I needed."

"That girl," Sue said with exasperation. "She called me from the trailhead out at the nature preserve, asking me to pick up her rig. She knows there's no riding out on that trail. I have no earthly idea what she is up to."

"She provisioned herself for a long trip," Mrs. Felz said. "She didn't use one of those little bitty saddles y'all use, either. She put a stock saddle on that horse."

"That's ridiculous," Sue said. "What does she intend to do, play cowboys and Indians three hundred feet from a major highway?"

Kate and Colar exchanged glances, then ducked their gazes.

"How are you two involved with this?" Sue asked, turning her keen gaze on them.

"Us? We were just wondering where she went," Kate said as innocently as she could.

"Uh-huh," Sue said, dryly.

Mrs. Felz spoke up. "Lynn said that it was something to do with Joe. I don't know any more than you, but if she is going to bring my son back, then I think we should be doing all we can to help her, not stop her."

"Something to do with Joe?" Sue said. There was something else in her expression now, some connection that Kate didn't get. "Interesting." She turned to Mrs. Felz and covered her hand with hers. She gave it a squeeze. "I knew your son. He was a good man. He was unjustly accused, and I think he just wanted to disappear, after all that. But if after all this time Lynn Romano has known where he was and hasn't told any of us, well, I think when she does come back from her little game, she is going to have to be more forthcoming with all of us, but especially with you."

Mrs. Felz looked on the verge of tears again. Kate was relieved when they heard a knock on the door.

"I'll get it," she said. She went through to the dark living room and peered out the screen door at the strange man standing there.

"Can I help you?" she said dubiously. He didn't look like a client or a client's father. He smelled of booze, and his clothes were worn and stained . . . *He's a crow. He's one of Marthen's crows.* Kate stumbled back, on the verge of screaming, and started to slam the front door shut.

"No, wait!" he cried out, tearing at the flimsy screen door and pushing back at her. "No, I'm here to warn you! Lynn Romano! Where is Lynn Romano! She's in terrible danger!"

He said his name was Gary. Mrs. Felz took one look, or one smell more like, and immediately put on water for coffee. Gary spilled the details, his hands and his voice shaking.

"Listen, the restaurant guy, Mike Garson, has it in for Miss Romano, and he said he would give the general guns if he would take her out. I didn't think he'd do it. I thought he was just leading Marthen on. But he brought the guns today, and they're all armed now. Marthen's crazy, man. I know I helped him some, but I was trying to get him to stop. I didn't let him kill that kid, and I swear I wouldn't help him kidnap that girl, that Kate kid."

"That would be me," Kate said with a dry voice. Gary looked at her, and to her horror he started to cry.

"I didn't know what he was like," he said, his words hard to understand. "I didn't know. I—I couldn't stop helping him. He got inside my head and made me crazier and crazier." He covered his face with his hands. "I wanted to stop drinking, and he just made it worse."

Sue Devin put her hand on his shoulder, patting him a little. Kate was impressed with the way she didn't ask any questions, just faced all the weirdness confronting her with equanimity.

"Sir," Colar said. "What is his plan?"

Gary lifted his tear-streaked face.

"He's sending two of the worst guys over here to kill Miss Romano and anyone else who's here, and to torch the place after."

The horses. Kate could feel the blood drain from her face. The barns going up in flames, the horses screaming in their boxes . . . She looked over at Sue and Mrs. Felz and saw that both women had the same expression.

Scorched earth. It was his solution to everything. *I have burned lots of villages,* he once told her.

"Not this time," she muttered. They all looked at her, and she realized that she had spoken out loud.

Sue Devin got to her feet. "Well, I believe this is a credible threat, and I'm going to call the police. In the meantime, we need to start evacuating horses, just in case the police can't put a stop to it."

"That's not all," Gary said. His broken whisper had become stronger. They all turned to look at him. "He's going to use the attack here as cover for when he goes after you, kid."

It didn't shock or frighten her as much as she had feared. Now that the moment had come, Kate became suddenly clear-headed. She looked over at Colar.

"This is it," she told him. "It's time."

He nodded.

"What?" Mrs. Felz, Sue, and Gary all said at roughly the same time. Kate looked around at all of them, all these well-meaning adults who could not fathom, not even Gary, what they were in for.

"He's my problem, and I'm going to take care of him once and for all."

Sue put the word out that there was a gas leak at Hunter's Chase, and all the area farms sent over their vans and horse trailers to evacuate the horses. Fancy Pendleton sent their head groom and stable girls to help, along with their biggest van. Howard Fleming also sent word that Hunter's Chase was welcome to any help he could offer. Kate and Colar got to work loading horses and notifying clients. Quite a few came out to help. Kate didn't know how many people would move their horses permanently when this new crisis was over, but the first priority was the safety of their charges. That's what Lynn would do. Horses first, business later.

Sue also put Gary on to talk to the police, and soon there were fire engines and patrol cars parked all around the farm. Helicopters rattled overhead. Spare, gray Lieutenant Spencer came and talked with Gary for a long time, the homeless man telling him where the camp was. The police sent out another response team to find the camp in the woods that they had been looking for all this time.

Under cover of the chaos, Kate and Colar plotted.

"Do you think they'll still try it, after all this?" she said in a low voice, after leading a pretty little Arab up the ramp of a High Hollow van and tying her with a safety knot. Colar faced her over the back of the horse—they had a bit of quiet to themselves for a moment. "Or will he call it off?"

"It might be out of his hands," he said, his face strained. "Once he sets the crows in motion, they may just come on of their own."

She nodded. She had seen the crows at work in the camp and then in battle. They were fearsome and fearless. The police would stop them—eventually. And if the police underestimated them, as they likely would, it could take too long. *And let's say the police take Marthen into custody,* she thought. She knew from her mom's cases that there would be little they could book him on. Attempted kidnapping? It was the word of a drunk accomplice against his. He had threatened to kill Austin, but he hadn't committed murder. They'd keep him for a while, maybe even a few years, but he would get out eventually.

And when he did, he would come after her again and

again. The only way she would ever be safe was if Marthen went back to Aeritan. No, scratch that; even the gordath couldn't stop him. The only way she would ever be safe was if he were dead.

Last winter, in a snowy clearing a few miles from where they were standing right now and a whole world away, she had picked up a rifle and held Marthen in her sights. She could have killed him then. By the laws of Aeritan, she had every right, not to mention every bit of sympathy. But she lived by the laws of her world. *And look where it got me,* she thought, stroking the mane of the pretty little horse.

Colar reached over and caught her hand. His fingers were strong and rough. She laced her fingers with his.

"I meant what I said," he said, his voice low. "I want you to marry me. Come to Aeritan. My father will give us his permission. You'll be my lady when I am lord of Terrick."

We're too young! she wanted to say. *We can't get married.* She swallowed against the lump in her throat, because the most important thing wasn't getting married, it was what she had to tell him, what she had been trying to tell him in the woods off Daw Road.

"So here's the thing," she said, fighting tears. "You know I'm supposed to go to Harvard, right?" Colar looked at her, but his expression was quizzical. She laughed a little. He couldn't help but know; her parents made sure the pressure was on all the time. "Yeah, well, I won't get in." There were too many hardworking girls with great GPAs and all the right bullet points on their résumés to compete with. She knew from Mojo that all the heart in the world only gets you so far. She looked down at their interlaced hands. "So it's tempting to go with you, because I know they'll be disappointed that I don't get in. But I can't use marriage to you as a—safety. I don't know what's going to happen to us, but I can't go with you. I want to become a doctor, and it's going to mean a lot of hard work." She blinked back tears. "I don't think that I can do that and be your lady."

He was quiet for a long time. The horse remained perfectly

still between them, her ears slack and her eyes drooping. The air in the van was thick with the scent of horses and manure.

"I think you could do anything and be a Lady," he said finally, and she could almost hear the capital letter. "I just don't want to lose you." He ducked under the mare's neck and came around to Kate's side, taking her in his arms in the narrow space. He kissed her, and she shivered, lost in the kiss.

"I don't want to lose you either," she whispered. "You have to stay. Colar, please." She tried to laugh. "You could go to Harvard for me."

He kissed her again. "If I stayed, it would be Annapolis."

She drew back, knowing surprise was written all over her face. When did he learn about Annapolis? He kind of shrugged. "Remember when you had to tell all the lords about how war is waged here?"

Boy, did she. It had been the end of a long ride as the army trundled off to meet Lord Tharp's men, not knowing what they were facing. Lieutenant Grayne had bundled Kate off to General Marthen's tent, and all the officers were there. Then they had been so big and frightening with their strange accents and clothing. She was too scared to distinguish between them then, but she eventually learned to recognize Colar's father, the gruff Lord Terrick; the almost grandfatherly Lord Shay, who loved to talk to her and Talios about his ailments, both real and imagined; and creepy Lord Favor with his avid eyes. That night, though, she told them what she knew about arms, warfare, tanks, jets and bombers, and—*aircraft carriers*. She looked at Colar, the question in her eyes. He grinned a little.

"My father told me later what you said. Floating cities that launched flying machines? It was like something out of a kitchen tale. Then at school Mrs. Patterson talked to us about colleges, and I asked her where I could learn to fly. She gave me a lot of brochures, and one was for Annapolis. And so I thought, wouldn't that be something, the son of the lord of Terrick flying jets?"

In the silence, "Kung Fu Fighting" blared out in the little

space. The mare tossed her head and whinnied, and Kate scrabbled frantically for her phone, prying it open. The sound cut off. Heart hammering, she snapped into the phone, "Mom! We're at *the stables*! What more do you want?"

The general's deep voice filled her ear. "It's time for you to come home, Kate Mossland."

Fourteen

The summer grasses were gray and gold, their tassels sweeping over Crae's stirrups and stroking Hero's flanks while they cantered, trotted, walked, and cantered again in a rhythmic, steady pace as they headed northeast. He had left the crow behind in the first hours, the man striding along as if he were a pilgrim on his way to a holy place, with a far different purpose than Crae's urgent one. Crae didn't need his cryptic guidance anymore anyway; once he had been set on his path, it unfurled before him, though he didn't know if he was hurtling himself toward the crow's prophecy or fleeing from it.

It sent a cold spike of fear down his spine. The trouble he had brought down on Trieve was nothing as compared to the grief Aeritan would suffer if the crow's prediction came true. If the Council fell, and the crows rampaged across the land, the stones themselves would weep for Aeritan.

It wasn't as if the Council were peaceful in and of themselves. As Jessamy had teased him, he had joined an unruly family. But the shifting alliances and small wars were enough to keep Aeritan from breaking up and feeding upon itself.

There was Brythern, too, ever itching on Aeritan's north-eastern border, its ambitions toward its squabbling neighbor always couched in diplomatic terms, and always clear. And no one really knew what happened to all those guns in last year's war. Crae knew the Brythern lord Hare had his heart set on those weapons; he even took Bahard off with him. If Brythern got the weapons or could forge them, based on what Bahard had with him, then all of Aeritan would need to come together to face this new enemy.

It was the only sense he could make of the old crow's prophecy, and his heart sank. He was one man, he needed to stop either a mad crow or an invading army, and if he turned aside to Red Gold Bridge to plead for help, he might not be believed. Now here he was, riding right into the strange country. If Hare came across him, he would not be pleased.

Amused perhaps, but not pleased.

Night fell, and Crae camped under the hazy sky, the stars few between the clouds. There was no moon. After lighting a small fire to heat up vesh and making himself a meal of flatbread and dried meat, he doused the flames and rolled himself up, making sure his crossbow and sword were near to hand. Hero munched on grain, and Crae fell asleep to the comforting sounds.

He woke at gray dawn. The wind had risen, and the mist promised by the night clouds fell over him. Everything was slick and cold and damp. Hero nudged him in his bedroll and whickered low, demanding breakfast. Crae sat up, and there in front of him sat the old crow, watching him steadily from across the blackened fire circle. He sat on his haunches, his legs crossed, as if he had been there for hours, which, Crae suspected, he had been. Crae grunted and got to his feet, rolling up his wet blankets. He grained Hero and had the fire going before he said anything to the crow.

"Vesh?" he offered.

"You break bread with me?" the man said, his voice raspy and thick. The chill and wet had affected him as well. He might have been able to move fast enough overland to catch up to a man on horseback on no sleep, but he was affected by the damp the same as anyone. Crae was inexplicably heartened. He was mortal, not the fearsome creature of kitchen tales. Well, he was that, too; Crae would do well not to fool himself.

"Why not?" he said. "You don't even have to tell me your name."

The man snorted. "Don't you know we crows have no names? Soon you will forget yours, you know."

Crae ignored the needling. He waited till the water in his small kettle boiled, threw in the ground herbs, and let it steep before turning to look at the man. "Lordless, landless, nameless. You travel light, to be sure."

"We give it all to our god," the crow said, his voice short. "And he carries us."

"If you ask me, he uses you ill for the privilege."

"No one asked you." The crow sounded irritable now, and Crae looked at him. He snorted with laughter. First a cold and now a temper. Fearsome kitchen tales notwithstanding, the crow sounded more and more human by the minute.

"We'll make a man of you yet, crow," he said, cheerful now that he had gotten under his companion's skin. The man just scowled at him, his eyes narrowed.

The aroma of the steeping vesh rose above them, rich and tantalizing. Vesh smelled better than it tasted, but out in the cold and after a hard day's ride and a night of sleeping on the damp ground, it tasted just fine to Crae. He poured the first cup of vesh for the old crow. The man sipped judiciously and nodded.

There was only one cup. Crae waited for his turn, making another meal of traveling bread and meat and breaking camp. The crow handed over the cup, Crae poured himself some now very strong vesh, and sipped down to the dregs.

He kicked over the fire, doused it thoroughly, and saddled up. With one foot in the stirrup, he looked back at the crow, one eyebrow raised. "See you tomorrow morning?" he asked.

"I can give no assurances, Lord Crow."

Crae made a pained face at his designation. He swung into the saddle and gathered the reins, pointing the horse north and east. He left the crow behind without a farewell between them, but he had the thought that if the old man wasn't at his campfire tomorrow morning, he might just miss him.

The sun was high when Crae stood at the lonely crossroads of northern Trieve. Brythern lay north, Red Gold Bridge to his west. The mountain range that flanked the stronghold's lands rose blue in the distance. He stood at the entrance to the Ring Road, the last of the great roads built in the days of the high king, and its cracked and broken surface stretched straighter than any trail. The road was flanked by two straight lines of trees, their branches stretching overhead and shutting out the sun. Dappled shadows played across the broken road as far as he could see, and the air was cool and pleasant.

He and Lynn had come this way last winter when they were taken hostage by Hare and led back to Red Gold Bridge. The gordath had reached this far, sending tremors that had toppled them like so many chess pieces on a board. Now the land was peaceful, if empty, the remnant of a last great kingdom stretching before him to his west, and a rougher, less-traveled trail heading north. He hesitated because he had a decision to make.

Go north and face the menace from Brythern alone. Or, turn west and beseech Lord Tharp's help, and convince the man who held him in disregard that danger came from Brythern and to call out the Council. Even if Tharp hadn't heard yet of Crae's brother's murder, he had little chance of success. *The first I tell him that a crow told me, he will likely have me clapped into his prison cells. Again.*

He almost wished the crow were here to help him make a decision, but he doubted the man would make it so easy on him.

Crae dismounted, hoping to find an answer. He stretched his back, loosened Hero's girth, and the horse heaved a sigh of release. As a reward the animal rubbed his head against Crae's side, trying to scratch an itch under his pesky bridle. Crae tolerated it while he thought.

Once as a young man, before he sought a position as a man-at-arms to one of the Houses of Aeritan, Crae had gone to Brythern. It was an adventure. He landed in the great city of Cai-sone along the banks of the Aeritan River, with its pile of old stone houses climbing on top of one another. Not even Red Gold Bridge was so big, and that stronghold was built out of the side of a mountain. Cai-sone had streets that were broad enough for two wagons to rumble along abreast, even rigs drawn by four or six horses. Its streets were made of flat stones, not the rough cobblestones of most of the villages he had been in, and there were covered gutters alongside the street. People bustled along to market, on errands, the merchant houses and shops with their gaudy signs thick with energetic crowds. There were taverns on every corner, and men and women of learning with great books and curious instruments at almost every table, talking animatedly with their hands.

Besides Brytherners the city was filled with foreigners from down the river and across the sea, some with faces browned by the sun, others as pale as if they were warmed only by the moon. The markets were roiled with a cacaphony of tongues as people haggled over goods from all over the world. Sometimes he saw something that was undeniably Aeritan, such as linens from Favor or mined ores from the mountains of Temia, and he felt a pang of homesickness, but mostly the markets were full of marvels he had never seen and could not afford to buy. Crae had stayed in a cheap inn, found romance with a barmaid, had his pocket picked, and drank and brawled, and when he shipped back upriver with an aching head and an empty wallet, he was full of wonder at what he had seen.

He had never gone back. He had taken his position at Red Gold Bridge shortly thereafter, and he no longer had the leisure for wandering.

Until now. For the first time he recognized that as a crow,
he was free. He had no duties. He could ride south or east,
or anywhere but north, away from the crow, his cryptic
words, and his maddening purpose. He could disappear into
exile, could even ship out and go downriver and out to sea to
the countries of the pale people or to the lands where the
people were darkened by the sun. He didn't have to follow
the crow and his prophecy and try to save his country from
a distant menace. He could just . . . go.

And watch Aeritan burn from a distance and know that he
had abandoned his promise to keep Trieve safe.

"Damn you, old man," Crae said out loud. He tightened
Hero's girth and swung back into the saddle. He turned the
horse's head west, toward the Ring Road that led to Red Gold
Bridge. Maybe he was a crow, and maybe he wasn't, but he
was a captain at heart, and a captain did his duty. He'd make
Tharp listen to him.

With a careful nudge from his mind, Joe
reached out and touched the gordath, closing it with a firm
touch. It almost zippered up at his direction. The forest
grew still and calm, and only the faintest rumbling shook the
ground.

What do you know—the gordath responded to a gentle
touch, after all. He glanced over at Arrim, and together they
lowered their hands and their guard. He let his mind reach
out. He felt the presence of the gordath, but it remained still, a
rattle of leaves the only sign that it had ever been open.

They had been practicing for the better part of three days.
They had the devil's own time closing the thing down at first.
After all the abuse it had taken—and they had taken, Joe
thought—the gordath resisted their efforts, but it finally sealed
itself. And then he and Arrim conferred, and Hare, Ballard,
and the rest of the men let them be.

They finally got it that they need us, Joe thought. At least
they weren't being stomped on regularly, though Arrim still
looked pretty bad.

Joe wiped his forehead of sweat and sat back on a nearby fallen log for a rest. The forest mostly stayed cool and green, but controlling the gordath was hard, even though it was all mind work. He squirted himself some lukewarm water, wincing at the taste of it from the leather skin, and passed the rest to Arrim.

The other guardian reached out for it, but his hand shook, and he fumbled at the neck. Joe looked him over with concern. He needed a good long bed rest and food.

"Hey, hang in there," he told him under his breath. Arrim made a sound like assent. Joe held up the waterskin for him and he finally drank, coughing a little.

"I don't know if I can keep doing this," Arrim muttered.

"You're doing fine," Joe said, but he frowned. *Had* he been doing most of the work? It was hard to tell. He had assumed that this gordath had been harder to work than the one in Aeritan, just—well, just because. But maybe he was sweating it out because Arrim wasn't pulling his weight.

Not that he could blame him, but it made him uneasy. If push came to shove and they had to close the gordath down fast, he didn't think he could do it by himself. If Arrim couldn't help, they could be back in the same trouble as before.

"So, it goes well," said Hare, coming over to them. He stood before them, his hands playing with the long knife, flipping it from point to pommel.

Joe snorted. "Subtle as always, Hare," he said. He nodded at the knife.

Hare stared at him levelly, but he sheathed the knife.

"Yeah," Joe said. "I think we might have it under control. Don't know how long we can keep it that way, but at least it's not trying to kill us anymore. Maybe."

At the last word he could see Hare react the smallest bit. The men listening to the conversation exchanged glances. It was mostly for their benefit he had thrown that last word in. The more uneasy they were, the more control he might have over Hare. Hare wouldn't back down in front of his captives, but he might listen to his men's protests.

From the back Mark made a rude noise. "You keep acting like it can think," he said. "It's just a—a *thing*. Hell, *I* had it under control last year."

Joe looked from Hare to him. He shrugged. "Feel free to give it a try," he offered.

"Fuck you, dumb ass," Mark said.

"Quiet," Hare said. He started worrying with the knife again, and then actually remembered and put it away in the small sheath on his belt. "Can it think?" he said for Joe's ears alone.

We're in this together now, and he knows it, Joe thought. He shoved away the feeling of triumph. If Hare knew what he was thinking, he doubted the man would appreciate the fellowship. "It might have only one driving impulse," he said. "It wants to be open."

"It wants to consume," Arrim said. He looked out over the forest, toward the now-empty air where the gordath had centered.

He said it loud enough for the men to hear. Joe saw a few of them make a sign—unfamiliar, but he knew what the signal meant. Every culture had a sign against evil. At Arrim's words he felt the sweat chill down his back.

"All things seek to consume," Hare said thoughtfully. "And pass on their seed. This gordath—can it reproduce?"

Joe was thunderstruck at what he was asking. Could a gordath make baby gordaths? God, he hoped not. His life was too complicated already. Maybe it was only half-sentient. It only wanted to eat a hole in between the worlds. He looked at Arrim, but the man gave a grimace and shook his head.

"Guess not," Joe said.

"Small mercy," Hare said, and Joe couldn't help it—he grinned. Then his grin faded as he got back to the original point.

"So, looks like what you want is to feed it. Give it just enough to keep it satisfied and controlled, not enough to set it loose."

"You are a most astute ally, Guardian."

Maybe. But how the hell they were going to be able to pull that off was more than Joe could come up with. He just nodded sagely at Hare. "Yeah, exactly. It'll be tricky, though."

Hare nodded. "Rest and food. You can try again later."

He was almost solicitous as he let them be. Joe took another swallow from the waterskin as the men set up the night camp, and he watched the activity around them. Even Mark pitched in, though he was sullen about it.

Well, he thought. *I have Hare right where he wants me. Now what?*

Kate closed the phone, all the color draining from her face. Her lips felt stiff. "Marthen's at the house. He has my parents."

They ducked out of the horse trailer and looked around. The farm hummed with activity, as vans pulled away with their precious cargo. It looked like the end of a horse show, she thought dazedly, with all the vans leaving.

More patrol cars had arrived, and more SWAT guys, too. At least they took the threat seriously. But the driveway was blocked. How were they going to get the Jeep out without calling attention to themselves? She moved purposefully toward the Jeep. She would ram through them if she had to.

Colar grabbed her. "Wait. Think. He wants you to go straight home and walk into his trap. You have to tell the police."

She could barely speak. "If he sees the police, he'll kill them." She knew he would because it would punish her, and if he couldn't have her, then he would settle for her pain. Sickness came up in her throat, and she wished she could unknow the knowledge of his madness. She felt complicit, guilty. She hated him, and she knew more about him than anyone else right now.

Use what you know, then.

She thought for a minute, then opened her phone and redialed home.

"What are you doing?!" Alarm made Colar's voice rise.

"He's not the only one who's crazy," she said, and she didn't even recognize her own voice.

The phone picked up, but there was no salutation. *Of course. What is he going to say? Hello?*

"You're nothing but a bully," she told him. Still silence. She snapped. "Talk to me. Or are you frightened?"

"I am holding a gun to your father's head. If you are not here soon, I will be forced to shoot him. And then your mother. And don't bother to tell your police, because by then it will be too late. They're much too far away to help."

Soldier's god. She stopped dead still. When she was able to speak again, it was with eerie, self-contained calm.

"Let me talk to them."

There was silence. Then her dad came on the phone. "Kate?" His voice was breathless, as if he had been running.

"Daddy—"

"Call the police, Kate! Call—"

The phone went dead.

Think, Kate, think. Had she just put her parents in even graver peril, or had she bought them time? It would serve him no purpose to kill them now. Only if he was under direct threat would he murder his hostages. *He didn't murder Austin,* she thought hopefully.

Of course, that was because Gary stopped him, and Gary was talking to the police fifty feet away from her. She took a deep breath and punched in the number again, her hands shaking. *Soldier god, please let me be right. Please. Help me protect my parents.* She didn't know if the soldier's god would or could help her in such a peaceful prayer, but he was the only god she had any familiarity with. They had been on speaking terms once, and she thought that maybe he would remember and come all this way and help.

This time when the phone was answered, she didn't wait for him to speak. "Marthen. I give in. I'm on my way." She closed the phone before she found herself begging him not to harm her parents, and willed herself not to cry. Without looking at Colar, she said, "All your gear is still in the Jeep?"

"Kate, you can't go face him alone."

"I have to. I have to. If he sees you or anyone else, he'll kill them in front of me." Her voice hardened. "I'll make sure I separate him from Mom and Dad. I'll let him take me to the new gordath. That's where you'll meet us. We need to keep three horses back. Allegra and, um, Cinnamon and Hotshot." They were two of the school horses: sturdy, quiet beasts who would bear up to a long ride. Allegra was more delicate, but she was Kate's, or practically so. Anyway, Lynn would understand. She was on the same mission. "You'll need to get the gear and the horses to the new gordath and wait for us there. I'm going home, and I'll bring Marthen there."

"There's a problem. I don't know how to get there," Colar said.

"That's okay. Gary does."

They both turned to look at the homeless man. He stood with the police, talking seriously with them. Somehow, the crying, desperate man had disappeared. He stood a little taller in his worn and dirty clothes, his back straight.

"Can he ride?" Colar said skeptically.

"Probably not, but you can put him up on Cinnamon on the way, and you can lead Allegra. Or Hotshot," she added hastily. Colar was a good rider. She could trust him with Allegra as she had trusted him with Mojo.

He grinned at her. He kissed her quickly and said, "I'll take care of your horse."

She shivered at the kiss and blushed. "I know." Determinedly she turned back to her task. She had to go rescue her parents and face down Marthen. "All right. Call me if you run into any trouble, and I'll call you."

"I don't like you facing him alone."

"Me, either," she said, wrinkling her nose. "But I don't want to push him too far. If he saw you, he could—he could—" She couldn't finish the thought. *Kill my parents. Kill you.* "Wait till we get to the gordath. We'll take care of him then."

She didn't say how, and he just nodded. He didn't look like a kid anymore.

They kept one eye on the cops as Colar got his gear and her backpack out of the Jeep, trying to keep the sword out of sight. He hustled the bags off into the lower barn, where the school horses were waiting their turn to be loaded onto the vans. Kate watched him go, then got behind the wheel and started the Jeep, bumping up the driveway and over the grass behind the hill barn. She turned out onto the road, accelerating away from the farm. All she had to do was go home, rescue her parents, and bring Marthen back through the gordath. Piece of cake.

Her house appeared silent and undisturbed from the outside, except that the garage door was open. Both her parents' cars were parked inside. She parked the Jeep in the driveway and steeled herself, walking up to the front door. It felt strange to have to knock on her own front door, but she wanted to alert him to her presence, let him feel he was still in control.

Well, he was, she admitted to herself. But he was expecting the quiet little mouse he had captured last year, and she would give him that, right up until the time she roared.

The door opened, and she was yanked inside. Kate stumbled forward, putting out her hands as she was shoved roughly to the floor, her face mashed down on the smooth parquet hardwood.

"Got her," a strange voice called out. So he had brought his crows. She thought about what Gary had told them. With the attack on Hunter's Chase foiled, he brought his worst men with him. Her stomach roiled at the thought of her parents having to face crows.

"Don't hurt her. Bring her in here."

That voice she knew. It had terrified her to her bones last year with its quiet menace, its softness hiding violence to come. The crow pulled her to her feet and pushed her forward into the kitchen.

Her parents sat at the table, her mom white-faced, with tears welling in her eyes. Her dad was curiously ashen and unwell. He had just been put on heart medication, and Kate felt a squeezing of her own heart. *Please hang on, Daddy. Please.* She hurried over to them, pretending to ignore the two crows and Marthen, and knelt and hugged them both.

"You shouldn't have come. You shouldn't have come," her mom said, her voice breaking. And her dad, low-voiced, "Did you call the police? Where are the police?"

"Shh, shh, it's going to be okay," she said, reaching around and patting them both awkwardly, trying to think. Two crows, both armed with rifles. Marthen, armed as well with a rifle of his own and a handgun tucked into his belt. She waited for a second, gathering herself before she had to face him. Finally, she stood and turned to him.

The meticulous man she had known last winter had transformed into a homeless drunk. His hair was long and tangled. He had not shaved. He stank. His clothes were no longer the fine clothes she remembered, pressed and brushed by his orderly. His boots were covered with mud. Only his eyes were the same, burning dark, almost black. Her back itched, and she clenched her fingers into fists, letting her fingernails bite into her palms. He had not wielded the whip that had been used on her, but he had ordered it.

"General," she said curtly.

"Kate Mossland," he said, and he gave her a courteous bow. She heard her mom gasp.

"So you have me," she said. "Now you can let them go."

"No."

Both her parents started protesting. Before Marthen could order the crows to silence them Kate raised her voice. "Mom, Dad, stop."

"Kate—" her father began.

"Dad, he's really dangerous. You have to stop."

Her mom put her hand on her husband's arm, and he subsided, but grudgingly. Kate turned back to Marthen.

"Again, let them go."

"Again, no. They are your safe-conduct."

"I'm not leaving them here with your crows." Despite her

attempt at calm, she could feel her mouth twist in disgust. "Let them go, call off your crows, and I'll go with you willingly."

"Kate!" her mother screamed. Kate held up her hand, and her mother began to sob. The crow who had knocked her down in the foyer advanced on her mother, and in one swift movement, Kate moved in front of her to block him, hands up to ward him off.

"Back off," she said, eyes and voice blazing. She didn't know where it came from, this sudden strength, but she reveled in it, and she let the crow see it. To her astonishment, he stopped, lowering his hand, and she could see uncertainty in his expression. She turned on Marthen. "Call them off."

His expression was soft, approving, and she felt sick to her stomach again. *Ewww. Ewww. Gross.* He nodded at the crows, and they stepped back by the fridge, but they kept their weapons trained on the little crowd.

"You have fire in you," he said. "I always knew you were strong. I think you have something of a warrior in you. Yes, we will do well together. The Aeritan Council will agree to our alliance, or will be made to agree, and then we will see. We will see."

With an effort, Kate kept from puking. Instead she said, her voice only shaking the least bit, "I propose this. We drive to the gordath, all of us. I go through with you and the crows. My parents stay here. I'll see if you or your men shoot them, and if that happens, not only won't I marry you, I'll kill you myself."

The only sound in the kitchen was her mom's crying and her dad's shallow breaths. The crows stood silently. Marthen considered her proposal.

"Where's young Terrick?" he said.

"Helping at the stables," she said.

He didn't believe her. She could see that. She kept her silence, challenging him.

"If he shows up at the gordath, I'll shoot them all myself."

She let herself shrug. "I have the car, and he doesn't even know where it is."

Again he considered, and again she kept her attention focused on him. Finally, he nodded.

"Done," he said. "But if there is any treachery, any trickery, if I see Terrick or the police, or anyone else, your parents will not live."

Kate just said, "We need to wait until nightfall."

Twilight came down over the peaceful barns at Hunter's Chase. The vans had all gone, and the stalls were empty, their doors swinging wide and the comfortable wood shavings bedding waiting for their occupants. Only three horses remained in the farthest stalls in the school barn. Allegra had been indignant at her move to rustic quarters, but Colar forked down a few flakes of hay, and that had mollified her. He tacked up the other two horses and left them in their stalls with their halters on, but he knew that it would drive the sensitive mare crazy to be treated that way. He'd tack her up last, when it was time to go.

The police kept a few squad cars at the farm and a fire engine, but Colar could tell that they thought the whole thing was a bust, and their interest in Gary had changed into disgust. Although he had told them the truth about the crow camp, by the time they found the place, it was empty except for a few tents, a few firepits, and a broken crate that had once held guns. Marthen must have already sent them on to the gordath.

Kate had not called, and he didn't dare call her, lest he ruin whatever she had going on. He hated letting her go alone, but he knew that Marthen would not hurt her, or at least not yet. The idea of the general touching her sickened him. *Had* she been his paramour in camp? Everyone thought so, but now he wasn't so sure. Kate would have been worse off if it had been so.

He started to notice a few stars in the twilit sky. Time to go. He gathered up his gear and Kate's backpack and lashed both packs onto Cinnamon's saddle. The chestnut gelding nudged him peacefully. He was a broad-backed horse and would do for a packhorse, though the small English saddles were not the best for the job. Colar balanced the load as securely as he could and bridled the horse.

He heard a noise. It was Gary, ducking into the barn. "We better go," the man said. "The police are talking about bringing me in for more questioning." He looked nervously at the horses. "Which one am I riding?"

Colar brought out Hotshot, another chestnut who had once been a police horse and could be relied upon to stay calm under stressful conditions. He could be stubborn, but he would follow the others, because that's what horses do.

"Here," he said, lowering the stirrups to the end of the leathers. He held the rein and helped Gary into the saddle. The man was awkward and leaned forward, grabbing the reins and the horse's mane in a big tangle. "You won't have to guide him," Colar said. "He should just follow."

He left Allegra for last. There was no way the light-boned, temperamental mare would go easily. He spoke softly to her, and though she laid her ears back, she let him saddle and bridle her. She got nervous around the other two horses, and it took a few minutes to sort them all out, Colar on Allegra, leading Cinnamon, Hotshot bringing up the rear so as not to be left behind.

They clopped softly out of the back of the barn, their stirrups scraping the sides of the narrow door, toward the trails. The little train wound up toward the roads.

"Can you get us there from here?" Colar said. Gary nodded, clutching the reins and looking around to catch his bearings.

"I think so. You want to stay off the roads, right?"

"As much as possible." To emphasize that, headlights showed up ahead as a car came around the bend. They waited for the car to pass. It never slowed down, the driver never catching sight of three horses and two riders on the side of the darkening road.

"All right then. Let's try this way."

They rode like ghosts in the night. Gary led them overland, from horse farm to horse farm, cutting cross-country and

and thrown into prison. With difficulty he kept his sword hand off the hilt of his sword.

The guardsman disappeared, though the two with crossbows held their position. Crae waited as men and women eyed him curiously as they passed by. The air was cool, the bridge mostly in shadow from the tall trees pressing in. It felt good after his long ride. Hero remained collected underneath him, neck arched against the light pressure on the reins. He didn't want to flee, but in case the two guards had been given orders to shoot, he wanted to have some chance to live to fight again.

Nor did he wish to have yet another good mount shot out from under him.

When the guard came back it was through the main gate, and he had Tal with him. The young captain's face lit up and he hastened over to Crae.

"Captain! My Lord, that is!"

They shook hands, and Crae said, "You've got the place well in hand, I see."

Tal beamed. "I made a few changes—but you have urgent business, you say. I sent word to Lord Tharp and Lady Sarita, and I wanted to bring you in myself. Here, dismount, and we'll have someone take care of your horse."

Crae did, with relief intermixed with wariness. "What news have you heard?" he said bluntly, shaking the reins over the horse's head and leading him through the gate. It would be best to know exactly where he stood before he stepped into a den of trouble.

Tal shrugged. "We have enough trouble of our own to be getting news from the rest of Aeritan."

The wariness increased, now with alarm. "What is happening, Tal?"

The young man, barely older than Alarin now that he noticed, looked at him frankly, his expression hard. "I'll let Lord Tharp tell you, lord to lord. It may be that your urgent matters mesh with his."

More likely, it only meant that with his own troubles, Tharp would be less likely to help him. In the courtyard, Tal had a boy take Crae's horse. Crae stopped the boy from leading him to the stables.

"Rub him down here, and grain and water him lightly," he told the youngster. "Have him waiting for me after I speak with Lord Tharp." He saw the way the boy checked in with Tal first, and the captain nodded his head slightly. Crae followed Tal to Lord Tharp's Council chamber.

Tharp had aged. The man had more gray in his hair and beard than brown, and he had gotten thick in the middle. His mouth drew downward disapprovingly at Crae's approach, but then, Crae had never known the man to be anything but disapproving. Next to him waited Lady Sarita.

Her exile had agreed with her. She had hardly aged. Her dark hair, uncovered, gleamed in the dim light coming from the window overlooking the woods, and her face still held the same youthful beauty, though she was no longer young. She was dressed in outlandish clothes, even more strange than Lynna's garb when he'd first seen her. They showed off her figure in a way that no Aeritan woman would ever be seen. *No wonder Tharp seethes,* he thought.

A strongholder came in with vesh, and they waited for the man to leave before setting to counsel.

"What brings you to Red Gold Bridge?" Tharp began abruptly.

"I have word of danger from Brythern. I've been told the lord of crows comes and intends to take on the Council, killing the lords and sowing chaos in his wake."

Tharp snorted. "You have been listening to kitchen tales."

"I wish that were true. But Trieve was beset by crows less than a half month ago, and I fear that this crow lord could bring upon Aeritan what my House faced." His breath caught. One lord was already down. Was his killing of Favor a portent of the war that would break out?

Tharp and Sarita exchanged glances. "So why Red Gold Bridge? Why not Kenery? Have you sent word to him?" Tharp said testily.

Lady Sarita gave a displeased snort. "Knowing Kenery, he is probably counting out all the alliances he intends to break before he makes them," she said.

Crae wondered if Lord Kenery knew that last year's games during Aeritan's war had put him in a position where no lord would ever trust him again.

Sarita wasn't finished. "And you ride alone, Lord Crae," she said. "A great danger comes, and yet you bring no men with you."

She would point that out. He looked from Tharp to Sarita. They were great lords, both of them, but Tharp had tried to take all Aeritan for himself, and Lady Sarita looked as if she had a foot still in her other world. And then there was Crae himself. A lord in name only, a brother murderer, led by a mad crow toward a destiny he didn't desire. They were in this together, like it or not.

"Well," he said. "That's quite a story." He proceeded to tell it.

To Crae's vast relief, they did not throw him into prison upon hearing of his kin murder.

"Lady Jessamy's daughter—did she recover?" Sarita asked, when he finished.

"She was on her way to recovery when they left for Favor."

She nodded as if that was all she required. Tharp cast a glance at his wife as if he could not understand her meaning but said only, "So the crow told you that this great danger was coming through Brythern, the lord of the crows himself. Why Brythern, do you know?"

Crae shook his head.

"You see, Lord Crae, we are having Brythern troubles of our own," Lady Sarita put in. "Just more than a month ago, smallholders told us they saw a troop of masked Brytherners moving through the Wood. Not long after, our guardians disappeared. Our guards—your old command—tracked them to the border of Brythern but lost the trail."

Crae's blood ran cold. If Brythern wanted guardians, it

could only be for one thing. They had a gordath to control. But what did a gordath and a crow lord have in common?

"I fear that Mark Ballard is up to his old tricks," Lady Sarita pressed on, and she pronounced the name the same way Lynna had. Her face went hard. "He is likely trading with the same merchant as you did, Eyvig. I knew him. On the surface he was nothing but an innkeeper, though well-respected." Her mouth became bitter. "Underneath he was very dangerous."

She didn't have to say more for Crae to know that she had faced this man and knew firsthand what he was like.

"So it's curious that your danger comes out of Brythern, too, as well as ours," she finished. She looked at her husband. "We will throw our lot in with yours."

"Sarita!"

"Eyvig, we're all outcast lords here. You because of the war you started last year, Crae now because of his stupidity. Yes, stupidity," she snapped at him, when he made to protest. "Lord Favor was nothing more than a bothersome gnat, certainly not worthy of death. I always thought Lady Jessamy should have been the one summoned, but there is no accounting for the high god's taste, or the Council's. No matter. You've been told there is this great danger coming through Brythern, and we know there is a gordath and now guardians to control it. I don't think it's far-fetched to combine the two and know that some evil is coming through the gordath itself. And believe me, we want to stop it as soon as we may, or this time Mike Garson and Mark Ballard may get their way."

Her words came to a close in the small room. Crae and Tharp looked at each other. Sarita regarded the both of them, her arms folded and one elegant eyebrow raised as she waited for them to make a decision. *No,* Crae thought, *she is waiting for us to give in.* He lifted his shoulders and gave her a crooked grin.

"You are as formidable as your mother, Lady Sarita."

She made a disparaging noise at the flattery, but he could tell she was pleased.

"Yes," said Tharp. He didn't look happy about it. "But we are one House, and while we could fend off one crow, we cannot hold off an army of Brytherners, no matter where they come from." He looked at Crae, disgruntled. "Since you didn't bring your men with you, I suppose you want ours."

"No," Crae said. "I will ride on ahead and scout out matters, and leave sign for your men to follow." He had to trust the crow and his cryptic words. They had led him so far. He looked at Lady Sarita. "Your husband may no longer be able to call on old alliances, and as for me—"

She nodded. "But my goodwill might not be completely in tatters. I will send word to my old friends and see what we can see."

"I'm sitting right here," Tharp said, with some irritability. Lady Sarita cocked her head and smiled at him sleekly.

"I know, Eyvig."

Crae pulled up Hero and looked down at the rough trail that led north and west. He had been following the sign for a day and a half, and it was clear enough. A company of men had come this way on foot, days earlier. Those were his Brytherners. He frowned. Tharp had said that his men had turned back after having lost the trail from Red Gold Bridge. He was no great hand at tracking, but he had found the trail easily enough. He clicked his tongue. Had Tal given up too easily? He would not have believed it of the man.

Or had the guard been drawn off at Tharp's bidding, perhaps? Tharp had never liked his guardians, for all that he had lordship over the one stronghold that faced Gordath Wood. He never liked Arrim because the man had a power that he could not understand or control. Arrim had crossed Tharp last year by trying to close the gordath against his orders. Now there were two guardians, one from the other side of the Wood. Crae had never met the man, not even during the aftermath of last year's war, but he knew the man had known Lady Sarita and had come back to Aeritan with her and Arrim.

And so it would stand to reason that Tharp disliked this

man also and might be jealous of him as well. So when they were taken, he might have thought good riddance and counseled Tal not to look too hard. That was until Crae came, and they learned they faced a greater danger.

Crae cursed under his breath. If that were the case, he lost all sympathy for the man. To be ruled so by jealousy . . . A thought struck him. If the new guardian knew Lady Sarita, had he also known Lynna?

When he found him, he would be sure to ask. He wasn't sure he wanted to hear the answer, though. He dismounted and grabbed the end of the Trieve banner he had been carrying and tore off another strip. He planted a small stake in the ground with the strip tied around it. He had been leaving the sign at intervals for the men Tharp had promised would follow. Now he trusted Lady Sarita more to come through on that account. Crae stood and swept his gaze over the trail one last time before remounting. His vision sharpened.

Oh ho, he thought, looking down at another set of hoofprints.

The Brytherners had another pursuer.

It was hard to tell how fresh were the hoofprints on the hard, dry terrain, but they held their shape and did not look too old or too crusted out. They overlay the trail he had been following. What game was Tharp playing at? Or was this a wild card in the game? Crae's curiosity was aroused. Whoever this man was, he was likely to be armed. Whether he was an ally or an enemy was less certain. Crae swung back into the saddle and pushed Hero after the horseman.

If the old crow were here, he would ask him, but even before Crae made his plea for help at Red Gold Bridge he had not shown up for his share of morning vesh. On the one hand, Crae was relieved to be free of his cryptic and sometimes annoying company. On the other, he missed the old creature.

He kept Hero to a walk, the better to watch for sign. The hoofprints became no fresher, but he came across two piles of dried horse manure and other scat. Crae pulled up alongside one pile and frowned, then identified it: dog shit.

A horseman and a dog, following a group of around a dozen men. The whole thing grew more curious. But he wasn't more than a half day ahead of Crae, if that. Crae made a decision and put Hero into a hand gallop. His horse snorted and bucked a little, then lit out, running strongly. The crow would just have to catch up as best he could, Crae thought.

Lynn topped a small rise at a walk, the trail leading down toward grasslands. They headed toward a narrow canyon as far as she could tell, and the trail undulated through the terrain, a pale scar etched out on the dry and grassy hills. She and the horse were covered with dust and sweat, and the dog flopped down as soon as they reached the top of the rise and halted. The setting sun was unrelenting, and she was grateful for her sunglasses. She lifted them and squinted, the better to catch sight of any sign of Joe and whoever he was with.

The land was empty except for herself and her beasts. Earlier they had passed a few homesteads, but they were tucked far off into the distance, and she hadn't stopped in, preferring to make good time. And she didn't trust Brytherners. Even though her encounter with Hare and his men last winter had been her only experience with them, she didn't want to find out that ordinary Brytherners were her enemy, too.

Something caught her eye, and she peered again toward the hills in the distance and the dark line of a canyon. A spark? It was hard to tell. Perhaps a bit of metal had caught some light. She looked hard, then remembered when she had closed her eyes and found the trail. *Well okay,* she thought. Lynn tried it again, closing her eyes and waiting.

Red Bird snorted and shied, and Lynn grabbed hard with her legs and for the saddle horn. Her eyes flew open, and she looked around wildly.

A man stood there, a skinny, scrawny man. A crow. Lynn grabbed for the saddlebag where she had stowed the gun, at the same time backing Red Bird away from the danger.

"Stand back!" she ordered, keeping her voice as firm as she

could, cursing herself for packing the gun so securely. Red
Bird snorted and half reared, stamping onto the ground. The
crow merely watched her, his cloak covering a body as skinny
as a rail. He carried a walking stick but not a maul or a spear.
"What do you want?" she said, her heart hammering.

He merely watched her. His eyes were dark, narrow slits
against the sun, and his skin was browned and scarred. Except for the tattered cloak he was naked. Finally, he nodded.
He pointed with his stick and she turned to follow his direction. Straight toward the canyon, where she thought she had
seen a flash of light.

She turned back, and he was gone. Lynn stared. "What—"
What the hell just happened?

Hoofbeats caught her attention, coming faintly over the
distance. She saw the tiny horseman in pursuit behind her. He
galloped up over one rise and disappeared as the trail dipped
down again.

Oh no. What do I do now? Brazen it out, confront the
rider, or make like a bat out of hell?

He was maybe twenty minutes behind her, at the most. She
didn't wait. She gathered the reins, clucked to Red Bird, moved
him into a gallop. Retreat first, ask questions later, she told
herself as Red Bird took off, the dog racing after them.

His quarry had seen him and broken into a
run. Crae bent low over Hero's neck, urging him on. Whoever
the man was, he couldn't let him get away. Whether he was the
vanguard of his mysterious army, or whether he was an
enemy of it, Crae needed answers. Hero answered his call for
speed, giving him a burst, foam flying off of his sweat-
darkened neck where it had been carved by the reins.

The trail narrowed between two ridges, and
the terrain began to rise. Red Bird faltered, and Lynn pulled
him up, keeping him to a walk. The trees grew thick again,
though these were not the tall trees of Gordath Wood but
wind-blasted scrub. Red Bird breathed hard, and she winced

for him, but she had to keep him walking. She ducked under low branches as the trail wound down from the ridge into another little woods. There. A tangle of vines cradled a massive rockslide. It jutted from the side of a cliff, and Lynn could see that it was supported by smaller stones, as well as the vines.

A cold shiver of recognition went through her, even as a rattling of wind came to her, along with a burst of static in her head. She had found the mate to the morrim on the hiking trails back in Connecticut.

The dog came trotting up, panting hard, and she shushed him, as if the morrim could hear and be woken. *It's already awake,* she thought. Awake along with the gordath that had brought her here.

The last time she was this close to a live morrim, she had jumped down a mountainside to get away from it. She began to back Red Bird away from the rock. The dog alternately growled and barked, its tail tucked between its legs. *I know, I know,* she thought. She had to get out of there, but Red Bird was spent, and the other horseman was right on her heels. She didn't want to lose Joe's trail, but she didn't know how she was going to get rid of this other guy.

The trees here were nothing like Gordath Wood, but they would have to do for cover. Lynn closed her eyes and tried to find the trail again. The spark was faint here in the woods, but she could see it. She turned to center it on her eyes and found her direction. Then she dismounted and led Red Bird and the dog off into the woods to find cover.

They backed themselves into a little copse, far enough away that she could no longer see the morrim or the trail. Red Bird halted willingly, and her heart pounded for him. He needed to be walked cool, but they had no time for that. Some horses could take such abuse. *Please be one of them,* she prayed. As if it now understood the need for quiet, the dog flopped down to the ground, panting tongue dripping. Lynn took the gun out of her saddlebag, unwrapped it, and edged forward as far as she dared, settling herself behind a green bush of thin, whiplike branches. She hoped it obscured her, but she knew she had to sacrifice cover for the ability to see her pursuer. She looked behind her; she could barely see the dog and the horse, and they were keeping still. Lynn thumbed the safety on the gun, then left it on. If she needed to shoot, it would take just a moment to flick it off.

Now she heard trotting hoofbeats scraping up the slot. She couldn't see her pursuer yet, and she took a deep breath, released it, breathed again, trying to slow down her heartbeat. If he went on ahead, she could reassess her situation.

The horse slowed to a walk, and Lynn bit her lip, keeping herself from bobbing up to take a look. He had to be just on the trail right where she turned off. If he saw Red Bird's hoofprints . . .

At the approach of a strange horse, Red Bird lifted his head and neighed, his nostrils quivering. The bell-like neigh rang in the woods. Lynn turned to look at her horse, aghast at his betrayal, then whipped around again, thinking curses about horses and their social needs, and what had she been thinking not to anticipate that? She held both hands on the gun, braced herself in her bushes, and aimed at the way she had come.

Whoever he was, he was being cautious. She heard a familiar sound, and it took her a moment to identify it. Of course. A crossbow was being loaded, its mechanism drawn back and locked into place. She knew what one of those could do; she had killed a man with one herself. At close range it was as lethal as her gun. So they were equally matched.

With grim determination, Lynn thumbed the safety off. She could see him now, a patch of dull-colored movement through the trees.

The neigh of the other horse still rang in his head. Crae swung his leg over Hero's saddle and slid to the ground. He waited, taking his time. He had the crossbow at the ready. He had one shot, and then he would have to use his sword. He didn't like the terrain. He was surrounded by woods and would have no clear shot for his crossbow. The trees were thick and squat, their branches a tangle reaching toward the sky. He glanced at the mess of rock and deadfall that cascaded down the side of the ridge. It made him uneasy, as if it could come loose and fall on him at any second. He scanned it carefully to see if the horseman was hiding in the underbrush, but he could see no sign of him.

Now he had a ringing in his ears. He shook his head impatiently and edged forward so he didn't have to stay near the rock. Anyway, it looked as if his quarry had gone ahead. He led Hero forward, looking for sign, but there was little to be seen in this wood. There was a trail, but no sign of hoofprints. He looked around, trying to make sense out of the woods, knowing he was taking too long. The horseman would have him in his own sights if he was armed as well.

High god, don't let that dog be a bear hound or boarhound. He'd have to use a bolt on it to stop it, and there would go his shot.

There. He saw a patch of chestnut. The telltale horse was imperfectly hidden, far back into the woods. And closer to the trail, barely visible through a patch of cloudy brush, clothing and a glint of something else, something small and metallic. Crae pushed back at Hero, seeking cover, his blood surging. That was neither sword nor crossbow. A knife—or did the man have one of Bahard's weapons?

Lynn watched from her vantage point in the cloud of vines. She could see him hesitate. He had moved his horse into cover, much as she had, and waited, crossbow loaded and cranked, ready to fire. She ducked down, waiting, willing him to give up and go away. She kept her breathing quiet, meditative. *I'm not here. I'm not here.* She could barely make him out through the woods.

He hesitated, still peering at her cover.

Then, bless his heart, as Mrs. Felz would say, Red Bird neighed again. The man looked that way and raised the crossbow. Lynn counted to five and stood, her hands shaking a little.

"Hold it."

He froze.

He remained obscured by the brush and the trees, but from what she could tell, he was tall and skinny, wearing standard Aeritan gear, a long sword at his side, a long knife in the other hilt. Hard to see anything else about him. She kept the gun steady, supporting it with two hands.

"Set down the crossbow," she said.

After a moment, he did. Those things were on a hair trigger, she knew. She breathed a sigh of relief when it was placed gently on the ground.

"Keep your hands away from your belt. Raise them."

He did.

"Now what?" he said. His voice sounded odd. He sounded as if he were—smiling? *Laughing* at her? She felt a wash of rage. What a jerk. *I have the gun, asshole.* And wait. Why did he sound . . . familiar?

"Why are you following me?" she said, her voice short.

"I would follow you anywhere."

She couldn't say anything for a long moment. Her breath came short. She thought it would be best to put the safety back on the gun, and so she did, and for good measure she set it on the ground, too. When she could talk, it took her a moment for her voice to work. Finally she managed.

"Crae?"

It came out as a whisper, but he still heard. He dropped his hands. She pushed through the woods, the vines and brush scratching at her and trying to hold her back, but she just pushed harder until she was in his arms and he folded them around her as if he would never let her go.

She tried to keep from crying. "Crae," she sobbed once more. He smelled of sweat and dust and leather and cloth, of the faint metallic scent of sword and knife and chain. She stayed in his arms, letting him hold her tight, their breathing coming together.

When they kissed, it was like the secret kiss they shared in Hare's camp, slow and sensual. Her knees weakened, and she tightened her arms around his neck. He pressed his whole length against her, and she remembered how tall and lean he was, every inch of him hard muscle, how good it felt when he wrapped his arms around her the few times they had shared an embrace. His hands were hard yet gentle. She remembered when he had bound her broken arm, taking as great care as he could. She remembered how she would watch him out of the corner of her eye on their long journey across Aeritan, attracted to him physically and liking him more and more, even as she missed Joe. And falling in love, finally, only to know that she would never see him again.

He ended the kiss, and they drew apart. He was so skinny. His beard had come in mostly gray. His clothes hung off of him. His smile was the same, though, the rare smile she thought she would never see again.

"High god, I never thought I would see you again," he said. "What are you doing here?"

Lynn felt a bittersweet pang. *Oh God, what am I going to do? How can I tell him?*

One crow drove her mom's car to the trail- head, and the other one sat in the back with her parents, and Kate was crammed in between the driver and Marthen. She shivered with revulsion at his nearness, at the smell of him. He didn't try to touch her, but they were pressed together, and she had to take deep breaths now and again to keep from throwing up. The ride was silent. Her parents were so frightened they had given up. They had lost hope. Kate wanted to tell them that they would be all right, that Colar was waiting for them, but she could only sit still and quiet, hoping they wouldn't do anything foolish in their fear.

When they pulled in to the little graveled lot, the crow turned off the car and got out, leaving the door open and headlights on. The car chimed softly. Only then did Marthen touch her. He put his hand on the back of her neck, immobilizing her. She heard her mother gasp at the familiarity, and she swallowed. *Keep still,* she told herself. *Just keep still.*

"Do not move until I say so." His hand was hard, gripping her as if she were an animal to restrain. Then he moved his thumb to stroke the nape of her neck, and she knew it was a caress. Tears leaked from her eyes, and she almost sobbed out loud.

No. Find anger. Anger. To her relief it came blazing up. She kept still, all of her muscles gathered, waiting for her moment.

The back door opened, and her parents were hauled out, their backseat guard following them. One of the crows came around and opened Marthen's door, and only then did he release her. He slid out. "Come," he said, and she followed.

She didn't look around for Colar. She kept her eyes on Marthen.

"You have me," she said. "Let them go now."

"We aren't at the gordath, and I know Terrick is here somewhere. Call him out."

"I told you, he's at the barn. I drove back to the house alone."

"Call him, Kate Mossland, or your parents die right here and now."

There was a loud thunk, and the crow guarding her parents dropped his rifle with a hoarse curse, holding his eye. Another rock came out of the woods, hitting the windshield of the car with an enormous crash. The car's alarm began whooping, the sound ripping at the peaceful woods.

Kate didn't wait. She rammed herself into Marthen, sending him off balance, and grabbed his rifle. They wrestled for it as the little parking lot exploded into chaos around them. He was much taller and stronger than she, but she held on to the gun with the grim determination of a Jack Russell terrier.

A war cry came from the woods. No, two war cries. She saw two bodies bursting out from among the trees. Marthen tried to bring his weapon to bear, but Kate screamed in his ear and backed her body up against his. He stretched his arms up over his head, and for a second her toes left the ground as she kept her hold on the stock. As he tried to bring them both around so he could shoot, she found his finger on the trigger, tilted the barrel up, and squeezed, shooting into the trees. Marthen roared with frustration. Kate jumped off her toes and swung her foot back, her heel catching the man in the shin. This time he roared with pain.

She heard gunfire and her mother screaming. Kate screamed herself, more in anger than in fear. The scream cleared her lungs, gave her strength. She let go with one hand and grabbed the handgun in his belt, wrestling it free.

Marthen finally pried her fingers off the rifle and threw her from him. She landed hard on the driveway, clutching the handgun. For a moment the breath was driven from her lungs. She couldn't scream, couldn't make a sound, could only watch as Gary dove for the loose rifle the crow had dropped, scooping it up and turning it on the other crow. For a moment the two homeless men faced off, weapon to weapon, and then the crow toppled, Colar's sword protruding through his belly.

One down, she thought. Two to go—and there were her parents, restraining the other crow, the one with blood running down his face. She wanted to yell in triumph, but her lungs still couldn't get air.

Marthen turned now, training his weapon on Colar. In the headlights the chain and leather armor gave the boy bulk. He pulled the sword free and held it up as if it could ward off bullets.

"No!" Kate found her voice. She lifted the handgun, aiming at Marthen, her hands shaking.

"Sword down, boy," Marthen called. "You can't win here."

"I challenge you, General, in a fair fight."

Oh, Colar, no. Even as she thought it, Marthen said, "Fighting is not about fair, boy."

"Don't call me boy."

Marthen laughed. It sounded surprisingly carefree. "Is that what this is about, Terrick? You think you are the one for her? She has the soldier's god in her, *boy*, and she wants a real warrior, not a child playing at soldier."

Time slowed. Marthen raised his rifle, and Kate shot him, the single crack reverberating in the night air.

Marthen staggered back a step, his arm flying up and blood spraying, as the rifle fell from his hands. He grabbed his arm, panting hoarsely. His eyes were wild but also, for the first time, uncertain. She stepped forward, ready to fire again.

"Kate, no!" her mother screamed, and she hesitated long enough for Gary to lunge for the fallen rifle, blocking her shot.

It was all Marthen needed.

The funny thing was, she knew what Marthen was going to do even before Gary got within reach. She could see it in his eyes and the way he held his body. She wanted to shoot him again, to kill him this time, but Gary was in the way, one rifle in hand, bending to pick up the other one. With a quick movement, Marthen kicked him backward, grabbed the rifle from him, and shot at close range. Gary cried out and fell to the ground with a grunt.

"No!" Kate pulled the trigger, but she did something wrong, and the gun didn't fire. Marthen sprayed gunfire over them, and everyone dropped.

He reached down and grabbed her by the arm, hauling her to her feet. She struggled, but he held the rifle close to her head, the barrel burning against her hair, and his arm was around her throat, so she couldn't breathe again. Her hand loosened, and the useless handgun fell to the ground.

"Quiet," he said, and his voice had gone soft with rage. Somehow, everyone in the parking lot heard. The only sound was harsh breathing and Gary's dying cries. "Weapons down, or she dies."

No, Kate tried to say, but she couldn't breathe. Her vision was starting to fade. Marthen dragged the both of them back into the woods, and she could hold on no longer. She let the darkness take her.

As soon as Marthen and Kate disappeared, Colar picked up his sword, sheathing it and heading toward the woods after them. Allegra was the fastest, but he already knew he would need to take one of the sturdier horses. Then he heard a gunshot from the woods and the scream of a horse.

Soldier's god. There was the sound of crashing hoofbeats, and his heart sank. Marthen had taken two of the horses, it sounded like, and killed the third. He could see it all in his mind's eye. Put them both up on one, and lead another for when Kate came to.

"Oh God, oh God," Mrs. Mossland stammered, and he wondered for the first time which one she meant here. Her eyes and hair were wild, but she knelt by Gary and held his hand, checking his pulse. "Where are the police? They have to find her!" Her voice rose into a scream, but even in the background they could hear the sound of approaching sirens. "Oh thank God," she breathed.

"The police can't find her," he said. "But I will."

He would be on foot, but he could track, and Marthen would have to ride carefully to avoid laming the horses. And he could not help but leave plenty of sign.

"Where is he taking her?" Kate's mom whispered.

"Back through the gordath. But I won't let him. I'll stop him."

Mr. Mossland said, "I'll go out to the road and flag them down. Cole, wait here. Tell the police where they've gone. Don't go after them by yourself." He limped off to the driveway entrance.

Mrs. Mossland looked at Colar. "What happens if he takes her through?" Her voice was very quiet.

"I'll follow him." He was itching to get moving, eager to get on the track.

"Can you bring her back?"

"I don't know if I'll be able to." He said it as honestly as he could. "I'll try."

She nodded. "Go. Bring her back if you can, but if you can't—just stop him."

He nodded. "I will. I promise." He leaned forward and gave her a quick kiss on the cheek, a guerdon of son to mother. He would have knelt, but she wouldn't have understood, and they didn't have time. "If I can't bring her back, I will take her to my parents, and they will never let her forget who she is and who her people are."

As the emergency vehicles turned in to the little parking lot, their lights strobing and their sirens blaring, Colar ran off into the woods.

The horse on the ground was poor Cinnamon, blood pouring like black ink from across his neck. Colar ran past him up the rocky hill. Behind him he could hear the chaos of the rescue, and then the sounds were lost in the deep woods. Soon all he could hear was his own breathing as he ran as hard as he could up the trail toward home.

Sixteen

Crae waited with Hero and watched Lynn as she fetched her horse and dog, leading them back out onto the trail. She was as thin as he remembered, the angles of her face pure and sharp. Her hair was pulled back into a braid, and she wore a strange billed cap that shaded her face and dark spectacles unlike anything he had ever seen. He didn't like not being able to see her eyes. All he could make out of her was her mouth, her lips chapped and broken from lack of water, and the tip of her nose, reddened from the sun. The horse was a sturdy chestnut, not nearly as tall as the big gray she had ridden the last time, and her saddle was tied down with supplies and a bedroll. This time she had come prepared for her journey through the gordath, including the weapon. She checked it once more and put it in the small saddlebag.

She tightened the horse's girth with the same competency he remembered and flipped the split reins over the horse's neck. She mounted with fluid ease and glanced at him.

"I was worried that you might have died. Those soldiers on the road that night—I should have stayed and helped."

"It was better that you fled. It would have all been for

naught, had you been captured." And he would not have been able to fight as well if she had stayed and he'd had to protect her.

She nodded. "So what happened?"

He shrugged. What could he tell her? "We fought. Stavin was cut down, and then there was a great earthshaking from the gordath, and the rest fled."

"Cut down?" Her voice failed her as she saw from the expression on his face the worst news. "Oh, Crae. I am so sorry. He was your friend. He was a good man."

"Yes," he said roughly. "And before he died, he gave me his chain of command and bade me take care of Jessamy and Tevani. I was made lord of Trieve upon his death. Jessamy and I are married."

And then I killed her brother, and so it is truly a marriage in name only. He didn't say any of that. She was thunderstruck, as he meant her to be. Hoped she would be. "Oh," she said at last. "I—congratulations." She turned away. "Oh God. I shouldn't have kissed you. I'm sorry."

"All our kisses end in sorrow," he said, bitterness lacing his words.

She looked back at him, and even with her eyes covered, he could see she was crying. "Crae, I *never* wanted to hurt you. I never meant to—let myself—" She broke off.

"Was it true, when you said you loved me?" He meant when he had kissed her on the snowy road outside Red Gold Bridge and watched her ride up the ridge into the woods.

She bit her lip and then said, "Yes."

High god, why wouldn't she let him see her eyes? "Uncover your eyes," he said, furious. He startled her. Her mouth dropped. For a moment she waited, chin up, and then she took off her spectacles and met his gaze. "Yes," she said again. "I meant it. I still do."

Her eyes were as he remembered, dark and direct. She did not look sidelong the way an Aeritan woman would but met him head-on. *We would have done well together.* He let himself think how it could have been, the two of them. He would not be a lord, but would be a captain still, and she his wife, and they would have lived in Red Gold Bridge or at any House that would have had them.

"Is that why you returned?" He kept his voice rough to hide his emotion. If she had come back to him, what would he do? But he needed to know, even though it would hurt both of them to have to say it and for him to have to turn her away.

She shook her head the tiniest bit. "I'm sorry," she said, and her voice was quiet. "The gordath had opened, and it looked like the guardians were in trouble. So I crossed, because I needed to try to help."

It stung, and he welcomed it because he knew he had deserved that, just for asking. "I know," he said. "I was just at Red Gold Bridge; they told me the guardians were kidnapped by Brytherners."

"Oh, I knew something bad had happened. I just didn't know what."

He frowned. "What news had you gotten of their trouble?"

"The dog." She nodded down at the thin mongrel, which wagged happily under their attention. "She showed up at the farm with a bit of Joe's shirt tied around her collar. I knew then he was in trouble. I didn't think—I didn't know what it was. But if the gordath was open, then I knew it was bad."

Joe, the other guardian. Crae recognized the name from the one she had whispered drowsily a year ago, under the influence of a pain draught for her broken arm and on the verge of sleep. She had come back, braved the gordath, for him. She frowned, looking at him.

"Crae, I don't understand. If you are Lord of Trieve now, what are you doing on the outskirts of Red Gold Bridge looking for kidnapped guardians?"

Well, she was being led about by a dog, and he by a crow. Crae stopped worrying about being believed. "A crow made me a prophecy," he said. "He told me that Aeritan was in great danger from Brythern and beyond. And so he led me here."

She nodded. "Really skinny, wearing nothing but a tattered cloak?" At his look of astonishment, she said, "Yeah, he pointed me this way, too. He didn't say anything about a prophecy. He didn't say anything, actually."

"You saw him? He was here?" *And he hasn't shown himself to me in days.* Perhaps some of his annoyance showed in his expression, because she looked a little puzzled.

"It must be another gordath," she said. "The Brytherners must have kidnapped the guardians because they want to control a gordath. And something's coming through it . . ." Her voice trailed off.

Still annoyed, he said, "Well, it's good to know there's truth to his words, I suppose."

She grinned. "That's something," she agreed, and just like that, they were comrades again, as they had been last year. He had missed her sudden smiles. "There's something else, too," she added. "A—spark. I can see it when I close my eyes. It's like a line leading me."

He hadn't seen any spark, but the sign was the clearest he'd ever tracked, and he wondered if that were somehow akin to her spark. "I've just been tracking. You, mostly," he added wryly. She gave a reluctant smile back.

"Okay, then," she said. "Let's go." She whistled for her dog, and the animal took point. Crae fell in behind her, watching her ride. She rode as elegantly as always, one hand down by her side and her body moving fluidly to the horse's flat-footed walk. It was as if she were the daughter of the horse god.

He knew that despite what she had said, if he kissed her again, she would kiss him back. They might even lie together, even though he would be breaking his vow to Jessamy, and Lynna would be breaking her handfasting to her guardian. They were neither of them free, and somehow that made them both free.

And then what? He had another glimpse of that other life, this time fleeing with Lynna, catching a river ship and sailing out for other countries, but their love would sink under their shame and guilt. They would cling to each other till their love dried up, and finally part in bitterness and rue. Cruel is the grass god's daughter, he thought, to give love where it could not be kept.

"He's going to have us open it for good to-day," Joe said, bending down to pull on his boots. They had been woken out of their light sleep a few minutes earlier. After quizzing them on the state of the gordath, Hare ordered them to be given a good breakfast, as if that would somehow help. Joe wondered if it weren't more like a condemned man's last meal.

Arrim laced up his thick and awkward boots, hiding his words, as Joe had, by bending down. "I think you're right, Guardian. Will you follow my lead?"

He didn't have much choice. He was out of ideas. He had bought them time and a relief from the physical abuse, but now they had to put up or shut up. If Hare wanted them to open the gordath, there was little they could do to stop it.

"What do you have in mind?" Joe said.

"Guardians!" Hare called to them.

Joe glanced at Arrim, who stood slowly. Arrim gave him a look that said, *Follow me.* He got up and let Arrim lead them over to Hare.

"Today's the day that you open the gordath and hold it open. You've quieted it as you said, and you've gotten it under control. Now it's time to reopen it." Hare paused, cocking his head to look at them. He had his hands behind his back, and he looked relaxed, as if he were addressing friends, but his men ranged themselves behind them. "I let you rest and restore yourselves, because you convinced me that you needed all your strength. But you are still captives, and you are still under my control. Remember, if you can't—or won't—control the gordath, you are useless to me. You may pray to your gods, forest or otherwise, that you continue to be useful."

Joe nodded judiciously. "Nice speech. You sure do know how to keep morale up."

Hare rolled his eyes and made a face. "Open it. Keep it open."

They were left to stand apart in the clearing, the others moving back. Joe heard a few swords scrape out of their scabbards and someone load a crossbow. Yeah, they weren't going to be able to get out of this one.

"So what was your plan?" he said under his breath to Arrim.

"Do as he says, and fail if we must," Arrim said. "But if it looks as if the gordath is out of control, then we let it rampage. With luck it will kill Hare and his schemes as well."

Joe fought for control of his voice. "Jesus, Arrim," he managed finally. "It'll kill us, too. And if it stays open, and we're dead, who's going to close it?"

Arrim grinned, but it didn't look like he was laughing. "Who wants to live forever?"

Me. "Arrim, don't do this," he said through gritted teeth.

"Guardians," Hare said in a warning voice. "I grow impatient."

So here it was. Joe would have to control the gordath on his own, and at a certain point Arrim would be trying to goose it wide open.

"Don't do this," he said again. "Don't try to push it out of control."

"You said you would follow my lead."

"That was before I found out you were crazy!"

"Guardians!" Hare said again.

The crack of a gunshot sang out through the woods.

Joe threw himself to the ground. *Hare's lost it. He's finally lost it, and he's shooting at us.*

The Brythern men exploded into shouting chaos. He could hear the twang of crossbow shots, Hare shouting orders to get into position. Joe rolled behind a tree and flattened himself, trying to make sense of everything. The shot had come from the woods. Was it the cavalry come at last? Had Captain Tal finally found them?

The woods quieted. He took a risk and peeked out. Men had found cover, and the clearing was mostly empty.

Hare shouted, "Show yourself! Who are you?"

"Back off, Brytherners, or the next one goes through your lord," a strange voice shouted from the woods.

Hare looked puzzled. "I know your voice, Aeritan," he said at last. "I know you. Name yourself."

"It doesn't matter, Brythern lord. Throw down your weapons, or we'll pick you off one by one."

Joe could see Brythern soldiers fading back into the woods toward the voice. The forest might be sparse here, but cover wasn't completely thin. He hoped his rescuer had plenty of company and a lot more guns.

Just then, to his dismay, he felt a familiar sensation, a kind of crawling inside his brain.

No no no. The gordath was opening, only he hadn't had anything to do with it. He looked around for Arrim. The guardian had found another tree and had pressed himself behind it, but his eyes were open and his hands were outstretched. He was opening the gordath. *Oh shit, Arrim, no.* The gordath shivered inside Joe, humming along to his heartbeat and the air that bellowed in his lungs. It pulsed inside his head and opened up in a flare of blinding light.

Marthen had trouble holding on to the girl. She wasn't completely unconscious, but she couldn't hold herself upright. He had her snugged in front of him, her hands lashed to the D rings on the front of the saddle, and he kept her secured by his sound arm for good measure. His other hand, blood dripping down from the shoulder wound where she had winged him, held the reins. They kept slipping from his bloody fingers. The rifle was slung across his back.

He had them up on the back of the stolid bay gelding, the flighty mare led by the rein. She was a bitch. She bucked and squealed and pulled against the rein, and he wished bitterly he had shot the mare and kept the other gelding, but it was too late now. She finally settled down as he kept them at a fast trot up the hill, past the muttering rock that hulked in the darkness, and down toward the gordath that he knew was there.

Kate began to recover, thrashing, but she couldn't loosen

her bonds. He tightened his grip. If she kept struggling she could bring down the horse.

"Give me any more trouble, and I will throttle you again," he said in her ear. To emphasize his threat, he brought up his arm around her throat, and instinctively she began to fight it, but she managed to calm herself, sobbing a little. He released her only slightly. He thought she might be exhausted and cowed, finally, and felt a pinprick of relief. It was better this way. Soldier's god knew, he didn't have time for her to fight him all the way to Aeritan.

"When we cross the gordath, you may ride alone," he said, a promise to lift her spirits. They were almost through. His men should be waiting for him at the entrance. It was a small enough army, but it was all he needed to take down the Council.

He could feel it now, the strange humming in his heart and head that signified the opening. The ground trembled a little, and the gelding snorted and shied, and the mare squealed. He kicked the horse harder.

He could see flashlights up ahead, the clear cold burning torches people used here. Better than fire, they gave off a more efficient light, and they could be extinguished in an instant. Marthen trotted into camp and pulled up the horses as his men surrounded him, armed with the weapons from the crate.

"It's the boss!" someone called out. They kept their flashlights low, but he could see their expressions as they took in the horses and the girl.

"Follow me," he said. "Look sharp. Fire on any pursuers."

"Wait—what about Chris and Sonny?" someone asked.

For a second his world reeled. These men weren't crows. They had names; they had lives. Yes, they were destitute, but not mad. *This is not Aeritan. They are not crows.* Maybe it was the pain from his wound, but Marthen's head cleared for the first time in months. What was he doing, leading these men, stealing this girl? He had never been a good man, but this was folly.

Stop this, he thought, and he opened his mouth to dismiss

them all. Then he heard faint laughter and shook his head to clear it. When he looked at them again, they were still watching him, their expressions puzzled and alarmed. The feeling of clarity faded as if it had never been.

"They are dead," he said, and his voice was harsh. "Let's go."

He had suffered momentary madness, he told himself, as he pushed the horses forward. That's all it had been.

The ground trembled underneath them, and then shook hard. Then light flared up around them and he, the girl, and his men burst through into daylight.

Joe peered through the black-limned opening that hung in front of them, its edges bleeding into the reality of the woods. The blackness focused, and he could see another forest, in darkness now, full of men on the other side. For a moment he thought he looked into a mirror, but these men were not Brythern soldiers. They were dressed like him, and they carried some serious weaponry, and behind them came two horses and one, no two, riders.

He was conscious of Hare and his men falling back.

The earth shook again, and he stumbled, and at his loss of balance the gordath jerked wider.

The men started coming through. Hare didn't wait. "Fire!" he shouted, and the crossbowmen set to work, firing their crossbows at this new army, who fired back, the gunshots rolling over the crossbows. Hare's men fell, and the army burst through.

The opening shuddered, and the gordath cranked wider. Then another earthquake hit the forest, and Joe lost his balance. The hole was growing, eating at the edges of the world. This was not the portal that gently gathered in wayward travelers. *This* was the gordath that he remembered from last winter. This gordath was full-bore, cutting open a direct hole between worlds. *The newcomers came through just in time,* Joe thought dazedly. Sure enough, one of Hare's soldiers screamed as he was caught in it, and he toppled in. Joe struggled for control, but the gordath had taken over his heart and his breathing now, speeding them up until he knew he was going to pass out. They were done for. Arrim's plan to take everyone out was going to work, and there would be another cataclysm for Brythern's history.

His vision turned black, and he fell to his knees. *Shhh,* he could hear his abuela say in his head. *Shhh, go to sleep, little Joe, go to sleep, let yourself sleep.* He could hear her little breathy lullaby and the Spanish words he had never bothered to learn. His breathing slowed, and his heartbeat slowed, and he knew he couldn't fight it anymore. *Okay, grandma,* he thought. *Okay.* As he slackened his grip both on the gordath and on consciousness, the last thing he thought was that the gordath had loosened its grip on him.

From her vantage point above the clearing, Lynn watched Joe fall. The gordath hung over him, a growing menace. He would be consumed like the man who had fallen into the emptiness. She began to slide down the ridge toward him. Crae yanked her back by the back of her shirt.

"No!" he shouted. She fought him, furious, but he wouldn't let her go.

"I'm not letting him die."

"What good can you do him if you get pulled in with him?" Crae went back up to the horses, scrambling for balance as the earth shook, and grabbed his pack. He dumped out his supplies, grabbing the thin rope he used to hobble his horse at night. He tied one end to a tree and tugged it, testing its strength. It held.

"All right," he said. He braced himself. "I'll get him. You cover me."

She tightened her grip on the handgun and watched him slide down the rope toward Joe. The entire clearing was chaos. Two men had fallen in the gordath, or been pulled in, and the Brytherners had scattered but were regrouping. There was a horseman, struggling to control two mounts and hold on to someone riding double in front of him.

Hey. That's Allegra. And my Hotshot.

Gunfire came through the gordath, and the Brytherners that had been firing their crossbows dove for cover. Hare caught sight of Crae's rescue attempt and brought up his gun, but Lynn aimed, took a deep breath, and fired. The shot went wide, but it got their attention. Hare stumbled back, ducking for a tree trunk.

She made herself calm down and aim for Hare's shoulder and side, all she could see of him through the trees. She prepared to squeeze the trigger when an arm came around her neck, hauling her backward. Lynn's scream was choked off, and she struggled against her attacker. The gun was plucked from her hand, and an unwelcome voice said in her ear,

"Hey, babe. Long time no see."

Mark.

Seventeen

Colar came upon the gordath just as Marthen and his men disappeared into it. He ran harder and dove through after them, disoriented by the rush of daylight he suddenly dropped into.

He landed in the middle of a war. Marthen's men faced off against a squad of Brytherners. Marthen was off to the side, holding Kate in the saddle in front of him. She jerked her hands, but she was tied to the saddle. Hotshot reared and backed up, and Allegra just bucked wildly at the end of her reins.

Colar ducked behind some brush. It was hard to make sense of everything, what with the ground shaking and the empty hole of the gordath behind him growing and contracting like a bellows, its edges wavering. It made him dizzy to look back at it. He grimaced, drew his sword, and wished he had a crossbow. Marthen would be an easy shot from behind.

He watched as a man fell into the gordath and disappeared, his scream choked off. Colar felt a little sick. He had just come through the portal, but he didn't think anyone would be getting back that way. If you tried to go through the gordath now, it didn't look as if you would get anywhere.

First things first, he told himself. He had to get Kate away from Marthen.

The Brytherners had received the worst of the attack, but they had taken cover and were regrouping under their orders. Whoever their officer was, he knew what he was about. Colar admired the way they regathered, taking careful shots and maintaining their cover. Marthen's ragtag handful of men were disoriented from their passage through the gordath. Here in the daylight they were not fearsome crows, despite their rifles. They were going to be easy targets for a disciplined fighting force.

"Retreat!" Marthen shouted, but they didn't know where to go. Two made to go back through the gordath but were immediately swallowed up. The men's screams were cut off as if they had never existed at all, and a shiver ran down Colar's spine.

The Brytherners laid down another rain of crossbow fire, and more men fell.

Colar watched the general cut his losses. He cuffed Kate hard to keep her from struggling, dropped Allegra's rein, leaving the mare behind, and kicked Hotshot into a gallop, away from the furious gun battle.

"Lower your sword!" someone shouted. He looked up at a Brythern soldier, who had him covered with a crossbow.

Mark hauled Lynn down into the clearing, keeping her arm pushed up behind her back. She bit back her pain, but she couldn't control her despair. *We lost,* she thought. *If the gordath doesn't kill us all, Mark and Hare will.*

The gordath hung before them, an eerie sight, and the earth shook violently. Joe and the other guardian lay unmoving, and dead men and wounded men were scattered all around.

"Take them," Hare ordered, and the rest of his men went about making prisoners of the confused homeless men, taking up their weapons and binding their hands. They had taken Crae, too, and surrounded him, several swords at his throat. They tried to disarm Colar, but the boy resisted.

"Don't try it, boy," Hare said. "I will show no mercy."

"Brythern lord, I mean no trouble to you," Colar said, still holding his sword, practically begging. Lynn's heart sank. *If he was here, where was Kate?* "You must let me go. My friend is in terrible danger—"

"Enough," Hare said.

"There's no time!"

Hare held up a hand, fury in his expression. He almost brought up his gun, then held himself back. "Your mission doesn't concern me right now. Be silent, or you will not leave this clearing." He turned to Lynn and Crae, shaking his head. "You two," Hare said in disgust. He looked down at Joe. "Is he dead?" he asked. Mark, still holding on to Lynn, dragged her forward and planted a solid kick in Joe's side. Lynn muffled a scream as Joe moved sluggishly and groaned.

"Nope, guess not," Mark said cheerfully.

As if the gordath sensed the abuse, the woods shook harder, and the hole in the air expanded again.

Lynn kept herself from telling him to stop; it would only egg him on. One of the Brythern guards dragged the other guardian forward. She recognized him. He was the one who had stolen her horse last winter in a mad bid to close the gordath. He looked past her, no equal spark of recognition in him.

"Good," Hare said. "Now, we get somewhere." He nodded at Mark. "So, you can go home now, go to your world, and begin the trade we talked about." He gestured at the hole between the worlds.

Mark's smugness turned to panic. "Wait—what? No! I didn't go through the gordath when it looked like that! Are you crazy? You saw what it did to Drav and those other guys!"

Hare looked impatient. "It's open. They are holding it open. What more do you want?"

"No! I'm telling you, that's not how it's supposed to work. It's supposed to be *invisible*. Not—not this black shit."

Hare turned on Arrim. "You! Is this how the gordath works?"

Arrim giggled. "Yes, Lord Hare. First earthshakings, then a hole that eats between the worlds, then death and destruction. Exactly how it's supposed to work. After you."

Hare slapped him with all his force. His studded glove drew blood as Arrim's head snapped back. Then he grabbed Lynn and began to shove her forward.

"You will go through," he said through gritted teeth. "You misbegotten bitch, if the gordath swallows you alive, so be it. I never want to see you again."

Lynn fought back, her heels sliding in the dirt, as he pushed her toward the hole between worlds. She could smell it now, a smell of death and decay, and she could hear it call to her with whispered cries. She grabbed for Hare's arms to keep herself from being pushed in. He struck at her to make her lose her grip, but she clung, digging in her fingers so that they grabbed at his shirt, armor, and skin. *If I'm going in, so are you.* Out of the corner of her eye she could see Crae struggling, Brythern guards pulling him back.

"Lynna!"

She grabbed at the gun at Hare's belt, and he knew what she was going for and redoubled his efforts to push her in. He was strong, but she was desperate. They fought over the gun, and she twisted it around so that it was aimed at his belly.

His eyes widened as she pulled the trigger, the muzzle jammed above his belt, the shot loud between the two of them.

Hare tumbled backward, holding his belly, a bewildered look in his eyes. He tried to keep his hold on her, but his arms released. Lynn pushed herself out of his deadly embrace, and Hare kept going, falling into the gordath, and was swallowed in the darkness.

Lynn took in air, gasping and sobbing, and stumbled back, even as the ground shook harder and the gordath expanded. The sound of hoofbeats and war cries made her turn around.

It was Red Gold Bridge. She saw Dungiven in full battle armor, ridden by Lord Tharp. The big horse rolled steadily forward in a controlled canter, his neck arched and his nos-

trils bright red. He was followed by another fifty or so horses
and soldiers.

The cavalry had arrived.

The pain of his broken ribs made it hard to
breathe, let alone move, so Joe just lay there while the fighting
raged around him. Besides, he figured he had learned a few
things about the gordath, and that's what he could do to help.

For one thing, control was overrated.

For another, he had been wrong all the time. It wasn't that
the gordath wanted to be open. It just wanted to be left alone.
He figured he could get behind that. And so he quieted it the
only way he knew how, by quieting himself.

Maybe he had his mother's mother to thank for that. It was
almost as if he could feel her cool, rough hand against his
forehead, the way she touched him when he was sick as a kid.
He couldn't remember all the words, so he sang what he could
remember and hoped that it would do the trick.

A la nanita nana, nanita ea, nanita ea,
A la nanita nana, nanita ea.

"Lord Tharp," Crae said, bowing lord to lord.
He looked up at the man, sitting the great gray horse. "It is
very good to see you."

It was. Tharp grinned in a rare good humor. The easy fight
had put him in a good mood. "Your crow didn't lie, then," he
said, resting his arms on the saddlebow as he looked around
with great satisfaction. The big horse pawed and snorted, froth
tossing from his bit. There were the Brytherners, many dead,
the rest being bound by his men, including Lord Bahard. There
were a few remaining crows as well, but the few survivors
were thoroughly cowed.

"Lord Tharp," said the boy. Crae had recognized him finally, the young Terrick. He wore blue trousers, the same
as Lady Sarita's, Lynn's, even the guardian's, but the rest of
his clothes and armor were Aeritan. The boy bowed, but he

shifted his weight anxiously. "Sir, I am Colar of Terrick. My friend has been carried off by General Marthen, who has gone crow, sir, and I followed them from her world back here, and I fear greatly for her life, and, sir, if I could have your men, I could bring him down, because I fear for her, and I promised her mother and father I would save her."

Tharp looked down at the boy. "I don't give out my army lightly, Terrick," he growled. "Especially to a House that has stood against me in the past."

"Oh, for the love of the high god, Eyvig," said Lady Sarita, taking off her helm and pushing her horse up next to him. She was a beautiful warrior in her armor, a long sword draping down her side.

The silence in the clearing rang like a bell. She leaned down to Colar. "Is he armed with Bahard's weapons?"

The boy nodded. "Yes, my lady. And he has at least a half hour's head start."

"All right. We can give you a dozen riders. Are you horsed?"

Colar cast around, and brought over the light-boned dark bay mare. He gathered the reins and leaped into the saddle. Lady Sarita looked at the horse, and her mouth dropped. And she laughed out loud.

War agrees with them, Crae thought, shaking his head. Perhaps their marriage will strengthen after all, although all the gods pity poor Aeritan if this was how they sought happiness. "I'll go with the boy, my lady. My business is with the general." If the crow was to be believed, and as Tharp had pointed out, he had been proved right so far, the general was his mad crow. Best to stop him now.

"Good," Tharp said. "We'll clean up here." He glared at Lord Bahard. The man fought his bonds halfheartedly.

"Look, Tharp, the guardians will bring the gordath under control again," the man wheedled. "Just let me go home, and we can forget all about this."

"Unfortunately for you, I have a long memory," Tharp said.

"As do I," put in Lady Sarita. "I think it's better for both worlds to keep you where you can do no more mischief." She looked over at the guardians and at Lynn. "I think it's time to close this once more, and please, keep it closed. Can you do that, Joe? Arrim?"

"Yeah," said the strange guardian. He struggled to sit up, and Lynn helped support him. "Yeah, we can do that."

Joe looked at the hole. It was no longer gap-ing, but gathering in on itself. He could feel it again, the control he and Arrim needed to keep it open just long enough for them to go through, though he didn't know how long his strength would hold out.

"You know, I figured some things out," he said. A lot of things actually, but this one was the most important.

Lynn looked at him quizzically.

"I can be a guardian on our side, too. Arrim can handle Aeritan, and I'll take New York."

"I know."

Huh. "You know?"

She smiled. "I met a whole bunch of guardians back home. You'll have to teach them what to do, but I don't think we'll have a problem with the gordath anymore."

He didn't know what to say. In the end, he just said, "Help me up."

Arrim hobbled over, and Joe took stock of him. He was in bad shape, as bad as Joe felt, covered with blood and dirt. Always shaggy, the man looked like a strange forest animal. Which, Joe reflected, he kind of was. Arrim was never happier than when he was deadheading through Gordath Wood. *Me, I'm a different kind of guardian.*

"Hey," Joe said. "I'm going to go back and take care of the gordath from the other side. We'll still be working together. We just won't be able to see each other." They'd each know the other was there, though. Even separated by the gordath, Arrim would still be his partner. His mentor.

Arrim nodded. "What will I tell your Corinna?" he

managed, and Joe shook his head. *I think he was really hoping we'd get together.*

"Tell her I said you two will make a great couple."

Lynn gave him a look, but she said, "Let me get my horse, and then we can go home."

There was just one loose end. "Mrs. Hunt!" he called out.

Lady Sarita turned to look at him, as did everyone else. He jerked his head at Mark. "Man's got something he can't use here, and we sure could to keep Hunter's Chase safe and sound."

Mark protested furiously, but it made no difference. The stacks of cash he had stowed in his pack were passed over to Joe, who couldn't help but grin.

"Thanks, buddy."

Mark lunged at him, cursing, but the dog came at him, snarling and barking, and he dropped back.

"Screw you, Felz," he muttered, and Joe just turned his back. He had to trust to Red Gold Bridge to keep Mark under lock and key, but the man was like a bad penny. He'd keep turning up. *We'll just have to keep the damn thing closed,* he thought.

Lady Sarita looked over at Lynn, who had brought up a sturdy chestnut horse wearing a western saddle. Another surprise, Joe thought. "I trust you found the rest?" she asked, her voice reproving.

"I did. Thank you. It's safe and sound."

"Good. It was not easy to reclaim my own dowry, but I kept an eye on Garson, and he led me to it." She smiled, and it was not a pleasant expression. "I think he knew, but he couldn't go to the police. I enjoyed that."

I bet you did, Joe thought.

Lynn nodded. "Mrs. Hunt, it's good to see you again, and Dungiven." The big stallion tossed his head and pawed the ground restively.

The ground jerked and rumbled, and brought them all back.

"Right," Lord Tharp said, testy once more. "Enough pleasantries. Close that thing, and let's go home."

Joe looked at Arrim. "You know what we need to do, right?"

The man nodded again. "It will work. I can feel it."

Lynn brought over the chestnut horse, and Joe smiled. "You know I can't ride."

She gave him a smile back. "That's okay. I'll steer." The horse snorted and sidestepped as she held the stirrup for him. "Steady, Red Bird, steady."

"Red Bird," Joe said. "Sure is a Texas name for a horse."

"Yeah, I know. Put your foot in the stirrup, there, and I'll give you a boost. Your mom named him."

"Wait—what? My mom what?"

Crae mounted Hero and prepared to ride out with Colar of Terrick and the dozen scouts loaned by Red Gold Bridge. They were hard warriors all, and they each picked up one of the weapons brought through the gordath. Marthen would not prevail. He was just one man, although he was a crow, and crows were just men, after all.

He looked over at Lynn, busying herself with the guardian and the horse, preparing to cross over to her world one last time. The guardian caught his eye, and for a moment the two men faced each other across the clearing. Crae knew he was figuring things out. Assessing him. The man's face went hard. Lynna looked from him to Crae.

The gordath rumbled again, and everyone jerked, almost falling off their feet. The horses scrambled backward.

"Ride out!" young Terrick called out, and they fell in behind him. Crae cast one look backward, and then she and the guardian were gone.

Marthen heard the thunder of hoofbeats chas-ing them. The gelding labored under the combined weight of himself and the girl, his wind broken, his gait choppy and uneven. Marthen glanced back. A small troop of outriders followed at full gallop. He kicked the horse brutally, but he could get no more speed out of the animal, so he pulled up. They were on the Brythern plains, a rolling terrain of grasses broken up by scrub, and there was scant cover. He turned the horse's head and pushed him toward a slight swale. He could shoot the horse if he had to and use the carcass for cover, but he was not a fool. There would be no escape unless he kept the girl as hostage. Even then, he was not likely to come out of this adventure alive.

Kate tugged fruitlessly at her bonds, but the ropes held.

"Stop," he said. He dismounted, stumbling a little as vertigo overtook him. He had not thought the small wound she had given him would sap him so much, but his side was soaked in sticky blood. He saw the way she took in his weakness, her expression calculating. "Don't get ideas," he said dryly. "I am still able to hold on to my prisoner."

"Not for long," she said, and cocked her head at the sound of their pursuit.

"If I die, so may you," he said, and this time her eyes went wide with shock. He took out his knife and cut her bonds, releasing her from the saddle. "Get down."

She dismounted stiffly, rubbing her wrists. Her hair was tangled, and she was covered with his blood, sweat, and dirt. Her throat was bruised and her face was swollen with tears. She looked, he realized, much the same as when he had first laid eyes on her. Then, he had thought of her as a weapon. Now he didn't know what to think of her. Marthen felt a great weariness. *What have I done?*

He waited for his thoughts to clear again, but they didn't. There was laughter in the back of his head, but he pushed it away, rubbing his eyes. He had listened to the madness for long enough. For a second, darkness sparkled, and then his vision came back. She stood there, watching him, and the soldiers in pursuit drew near, so that now he could hear the jangling of harness and the shouting of the men.

"Kate Mossland," he said, the strange name still so foreign

to his tongue. He nodded at the horse, the animal's head hanging low. "Take him and go, and do not look back."

He half expected her to protest and almost laughed at his own foolishness. Still a lovesick old sot, he told himself. Who would have thought it?

He unslung the rifle from his back. Just because he was surrendering didn't mean he would go easily. He was the mad general after all, and he had his pride. He didn't watch her go. All his attention was focused on the enemy.

They came over the hill, a fast-galloping mass of horses, men, armor, and weapons. Marthen knelt and fired, dropping the first horse, but they spread out, returning fire. His last conscious thought was of the soldier's god, welcoming him home.

Eighteen

Lynn watched Joe sit down cautiously at her kitchen table, the first time he made it out of the bedroom since she brought him home. She smiled. He looked good, sitting in the morning sun. He looked *right*. As his bruises faded and his ribs healed, he looked more and more like himself. She had missed him. *I want him here. He needs to be here.* He caught her smile, and smiled back.

"What?" he said.

"I was just thinking how you look like you belong there." She slid into the chair next to him. She bit her lip, half-guilty, half-smug. "And I was thinking maybe we moved too fast. Your ribs okay after earlier?"

He grinned. "Not complaining." He looked around. "I don't think I was in this house but once or twice, and sure never in here." Lady Sarita kept her privacy.

"Me neither. She really was something else." Lynn had told him about the fortune in the attic. The dowry plus Mark Ballard's loot would keep the farm going for a good long time. And this time Garson had skedaddled for good, after the cops connected him to the crate of illegal rifles in the woods. Maybe they would have to worry about him eventually, but not right now.

Lynn knew Kate's parents would never forgive her for coming back without their daughter, but she told them what she knew, that Colar had taken a dozen armed men in pursuit of the general. Kate wouldn't be able to come back, not if Arrim, Joe, and the perambulators did their jobs. And if they couldn't, things could only get worse. This time the gordath nearly killed the guardians. Who knew how bad it could get the next time it opened?

Joe looked up at her, and he wasn't smiling anymore. "I figure I'm a damn fool for asking, but I gotta know. You sure looked like you had something going on with that other guy."

Her throat closed. She waited a moment to compose herself. She knew he would ask about Crae, or she would have to bring it up. She just didn't think it would be so soon. She looked straight at him. "Yes. But." She chose her words carefully. "I went back for you, not him."

"Any regrets?" He said it softly.

"God, Joe. Don't—" *Don't do this to me.* She blinked back tears. "I love you. I loved him. I don't know how to explain it any other way. I can't tell you what you want to hear. I loved him, yes, and you'll have to make peace with that. But I came for you. Please don't—" She couldn't continue. *Don't leave me. Please, don't leave me.*

He reached out and pulled her close, holding her tight, even though it must have been painful. His hand tangled in her hair, as if he was trying to pull her inside him, and his breath was warm against her neck.

"Knew I was being an asshole," he said, and his voice was muffled. "I just can't stand the idea of losing you again."

"You won't," she said. "I swear it, Joe Felz. I won't leave you."

But you can't make me stop loving him, too.

The householders told him he would find Jes-samy up in the high sheep fields where they buried the crow.

He left the crow king at the bottom of the terraces, the
skinny old man turned somber, his keen eyes watchful. Crae
turned Hero and pushed him for the hard climb up the terraces, letting his horse take his time. At the House, he
dismounted and let the grooms take the horse; with the help
of his walking stick, he climbed the rest of the way by
himself.

A cold wind blew across the hill, zigzagging through the
grass. Close-cropped grass hugged the contours of the land.
Rocks poked through everywhere, white and streaked with
moss. The burial cairn looked like one of the ancient rocks,
except for the uneven tower it made. A vine of pink and yellow flowers trailed over it. Crae had never seen that weed before. A curlew called, and another answered, the birdsong
lonely and sweet in the high upland pasture.

Jessamy sat on a rock looking out over the distant lands.
The mountains of Kenery were blue in the distance, and far
below the silver line of the Aeritan River curled off toward
the sea. She turned at his approach. She had her kerchief in
her lap, and her brown hair flew around her face, catching the
sunlight with strands of red and gold mixed with the brown.
Her lips and cheeks were red, but her eyes, usually so filled
with spirit and drive, were narrowed with strain. Crae sat down
next to her, and she didn't move away.

Finally, he said, "Tell me what happened."

She sighed. "We brought him home. We buried him next
to our mother and father. Favor was a dreadful place. I had
forgotten all the ghosts we lived with. I thought, I will not
raise my children here. So I came home." She looked at him
challengingly. "I will not be driven from my home again."

"Never again," he agreed. "How are the children?"

"Well. Tevani misses you." She smiled a little sadly. "She
isn't as lively as she once was. Perhaps when she sees you,
some of that will come back."

He thought he would do anything he could to make that
happen. But could he return? "Did Alarin bring you my
letter?"

She nodded and pulled the chain from around her neck. "Here."

He reached out and held her wrist, stopping her. "No. It's yours. I gave up my lordship to save Trieve from the Council's wrath. You are Lord of Trieve now." He added roughly, "They will not attack Trieve for my crime if I am no longer lord here."

To his surprise, she laughed and sobbed together. "Oh, the Council. First they take Trieve from me, and now they take Trieve from you. It is a wonder they do not throw up their hands and let it all go back to the grass god."

He grimaced. "They may well try," he said. "But I will not let Trieve go without a fight. If you will still have me, Lady Jessamy, I will be your consort and serve you well."

He waited, heart hammering. She was lord now. She could dissolve their marriage and take another man to husband if she wished. He couldn't blame her if she did, but he hoped she wouldn't.

Jessamy didn't speak for a long time, and the only sound was that of the curlews and the wind. At length she poured the chain from hand to hand, the silver links running like water between her slender fingers.

"When I was eighteen and my parents died, Jori married me to Stavin. When Stavin died, the Council married me to you. My life was never my own to dispose as I will." She looked into the distance, and now her gaze was hard. "Trieve is mine now, and no one will take it from me. Let the Council fight over Favor, not Trieve. This House is mine, and I will hold it for my children." She turned to Crae and smiled thinly. "Since you are on speaking terms with the high god, tell him for me I am lord here, not you."

The high god was silent on the matter; probably, Crae thought dryly, he knew when he was bested.

"As for the other," she said, and breathed out a sigh. "You are an upstart, disreputable captain. Yet you are the only person who never treated me as if I were a chess piece. Not my mother and father, not my brother, not even Stavin." She tried to keep back tears but failed, and her voice cracked. "All I ask is that you keep crows from my kitchen, please."

He pulled her close, tucking her under his chin, and resting his cheek on the top of her head. After a moment she lifted her face to his, and they kissed, the taste of tears salty on his lips and tongue. Crae lost himself in the kiss, his heart hammering.

He was no longer a lord. He might even be crow. But they both deserved another chance to make things right, if not for themselves then for Trieve. Jessamy deserved all of him, as captain and husband both. He would strive to give her all he could. Crae let himself think one more time of Lynna and then let her memory go.

Elms lined the avenue approaching the House of Terrick. Allegra and Hotshot clomped steadily toward it, and even though the house was unfamiliar, their pace increased. They knew what houses meant: water and grain and a comfortable loose box.

Kate took it all in. It was drawing on toward evening, the sky was gray, and the air was raw and chill. She was grateful they would be out of the weather soon. Her body ached, she was bruised, hungry, and filthy, and she thought with longing of her careful pack of supplies they had left behind at the trailhead. She supposed the sooner she adjusted to her new life the better, but a toothbrush would have been nice.

She swallowed against the thick lump in her throat that hadn't moved since she watched from a distance as Marthen was cut down by gunfire. She was safe at last, and her parents were safe, and the price she had paid was that she would never see them again.

When her rescuers reached her, Colar had thrown himself from the saddle and taken her into her arms, and she had cried at last, all the tears coming after being pent up for so long. She had freed herself after a moment and went over and looked at Marthen. A tall soldier tried to hold her back, but she shrugged herself loose and stood over the body.

He was covered with blood and dirt, and his sightless eyes stared at the sky. His hair had gray in it. Colar came up behind her and took her hand, closing his fingers around hers.

"He let me go," she said, her voice thick and wobbly. "He looked really tired and sad, and he just said, 'Take the horse.'"

"He turned crow," someone said, but she shook her head.

"Not at the end."

They took the body away, and then the tall soldier, who turned out to be a lord, gave them some of his supplies for their long journey to Trieve.

First they had gone back to the gordath, though, but Lynn and Joe had already gone through, and the hole between the worlds was closed up tight.

Tears burned in her eyes at the memory. She glanced over at Colar. He looked calm, but his hand tapped his jeans in a nervous tattoo. Their circumstances had reversed. Now she was foster daughter. Her stomach tightened nervously amid her sadness and homesickness. She wondered when she would stop missing her parents. The tears welled up again, and she blinked them away, looking around at her new home.

The house rose in front of them, a stone keep with a high wall and narrow, slotted windows. It was a small castle, built for defense. Fields stretched out all around it, planted with hay. There were plenty of haystacks dotting the field, not the round rolls of a mechanized field but uneven stacks that had been put in place with human labor. Even as she watched, a team of four heavy horses drew a hay wagon towering with its cargo toward the castle.

"I forgot how much I missed the haying," Colar said, wistfulness in his voice. She glanced at him, startled.

"You helped?" she exclaimed, feeling foolish. *A lord's son . . .*

He grinned. "Everybody helps. We have to get the hay in, or it will get rained on and ruined, and then all the horses will die. You wouldn't want that, would you?"

She felt herself go pink at his teasing.

"And you'll have to help, too, you know. Even my mother

and sister help, though my mother is so busy, and my sister is so little, she mostly gets in the way." His voice trailed off. "She'll have grown, I bet."

"I'll help," Kate said a little nervously. She wasn't afraid of hard work. She had mucked plenty of stalls when she helped pay for Mojo's board. But this was different. She knew how hard life would be here. This was Aeritan.

I'll be welcome here, and I'll work hard, she told herself. *But I won't lose sight of what I want to become, even if it means I lose Colar.* She didn't have his same sense of assurance that his parents would agree to let them marry, let alone allow her to study to become a doctor. And that would be down the road. She couldn't marry anyone, not yet, not for a long time.

They had caught attention from the people in the fields now, and they turned and pointed. Kate could hear faint cries of surprise. Colar kept their gait steady and slow, but he reached out and held Kate's hand. He looked at her.

"I had it easier," he said, and his mouth quirked. "I was unconscious. It will be all right. I promise. They'll be so happy I'm back, they won't even notice you right away."

He was teasing again to reassure her, and she tried to smile, but she was too frightened. *I want to go home,* she thought, then she took a deep breath and straightened her back.

A great stream of people poured from the house, all running toward them. Kate saw three kids in front, two boys and a girl. His brothers and sister, running as fast as their legs would carry them, the girl almost keeping up with her brothers. She scanned the crowd and halted Allegra as the nervous horse snorted and tried to backpedal from the onrush. The voices came clearer now, the high-pitched voices of the kids rising above all.

"Colar! Colar! He's home!"

Allegra rose on her hind legs, and Kate rode it as if the mare stood still, crouching on her back till the horse came down. She drew back, giving them distance, as the people of Terrick swarmed around Colar. Hotshot took it better than

Allegra did, but even he crouched slightly and his eyes rolled wildly.

There was Colar's mother. She had on a red dress and an apron over it, her dark blue kerchief hiding all of her hair. Her face was tan and freckled, as if she spent a lot of time outside, and her eyes were brown and bright. Colar looked like her; it was there in his mouth and nose and the shape of his face. She scanned the crowd from her perch on Allegra's back. There was Lord Terrick, looking more gray and sour than she remembered. He waded through the crowd to his son, and he and his wife reached out to the boy. Colar dismounted and knelt before them; they knelt as well and took him into their arms. The brothers and sister waited in a circle around them, bright-faced and solemn.

The crowd fell silent and drew back a little. A few people looked over at Kate, and she busied herself by dismounting and running up her stirrups, tucking them neatly against the saddle flaps. This was Colar's moment. All she wanted to do was disappear. Nervous butterflies quivered in her stomach.

First Lord Terrick and then Lady Terrick rose and tried to raise up their son, but he stayed and put out his arms to his brothers and sister. They practically jumped on him, and Kate laughed and cried both, putting her hand over her mouth.

The crowd let out a huge "Huzzah!" and Allegra freaked again, so that she had to get her under control, walking her in circles to calm her down, the mare's long-legged walk carrying her smoothly. When she had her settled, Kate turned.

Lord Terrick was looking at her, his expression unreadable. She steeled herself and walked over to him. She held her hand out, and to her surprise, he took it.

"Mr. Terrick," she said, as her parents had taught her. "I'm glad to see you again, sir."

He regarded her silently for a moment, and then he smiled. It made him look years younger, and she smiled back.

"I am also glad to see you, child," he said, his voice still peremptory as ever, but kind at the same time. "My thanks.

My thanks from all of my heart that you have returned my son to me."

Lady Terrick came over now, and Kate felt her butterflies increase. She knew nothing about this woman. For all she knew, she could have been told terrible things about Kate. *Like that I was the general's whore,* she thought. She raised her chin.

"Mrs. Terrick." She tried, as bravely as she could, but her voice faltered.

"Kate Mossland, is it?" Lady Terrick said, her voice sure and strong. She cocked her head, looking Kate over. "I have heard a great deal about you from my husband."

Oh shit, thought Kate.

"I was sad indeed that I never got a chance to meet you before now, but my husband assured me that our son was in good hands. Are your parents well?"

Kate burst into tears.

It turned out it was the best thing that she could have done. Someone took Allegra from her while she covered her face and tried to get her composure, and Colar came over and stood by her, putting his arm around her and holding her close.

"Everyone, away, away," Lord Terrick said testily. "Give the girl room."

"Why isn't she happy? Doesn't she like us?" Colar's little sister stage-whispered, and again Kate laughed and cried. She wiped her face with the back of her hands and dried them on her jeans.

"I'm Kate Mossland," she said to the girl, who looked to be about ten. "What's your name?"

"Erinya," the little girl said, wide-eyed. Colar gestured to his brothers, making a *get along* movement. One after another the boys stepped forward.

"I am called Yare," said one, and bowed.

"I am Aevin," said the other.

"I am very pleased to meet you," Kate said. She looked back at Colar's parents. "Really, I am. It's just, a lot has happened."

"And you will tell us all about it," Lady Terrick said firmly. She took Kate by the arm. "Kate Mossland, the House of Terrick gives you guesting. Now come, both of you, to wash up and eat."

Colar sipped his vesh and felt unfamiliar warmth course through him. He lifted his eyes in surprise. His father had spiked it with some of the regional brandy. Lord Terrick gave him a look that was half smile, half grimace.

"You looked as if you needed that," he said, his voice a growl.

"Yes, sir. Thank you, sir."

His father grunted and sipped his own vesh. They sat in front of the fireplace in his father's writing room, where he handled Terrick's accounts. The hearth was bare, the fire unlit. It was high summer after all, though in Terrick the summers could be gray and cloudy and not much warmer than the winter months. It was no colder, at any rate, than the Mosslands' air-conditioned house. Colar stretched his legs out, then hesitated. He wore jeans, not good trousers. He saw his father give his strange clothes a look.

"So you led a dozen men in pursuit of Marthen," his father said, and there was a glint of approval in his eye.

"Yes, sir."

"I'm surprised Lord Tharp handed them over to you."

"Lady Sarita made him."

His father gave a crusty laugh. "Well. It was a good deed and a necessary one, though what a waste. The general wasn't always mad. Once he was the greatest strategist in Aeritan." He shook his head.

"It wasn't her fault," Colar said quickly, and his father shot him a look.

Colar almost quailed, but his father said only, "Looks as if you've grown a hand since you've been away."

Colar had. He towered over his father now. It had both pleased and saddened him. His father's hair had thinned over the last year, and his beard had come in gray. He was younger than Mr. Mossland, but Kate's father used something on his hair to keep it growing, and he still played games. He was the one who had nudged Colar into lacrosse and basketball. Colar thought that maybe he had wanted a son, and he felt a pang. He hoped the man was all right. He had been good to Colar, as had Mrs. Mossland.

As if he knew what his son was thinking, Lord Terrick said, "Were you a good foster son?"

He thought so, right up to the end, when he promised his foster mother that he would rescue Kate, and disobeyed his foster father. Colar sipped his brandy and vesh. His lips had gone slightly numb. This wasn't the first time he had sampled Terrick's famed brandy, but it was the first time he had taken so much. "Yes, sir," he said at length. He had done what he promised, after all. Kate was safe, and she would be a part of Terrick now.

"Were they good foster parents?"

Colar looked up and blinked. His father's voice was uncharacteristically uncertain.

"Yes," he said firmly. "Father, they treated me well. They treated me like a son."

Lord Terrick looked down at his cup. "I never thought we would see you again. I thought you would die. I never thought—" His voice broke. "I thought I had lost you."

Colar looked away. The old man never cried, not even when Colar's littlest sister had died of a fever when he was ten. *He cries,* he corrected himself. *Just not in front of anyone.* He cast about for a way to change the subject and let his father recover.

"I should show you my scars," he said. He set down his vesh and stripped off his jacket and shirt. It was dim, the only light from the windows overlooking the Terrick lands, but there was enough light to see. Colar was skinny, and the scars were clear, the long, fading red lines where his wounds had been stitched up etched across his stomach and back. His father caught his breath. Surgeons in Aeritan would have been hard-pressed to repair the damage. "They saved my life," Colar said awkwardly.

He was getting cold, but he let his father take a long look. "So it was the right decision."

His father nodded. "Put your shirt on, boy," he growled. Colar hastened to comply. His father changed the subject abruptly. "Now, what of the girl?"

Kate was upstairs in Erinya's room. The two girls would share a chamber. She had asked for a bath after dinner in a quiet voice, and his mother had ordered the householders to prepare one. He hoped she would know that it wasn't like showers back home. Baths were a lot of work here. He hoped she would adjust to her new life. He wanted to make her happy.

Better bring it up now; it wouldn't get any easier. "We wish to marry," he said. "Much later, when we're older, as people do in her world. Only Kate has set a condition, that she be allowed to study medicine, in Brythern if need be. She feels that she can do much good here, as she did in camp, by using her knowledge from home along with Talios's teachings. And father, I think she is right. The learning they have there, it far outstripped anything here and anything in Brythern even. The things I learned, the things I could do . . ."

He trailed off. There was no way he could explain it to his father, and Lord Terrick's expression had grown pained. He didn't want to know. He didn't want to hear that his son had left something of value behind. Colar's Annapolis brochure was still folded and stuffed into his back pocket. It was probably in tatters. Soon he wouldn't be able to read it, and the photos of the jets and the aircraft carriers would fade, and his sojourn on the other side of the gordath would fade as well.

"Well," his father said. "You will be her husband. Can you live with that?"

I'll have the greatest lady in all of Aeritan. He nodded solemnly, his heart pounding. He hoped Kate didn't want to wait too long. The custom of late marriage would have to give way to Aeritan, after all. "I can, sir."

Of all the responses his father could give, he didn't think he could be any more surprised.

"Well, I had thought as much, with the two of you." At Colar's expression, his father shook his head. "Just don't tell your mother yet. Let her have you back for a little while."

"Yes, sir."

Lord Terrick hauled himself heavily to his feet. "And here I've monopolized you far longer than I should have. Your mother wants you, and your brothers and sister, and I am sure your new lady as well. You have returned to us, son. Maybe one day you will understand what that means."

When he was a father himself. Colar followed his father down the stairs where his family waited to welcome him home.

The afternoon sunlight streamed across the lawn at the farmhouse at the newly renamed Red Bird Stables. A rented white pavilion gleamed in the rich, lowering sun, and wedding guests gathered in clusters on the neatly mown grass, their heels sinking into the damp earth. People laughed and chattered, holding glasses of champagne. From his vantage point on the front porch of the elegant old house, Joe looked out over the view. It was like Mrs. Hunt's gala, except that the old Hunter's Chase Stables took its formality and cold beauty from its owner. Red Bird Stables was comfortable and worn, like a pair of favorite boots. Weeds had sprung up alongside the gravel drive, but they were Queen Anne's lace and caught the gleam of sunlight with an ethereal air. The barns were comfortable and slightly worn, the fences tight and safe but no longer bright white. The horses browsed in the fields, a few watching the proceedings at the house with a quiet curiosity.

Across the cross-country jump course massed the trees of Gordath Wood, and his senses quivered. The gordath hadn't yet been completely quieted but was merely quiescent. *I reckon I can handle it from here,* Joe thought, along with the old folks that Lynn had introduced him to. They called themselves a fancy word, perambulators, but it turned out they were guardians just like him.

And with Arrim on the other side, well, that was the best

they could do. He looked over at Lynn, talking with elderly relatives on the lawn. She looked lovely in her wedding dress, a long, slim, white sheath that set off her dark hair and fine figure in a way that made him go weak at the knees.

They might even have started on the next generation of guardians already. They neither of them considered birth control when they got home. Lynn just put him to bed and joined him there when he was rested from the ass kicking Hare had given him. She gave him a glance just then and a smile over her flute of champagne, and he gave an answering smile back.

She looked happy, he couldn't help but note, and he damned himself again for a fool. She told him what was between her and that captain or lord or whatever he was, and he knew better than to let it get to him. Still, it was hard, seeing the way they had looked at each other. *Careful,* he thought. *You'll end up like Lord Tharp. Best just let it go and make damn sure the gordath stays closed.*

Something cold and wet nudged his hand. It was the dog. They had named her Cissy, and she answered to it eagerly. She panted and wagged, her eager brown eyes looking up at him. She was shiny and clean and had filled out, and took her job as guardian of the stables as seriously as he took his. He rubbed the dog's soft ears. Women might need horses, but a man needed a dog sometimes, especially when he was lost in the woods. He wasn't lost anymore, though. He had Lynn and the farm and the gordath to keep quiet.

He didn't need to run anymore.

With Cissy at his side, he came down the porch steps, accepting the handshakes and congratulations from the wedding guests. The grass was soft under his dress shoes, and he could feel the cool seeping up into the soles. Felt strange not to be wearing boots, but his old boots hardly went with fine clothes.

"Joe!" His mother came up, wearing a lavender dress that didn't suit her except for the beaming happiness that she wore with it. She gave him a kiss, and he held her. "What are you doing, leaving your wife alone on your wedding day?" she scolded lightly. She was a little tipsy.

"Just going to get her now," he promised.

Isabella became serious now. "She's a good girl. You treat her right." The unspoken context, *Not the way your father treated me,* bounced between them. He gave her another kiss on the cheek.

"Always, Ma."

At that moment Abel Felz stumped up to them. Joe had gotten his father's height, which was to say, not so much, but Abel had thickened, his neck and jowls sagging and his belly straining at his old blue suit.

"So this is where you'll be. I guess we'll never see much of you." His words were a bitter accusation.

Joe didn't say anything. His dad was in one of his moods, and nothing he said could appease the old man. He and his mother exchanged a quick glance and then he caught movement out of the corner of his eye. Lynn. He was about to wave her off, but she came up to them, the deepening twilight making her almost glow in her gown.

"Mr. Felz, I didn't get a chance to talk with you before," she said, taking her father-in-law's hand. "I'm really happy you could make it up for our wedding."

"Big waste of time," the old man snapped. "You don't know anything about farming, and Joe should know better. Farmers can't leave their land. Now who knows what's happening back home. And Isabella gone all these weeks. People can't just leave. It all goes to hell. People coming back and forth, crossing over. By the time I get home, it'll be hell to put to right and quiet everything back down." He glared at Joe and Lynn. "What are you looking at me like that for?"

Isabella took her husband's arm. "That's enough, Abel. Leave these poor children alone. You're like to give me a heart attack with that rant. Let them be on their wedding day."

She led him off, Abel still growling, and they stared at each other, dumbstruck.

"Well," Lynn said at last. "I think that was a piece of the puzzle."

Joe nodded. "He's a bitter old bastard, and he made my life miserable. But he is a guardian."

She folded her hand in his, and he pulled her to him and kissed her. It was a real kiss, a bedroom kiss, and they could hear the cheers and laughter of the guests as people turned to look. They both blushed and laughed and broke apart, but he kept hold of her hand. Joe thought that it was nice to finally stop moving. It was good to be home.